I've travelled the world twice over,
Met the famous: saints and sinners,
Poets and artists, kings and queens,
Old stars and hopeful beginners,
I've been where no-one's been before,
Learned secrets from writers and cooks
All with one library ticket
To the wonderful world of books.

© Janice James.

The wisdom of the ages
Is there for you and me,
The wisdom of the ages,
In your local library

There's large print books
And talking books,
For those who cannot see,
The wisdom of the ages,
It's fantastic, and it's free.

Written by Sam Wood, aged 92

YEARS OF THE FURY

The third volume of the saga which began with RAGE OF THE INNOCENT and continued with IN PRESENCE OF MY FOES.

The First World War has ended and, with Harry Miles back from France, he and Mary are hoping to settle down to their married life at last. But they have not taken account of their two unrelenting enemies. Michael Chadwick, who made Harry's life hell in the trenches, is now planning to settle a score with the couple. And Ethel, Mary's domineering mother, begins a campaign to steal their daughter, Elizabeth, from them. When Ethel and Chadwick join forces, not only the young couple's livelihood but their daughter's life is put in jeopardy.

Books by Frederick E. Smith
Published by The House of Ulverscroft:

LYDIA TRENDENNIS
THE DARK CLIFFS
OF MASKS AND MINDS
THE GROTTO OF TIBERIUS
A KILLING FOR THE HAWKS
THE WIDER SEA OF LOVE
THE STORM KNIGHT
THE OBSESSION
THE SIN AND THE SINNERS
WATERLOO
THE DEVIL BEHIND ME
LAWS BE THEIR ENEMY

633 SQUADRON:
OPERATION VALKYRIE
OPERATION CRUCIBLE
OPERATION COBRA
OPERATION TITAN

TRILOGY:
RAGE OF THE INNOCENT
IN PRESENCE OF MY FOES

FREDERICK E. SMITH

YEARS OF THE FURY

Complete and Unabridged

CHARNWOOD
Leicester

First published in Great Britain in 1989

First Charnwood Edition
published 1997

British Library CIP Data

Smith, Frederick E. (Frederick Escreet), *1922 –*
Years of the fury.—Large print ed.—
Charnwood library series
1. English fiction—20th century
2. Large type books
I. Title
823.9′14 [F]

ISBN 0–7089–8941–1

Published by
F. A. Thorpe (Publishing) Ltd.
Anstey, Leicestershire

Set by Words & Graphics Ltd.
Anstey, Leicestershire
Printed and bound in Great Britain by
T. J. Press (Padstow) Ltd., Padstow, Cornwall

This book is printed on acid-free paper

To Moe
In appreciation and friendship

Acknowledgements

The author wishes to acknowledge his debt to the following works of reference:

My Father's notes,
My Mother's autobiography,
History of the English Speaking Peoples. Churchill. (Purnell)
A History of Everyday Things in England. Ellacott (Batsford)
A History of Hull. Gillett & MacMahon (Oxford University Press)
Young in Hull. J. D. Wright.

Prologue

THE storm was advancing on the city like two Norse gods in mortal combat. Dazzling swords split the night sky and roars of rage made the ground tremble. As a brilliant flash penetrated the blinds of a thousand bedrooms, a young girl in the besieged city sat up sharply and gave a scream. "Grannie! I'm frightened! Grannie, help me!"

A massive peal of thunder drowned her screams. As it rolled away, running footsteps and then a woman's soothing voice could be heard. "It's all right, darling. Mummy's here. It's only a storm. It won't hurt you."

Another flash lit up the bedroom and showed a young woman in her night clothes comforting the terrified child. As thunder crashed again, the girl tore away and gave another scream. "Grannie! I'm frightened! Where are you?"

An older voice sounded from the doorway. "Grannie's here, my dear. Everything's all right now."

The light switched on and a woman in her middle fifties, also in night clothes, was seen walking towards the bed. As the terrified child tried to reach her, the younger woman drew her back. "It's all right, Mother. You can go back to bed. I'll stay with her until the storm's passed over."

The older woman ignored her and spoke only

1

to the child. "My poor little girl. It is a nasty storm, isn't it? Would you like to come into my bed for the rest of the night?"

The sobbing girl nodded eagerly. "Yes, please, Grannie."

The voice of the second woman sharpened. "Mother, I don't want you to pamper her like this. She'll suffer too much in later life if you keep on with it. I've said I'll look after her until the storm's over."

Again the older woman ignored her. "I'm sorry, dear. Your mummy won't let me comfort you. But never mind. Grannie's close by and she won't let the nasty storm harm you."

Without a glance at her daughter, she left the bedroom. As lightning flashed again, the child began sobbing bitterly. "I want to go to Grannie. Why won't you let me, Mummy? Why are you so mean?"

Unable to speak, the younger woman drew her closer so that the child could not see the tears trickling down her cheeks. A moment later a roar of thunder came like the crack of doom before it reverberated away. Listening to the battle raging above, a shudder ran through the young woman and her arms tightened protectively around the terrified child.

Part One

Part One

1

HARRY MILES could feel his heart beating faster as he neared the small house in St. George's Road. As he stood before the front door that abutted the pavement, the biting February wind swirled down the road and threw particles of hail into his face. Shivering, turning up his raincoat collar, he glanced upwards. The late afternoon sky was threatening more than darkness. There was every possibility it would snow during the night.

He glanced back at the door. With peeling paint and rusted letter box, it had an unfriendly, almost hostile appearance. Nor did the half-curtained windows upstairs disclaim the image. Loveless was the word that entered his mind until he thrust it impatiently away. He had always been impressionable to weather. He must not let it affect him now.

Yet he could not deny his dread of the ordeal ahead. Glancing round, he saw there was both time and excuse to escape. Apart from four children playing with whips and tops and a lamplighter who was just entering the street on his bicycle, no one else appeared to have seen him, unless the curtained, illuminated windows opposite hid prying eyes. And the unlit house that stood before him gave no evidence of life, making him wonder if it were unoccupied.

He knew he hoped it was and despised himself

for the thought. The thing had to be done or it would continue to prey on his mind as it had preyed for the last few months. Without further thought he turned and swung down the door knocker.

★ ★ ★

Mary Miles put the cover over her typewriter and gazed again through the office window. In the gas light that shone through it, the rising wind was making arabesques of snowflakes before allowing them to sink to the warehouse yard one storey below. She wondered why Harry was late tonight and whether she ought to phone her mother. If Ethel's dinner were spoiled she would have yet another excuse to berate Harry.

A faint whimper made her turn. A child's cot, an incongruous object among shelves of bottles and pill boxes, tables and filing cabinets, stood in the far corner of the office. Rising, she walked quietly towards it, a tall graceful girl in her late twenties whose blond hair could reach down to her waist when the pins that at present held it in a chignon were released. Seeing the child was still asleep, she gently adjusted his blankets. As she straightened, the wind buffeted the window and brought a cloud of acrid smoke from the coke stove that stood in the centre of the room. With an exclamation, the girl hurried to the stove and raked over the cinders.

She returned to the window and gazed out again. Earlier, the moonless evening had hidden the scene below but now a covering of snow

6

delineated the stables, the storage sheds, and the lane that led past No. fifty seven and its adjacent houses to the distant street. If it fell much longer it would make cycling difficult, if not impossible.

Even as things were, she felt the conditions would be exhausting for Harry. Only recently out of military hospital, in her opinion he was not yet fit enough to cycle all day looking for new orders.

At the same time she knew that the business could not survive for long without those orders. If only petrol would become available again, she thought, so that he could use the old Ford her father had bought.

As the minutes passed and the snowflakes thickened, her fears grew that he had suffered a relapse or had an accident. Her reason argued such fears were absurd, that some customer had kept him talking or he had found a likely one who needed winning over. But to Mary Miles, who had lived for over eight months with only faith to sustain her when everyone else had been certain Harry was dead, her reunion with him still had the aspects of a dream. Time and again she would wake in the night in an icy sweat, with the need to clutch and hold him as proof of his flesh and blood existence.

In many ways she knew she had been lucky. With conditions in Germany chaotic by the time the Armistice was signed, with many half-starved prisoners having to find their way home themselves across a continent in ferment, it had been almost a miracle that Harry had

7

been found by the Red Cross and returned to England before the end of 1918. Nevertheless, the traumas that Mary Miles had suffered since Harry had enlisted in the Army in 1915 had left their mark on her and her anxiety grew as the slow minutes came and went.

★ ★ ★

It was over forty minutes before Harry left the house and collected his bicycle. As he was about to mount it, one of the boys playing in the street ran up to him and held out a grubby hand. "You spare a ha'penny, mister?"

He fished into his pocket and gave the urchin one. Seeing a second child hanging back, he called him over and gave him a similar coin. The child's face lit up as if a switch had been thrown. "Gee, thanks, mister. Thanks a lot."

Seeing all the street lamps were now lit, Harry paused to light the acetylene lamp of his bicycle. Before riding away, he took a last backward glance at the house. It was anonymous now, one of dozens merging together in the winter darkness. He blamed the icy wind for the shiver that ran through him as he rode away.

Although fifty seven Ellerby Road was barely a mile away, it took him fifteen minutes to reach it. It was not so much the snow that impeded him, although the flakes were growing larger, but the wind that drove the flakes into his face and made him strain on the pedals.

There was little traffic about. The rush hour was over and, with fuel still scarce, most of the small shops he passed were in darkness. Nevertheless children, some barefoot, were still playing on the pavements and he kept passing small groups of men, some huddled in shop doorways, others grouped under street lamps with their chilled hands thrust deep into their pockets. Some were in uniform, others were anonymous in caps, overcoats or shabby raincoats.

The soldiers were starting to come home, he thought. As yet a trickle but one that would soon turn into a flood. Nearly four million men from the British Army alone. A tide of men that would soon sweep through every town and city in the land. Not for the first time, Harry Miles counted his good fortune. He might have suffered near starvation for over eight months while a prisoner of war but in his case it had at least resulted in quick repatriation and a return to his family and his work.

He had good reason to be grateful. As the most destructive war in history had devoured more and more men and national wealth, thinkers and statesmen on both sides had become fearful that European civilisation itself might be the final price to pay when the exhausted nations were finally compelled to lay down their arms. The Austro-Hungarian Empire, once composed of eleven ethnic groups, was already breaking into fragments and even Germany, once so obedient under the iron grip of militant Prussia, was in turmoil, with food riots in its cities and Soldiers' Councils and other revolutionary groups struggling to wrest power

9

from a weakened central government.

Although the victorious powers were not facing challenges of this magnitude, their need to demobilise and release millions of men into economies weakened by four years of war was a massive problem in itself. In Britain and America it was soon to lead to widespread disillusionment and in Italy, as in defeated Germany, it was eventually to provide willing recruits to Fascism.

The British demobilisation plan, drawn up by the newly-elected War Minister, Winston Churchill, was perhaps as fair as could be expected but even this scheme could do nothing to ensure a soldier received fair play from his one-time employer. As Churchill said himself, fair play was something no government could legislate for and rogue employers would always exist.

To Harry, who in spite of his egalitarian instincts had the ability to see both sides of an argument, it seemed some measure of disillusionment was inevitable. Soldiers throughout the history of the world had always romanticised their home life when they were subjected to the harsh disciplines of war. Wives they had once seen as shrews became doting creatures with soft, inviting arms, if not outright sex goddesses. Screaming children who once had made them wish they had been born eunuchs were transformed into endearing cherubs who obeyed their every dictate. The home that at times had seemed like an ante-room of hell became a shimmering haven for which a man would give his right arm as shells tore up the tortured earth around him. Such fantasies could not be expected to survive for long in a world of human frailties.

Employment belonged to the same fanciful world. For four years employers had been forced to take on new staff, some of whom had proved as good or even better than the old. The problem of whether to sack or keep them was not simply one of divided loyalties. Men who had spent years learning how to kill one another and had risen in rank and importance as these lethal skills developed were not always the ideal replacements for men or women who had never known the revolutionary and sometimes anarchistic urges of the combat soldier.

The wind eased a little as Harry turned into Ellerby Road. The pavements were white now, with black footprints betraying the passage of pedestrians. As he reached a street corner, he saw a group of shabbily-dressed men waiting outside a pub for opening time. They appeared to be quarrelling and as he passed them he caught a few of their angry comments. The discontent was already here, he thought. And there were still three million more men to return.

★ ★ ★

Ethel Hardcastle glanced at the gilt clock on the mantelpiece and gave a tut of annoyance. The young girl sitting beside her on the sofa shifted

11

restlessly. "Why are they so late, Grannie? I'm hungry."

Ethel turned towards her. A woman in her early fifties, she was handsome rather than beautiful with well-proportioned features and a mass of glossy brown hair streaked only here and there with grey. Her clothes, a beige skirt and high-collared blouse, were perfectly matched to the somewhat prim image that she favoured. "I've told you, dear. Your father isn't back from his rounds yet."

"But it's half past six! Why can't I have my dinner? I'm ever so hungry."

"I'm sorry, dear. If it were my choice you'd have had it half an hour ago. But I can't go against the wishes of your parents, can I?"

The girl, a pretty child with long, golden hair like her mother's, pouted. Although only six years old, she spoke like a much older child. "I don't see why they always want me to wait for them. Why can't I just have it when it's ready like some of my friends do?"

"You must ask your mother that. Or better still, your father. I'm sure he's the one who insists on it."

"That's not what Mummy said when I asked her. She said that because Daddy had been a prisoner of war and been away from us all so long, it was only fair to him that we shared our meals together."

Ethel gave her a patient smile. "I sometimes think your mummy likes to take the blame for things your daddy does. But that's a little secret we can keep between the two of us, can't we?"

Before Elizabeth could answer, Ethel reached out for the picture book the girl was holding. "Would you like me to read you another story until they arrive?"

The girl nodded. "Read me the chapter about the grizzly bears in the Rockies, will you, Grannie? The ones Mr Watson used to talk about."

Ethel turned over the pages until she had found the chapter. Pausing, she gazed fondly at the expectant girl. "You'd love to go to America, wouldn't you, dear?"

Elizabeth's face lit up. "More than anything in the world. More than absolutely anything!" Her voice turned pleading. "Won't you take me, Grannie? Please! I'd be ever so good. You wouldn't know I was there."

Ethel sighed. "I'd take you like a shot if I could. But you know what your mummy and daddy have said. I can't go against their wishes, can I?"

The girl pouted again. "I don't see why they should stop me. I think it's horrible of them."

Ethel tut-tutted again. "You mustn't say things like that. I'm sure Mummy and Daddy think it's the best thing for you."

The child was close to tears now. "How can it be the best thing when it's the thing I want most in the world?"

Ethel put an arm around her shoulders. "Never mind. Perhaps Grannie will be able to take you another time. If Grannie lives to go another time, that is."

The girl showed immediate alarm. "You're

13

not going to die, are you, Grannie? Not the way Grandpa did?"

Ethel sighed. "I hope not, dear. But as one gets older one must take it into account."

The girl's blue eyes were suddenly clouded with fear. "But you're not old, Grannie, are you? Not like old Mr. Foster is."

"You don't have to be very old to die, dear. Your Grandpa wasn't old and look what happened to him."

With a sob Elizabeth threw herself into her arms. "You mustn't die, Grannie! You mustn't!"

Ethel hugged her tightly. "I don't want to, dear. I don't want to leave you, just as you don't want to leave Grannie, do you?"

The girl, who had her face buried in Ethel's whalebone-stiffened bosom, shook her head in distress. "No. I want to be with you always."

Ethel sighed again. "That's not possible, dear. But it's a great comfort to Grannie to know that when God calls me to join your grandfather in heaven, you'll remember me by visiting my grave, just as we visit Grandpa's grave. You will do that, won't you, my darling?"

The tearful girl nodded. "Yes. Every week. I promise."

"That's a good girl. It'll please Grandpa as well. Shall we go tomorrow and take him some fresh flowers?"

When the girl nodded again, Ethel's tone changed. "You mustn't fret about Grannie. You pray every night for her, don't you, when you pray for Mummy and Daddy?"

"Yes. Just as you say I should."

14

"Then I'm sure God will look after me for a few years yet. After all, God knows how much you and I mean to one another. So He's not going to take me from you yet, is he?"

Elizabeth raised her tear-stained face. "Don't you think so?"

"I'm sure He's not. Not if you're a good girl and love Grannie and do as she says."

In the way of children, Elizabeth's mood changed immediately. "Then it's all right, isn't it? Because God must know I love you."

Ethel took a cambric handkerchief from her sleeve and carefully wiped the child's eyes. "Just as long as you're a good girl and do as Grannie says, God will take care of her, dear. Only God doesn't like our secrets to be given away, so you must promise Grannie you'll always keep them and tell nobody."

"Does that mean Mummy and Daddy too?"

"Everyone, dear. Secrets are just between God, you and me. If you were to tell Mummy or Daddy, He might become angry and take Grannie away. So be a very good girl, tell nobody, and you and Grannie will have many more years together."

Comforted, her earlier mood restored, the girl snuggled against the woman. "Will you read me that story now, Grannie?"

2

MARY was only able to relax when she caught sight of Harry cycling down the lane. Reproaching herself for her fears, she watched him park his bicycle in the garage and make his way to the warehouse door below. With his raincoat collar turned up against the wind, she thought how tired he looked. As his footsteps sounded on the staircase, she hurried to the office door and opened it.

Knowing her anxieties upset him, she made no mention of them. "Hello, darling. What a dreadful night."

He smiled and kissed her. "Sorry I'm late but at last I got round to seeing Arthur Turnor's wife."

She helped him remove his snow-covered raincoat. "How did you find her?"

He did not reply immediately. "What sort of a day have you had?"

"Not too bad. I've managed to get that order ready for Tysons." Her tone changed as he dropped into a chair and pulled off his bicycle clips. "You look tired. We shouldn't have dismissed Willis."

"Rubbish. We'd have gone bankrupt if we kept him much longer. He wasn't earning his wages."

She knew he was right. The plump, self-indulgent Londoner she had been forced to

16

employ during Harry's wartime absence had caused her endless problems. "Yes, but it means you have to work that much harder."

His laugh made light of her concern as he handed her his order book. "We'll manage. I got that order from old Morfitt this afternoon. That should keep the men downstairs busy for a day or two."

She reached down and kissed him. "Thank heaven you're back. I don't think I could have carried on much longer."

He shook his head. "You'd have managed, just as you have for the last three years. Your dad was right. You're as good a businessman as the best of us."

A dimple showed in her cheek. "I'm not sure I like the sound of that."

He grinned. "Come off it. You don't like helpless women any more than I do." Turning, he nodded at the cot. "How's the little fellow been today?"

"Very good. He cried a little this morning but he's been sleeping ever since his mid-afternoon feed."

He pulled off his scarf. "You must have given him a good one."

It was a comment that made her blush. Although she had overcome her earlier sexual inhibitions when they made love, like so many of her generation she still found difficulty in discussing aspects of sex in everyday conversation. "I think he does quite well."

His smiling eyes moved down to her full bodice. "I'm sure he does. One way and another

I think he's a lucky boy."

Along with her embarrassment she knew his words excited her. Since she first became conscious of men, there had been no one else for her but Harry Miles. She watched him walk across to the cot, a wiry man of medium height with wide-set brown eyes and a smiling, shapely mouth. Thinking again how tired he looked, she heard him laugh. "What is it?" she asked.

He pulled off his wet cap and shook it, uncovering his dark, curly hair. "When I bent over him, a drop of water fell from my cap on to his cheek. You should have seen the face he pulled."

She bent down. "Has it woken him?"

He grinned. "Just for a moment, to give me a look of disgust. But he seems to have gone off again."

She saw he was right. "We'll have to go in a minute or Mother will start moaning about dinner. But tell me quickly about Mrs Turnor. What is she like?"

A frown crossed his face. "I don't know what to make of her. If Turnor hadn't been killed so long ago, I'd say she was still in shock."

She gave a shudder of sympathy. "I can believe that. I felt the same way for weeks after the telegram came about you."

"Yes but it's nearly a year now She's painfully thin, her hair looks as if it hasn't been combed for days, and her clothes are nearly in tatters. She acts as if she's no further interest in life and yet she's little more than a kid, twenty-two or twenty-three at the most."

"Perhaps she isn't interested," Mary said. "Perhaps in losing her husband she's lost her reason for living."

He frowned again. "That's all very well but life has to go on. She needs help of some kind. There was no fire in the house when I arrived and from what I could see everything movable has been pawned."

"Pawned?"

"Yes. Not that she said so. But it's obvious enough she can't make ends meet."

"Did you offer her help?"

He gave a wry shrug. "I tried but she didn't like it. She seems fiercely independent."

"You don't think that was because . . . ?" She paused, suddenly aware what she was saying.

His wryness grew. "Because Turnor might not be dead but for me?"

For a moment she showed anger. "Don't start that nonsense again. If Turnor acted against your orders, how can you blame yourself? I meant just the opposite. She might have felt if she accepted your offer, it could be interpreted that you owed her something." When he did not reply, her voice sharpened. "She didn't blame you, did she?"

He turned away. "No. The poor kid didn't look as if she'd the heart left to blame anybody. She looked burned out with grief."

"Hasn't she any relations to help her?"

"No. Her parents threw her out when she married Turnor. And I suppose his relations are as poor as he was. Not, I feel, that she'd ask for help if any was available. But she did

19

say Chadwick had been round to see her."

She gave a start. "Chadwick?"

He shrugged. "Why not? Turnor was in his team too."

"What did he want?"

"The same as I wanted, I suppose. To see how she was getting on. He told her he believed she was entitled to some government help and he'd try to find out what could be done."

"Do you believe he will?"

"Yes, I think so. Visiting bereaved relatives seems to be one of his better traits. After all, he came to see you after they thought I'd been killed, didn't he?"

She bent over the cot so that he could not see her expression. Chadwick had come to see her, that was true, but what had happened afterwards still gave her nightmares. "He sees them after their sons or husbands have been killed, Harry. I don't think that's much consolation to them, do you?"

His voice was mildly reproving. "That's rather hard, isn't it? It's surely the war that killed them, not Chadwick."

She straightened. His ability to forgive was one of the things she loved about him. But not forgiveness of Chadwick. "Harry, he gave you hell over in France. You hated his bloodthirsty ways so much you had to go back to the Front to prove you weren't like him. So how can you stand there now and make excuses for him?"

His eyes were on her. "You really do dislike him, don't you?"

You can't know how much, she thought.

20

"What do you expect after all he did to you? I don't just dislike him, Harry. I hate him."

Her outburst, so unlike her, was holding his attention. "I'm not exactly in love with him myself. But I can't deny he has his good side."

"He's probably doing it out of guilt. From the way he threw men into battle, even he must have a twinge of remorse now and then."

"Love, it wasn't his fault Turnor was killed. He gave us strict orders to stay at our post. I was the one who disobeyed the order. So if anyone's to blame, I am."

"And I've told you time and time again that's stupid. You went out on an act of mercy and that's why Arthur Turnor tried to help you. It wasn't your fault he was seen by a sniper. So stop blaming yourself."

The way he changed the subject told her he was not convinced. "Didn't I see a letter with an American stamp on the kitchen table this morning?"

"Yes. It was for Mother. It must have been from Jack Watson."

He frowned. "I hope that doesn't mean Ethel will be giving Elizabeth fresh ideas about having a holiday in America with her."

It remained, she knew, a highly sensitive issue with him. During the time he was missing, an officer in the American Expeditionary Forces, Jack Watson, a friend of one of Ethel's brothers-in-law, had paid Ethel a visit.

To Mary's great surprise, the prim Ethel had taken a liking to the middle-aged officer and eventually accepted his invitation to spend a holiday with him in America after the war.

At first Mary had welcomed her mother's new emotional interest until Ethel, without Mary's sanction, had promised to take Elizabeth with her.

It was the kind of situation in which Ethel specialised: one that put Mary or Harry in the wrong no matter what action they took. Forced to refuse Elizabeth permission on the grounds her father might still be alive and want to see her on his return, Mary had only succeeded in antagonising the disappointed girl. Worse than that, Harry, a highly sensitive man, had been unable to shake off the thought that his daughter, consciously or unconsciously, saw his return home as the principal factor depriving her of the promised visit to America.

His concern was showing now. "Perhaps we ought to let her go. I don't like the feeling I'm the one holding her back."

Her refusal had never been more emphatic. "No! It would mean she'd be entirely under Mother's influence while they're away and I'm not having that. God knows, Mother's spoilt her enough already. And she's making her older than her years with her sanctimonious ways and her morbid talk about Dad and visiting his grave. In any case who can say how long Mother would stay away?"

He shifted restlessly. "I know all that but what's the girl going to be like after Ethel goes? She's got an obsession about America and she's going to break her heart when she's left behind."

She knew he was right. But she also knew she must act on her own instincts. He had not been home for the last three years to witness the frightening influence Ethel had exercised on the young, impressionable child.

"I'm sorry, Harry, but Elizabeth has to learn she can't always have her own way. She's young and she'll soon get over her disappointment."

He looked unconvinced but lit a cigarette instead of continuing the argument. He walked slowly across to the window, then turned. "Do you still think Ethel will sell the business if we move out into a house of our own again?"

She showed no surprise at the question. It was one they had asked themselves many times. "If we took Elizabeth with us, I'm sure she would. She told me so the last time I threatened to leave, when you were away."

He exhaled smoke. "We're hardly likely to leave Elizabeth behind, are we?"

"No, but Mother would go half out of her mind if we took her to live somewhere else. She worships the child."

He grimaced. "Worships?"

"Yes. I know it sounds unhealthy but she does. Losing her would be a dreadful blow."

"So you're saying she'd sell the business out of spite?"

"Yes, I suppose I am. The only thing that might stop her is the income she gets from it. And the percentage that goes to my sister."

"But Connie doesn't need the money, does she?"

"Probably not. Her husband has a good job,

although I hear he hasn't been well lately."

"So that's not likely to stop her?"

Mary sighed. "Mother's so unpredictable who can say? But I don't think so. She'd be so upset and furious at losing Elizabeth that she probably wouldn't stop to think of anything or anybody."

He frowned and continued to smoke in silence. Knowing the way his thoughts were running, she crossed the floor and pressed his arm. "I know how you feel, darling, but good jobs aren't easy to get. And you've only been out of hospital four weeks, so you couldn't possibly do manual work yet. Leave it a while longer until you've fully recovered. Then we'll talk about moving again."

He shifted restlessly. "I know all that. But don't forget, every day Elizabeth is getting older."

As if I'm not aware of it too, she thought. "I want to leave as much as you do. Perhaps even more. But we have to be sensible." Feeling it vital she won the argument, she used his affection for Elizabeth to support her case. "Elizabeth does like her private school, you know. It would hurt her to leave it. And she'd have to if we both lost our jobs."

He gave a grimace. "There's no way we can win, is there? All right, then what about you giving up your job and spending your days with Elizabeth? At least that would help to counter Ethel's influence on her."

"Harry, as things stand now you come back every night looking worn out. So how could you manage the business and be a salesman as well?"

"I'd manage," he said. "One way or another we have to break your mother's influence over the child."

She fought back the temptation. "Wait a little longer. Remember she's probably going to America this spring. That's not long now and it'll give us at least two months' rest and time to work things out."

He brightened at the reminder. "I'd forgotten that! God bless America. All right, love. We'll stick it out until the spring and see what happens then. Now we'd better get over, hadn't we, or she'll give us hell for burning the steak or whatever we're having?"

Unsure of the extent of her victory but relieved at his change of mood, she laughed. "Nothing so splendid. It's pot roast tonight."

Giving her a rueful grin in return, Harry threw his cigarette into the stove and pushed in the damper. Then he picked up the baby and carefully wrapped the blankets round him before venturing out on the landing.

He waited until Mary had switched off the gas light and locked the office door. Then, with the wind driving snow into their faces, they made their way down the lane that led to the back garden of No. fifty seven.

3

ETHEL made her announcement after the table had been cleared and Harry had settled in an armchair with the evening paper. "I'd a letter from Captain Watson this morning. He asks if I'll take my holiday over there in May. He's made enquiries and although the shipping situation is going to be difficult for the rest of the year, he thinks he can arrange it so that I get a passage on one of the ships taking back American troops."

Mary was sitting on the sofa with Elizabeth at that moment, helping the girl with a jigsaw puzzle. As she glanced up, she saw Harry lower his newspaper. Knowing he did not want to make any comment that could be held against him later, she gave her mother a smile. "That sounds rather exciting. What are you going to do, Mother? Take him up on his offer?"

The look Ethel gave her contained its own coded message. You want me to go, don't you, so that you can have this house and Elizabeth to yourself? "I haven't had time to think about it, dear. But I think Jack will be disappointed if I don't go."

"I'm sure he will," Mary said. "He talked about nothing else the last time he came to see you."

Before Ethel could reply, there was a wail from Elizabeth. "Can't I come too, Grannie? Please!"

Ethel's eyes moved to her. "Darling, we mustn't go into all that again. Your mummy and daddy say you can't go and that's the end of it. There's nothing I can do."

"But you promised me, Grannie. And I want to go to America so much."

"I know you want to go, darling. That's why I offered to take you in the first place. But we mustn't do things your mummy and daddy don't want, must we? So be a good girl and Grannie will bring you back a nice present."

"I don't want a present. I want to go to America with you. You promised I could. And you always say no one should break a promise."

Ethel sighed. "You can't blame Grannie, dear. It's not my fault I have to break my promise."

The girl began to turn hysterical. "It is your fault. You don't want me to go any more than Mummy and Daddy do. If you did, you'd take me."

"That's silly, child. I've told you often enough I'd take you if I could. So don't start blaming me now."

Before the girl could reply, Mary broke in sharply. "Stop this nonsense, Elizabeth. You're upsetting everybody. Stop it or you'll go up to your room."

The girl jumped to her feet. "I won't stop it. Grannie promised me and I've told everyone at school that I'm going. What am I going to tell them now?"

"You should never have said such a thing. I told you the same day that you couldn't go. So why do you keep on about it?"

"You didn't. You said I had to stay home in case Daddy came back after the war."

Without knowing why, Mary felt her cheeks turn hot. "I said you must be here when Daddy came home, yes. But not that you could go off a few weeks afterwards."

"Why not? Daddy's seen me now. So why can't I go?"

Before Mary could answer, she heard an exclamation and saw Harry rising from his chair. Catching her glance, he laid down the newspaper. "I think I'll go over to the office for a while."

She stared at him. "At this time of night?"

"Yes. There are a few jobs I ought to do before tomorrow."

"But it'll be cold over there. The stove will be out."

He shrugged. "I'll be all right. I won't be that long."

Without another word he fetched his coat from the hall. Then, stooping a moment to kiss Elizabeth, he left the room. As the house door closed, Mary swung round on the child. "Now you see what you've done. You've hurt Daddy by all this talk about America. I've told you before not to mention it in front of him."

The child was looking both tearful and guilty. Before she could speak, Ethel put an arm around her shoulders. "Don't put the blame on her if Harry's in a mood tonight. Sometimes I think you both forget she's only a child."

Mary's temper snapped. "We don't forget

28

anything of the sort, Mother. Any more than I forget you're to blame for all this nonsense. If you hadn't made her this ridiculous promise in the first place, none of this would have happened."

Ethel drew herself to her full height. "So it's my fault again, is it?"

"Of course it's your fault. You spoil and pamper the girl and make her promises you've no business to make, and then she turns on us when she can't have her own way, Can't you see how bad it is for her and the trouble it causes?"

With a sniff Ethel bent over the tearful child. "Your Grannie can't do the right thing, can she, dear? Perhaps it's as well she's getting old and won't be here forever."

The child burst into sobs and clutched at her skirt. "Don't talk like that, Grannie! Please don't talk like that!"

Mary found herself trembling with anger. "How dare you say such morbid things to a child? You ought to be ashamed of yourself."

Elizabeth, hysterical in her distress, was burying her face in Ethel's skirt. Bending down, Ethel caressed the child's golden hair. "There, there, dear. Don't be upset. Grannie's not going to leave you yet." Lifting her head so that the child could not see her expression, she gazed at Mary. "In fact perhaps Grannie might change her mind and not go to America at all this year. After all, I can't upset my little girl, can I?"

The child's sobs ceased and she raised her

tearful face. "Do you mean that, Grannie?"

Taken by surprise by the pronouncement, Mary could not hide her dismay. For a moment she saw a gleam of triumph in Ethel's slightly protruding eyes. Then the woman gazed down fondly at the child again. "I shall have to write Captain Watson and find out if I can go over later. But I'm sure he'll understand if I have to change my plans."

★ ★ ★

As always after a quarrel with her mother, Mary found it difficult to sleep. Until that evening the belief that she and Harry would soon have a few months of freedom from Ethel's molestation had been the one strong case in her argument to persuade Harry to remain at No. fifty-seven until his health fully recovered. But now, if Ethel meant what she had just said, the situation had drastically changed. With Ethel sniping at Harry at every opportunity, how could she, Mary, justify his harassment for another six months or even longer until she felt he was strong enough to face the rigours of unemployment? Ethel had the weaponry to drive a saint to drink or even murder.

Yet Harry was patient with her, God knows he was. After the nightmares he had suffered in France, Mary had often felt she could forgive him if he picked Ethel up and threw her out of an upstairs window.

She lay listening to him sleeping quietly alongside her. After learning of the horrors

30

he had endured, she had been prepared for a different man to return to her from hospital. Exactly how different she would have found difficult to define but the expectation had been there.

She had quickly discovered his love for her had not changed. Nor had his sensitivity, a thing that had surprised her after the hell of trench warfare. He could still suffer from the pain of others and his capacity to forgive remained as deep as before. The only change here was the container in which he carried these qualities. Inevitably the war had taught him if the package were too thin, the contents could break out and leave only a shell behind.

The outer man, then, gave less away than the younger man who had courted her before the war. This she did not mind, indeed this tougher shell pleased and excited her once she had established the inner man had lost no sensitivity.

But there were some changes. For him, she felt the most profound was the loss of religious belief that his gentle, hard-working mother had once so diligently cultivated. It was a thing he had never spoken about or even hinted at but even before she found out he no longer attended chapel, she was close enough to him in mind and body to be aware of his loss.

Although she had religious faith herself, buttressed by his survival after being thought dead, this loss did not affect her personally, probably because in most other ways he remained the man she had married. Also, her faith had always been an intimate thing that had found no need for temples of worship or the high-toned words of the prelates. But because she believed it had once been an important part of Harry's life, his loss saddened her. Any loss her husband suffered was a loss to Mary Miles.

Although Harry had never shown the slightest objection to Elizabeth's being brought up in the Anglican faith and attending church with her grandmother on Sundays, Mary was only too aware that to Ethel their own failure to worship publicly had humiliating significance. Religious attendance to Ethel was positive evidence of one's respectability and absenteeism was not only to declare one's impiety but one's moral turpitude as well. That her own daughter should behave in such a way and that behaviour be witnessed by her neighbours was a personal affront to Ethel. Having brought up her two children as God-fearing, respectable girls, there could be only one reason why Mary had become an apostate herself: the influence of a Socialist. In other words Ethel had found yet another stick with which to beat Harry.

The other change in him, if it was a change, was bound up with his military service under Chadwick, the local squire's son with whom Harry had clashed when the two of them had been children and who had been made his commanding officer when they had joined up. Contemptuous of Harry's religious background, Chadwick had made him a machine gunner to ensure he would kill his full quota of the enemy. What inner torments the slaughter that followed had inflicted on Harry, she could only guess but she had little doubt it was one reason for his loss of faith.

But worse was to come when Chadwick had Harry's best friend, Gareth Evans, executed for cowardice in the face of the enemy during the battle of the Somme. Although she had needed to prise the facts out of Harry, she had learned that he had spent the last night with his friend and been present at his execution and burial the next day.

Although she had not known it at the time, the effect on him had been traumatic and all his pent-up bitterness had exploded in an inhuman act against the enemy that Chadwick had witnessed. Harry's shame had been so intense that after recovering in hospital from a head wound, he had requested a return to active service rather than take the home leave to which he was entitled.

In the end it had been a Frenchman, the husband of Nicole Levrey with whom he and Gareth had been originally billeted, who had persuaded him to go home and accept a discharge.

Lying there, listening to Harry's quiet breathing, Mary remembered her initial joy at his safe return. But it was a joy short-lived when he confessed to her that some secret compulsion was urging him back to France. Believing at first it was patriotism or a wish to be with his men when the expected 1918 German offensive began, she had at first used her problems with Ethel as a weapon to hold him back. But when

33

she saw how urgent his compulsion was, she had given way and he had written to ask Chadwick to help him.

By this time Chadwick had high regard for him as a soldier and been only too glad to aid his return. But conflict between the two men had surfaced again when Harry, unable to listen any longer to the screams of a German he had bayoneted, had disobeyed Chadwick's orders and gone out to help the man. It was when he was trying to drag the German the last few yards to safety, that Arthur Turnor had left his post to help him and received the wound that had ultimately killed him.

Furious at Harry's insubordination, Chadwick had put him under open arrest until the offensive was over. Yet the letter Mary had received from Harry had betrayed no apprehension of the punishment he might receive. Instead it was full of heartfelt relief. That night he had found out why he had needed to return to France. Chadwick had often taunted him that beneath the skin the two of them were alike, and after his inhuman act the previous year Harry had begun to believe him. The incident with the wounded German had expurgated that fear. Whatever happened now, he could live with a clear conscience. Nothing Mary had known about him before had revealed such sensitivity as that letter and nothing had revealed more the ordeal the war had inflicted on him.

Neither of them was ever to know if Chadwick would have punished him. A few days later Harry's gunpost had been overrun in a fierce battle. Respecting his courage and certain he was dead although his body was never found, Chadwick had dropped the charge.

Although the telegram Mary received only stated Harry was missing, she had known well enough what it implied. Refusing to accept his death, she had asked to see Chadwick when he was home on sick leave to learn all the details of the battle.

At first she had found him courteous and helpful. Telling her his father, Sir Henry Chadwick, had influence in high places, he promised to do all he could to get further news of Harry.

Grateful to him, she could not object to his frequent visits, although her mother's delight at the attention of the highborn young officer infuriated her and caused many a quarrel. At the end of his sick leave, Chadwick asked her to have dinner with him. Afraid he would drop his enquiries about Harry otherwise, she felt unable to refuse.

The outcome was a disaster. On the way home he stopped his car and asked her to become his mistress. Her reminder that she already had one child and was carrying another made no difference. If she would become his mistress, he told her he would ensure that they went to the best schools in England.

As always at this point her recollections disintegrated into confused scenes of outrage at what he had done next. She had never told Harry about it. At first she had used his convalescence as her excuse but now she was more honest with herself. The knowledge there was steel beneath his gentle exterior, that he could be violent under provocation, made her afraid of what action he might take against Chadwick. Chadwick had both political and economic power, particularly now that his father had died and he had inherited both his title and his estate, and so could be a dangerous enemy.

The thought reminded her she must be more careful when Chadwick's name was mentioned. In the warehouse she had drawn Harry's attention by the intensity of her dislike. More of those mistakes and his suspicions might be aroused.

A low whimper disturbed her thoughts. Slipping out of bed quietly so as not to waken Harry, she picked up a torch and tiptoed to the cot. Shading the light with a handkerchief, she bent down and saw the baby's face was screwed up in pain. Reaching down, she tried to soothe him but a moment later he gave a louder cry. As she picked him up, Harry's voice at her elbow made her start. "What's wrong? Why is he crying like that?"

She put the baby over her shoulder and patted his back. "He's probably got wind."

"I've never heard him make that sound before. Is he in pain?"

"Probably. Babies often get odd pains after a feed." Seeing his expression, she laughed. "Stop looking so worried. It's nothing serious."

The baby gave a sudden burp and she felt his

small body relax in her arms. She glanced at Harry. "There you are. He'll be all right now. You go back to bed."

He gave the child a last concerned look and then obeyed. She rocked the baby in her arms until he was asleep and then lowered him into his cot.

Harry was still awake when she returned to bed. As she slipped in between the sheets he drew her towards him. "You're not too tired, are you?" When she shook her head, he leaned forward and kissed her. A minute later their bodies fused together as they made love.

She lay awake when it was over although after a while she could tell from Harry's breathing that he had fallen asleep. Her sleeplessness was not because of his lovemaking: she had always found their union fulfilling in every way. It had been the necessity to stay quiet when the great white star to which he had carried her had burst into a million shimmering fragments. The moment when she had wanted to cry out her love for him and had been too inhibited in case her mother overheard her in the adjacent bedroom.

Her mother, she thought. The only person in the world who knew what had happened between her and Chadwick that night. Ethel had promised to say nothing and to date appeared to have kept her word.

Yet how much of her silence was due to fear of Chadwick's response if the scandal came out? Mary did not know but as she listened to Harry's steady breathing beside her, she was certain of one thing. Ethel's desire to hurt Harry seemed boundless and if she ever found an opportunity to tell him without risk to herself, she would do so.

4

HARRY ran into Chadwick early in April when travelling in the middle-class suburb of Welton. Still unable to obtain petrol, he had just emerged from a grocery shop and was crossing the pavement to collect his bicycle when a large Lagonda swung in and parked against the kerb a dozen yards away.

Although the man who stepped out was wearing civilian clothes, Harry would have recognised him anywhere. Tall and dark, wearing a small military moustache, carrying a malacca cane and impeccably dressed, Chadwick looked the archetypal young ex-officer. Standing there in the spring sunlight as he gave orders to his chauffeur, he was drawing the eyes of every female that passed by. Even Chadwick's enemies could not deny that the man was handsome and had style.

He caught sight of Harry as he was about to cross the pavement. For a moment he appeared to hesitate. Then he turned and walked towards him. "Miles! It is Miles, isn't it?"

Harry took a deep breath before replying. "Yes, it's me. Hello, Chadwick."

If Chadwick resented the omission of his military or civilian titles, the only evidence of it was a half-smile. "It's good to see you again, Miles. I heard you'd survived and got home safely."

Harry had often wondered if he had known. In spite of the enmity between them, Chadwick had taken the trouble to visit him when he had been hospitalised in France and he had half expected a similar visit on his return home, particularly as Chadwick's family estate was not far from Hull. That Chadwick had known he had survived and not paid him a visit seemed a contradiction of the man's normal behaviour.

He pushed the thought aside. The war was over and civilian customs were now the order of the day. And titled squires, he reflected dryly, were hardly famous for fraternising with the rank and file. Yet for a moment he imagined Chadwick had looked embarrassed, an almost unheard of thing in the self-confident officer he had known.

The young squire was holding out his hand. "I'm glad you made it, Miles. Congratulations."

Harry felt he had little alternative but to reciprocate. "Thanks. I'm glad you made it too."

"I ought to have looked you up but I don't seem to have had a minute to spare since I was demobbed. My father died last year, so I've had to take over the estate. I hadn't realised before how much the old boy had to do."

Harry wondered why he did not find the reason adequate. "Yes, my wife told me about him when they brought me back last year. I'm sorry. I liked Sir Henry."

Chadwick smiled. "If memory serves me right, he liked you. Certainly he did everything he could to find out if you were alive."

Harry was only too aware of the sensitive ground on which they were treading. Sir Henry Chadwick's liking for him, and his son Michael's dislike, had been born at the same moment, in their childhood during a boxing match Sir Henry had arranged to settle a quarrel between them. Outmatched by Michael, who had been taught boxing at his public school, Harry had been knocked down time and time again until he could no longer stand. It was his bravery in defeat which had earned him Sir Henry's respect, and when Michael had taunted Harry for finally being unable to climb back to his feet, the squire had denounced his son for unsportsmanlike behaviour. With Michael's deep if grudging respect for his father, it took no deep knowledge of human nature to explain his treatment of his former opponent once the war had made him Harry's commanding officer.

Wondering if Chadwick was thinking about the childhood incident too, Harry nodded. "Yes, I've always appreciated that. And the part you played in it too, of course. From what Mary tells me, you spent a good deal of your time trying to help her."

Although Chadwick's good-looking features did not change, Harry had the odd feeling that the man behind them relaxed. "I'd have been a poor officer if I hadn't, wouldn't I?" Turning, Chadwick pointed at a sign down the road. "I think this calls for a little celebration. And the White Hart's a pleasant old pub. Let's go and have a drink."

The lounge bar was filled with locals, mostly

41

middle class, plump, and self-satisfied. As Chadwick, chatting to Harry, approached the bar, Harry noticed how their voices dropped and how they moved aside to let him through. Gareth had been right about the English, he thought. "It's the way you speak, boyo, that counts here. Not your clothes or your money, although they help a bit too. It's your accent, boyo. That's what makes 'em stand to attention and say sir."

Dear old Gareth, he thought. Condemned to death by this same man I'm drinking with. Is it right what I'm doing? Was he, as Mary had so often said, a fool in his capacity to forgive? Yet Mary had not stood shoulder to shoulder with men like Chadwick and profited from their courage.

Not that their courage should confer on them a general amnesty for their sins, as the Army chaplains were ordered to promise. But Harry could not deny that when a man was facing death, there was no greater comfort than to have brave men by his side. Their failings, however grave, could wait until the morrow.

Chadwick's educated and pleasant voice interrupted his thoughts. "What will you have, Miles?"

"I'll have a beer, thanks."

Chadwick sounded amused. "A beer? On an occasion like this? Have a whisky along with me."

Harry shrugged. "All right. I'll have a whisky."

The voices around them were still subdued, making Harry wonder if Chadwick's identity were known. Possibly, but not necessarily, he thought. The man's background lent confidence and authority to his manner.

The whisky set before Harry was a double. Chadwick clinked his own glass against it. "Cheers, Miles. Good luck."

Harry felt the spirit warm his stomach. Whisky had been William's drink and when Ethel, who disapproved of alcohol, had been absent, Harry had occasionally enjoyed a tot with him. But since the war and his homecoming he had not tasted the spirit again. The wages he and Mary received from Ethel did not run to such luxuries.

Chadwick held out a gold cigarette case. "Turnor's wife tells me you've paid her a visit. What did you make of her?"

So he had visited Eleanor Turnor again. Harry accepted a cigarette. "She gave me the impression she was still in shock."

Chadwick clicked his lighter and held it out. "I thought the same. But dammit it, it's well over a year since he was killed. She ought to have pulled out of it by this time."

"I think they were a very close couple. And she had left her parents to marry him."

Chadwick's dark eyebrows came together. "Left her parents?"

"Apparently they're quite well off and didn't think Turnor was good enough for her. When she insisted on marrying him, they threw her out and cut her off without a penny."

"Did she tell you this?"

"No. Turnor told me. Just before Jerry

43

attacked us on the railway embankment."

Chadwick frowned. "It's hard to believe she'd give up so much for a man like that. I always found him a dull fellow. Whereas she must have been an attractive girl at one time. For that matter she still could be one if she'd pull herself together."

With the conversation reawakening Harry's sense of guilt, he had to stir himself to answer. "Yes, I suppose she could."

Chadwick eyed him a moment, then changed the subject. "What exactly happened to you, Miles? The last sight we had of you was when your post was being over-run. I saw a couple of Jerries jump into the post and then smoke hid everything from sight. I couldn't check afterwards because I was knocked out myself and taken to a field hospital."

Harry nodded. "A tank shell hit a wall close by. Dunn was killed and Apse had an arm blown off. Swanson was half-buried and I was knocked flat and winded. I remember a big German jumping into the post and lunging at me with his bayonet. He got me in the shoulder and was going for my stomach when I blacked out. I heard later one of his officers pulled him away and saved me."

Chadwick's laugh was a mixture of respect and amusement. "So you owe your skin to them! I think you must have a charmed life, Miles."

Harry shrugged. "Listen who's talking! I used to think you were immortal until I heard you'd got it in the leg. Does it worry you much?"

"No. Just a twinge now and then when

44

I'm riding, that's all. Am I right in thinking Swanson was in the same POW camp as you?"

So he had made enquiries, Harry thought. "Yes. They brought us back together but put us in different hospitals, Swanson went to London for a time but he's back in Hull now, working in his father's business."

"Is he, by Jove? Do you ever see him?"

"Yes. We meet every two or three weeks when he can get away. His father gives him a hard time."

Chadwick raised an eyebrow. "A hard time? I always thought his family was well off."

"They are but his father never forgave him for not avoiding conscription, which apparently he could have done because of the essential nature of the family business. So he's been given a rank-and-file job as punishment. I don't think it worries him too much. He's a happy-go-lucky character and knows he'll inherit the business one day."

Chadwick grimaced, took a sip of whisky, then changed the subject. "How are you finding things now it's all over?"

"Finding things?"

"Yes. Life in general. Are you happy?"

"Yes. Why not?"

"You don't miss the comradeship and the excitement? Never knowing what each day will bring?" Before Harry could answer, Chadwick gave his cultured laugh. "You do. I can see it. We all do."

Harry shook his head. "I might miss the

45

comradeship. But you can keep the rest."

For a moment there was a twinkle of malice in Chadwick's eyes. Then his tone changed. "I know I'm getting damned bored with it all. All this filling in of forms and handling tenants' complaints. At times I wish I'd never handed in my commission. If I hadn't, I might have been over in Ireland dishing it out to those damned rebels."

Harry knew he was referring to the Irish struggle for independence that had flared up again since the end of the war. "You wouldn't want to get involved in that, would you?"

Chadwick took another sip of whisky. "Why not? I'd enjoy shooting the brutes."

Harry could feel his dislike of the man's character returning. "Didn't you get enough of that in France?"

Chadwick stared at him. "Enough of what?"

"Killing. Personally I never want to see a gun again in my life."

Chadwick eyed him quizzically. "Come off it, Miles. You were the best soldier I ever commanded. You probably shot more Germans than I did. So don't pretend you hated it."

"You know damn well I hated it. And so did most of us."

Chadwick laughed. "Did you, Miles? All the time?"

Believing he might be referring to his own personal nightmare, Harry drew hard on his cigarette. Emptying his glass, he motioned at the barman. "Two more double whiskies, please."

Chadwick checked him. "Let me get them."

46

Harry's voice was brusque. "No! It's my round."

Glancing at him, Chadwick shrugged and drew back. "You haven't said anything about your work yet. I take it you have gone back into your mother-in-law's druggist business?"

Harry had the feeling the man knew the answer before asking the question. "Yes, I'm still there."

"And your wife?"

"She works there too."

"What about the baby? Did she have a boy or a girl?"

"A boy."

"So you've got one of each? You must both be pleased about that. How old is the girl now?"

"Six," Harry told him. As he paid for the whiskies, he decided it was his turn to ask a few questions. "What about you? Have you married yet?"

Chadwick pulled a fastidious face. "No. I can't bear the thought of being tied down. In any case I've got plans for the estate and they'll take up most of my time." When Harry made no comment, he went on: "I'm going to diversify. I wanted the Old Man to do it when he was alive but he was a landowner to his finger tips. I find it too boring. I'm thinking of buying a business here and there and putting a bit of money into others. I might even buy myself a deep sea trawler."

He could not be faulted for lack of enterprise, Harry thought, unless he was only indulging in pipe dreams. He knew his comment was malicious but could not hold it back: "Don't you get enough excitement from your fox hunting?"

Chadwick's pleasant laugh sounded above the buzz of conversation. "You hate blood sports, don't you, Miles? That's only because you've never tried them. If I could get you on a horse and get a stirrup cup inside you, you'd be tallyhoing with the best of us."

Alcohol was having its usual effect on Harry, increasing his tolerance and ironing out his resentments. "I can't think of anything more unlikely."

"How can you be so sure until you try? Why don't you visit us at The Grange one of these days?"

Thinking of Mary's expression if he were to suggest such a thing, Harry could not help smiling. "What, and go fox hunting?"

Chadwick laughed again. "You might be tempted, who knows? But seriously, why don't you? I might have something to interest you." When Harry looked curious, he went on: "If I start up a few enterprises, I'm going to need good men to run them. You might be just one of the chaps I'm looking for."

Harry decided he was not the only one the double whiskies were affecting. "Aren't you forgetting I've got a business to look after?"

"I hope you're not doing it for the sake of that mother-in-law of yours. From what I saw of her, she'd pour you down the drain as fast as look at you."

It was a remark that reminded Harry of the jarring rudeness Chadwick's kind could

48

sometimes show. "It's got nothing to do with the old girl. Mary kept it going through the war and I don't intend to let it go under now."

Chadwick's nod was a mixture of respect and mockery. "You haven't changed, have you, Miles? No matter how you hate a job, you'll stick it out to the end. I'll agree it was an asset during the war. In fact it made me put you up for that Military Medal. But you aren't at war now. You're never going to make that business really pay unless you get the capital to expand. I could see that right away on the few visits I made."

Without the whisky he had drunk, Harry would never have made the confession. "It's not just that. Mary knows how much the business meant to her father. If we were to walk out now, it wouldn't last five minutes. Her mother hasn't a clue how to run things."

"For God's sake, man, you've two children to consider. You have to think about your future, not a dead old man." When Harry did not answer, Chadwick's tone turned sarcastic. "You haven't gone back to that religious rot of yours, have you?"

Harry wondered why he had bothered to hold back the truth. "There is another reason Mary would never agree."

Chadwick gazed at him, then lit another cigarette before glancing back. "What's that?"

"Let's put it this way. We both know our relationship during the war wasn't the happiest in the world. Mary knew about it too, so she'd hardly be full of joy if I started it all over again, would she?"

49

Once again Chadwick appeared to relax. "You don't let a wife determine your future, Miles. You do what you want and the woman follows you. Surely you know that."

Harry's old dislike of the man was growing apace. "You're making some pretty big assumptions, aren't you? Why do you think I'd want to work under you again?"

"I could think of half a dozen reasons. To start with you'd make more money. Your wife wouldn't have to work. And you wouldn't have to cycle around all day. In fact if you worked for me, I'd probably get you a car. I can get all the petrol I want."

"I've noticed that already," Harry said. "You people were always good at skimming off the cream, weren't you?"

Chadwick laughed. "Don't tell me you still believe that rubbish about the Brotherhood of Man. Didn't the war teach you it's every man for himself and the devil take the hindmost?"

Although on the surface both men were still affable, Harry knew that their temporary armistice was drawing to a close. He drained his glass and rose from his stool. "All the war taught me was what ruthless bastards your kind are. If I worked for you, I'd be scared of catching the same disease."

"But you've caught it already, Miles. You showed it a dozen times during the war. That's why I want you. Work for me and you'll be a rich man in no time."

Harry crushed out his cigarette. "Thanks for the offer but I'll stick to my bicycle. The air's

50

cleaner out there than in the cars you people drive."

Chadwick showed mock regret. "I thought the last few years had taught you something about life. You disappoint me, Miles."

Harry turned back to him. "I'd disappoint you a damn sight more if I worked for you. I'd expose every fiddle that you made. Do you still feel like taking me on?"

"No, you wouldn't, Miles. That code of yours wouldn't let you."

"Try me!"

Chadwick smiled. "I'm prepared to. Any time. All you have to do is ring me."

Harry gave him a look and turned away. "I'll have to go. I've got work to do. Thanks for the drink." Pushing through the curious onlookers, he made for the door. The last thing he heard before it swung behind him was Chadwick's quizzical laugh.

5

LATER that day, reminded of her by Chadwick, Harry called round again to see Turnor's widow. "Hello. I'm travelling in this area this afternoon so thought I'd just pop round to see how things are going. You don't mind, do you?"

She looked surprised to see him. Slightly above average height, painfully thin, she was wearing the same shapeless dress as on his previous visit. Her hesitant voice, devoid of accent, reminded him that her parents had given her a good education. "No, I suppose not." A moment's hesitation and then she said: "Do you want to come inside?"

"If I may. Just for a few minutes."

She led him into a tiny hall. Ahead was a flight of stairs, to the left the sitting room. With almost all its ornaments gone, he felt its bleakness again as he followed her inside.

He felt embarrassed as he turned to her. As before, her appearance and behaviour gave the impression of a young woman whose spring of youth had died and whose life now was a penance. It showed in the indifferent gesture she made at one of the shabby armchairs. "Do you want to sit?"

Feeling it might relax them both, he sank down. "I saw Chadwick this morning. He said he'd seen you and I wondered if he'd brought you any good news."

The question seemed to surprise her. "Good news?"

"Yes. You said he was going to see if there were any government grants you were entitled to."

"Oh that! Yes, he has been round a couple of times but it seems there aren't any. I didn't expect there were."

He gave a start. "Are you saying you can't get any help?"

She frowned slightly at his question. "Sir Michael says there is a charity who will let me have five shillings a week for a year or two. He brought me the papers to sign."

"Did you sign them?"

Her apathy was giving way to resentment at his questions. "I don't like charity, Mr Miles. But Sir Michael persuaded me that I should sign."

One up for Chadwick, he thought. "Just the same it isn't much, is it? Not if you have a mortgage to pay off. Is Chadwick going to go on trying?"

"He said so but I don't believe there is anything more he can do." She frowned again as if embarrassed by the offer but feeling credit should be given for it. "He did make me an offer of his own money but of course I couldn't accept that."

"Why not? Chadwick's a rich man. He wouldn't miss anything he gave you."

Her glance discomforted him. "Would you accept charity of that kind, Mr Miles?"

"I know how you feel. But just the same, five shillings a week isn't going to be enough, is it?"

She ignored his question. "There's a possibility now that I might be able to move in with an old uncle who lives in Hebden Bridge. He always liked Arthur and he's suggested that I go as a housekeeper. His wife died last year and his daughter is abroad, so he needs someone to look after him."

"Will he pay you for your help?"

For the first time since he had known her, she smiled. "Uncle David? He was always the poor one of the family. No, but I shan't need payment. If I let this house and we put our pensions together, we should be able to manage."

"When will you go?" He was thinking what an attractive smile she had and what a difference it made to her personality. On his first visit she had seemed almost a non-person, someone from whom the very elements that constitute a human being had been removed or destroyed. Because of this, her incarceration in the house had not made its full impact on him: it had been like finding a rag doll in a cobwebbed attic. But that one smile had made her what she was — a young war widow without support from her family and needing to pawn her few possessions to stay alive.

At the same time, he thought, there was no indication from her plans that she was ready to face life again. Moving to stay with an old man to be his housekeeper and nurse was hardly the sign of a regenerated personality.

Her reply broke into his thoughts. "Not until the winter. He has an old friend from Australia staying with him at the moment and his cottage has only two bedrooms. But he expects his friend to be going back in December or January and that's when I can move in."

"And you say you'll let this house?"

"If I can. I don't want to sell it."

He believed he knew why. "Are you going to be able to manage here until then?"

"Yes, of course." Before he could pursue the point she rose. "Would you like a cup of tea?"

He rose with her. "No, I've a few more calls to make before I go home." As he moved towards the doorway, a framed photograph standing on a rickety table caught his eye. It was a photograph of Turnor in uniform and as he picked it up he saw the words 'To Lena, with love' written across it. He turned to the girl. "I didn't see this the last time I came."

She nodded. "I brought it down from my bedroom today to clean the glass."

He gazed at the picture again. "I see he called you Lena. Yet when he spoke of you to me, he called you Eleanor."

"That's because I never liked Eleanor. I made him call me Lena."

In the tiny hall he paused. "Will you do me a favour?"

Her brows furrowed. "What kind of favour?"

Self-consciously he drew out his wallet and pulled out three pound notes. When her face set and she drew back, he went on quickly:

"Please, Mrs Turnor. If you want to, you can pay me back when things get better. But please take them now. Arthur would have done just the same for me."

There was dislike in her eyes now. "You're doing this because you feel guilty about Arthur's death, aren't you? Well, there's no need. I don't want your sympathy or your charity."

He felt as if she had struck him across the face and it took him a moment to recover. "Perhaps you're right. Perhaps I do feel guilty. But I did order him not to help me. I would like you to believe that."

For a few seconds she did not move. Then her expression changed. "I'm sorry. I shouldn't have said that. But I was brought up never to accept charity and it makes me angry when people keep on offering it to me."

Shaking his head, he returned the notes to his wallet and buttoned up his coat. At the door he scribbled on a piece of paper and handed it to her. "At least take this. If you should need anything at any time, write or ring my office. This is the address and the number."

She barely glanced at the paper before slipping it into a pocket of her dress. "I shan't want anything, Mr Miles. But thank you for coming round again to see me."

★ ★ ★

Mary awoke to find Harry sitting bolt upright in bed with his cry of protest still echoing round the dark room. As she put a hand on his arm,

56

he jerked violently away. Then he recognised her voice and his taut, sweating body relaxed.

"What was it, darling? That nightmare again?"

For the moment he seemed incapable of speech. She struggled to sit up beside him. Awoken from a deep sleep, frightened by his nightmare, she had no chance to choose her words with care. "You weren't yourself, darling. It was such a terrible thing to happen to your men. Even Chadwick understood that."

The nightmare still had its grip on him. His harsh voice betrayed his shame. "It was murder. I must have killed hundreds of men before it but this was murder."

As she shuddered, his tone changed and he turned towards her. "I'm sorry, love. Did I frighten you?"

Realising he had recovered, she sank back. "You haven't had that dream for a long time, have you? What could have brought it on?"

It was a few seconds before he answered her. "Perhaps because I ran into Chadwick today."

She gave a start. "Chadwick? Where?"

"When I was travelling round Welton."

"Why didn't you tell me? Did he speak to you?"

"Yes. In fact he invited me to have a drink."

"Surely you didn't accept?"

"I hadn't much choice, had I? Yes, I had a couple of whiskies with him."

She took a deep breath. "Sometimes I think you'd drink with the devil, Harry, if he apologised for his sins. What did you talk about?"

"This and that. He wanted to know what happened to me before I went missing. Then we'd a chat about blood-sports and finally he offered me a job."

She sat up at that. "A job? Chadwick?"

"Yes. He says he's buying into industry and commerce and he's looking for staff." Wry humour entered his voice. "It's a bit of a joke, isn't it? I thought he was pulling my leg at first."

"What did you say?"

"I said I had a job but he didn't let up. He said he'd give us a car and God knows what else if I went over to him."

"That doesn't surprise me. He knows what a marvellous job you did for him during the war. What amazes me is that he has the nerve to ask you."

His laugh told her he had fully recovered from his nightmare. "He went further than that. He invited me round to The Grange for a day."

She could not hide her anger any longer. "Don't tell me you agreed to go?"

"Don't be silly. Of course I didn't."

"I should hope not. I wouldn't go there if the King himself ordered it."

She realised she had gone too far when he turned towards her. "What is it, love? Why do you hate him so much?"

She affected surprise. "How can you ask that after all he did to you?"

"That's all over now. We can't keep grudges going forever."

"I never said we should. But working for him

58

is different. It would put you at his mercy again, just as you were during the war?"

He laughed at her fears. "I'm not going to work for him. Nor are we going to visit him. You asked me what we'd talked about and I've told you. That's the beginning and the end of it."

"Then that's all right," she said. "Only you had me worried for a moment. I know how plausible he can be." Giving him no chance to question her further, she climbed out of bed. "You'll have to change your pyjamas. Those are soaked through. I'll get you another pair."

He was asleep five minutes later, exhausted by the nightmare. She took longer to sleep. One chance meeting with Chadwick, she thought, and all the dark memories of the past were brought back. Did that explain her present fear that his influence on their lives was not yet over? Or were there more tangible reasons behind her premonition? The thought was sufficient to keep her awake half the night.

★ ★ ★

Swanson shook his head when Harry finished speaking. "I think you're off your rocker, old lad. I'd jump at it like a shot if the Major offered me a job."

"Then you'd be a damn fool," Harry said. "Your old man isn't going to keep you a tally clerk for the rest of your life."

Swanson grimaced and took a sip of beer. "He hasn't done a bad job so far, has he?"

"Come on. The war's only been over a year. He's bound to relent soon."

"He's not going to relent enough to give me a decent job. He's going to make me work my way to the top. Step by bloody step. He's already told me that."

Swanson's expression brought a smile from Harry. During their darkest days in France Swanson had always managed to find a joke somewhere and his humour had been a godsend during their months of privation in a prisoner of war camp. The same age as Harry, he was a lanky, sandy-haired man with a permanent twinkle in his eyes. At the moment the two men were seated in the Hare and Hounds, a pub that was midway between No. fifty-seven and Swanson's lodgings.

"Step by step or not, you'll be at the top one day," Harry pointed out. "So you'd be a damn fool to antagonise your Dad again and risk losing everything."

Swanson's scowl as he tossed a cigarette at Harry acknowledged the soundness of his reasoning. "That doesn't apply to you though, does it? Not when you've all these problems with your mother-in-law."

A sudden crash of glass, followed by a loud burst of laughter, made both men turn. A barmaid carrying a tray had stumbled and a pint of beer had shot all over a seated man's trousers. As the blushing barmaid led the man behind the counter, Swanson gave a wicked chuckle. "Daisy'll do anything to get a man's trousers off. Why don't we sit over there the next time? One of us might be lucky."

As the laughter died down, he turned back to Harry. "So you're not going to take up Chadwick's offer?"

"Not a chance. Mary would murder me if I even thought about it. She hates Chadwick."

Swanson struck a match and lit their cigarettes. "Yet he did help her, didn't he, after you were reported missing?"

A faint line appeared between Harry's eyesbrows.

"Yes, but she can't forget some of the other things he did. Like having Gareth court-martialled and executed."

Knowing nothing about Chadwick's earlier persecution of Harry, Swanson almost pointed out that Gareth had committed the cardinal sin of fleeing the field of battle. Instead his friendship prevailed. "All the same, you have to admit he was a bloody good officer." At Harry's grudging expression, he grinned. "At least I thought he was. So why shouldn't he be a good employer? Wouldn't you prefer a job with him than slogging around all day on a bicycle and facing that mother-in-law of yours every night?" As Harry slowly exhaled smoke, Swanson laughed aloud. "Admit it, old lad. You're as fed up with your job these days as I am of mine."

"Being fed up is one thing," Harry said. "Working for Chadwick is another."

Swanson looked unconvinced. "Even when that old witch keeps threatening to sell the

61

business? Jobs aren't easy to get these days, old lad."

Harry had a rare moment of irritation. "For Christ's sake stop talking about Chadwick. Get off your backside instead and get us another round of drinks."

6

ETHEL did not go to America in May of that year. She wanted to go — of that Mary had no doubt — but in spite of Jack Watson's supplications, she held to her announcement that she would go the following year 'all being well'. As 'all being well' was to Ethel a multi-purpose comment that gave her full licence to change her mind according to her mood, Harry and Mary could only hope that Jack Watson's entreaties would eventually prevail, although both began to wonder as the months slipped by. Of the two, Mary was the more hopeful. "She'll go one of these days, darling. You weren't here to see it but she really fell for Jack. I can't see her risking losing him."

During this period Harry paid occasional visits to Lena Turnor. In spite of Mary's protests that he was being over-sensitive, the guilt he still felt over Turnor's death made him need the assurance that his widow was coping with her situation.

In turn, Lena began giving the impression his visits were not wholly unwelcome, although at first he believed this was only because they provided an interlude in the dreary and lonely routine of her life.

For his own part, Harry discovered that the visits began to provide a personal reward. With the problem of Ethel and Elizabeth constantly on his mind, now and then he had felt a human need to discuss it with someone outside his own family and, until he had met Lena Turnor, Swanson had been his only confidant. Swanson, however, was a bachelor and his understanding and comments on family life were consequently limited. In addition, he was a wartime comrade who had served under Harry, and the disciplines of war had demanded that a senior NCO betray a minimum of temperament and sensitivity, particularly when under stress. The reaction of both Chadwick and his crew made Harry believe he had acted this role tolerably well, which made it all the more difficult to reveal himself to Swanson today as the sensitive, self-critical human being that he really was.

With Lena Turnor no such problem existed. She had not known him as a soldier and they could hardly be called friends. In the way, therefore, that a man or woman shares with a stranger on a train thoughts that they would not dream of sharing with their wife or husband, he gradually found himself making comments and admissions that helped him to clarify his problems.

In turn he began to hope that if he continued to show such trust in her she might eventually be encouraged to confide in him, and that might open up her self-made prison.

But here he was disappointed. Only once or twice did she relax and allow him to see beyond the tightly-locked gates of her grief. Nevertheless she made it clear that she liked him to talk and at each visit he found himself adding one more small piece to the overall picture of his life.

Encouraged by this thaw in their relationship, he had a talk with Mary and on his next visit took a parcel with him. "I hope this isn't going to offend you but my wife made this up and asked if you'd accept it." When she made a sharp exclamation, he went on quickly: "Please don't be angry. I know how you feel about charity but it's only a few groceries and things. As Mary says, we've been lucky in the way we came out of the war and we'd like you to share a little of that luck with us."

Aware he was using Mary to mollify her, even though it was with his wife's consent, he waited for her reaction with some embarrassment. Her first words surprised him. "Is this the truth, Harry? Did your wife really make up this parcel?"

"Yes. She knows all about Arthur and I've told her all about you. She doesn't see this as charity, any more than I do. Please accept it, Lena. It'll please her very much."

She glanced at the parcel again, then gave a faint shrug of resignation. "Very well. If Mary made it up for me, I will. Please thank her for me."

He felt he had won a major victory. "Mary also asked if you would visit us sometime. I would fetch you and bring you back."

She shook her head before he had finished speaking. "No, thank you. I never go out visiting these days."

65

"But isn't that a mistake? Wouldn't a change do you good?"

"I'll be getting a change. It isn't that long before I go to Hebden Bridge."

He wanted to tell her she needed the company of people of her own age. "That's still six months away. Won't you change your mind? We'd enjoy your company."

For the second time in their acquaintance she smiled. "You'd enjoy my company, Harry? That I do find very hard to believe." Before he could protest, she went on: "It's kind of your wife but really I can't come. So please don't ask me again."

Although she had shut the door on his invitation, he realised that her passive resignation was not as complete as he had at first imagined. She was capable enough of making positive decisions and holding on to them with tenacity, but only decisions that were self-destructive. There were, he thought every time he visited her that year, no higher prison walls than those the mind erects when it loses faith in its stars.

★ ★ ★

In early October Harry and Mary took Elizabeth to the Hull Fair. Although for the young in the city it was the event of the year, it was Elizabeth's first visit and Ethel, who hated 'being jostled by the rabble' as she put it, had offered to look after Frank for the evening while her parents took her.

The child's face betrayed her growing

66

excitement as Harry and Mary, holding her hands, led her down Walton Street. On either side rickety stalls, lit by naphtha flares and manned by brass-throated vendors, stood cheek by jowl. The misty October night, stained crimson by the flares and the fairground ahead, was alive with chatter, laughter, and raucous barrel organ music. Harry glanced at Mary. "Do you remember when we used to come?"

She nodded and laughed. "It's fun to be back, isn't it?"

The crowds were dense along the narrow street, allowing them to move only at a snail's pace. As they passed a brilliantly-lit stall surrounded by a packed crowd, Elizabeth turned up her excited face to Mary. "Is this the fair, Mummy?"

"No, darling. We've a long way to go yet. These are just stalls selling things."

"What kind of things, Mummy?"

"Oh, sarsaparilla, coconuts, pomegranates, balloons, fish and chips, brandysnap . . . "

"What's brandysnap, Mummy?"

Mary glanced at Harry, who laughed. "I don't know what it's made of, love, but you can have some later if you like." Bending down, he swung the child up on his shoulders. "How's that? Can you see better now?"

The girl nodded, her fascinated eyes taking in the brightly-lit stall. "What are all those people doing, Daddy?"

"It's a raffle, love. They've bought tickets with numbers on. Do you see that big wheel at the back of the stall? In a minute the man will spin it round and whichever number stops opposite the pointer will be the winner. There — he's spinning it now. See if you can read the number."

"89," the girl announced a moment later.

"That's it. And there's the winner — that man in the cap and grey overcoat. See him?"

The excited girl nodded. "They're giving him a garden spade."

"That's right. He can choose his own prize."

It took them a further ten minutes to reach the entrance of the fairground. From her perch on Harry's shoulders, the girl gave a cry of delight. "Is this it, Daddy?"

"This is it, love. People come from all over the country to see it. It's big, isn't it?"

The girl's eyes were huge and shining. "It's enormous, Daddy. Absolutely enormous."

Lights shone everywhere on the huge, cinder-covered field, circling on roundabouts, running up dippers and big wheels, and coruscating in the evening sky. Steam engines hissed and pounded and organs bellowed out popular tunes. Crowds surged, swayed, laughed, and sang. Boys chased squealing girls and blew toy snakes into their faces. The night air, full of gaiety and oily smells, was intoxicating.

Harry swung Elizabeth down from his shoulders. "What would you like to do first?"

The girl, her cheeks flushed with excitement, pointed at a nearby roundabout on which artificial horses were gyrating. "Can I go on that, Daddy?"

Harry grinned at Mary. "We'll all go on it. Come on."

Mary threw up her hands in mock protest. "You're not serious?"

He caught her hand and pulled her towards the roundabout. "If we're going on, you are too. Isn't she, Elizabeth?"

The child was in fits of laughter. "You must, Mummy. You must."

Elizabeth had two rides on the roundabout. During the first Harry shared a horse with her. For the second he swung her in front of Mary and stood watching the two of them from the cindered ground outside. Each time they raced past him, with their long golden hair rising and falling in unison, Elizabeth waved at him and he waved back.

The difference in the child tonight, now that she was alone with them, had to be seen to be believed, he thought. He also thought how beautiful they both looked, the tall, graceful mother and the child who was almost a miniature replica of her. At that moment Harry Miles' gratitude to have survived the war and be returned to his family was almost overwhelming.

They went on the helter-skelter next and slid all the way down on coconut mats. Then to the steamboats, the cakewalk, and to Bostock and Wombwell's big marquee to let Elizabeth see the animal menagerie. Finally, after playing darts and rolling pennies for prizes, they bought fish and chips and a large bottle of sarsaparilla which they shared between them. As they were making towards the Walton Street exit, the child pointed at a stall ahead. "What are they doing, Daddy?"

The stall was a shooting gallery and half a dozen men were lined up firing at fixed targets. Thinking Harry had not heard the girl, Mary answered for him. "They're shooting with guns, darling. Trying to win prizes." Without thinking, she turned to Harry. "You ought to be able to win her something there, darling."

He did not hear her. Before his eyes the gallery had turned into a firing trench and the men into muddy khaki figures. As the scene grew more vivid, the fairground lights became star shells, grenades, and bursting mortar bombs.

Mary's cry and her hand on his arm brought him back to the present. "Harry, what is it? You've gone as white as a sheet."

He pulled himself together. "It's nothing. Don't let it spoil things. I'm all right."

Noticing his eyes were still fixed on the shooting gallery, she understood. Gripping his arm tightly, she glanced down at the puzzled Elizabeth. "Come along, darling. It's getting late and we promised Grannie we'd be home by ten."

The child gave a wail of disappointment. "Can't we stay just a little longer, Mummy?"

"No, darling. We mustn't make Grannie cross and we've both got a hard day tomorrow. So be a good girl and hurry along."

70

7

IT was December when Lena Turnor told Harry her uncle had written to say she could move into his cottage early in January. Knowing tenants for her present house would not be easy to find with so much unemployment about, and wanting her to get as good a rent as possible, Harry told her he would begin making enquiries for her while on his rounds.

During this time Ethel had made no further move regarding her American trip. To compensate for her influence over Elizabeth, the young couple gave all their spare time to the child but that spare time was severely limited. Trade was picking up only slowly after the massive injuries Europe had inflicted on itself, and both Harry and Mary were forced to work long hours just to keep the business afloat. In addition, Mary had her young baby to look after. Although the doctor pronounced him basically a healthy child, after Christmas he went down with an illness that for a while was suspected of being the dreaded influenza that had first appeared in 1918. A virulent strain, perhaps caused and certainly abetted by the carnage and the food shortages of recent years, it was sweeping unchecked across Europe and Asia and before its course was run was to kill over fifty million people.

Although eventually Dr Armstrong decided he

was not suffering from the disease, the boy was nevertheless confined to bed for nearly a month. For the first two weeks, until influenza was no longer suspected, both Mary and Harry kept Elizabeth well away from the boy's room and it was only after Armstrong and a fellow doctor declared a visit would put Elizabeth under no danger that they let the girl see her brother.

Ethel, however, who had not paid a single visit to the boy during his illness, hotly disagreed with their decision. "You can't risk the girl's health in this way. It's quite irresponsible."

At first, aware her concern was for Elizabeth's well-being, Mary was patient with her. "It's quite safe now, Mother. Whatever was wrong with him, and it wasn't influenza, is over now. Both doctors have confirmed it and told us it's quite safe for Elizabeth to see him."

Ethel's exclamation was one of pure contempt. "Doctors! You've already told me they don't know what's been wrong with him. So how can they know what's safe and what isn't?"

Aware she had a point, Mary nodded. "They haven't known what the illness has been, that's true, but they're now quite sure it was never an infectious or contagious disease. So it's quite safe to visit him. If I thought there was any danger, I would hardly let Elizabeth see him myself, would I?"

Ethel's sniff had contemptuous connotations that never failed to put the hackles up of anyone with whom she was arguing. "That's as maybe. But I believe it's wrong to take the slightest risk with a child's health."

"So do I, for heaven's sake. But I keep telling you, we're not taking a risk. Two doctors say so."

"I don't care what two doctors say. Why must Elizabeth see the boy until he's fully well again? What's the great urgency?"

Mary could feel her temper beginning to fray. "Mother, Frank is Elizabeth's brother. And she's not seen him for nearly three weeks. Why do you like to keep them apart? It's not the first time I've noticed it."

Ethel bristled immediately. "What do you mean by that? Why would I want to keep them apart?"

"I don't know why, but you do. I've noticed it when Elizabeth wants to help me bath Frank or change his clothes. It's almost as if you don't want the two of them to grow up like a normal brother and sister."

There were two red spots high up on Ethel's cheekbones now. "That's a wicked thing to say. When do I come between them?"

"You do it all the time. Often by example. How often have you been in to see Frank while he's been ill? Do you think Elizabeth won't have noticed that?"

Ethel's laugh was bitter. "Were you disappointed, dear?"

Mary stared at her. "What does that mean?"

"You thought for a long time it was influenza, didn't you? Were you hoping I'd catch it too?"

Mary's eyes widened in astonishment. "That's a dreadful thing to say."

"No more dreadful than your suggesting I'm

73

trying to influence Elizabeth against her brother. Who put you up to it? Was it Harry again?"

"No, it wasn't Harry. I notice these things, not Harry."

Ethel gave her sniff again. "Nothing's ever Harry's fault, is it? He's not a saint, you know."

Mary was breathing hard now. "He's a saint to live with you, Mother. I don't know another man in the world who could put up with you."

No remark could have stung Ethel more. "Put up with me! Is that what he's doing? I'll tell you why he puts up with me, my girl. It's because he knows which side his bread's buttered on. I gave him a job and a home for his family and this is the gratitude I get. Put up with me indeed!"

The injustice of the accusation killed the last of Mary's self-control. "Are you saying that is the only reason he works for you? And that he lives here out of choice? My God, Mother, he can't wait for a home of his own. Nor can I. You've done nothing but make our lives a misery ever since we've been with you."

Ethel's unstable temper snapped. "Then you know what to do! Get out! Get out, but don't expect to have a job when you do. I'll sell the business and your Harry can get into the dole queue where he belongs. And don't think you can come back with your tails between your legs when you can't pay the rent. It'll be all over, my girl. You'll find out what a cold world it is out there."

Aware the crisis both she and Harry had expected had arrived at last, Mary could feel her heart thumping hard. "I already know what a cold world it is, Mother. If the war hadn't taught me that, you have. Very well. I'll tell Harry tonight to start looking for a house. We'll try to be out as quickly as possible."

It was only then that Ethel remembered her Achilles' heel. "I suppose that means you'll take Elizabeth away too?"

"Of course we'll take Elizabeth. You don't think we'll leave her behind, do you?"

Ethel's face was now a study of emotions. Hostility was still dominant but alarm was beginning to merge with it. "Have you thought how she might feel about this?"

It had been Mary's first thought but she did her best to hide it. "How would she feel if we left her behind? We're a family and we're going to stay a family. She'll be able to see you from time to time."

"From time to time! Do you think that's going to be enough for her?"

Fear that Ethel might be right drove all compassion from Mary. "You talk as if she were your child. She's ours and she's going to live with us in the way she should. That's something you'll have to live with."

"But that would be cruel to her. You know how attached she is to me."

"Who are you feeling sorry for, Mother? Elizabeth or yourself?"

"That's a wicked thing to say. You know how much I care for the child."

"Then you shouldn't cause trouble the way you do. You can't have your cake and eat it."

Ethel's reply was a mixture of hostility and bitterness. "You've been glad enough to have me look after her all these years. So how can you suddenly turn round and do this to me?"

"We're not doing anything, Mother. You're the one who's just told us to get out."

The working of Ethel's features betrayed her emotional conflict. From the way she braced herself, her recantation was as painful as the drawing out of teeth.

"Perhaps that was a little hasty of me, although heaven knows the things you said were enough to provoke a saint. Very well, you can stay if you wish. I don't expect your father would want me to put you out into the street."

Mary was in no mood to let her off the hook. "Don't bring Dad into it, Mother. If he'd been alive he'd never have let you behave this way in the first place."

Ethel's face set again. "Do you want to stay or don't you?"

Mary had already made her own decision. "I'll talk to Harry tonight and tell him what you plan to do if we leave. I'll let you know what he says tomorrow."

Ethel's laugh of hostility was tinged with dismay. "If you let him decide for you, you're sure to leave. He's always disliked me."

"A moment ago you were accusing him of sponging on you. Why would he want to lose his job and his home if you were right?"

Ethel's temperament, which made her her own worst enemy, was never more obvious than at that moment. With an exclamation of disgust she walked stiffly to the kitchen door, then turned. "I've no more time to stand here arguing with you. Talk to your precious Harry and do what he wants! But remember what I've told you about Elizabeth and what I'll do with the business. Mark my words, you'll be both coming back to me with your tails between your legs in six months time. And when you do, don't expect any mercy from me."

8

THAT evening Mary barely gave Harry time to hand over his order book before she told him about her quarrel with Ethel. He listened in silence, then shrugged his shoulders. "It had to come, hadn't it? Only I'm surprised she was the one who gave the ultimatum. I always thought she was so afraid of losing Elizabeth that she'd keep a hold of herself."

"She is afraid of losing her. But sometimes she can't control that terrible temper of hers. She did this once before, when you were in France."

He nodded. "I remember your telling me. But she did back down, didn't she?"

"Yes. And for Elizabeth's sake she probably will again. But do we want her to this time?"

He gave a start as his brown eyes searched her face. "Are you saying what I'm hoping you're saying?"

It all burst from her then. "Yes, I am! Oh, God, yes, I am! I'm sick to death of her interfering with our lives. I'm sick to death of her constant sniping at you. I want to be free to be a proper wife to you. I want to be able to love you without thinking she's listening to us. I want . . . " She choked on her words and threw her arms around him.

He laughed aloud as he held her tightly. "Why

haven't you come out with all this before?"

She was sobbing freely now. "Because I hate the idea of your having to scratch around looking for a job. You've gone through enough these last four years without that."

He laughed again and kissed her wet face. "That's the least of our problems. If the worst happens I can always go back to carpentry."

"Yes, but how will we get a house? If she sells the business we'll both be out of work, so how can we get a mortgage?"

"We won't bother with a mortgage. We'll rent a house for a while. I know of one already in St George's Road, not that far from Elizabeth's school."

Ashamed of her tears, she tried to find a handkerchief but failed. Smiling he held out his own. She blew her nose, then stared at him accusingly. "You fraud! You've been keeping an eye open all this time for empty houses, haven't you?"

He grinned. "Are you surprised? Living here has been a bit like living on a volcano."

She thought he already looked ten years younger. "I don't know any other man in the world who could have stood it so long."

He shrugged. "She hasn't given us much choice, has she?"

Her anger returned. "No. Not after she stole Dad's new will that would have given us control of the business. But it's all over now. Let's go and tell her so." Then she paused. "But isn't St George's Road too near her? We want to get Elizabeth as far away as possible, don't we?"

He shook his head. "Not at first. It could hurt her too much if she can't see Ethel occasionally. We can take a house further away when she gets used to the move."

She realised he was right. "What sort of a house is it?"

"Quite small but then we don't want a larger one until I've got a job. It needs painting and a few other small jobs but I can do all those myself. I think you'll like it."

She was thinking that a mud hut would seem like paradise after No. fifty seven. "When can I see it?"

"More or less any time, I should think. She always seems to be home."

"She?"

He stared at her, then laughed apologetically. "Sorry. I thought you'd guessed from the address. It's Lena Turnor's house."

"Lena Turnor's?"

"Yes. Don't you remember my telling you she's going to her uncle in Hebden Bridge as soon as she lets her place?"

"But you said she's pawned most of its contents?"

"She has, but the basics are still there." When she hesitated, he went on: "It couldn't be better situated, not just for Elizabeth's school but for the business as well. After all, I suppose there is just a chance your mother might not sell it."

She had recovered from her surprise. "I expect it will help Mrs Turnor if we take it?"

"Of course it will. She needs the money to pay off the mortgage."

Her hesitation was too brief to be noticed. "All right. As soon as we can, take me round to see it." Her eyes moved to the clock over the doorway. "Now I suppose we'd better get over and tell Mother. I daren't think what she's been saying to Elizabeth since she got home from school."

He winced and hurried over to damp down the stove. "You're right. I'd forgotten that. We'd better get over."

Five minutes later they were hurrying down the darkened lane. As she paused at the back garden gate of No. fifty seven, he laid a hand on her arm. "What's the matter? Are you nervous?"

She nodded. "It's that temper of hers, Harry. You never know what she'll do next.

He sighed ruefully. "I think I'd rather face a Jerry whizbang myself. But it has to be done, so let's get it over."

* * *

Their fears were realised almost before they entered the house. Elizabeth, who had clearly been waiting for them, burst open the door that led into the living room and ran frantically towards Mary. "Grannie says you're going to take me away from her! You can't, Mummy! You can't!"

Glancing at Harry, Mary bent down to take the distraught girl into her arms. "Wait a minute, darling. Give us a chance to explain."

The sobbing girl jerked away from her. "Then

81

you are! You're horrible, both of you. I hate you!" Turning, she ran back into the sitting room and threw herself into Ethel's arms.

The young couple followed her. Mary, breathless with nervousness and distress, stared at Ethel accusingly. "What have you been saying to her, Mother?"

Ethel, whose expression indicated that she was ready for mortal combat, sat quite still on the sofa and gazed back defiantly. "I've only told her what you told me. That if your husband chooses to leave here, you'll be taking her with you. Isn't that what you said?"

Mary tried again to take the child in her arms. Instead she clung to Ethel. "Leave me alone! I'm not going to leave Grannie. I'm not, I'm not! You can't make me."

"Darling, listen to me. We'll only be going a few streets away. You'll be able to walk over to see Grannie. That won't be so bad, will it?"

Ethel had gone white to the lips at her words. "Then you are leaving?"

Mary nodded. "Yes, Mother. You've left us no choice."

Elizabeth's hysteria grew. "I'm not going! I won't, I won't!"

Harry moved to Mary's side. "Love, you wouldn't want us to leave you behind. You'd think we didn't care for you if we did that. Mummy's telling the truth. You'll be near enough to walk over to see Grannie."

The girl squirmed away as he tried to take her into his arms. "That's not true. Grannie says you want to take me away for good. And I won't go. I won't!"

Mary turned accusingly to Ethel. "Did you say that to her, Mother?"

Behind Ethel's haughty stare, Mary could see a glint of triumph. "What if I did? It's true, isn't it? You do want to take her away from me. I've known it a long time."

Mary's voice shook. "You're wicked, Mother. I've never realised before just how wicked you are."

"And you don't think it's wicked to take a child from her grandmother who might not have long to live? You're a fine one to talk."

There was an immediate cry of protest from Elizabeth. "You mustn't die, Grannie! Please don't die."

Harry, whose face had set at Ethel's words, took another step towards the child. "Your grandmother isn't going to die, Elizabeth. Her kind live for ever. You can be sure of that."

Ethel, with her arms wrapped tightly around Elizabeth, stiffened in outrage. "How dare you talk to me like that? You, whom William took from the gutter and made what you are today."

Harry nodded quietly. "I know what William did. And I know what he'd do today if he saw you trying to come between a child and her parents. You ought to be ashamed of yourself, Mother."

The accusation, coming from him of all men, drove Ethel's unstable temper over the edge. "You're a fine one to talk about people living forever! When I think of all the fine men who were killed in the war, it's a disgrace that you ever came back. But I suppose that's because the devil looks after his own."

There was a gasp from Mary. Ignoring Ethel, Harry turned to Elizabeth. "You can stop your crying, love. It won't do you any good because we're moving from this house as soon as possible and you're coming with us. Now leave your Grannie and come upstairs with me and Mummy. We've a lot of things to talk about."

Ethel's arms tightened round the child as Elizabeth shrank away from him. Harry's eyes moved to the woman. "I want you to let her go, Mother. If you don't, I shall take her from you. So make up your mind one way or the other."

Mary had never heard him speak this way before and neither had Ethel. For a moment she seemed about to refuse. Then, as Harry took another step forward, she released the girl and stood up. Although her words were addressed to Elizabeth, her eyes were throwing daggers at Harry. "Do as your father says, dear. But don't be afraid that you're not going to see your Grannie again. I promise you that will never, never happen."

9

MARY had little sleep that night. Elizabeth's hysteria at the thought of being parted from Ethel did not cease on her being put to bed. Her cries and sobs, which Mary was only too aware were being heard with satisfaction by Ethel, forced her to remain in the child's bedroom in case Ethel compounded the situation by coming to the child herself.

It was after one thirty when Harry entered the darkened bedroom. Elizabeth had fallen into a fitful sleep that was interrupted by muted sobs and spasms of her small body. Motioning Harry to stay where he was, Mary tiptoed across to him. "It's all right," she whispered. "Go back to bed. I think she'll sleep now."

His whisper betrayed his distress. "I've never heard her cry that way before. Are you sure she's all right?"

Until now she had kept her patience with the girl but his concern changed her mood. "Of course she is. She's playing up, that's all, to get her own way. The best thing to do is not to let her think she's upsetting us."

He was clearly unconvinced. As another sob broke from the sleeping girl, he switched on his torch and tiptoed towards the bed. He bent over her for a moment, then glanced at Mary. "She's very hot. Are you sure she's not feverish?"

85

She shook her head, drew him away, and led him back to their bedroom. Unable to switch on the light for fear of awakening the baby who was sleeping in his cot along-side the bed, she took the lighted torch from him. "She's hot because she's been throwing a tantrum for the last three hours. You don't have to worry, there's nothing wrong with her."

He dropped on the bed. "I expected she'd be upset if we took her away but I never thought it would affect her like this."

She sat down beside him. "I did. That's why we must get her away. But stop worrying. She's only a child, even if at times she doesn't talk like one. She'll get over it in a week or two. Children do, you know."

He shifted uneasily. "I hope you're right. She sounded brokenhearted to me."

"That's what Mother's done to her," she said bitterly. "Made herself indispensable in every possible way." Then, noticing how tired he looked, she drew back the bedclothes. "You're not well yet, Harry. Get into bed and stop worrying about her."

He resisted her for a moment, then obeyed. She went out on the landing again and stood outside Elizabeth's door. By this time the girl's sobs had ceased and her breathing was steady. Satisfied, she returned to Harry. "She's all right now," she whispered. "She's fast asleep."

As she slipped into bed, he drew her towards him. Remembering she had left the door open so as to hear Elizabeth should she awaken, Mary did not immediately respond. Had he persisted she would have closed the door and given him her body but he was too sensitive a man to ignore her hesitation. Making no complaint, he kissed her and sank back on his pillow.

She lay staring at the dark ceiling as his breathing quietened into sleep. Every aspect of their married life was being blighted by Ethel's presence, she thought. No matter how Elizabeth behaved, it was vital they left No. fifty-seven before the damage became irreparable.

* * *

There was no relief from tension the following morning. Elizabeth, sullen and sniffing, complained she wasn't feeling well and couldn't go to school while Ethel, usually one of the first up, remained in her room. As Molly, the maid, set the breakfast table and then disappeared into the kitchen, Harry turned to Mary. "What do you think? Is she only playing up?"

She knew he was referring to Elizabeth. "She is, of course, but she has a touch of fever too. She's brought it on herself by all that hysteria last night."

"So you think we should keep her from school today?"

"I think we'll have to. If she went, she'd be such a misery they'd probably send her home."

He shook his head as he sat down at the table. "I don't like to see her so upset."

Her anger returned. "I'll bet mother was loving every minute of it last night."

"Why isn't she down this morning?" he asked.

"She's sulking too, I expect." Then her tone changed. "If we're leaving, let's do it quickly, Harry. Otherwise life's going to be impossible here."

He nodded wryly as he reached out for the teapot. "I've had the same thought. When can you take a look at the house?"

"I suppose I could go this morning. I've only two appointments in the office and I could put both of them off."

"What about Frank?"

"Molly can look after him. We won't be long, will we?" When Harry shook his head, she went on: "But will it be all right for Mrs Turnor?"

"I don't see why not. Why don't we go round and find out?" As she hesitated, he read her thoughts. "I know it means leaving Ethel and Elizabeth alone together but that's something we can't avoid until we move out. So the sooner we get things settled the better."

She hesitated no longer. "All right. I'll have a word with Molly and cancel my appointments while you finish your breakfast. Then we'll go and get it over."

★ ★ ★

They returned to the office from St George's Road two hours later. Both were drenched: they had walked there and back and it had begun to rain only a few minutes after they started out. As Harry removed his sodden coat and picked

88

up his oilskins, Mary checked him. "You can't go on your rounds like that. Dry yourself first and wait until the rain eases off. You'll catch your death of cold otherwise."

"Rubbish," he said.

"It's not rubbish. Dr Armstrong said it would be another six months before you got your health back."

"Armstrong doesn't know what he's talking about. I'm as fit as a lop these days."

She pulled off her sodden shoes. "What's a lop?"

He laughed. "Come to think of it, I've no idea. It's something my father used to say. Probably it's a flea."

She sank into a chair and began running a comb through her long, blond hair. "Anyway, there's no point in working ourselves to death, is there? Not if Mother intends to sell the business." Then her voice changed. "Why are you looking at me like that?"

He lit a cigarette before answering her. "You aren't too keen on the house, are you?"

She took a few seconds to reply. "If you want me to be honest, I would prefer something a little bigger now that we have a boy as well as a girl. But on the other hand it is ideally situated for Elizabeth's school. And for us too if Mother should have second thoughts about selling out."

He gave a wry grin. "I shouldn't think that's likely, would you? Not after last night."

She winced as the comb snagged in her wet hair. "Likely, no. But Connie's husband's health

89

seems to be getting worse, so she might just stop to think. But that's only supposition. I still believe she'll sell."

Her conviction made him change the subject. "You haven't said anything about furniture yet. Can we manage there until we've the time and money to do some shopping?"

"I think so. There are two beds, chairs and a table, and cooking facilities. Yes, we'll manage."

"What did you think of Lena Turnor?"

"I thought you'd described her quite well. Apathetic and lost." She gave a faint smile. "Much as I'd have been if you hadn't come back."

He frowned at that. "Life has to go on. And you'd have had Elizabeth and Frank to think about."

"That's true. She isn't as lucky as I am. I wonder if that was why she wasn't very friendly? Did you notice she hardly spoke to me?"

"That seems to be her normal behaviour when she meets someone new. She was the same with me at first."

"Yet she seemed pleased enough to see you today."

He shrugged. "I suppose she's got used to me. And I could tell she's delighted to let the house. At least she'll have enough money now to be a little independent when she moves."

She did not tell him it was her main reason for agreeing to take the house. "Does she intend to stay with her uncle for good now? Or has she other plans?"

"I don't think she knows what her plans are.

90

She just seems to live from day to day. But perhaps she'll meet someone over in Hebden Bridge. I hope so."

When she did not reply, he turned to the window and gazed out. "I wonder what's happening at No. fifty-seven. Do you think they'll both be up by this time?"

"Mother would be up the moment we left the house," she said. "And then straight into Elizabeth's room."

He frowned. "It's going to be hard on the girl. I can't help feeling sorry for her."

She put down her comb and pulled him round to face her. "It's because we feel sorry for her that we must get her away. Are you listening to me?"

His shapely mouth gave her a smile. "Yes, I'm listening."

"Good. Then stop worrying." Seeing the rain was easing off, she crossed the office to collect a dry coat. "I'll have to go and pick up Frank now. How much notice do you think we should give Mother? Mrs Turnor said we could move in this coming weekend, didn't she?"

"Yes, but I think we ought to give Ethel at least one more week. In case she wants to let our rooms."

At any other time she would have agreed but her mother's behaviour the previous night had hardened her heart. "Harry, it's she who's throwing us out. And in any case, can you see Mother turning into a landlady? Let's tell her we're leaving this Saturday. If she doesn't like it, she's only got herself to blame."

10

FROM her office window, Mary saw Ethel marching down the lane towards the warehouse the following morning. The double-breasted, high-collared coat her mother was wearing made Mary think of an armoured Roman centurion advancing into battle. Nor did the umbrella she was carrying like an offensive weapon do anything to banish the impression.

Mary could feel her legs trembling as she sank down into her chair. She had hoped that Ethel's behaviour the previous evening when she and Harry had announced their intention of moving out that weekend would last for the remaining four days. Ethel had been grim-faced and curt but there had been none of the fireworks both Mary and Harry had expected. It almost seemed as if Ethel had accepted their decision and had no further intention of contesting it.

Not that her mood had suggested any weakening of her resolve to punish them. On the contrary every curt remark she had made had seemed to carry a barbed threat. But with both Mary and Harry resigned to losing the business and expecting into the bargain more bitter quarrels over the custody of Elizabeth, the woman's silent hostility had come almost as a relief.

But that had been last night, Mary thought, when Harry had been at her side to give her strength and support. In the cold, early light of a winter morning, facing a hostile Ethel was a very different proposition.

She wondered if her mother's appearance had anything to do with Elizabeth. The girl, who still refused to go to school, was complaining of severe headaches and stomach pains. Convinced hysteria was the cause, Mary had decided to allow her to remain at home for the rest of the week. If she complained of pains after that, she would call in the doctor and let him make a diagnosis.

The sound of Ethel's footsteps on the stairs scattered her thoughts and started her heart racing. A few seconds later Ethel entered the office.

Mary made an effort to keep her voice steady. "Hello, Mother. What can I do for you?"

The stiffening of Ethel's erect figure and the snap of her tongue convinced Mary that all her fears were justified. "Do for me? What does that mean? Haven't the two of you done enough already?"

Dry-mouthed, Mary rose to her feet. "Mother, don't begin another quarrel, please. You are doing what you feel you must do and we're doing the same. So can't we just leave it there without any more bitterness?"

Instead of the immediate counter-blow she expected, Ethel took a deep steadying breath. For a woman as short-tempered as Ethel, it was behaviour that told Mary she had misread her intentions. Ethel had come to bargain, not to fight, and it had been Mary's initial question, although innocent of intent, that had brought her simmering resentment to the surface.

"And what am I doing to you, my girl? Tell me that."

Prepared for a fight, Mary was obliged to lower her defences. "Let's not go over it all again, Mother. It's all been said so many times. It only causes more distress and it won't change anything."

"That's all right for you. You've got a husband and a family. But what about me? What have I got?"

Realising she was facing a new strategy, Mary began to wonder if she would not rather have faced the old. "I know that, Mother. It's a terrible shame Dad died so young. But you can't expect us to compensate you by leaving one of our children behind and risk losing her love forever, can you?"

"Risk losing her love? This is the way you're going to lose it, my girl. By tearing her away from a comfortable home and a grannie who loves her. She's breaking her heart at the thought of going. Can't you see that?"

Mary shook her head. "Mother, what have you come for? To have another quarrel or is there something you want?"

Ethel's effort to contain her temper was praiseworthy. "I've come to try to talk some sense into you while that husband of yours is at work. Do you both still want to work for me or not? I need to know before this weekend."

Mary felt both curious and apprehensive as she sank down into her chair. "Of course we still want to work for you. The business means a great deal to both of us, just as it did to Dad. It's you who says you're going to sell it."

"And why have I said that?"

"Mother, it's no use. Elizabeth's our child, just as Frank is. As a mother yourself, you must know how wrong it is to treat one child differently from another."

If Ethel felt shame at being reminded how she had always made Mary's sister, Connie, her favourite, she hid it well as she nodded at the cot at the far side of the office. "Frank's still a baby. When his turn comes he'll be treated the same way as Elizabeth."

"That just isn't true, Mother. You've never paid the slightest attention to Frank, whereas you started spoiling Elizabeth from the day she was born. But there's much more to it than that, and you know it. Elizabeth wouldn't be behaving the way she is today if you hadn't turned her against Harry. Or against both of us, for that matter."

Ethel's face set. "You keep on saying that but it's only in your mind. I've never said a word against either of you in front of Elizabeth. Ask the girl if you don't believe me."

"That's not the way you work, Mother. You do it by hints and innuendoes. And by making it look as if we're two spoilsports, as you did when you promised her that trip to America. You've given us no choice but to leave you."

Ethel held down her temper well. "Why don't we stop blaming one another and think about the child instead? If we came to an arrangement

95

that she stayed half the week with you and half the week with me, she might not feel so bad about moving. And you could both keep your jobs. Isn't that much more sensible?"

Mary stared at her. "You realise this is blackmail, don't you?"

Ethel stiffened. "It's all right for you, my girl, but if Elizabeth goes I'll be alone in that big house. It wouldn't leave me any choice but to sell out, and in that case I might as well go over to America for good. But if you'd both be reasonable about Elizabeth, I'd leave things as they are. I can't be fairer than that, can I?"

Mary was wondering how much of this she had discussed with Elizabeth. Before she could reply, Ethel laid the advantages before her. "You're being forced to take a little house that you say is virtually unfurnished. By keeping your jobs you could afford a bigger and better one. It wouldn't be such a cruel wrench for Elizabeth and you could afford to keep her at her school. And as you always seem to be worrying about Harry, it would save him having to take a job that might harm his health. After all, what else is he trained for but to do manual work?"

Mary was never certain what prompted her sharp refusal although she suspected Ethel's contemptuous mention of Harry was a factor. "No, Mother. That would be the worst thing possible for Elizabeth. By going backwards and forwards like that she wouldn't know where she belonged or who cared for her. I'm sorry but it's out of the question."

It was clearly not the answer Ethel expected.

Dismay was written all over her face. "Don't you think Harry has a right to hear the offer before you turn it down?"

Since when have you accepted Harry's right to be consulted, Mary thought. "I'll tell him, of course, but I know he'll give you the same answer."

Ethel made a final try. "Why don't you ask the child herself how she feels about it?"

"I don't need to, Mother. I know you already have."

Her words struck home and Ethel bristled. "Don't you think the girl should have some say in what happens to her?"

"No. She's too young. That's what you can never understand. You're trying to make an old woman out of a child."

In spite of her hostility, there was naked fear in Ethel's eyes now. "So you're determined to take her away from me no matter what it does to any of us?"

"Yes, we are, Mother." Feeling some sympathy for her now, Mary softened her tone. "You're still going to see plenty of her, you know. For heaven's sake, we're only going a few streets away. You'll probably see too much of her when she grows into a noisy adolescent."

Ethel stared at her for a long moment, then went to the door. There she turned. "You'll break two hearts when you take her away. Make no mistake, that's what you'll do and it's a wicked thing. I can only hope God can forgive you and won't punish you for it." With that and a muted sob, she disappeared down the stairs.

97

The warehouse foreman, a brawny, red-faced local man named Brown, was in the office that evening when Harry arrived back from his rounds and Mary had to wait until he returned to the warehouse before she could tell Harry about Ethel's offer. His response was the one she expected. "Of course you did right. The child wouldn't know whether she was coming or going with an arrangement like that."

Although relieved that he was of the same mind, she was unable to forget Ethel's last words on leaving the office. "The only thing is, Harry, I'm wondering what she might do next. She's such an unpredictable and unstable person."

He stared at her. "She's told us what she'll do. Sell the business and go to Jack Watson in America. What more can she do?"

"I don't know but I'm just a little worried. It's not like her to plead for something but that's what she was doing today."

He frowned and began removing his coat. "Isn't that just another ploy of hers? We both know she'll stop at nothing to get her own way."

She realised he was tired and her tone changed. "Sit down and I'll help you to pull off those leggings."

They made no further mention of Ethel until Mary had cashed up and they were preparing to leave. As she was rising to her feet after locking the safe, he put his arms around her.

"I'm sorry if I sounded callous. After all, she is your mother. But I don't think you need worry. In a couple of months when this affair's blown over, you'll probably find you've never had a better relationship with her. She's one of those women who can't help quarrelling with people around her. But once we've gone from her house and the business is sold, she'll have nothing to quarrel with us about."

His words reminded her of her effort to ease his mind about Elizabeth. Did either of them believe their own reassurances? she wondered. "According to Mother, she won't be here. She'll be in America."

"If that's true, she can't think as much of Elizabeth as she claims. She'll be completely cut off from her there."

The same thought had struck Mary. "Does that mean you don't think she'll go?"

He shrugged. "God knows. But if she does, it must show she's insincere about Elizabeth. So you'll have no cause to worry about her, will you?"

She shook her head. "On anything else, I'd say yes. But I'm certain about her feelings for Elizabeth. That's why I can't help feeling a little sorry for her."

He gazed at her quizzically. "But not so sorry that you've changed your mind about this weekend?"

She threw her arms around his neck. "Don't be so daft. I can't wait to move out."

★ ★ ★

Lena Turnor left for Hebden Bridge on Friday that week. With little more than her clothes and a few private possessions to take, it was not an arduous removal but nevertheless Harry helped her to Paragon Station with her suitcases. Characteristically she had protested but his answer defeated her. "You're doing us both a favour by leaving so quickly. So the least I can do is help you into the train."

The station was full of bustle, the clank of steel pistons, and the hiss and smell of steam. He identified her train and with the help of a porter found her a seat and loaded in her luggage. Then, standing on the platform outside, he handed her a magazine he had bought earlier. "Just in case the journey drags."

He had half expected her to remain in her seat once the suitcases were stored but instead she stood by the open carriage window. She was wearing her better clothes for the journey, a grey suit with a matching cloche hat, and in spite of her pallor he thought she looked quite pretty. "You shouldn't have come," she said. "But it's very kind of you."

"Don't be silly. Will someone meet you in at the other end?"

"Yes, my uncle's promised to be there."

"Drop us a line to tell us how you're getting on, won't you? We'd both like to hear."

"Yes, if you like."

"And we'll post you the rent weekly. Mary will handle it. She's very reliable on such matters."

She smiled. "I'm sure she is. Tell her I hope she'll be happy in the house. I know it's only small but Arthur and I were very happy there."

He knew she had spoken without thinking. As her eyes suddenly misted over, he tried to find something diverting to say but his words sounded both evasive and banal and he began wishing the train would leave. It was a relief when the guard's whistle blew five minutes later.

Even so he found himself walking alongside her carriage as the train jerked forward. "Take care of yourself and don't forget to write."

He was sure she could not hear him for the noise but she nodded. He expected her to sink back out of sight as the train moved away but she remained at the window until a cloud of steam hid the carriage. By the time it had blown away, the train had rounded a bend and she was gone.

11

HARRY and Mary moved as planned on the Saturday of that week. With all their furniture destroyed in a Zeppelin raid four years ago, they had little to take with them but their clothes and the children's toys, and for these and other sundry items, Harry used one of the warehouse carts. Although both knew the undignified mode of removal would do nothing to enhance their image in Ethel's eyes, both were also aware that they might need every penny in their possession before Harry found a job.

The physical side of the removal posed no problem because beforehand Mary had managed a quiet word with the warehouse foreman and he had arranged for two of his men to wheel the cart to St George's Road. Harry, who had been given the house key by Lena Turnor the previous day, was walking along the lane with the two men when Mary came running after them. Her distressed shout made him turn. "Harry! Come quickly, please! It's Elizabeth."

Giving the key to the men, he ran towards her. "What's the matter?"

She was breathless with distress. "Elizabeth won't come. She's locked herself in her room."

"Locked herself in? But how could she do that? There wasn't a key in her door, was there?"

She pulled him towards the back garden of

102

No. fifty seven. "I don't know but I can't open the door. I'm scared, Harry. Please hurry."

He ran into the house and up the stairs. He tried the locked door, then shook it. "Elizabeth! Unlock the door! Do you hear me?"

There was no reply. He shook the door again. "Elizabeth! You're frightening your mother. Open the door!"

Again there was no reply. Mary was at his side by this time, her face white with alarm. "What's happened to her? Why doesn't she answer?"

Harry hurled himself against the heavy door. When it would not give, he turned and ran downstairs, to find Ethel standing in the living room. "How did she get the key, Mother? Did you give it to her?"

Ethel stiffened in indignation. "Of course I didn't. The poor child is so upset she must have taken it from the kitchen herself."

He did not stop to argue with her. "Do you have another key?"

"Not that I know of. There might be one in the shed but I've no idea where."

He gave her a look, then ran out into the back garden where the curious maid was hanging out the day's washing. "Molly, do you know where spare keys for the rooms are kept?"

The girl shook her head. "No. I didn't know there were any."

Wasting no more time, he flung open the door of the shed. A moment later he ran into the living room carrying a heavy axe. Ethel let out a gasp. "What are you going to do with that?"

Pushing past her, he ran upstairs to the locked

door. Motioning Mary back, he swung hard at the lock. Splinters flew from the door but the lock held. He swung again and this time a panel split and opened. Pushing his hand through the splintered wood, he reached the key and turned it.

He found Elizabeth huddled against the wall at the far side of the bed and dropped on his knees beside her. "What is it, love? What's the matter?"

Her body was jerking convulsively but she was making no sound. As he tried to take her tear-stained face in his hands, she pulled violently away. Alongside him he heard Mary's distressed voice. "She hasn't hurt herself, has she? Let me see."

He moved aside so that Mary could kneel beside the girl. "Darling, what's the matter? Why did you lock the door like that?"

The girl buried her face into the coverlet of the bed. With an anxious glance at Harry, Mary tried to draw her back. "You mustn't be so upset, darling. We're only going a few streets away. You'll still have your own room and your toys."

At that the girl turned and flung herself into Mary's arms. She tried to say something but the words were drowned in the violent sobs that racked her. Harry dropped on his knees again. "What is she saying?"

Mary shook her head. With the child in her arms she gently rocked back and forth. "There, there, darling. You mustn't cry. Everything's going to be all right."

Again the girl tried to speak, only for the violence of her sobs to defeat her. As her breath caught and she began coughing, Harry turned in alarm to Mary. "Shall I call the doctor?"

She shook her head again. "No. You go and fetch Frank." As Harry ran out, she patted the hysterical child on the back. "Come now, darling. You'll make yourself ill if you go on like this. We're not going a hundred miles away so there's no need for all these tears."

Her admonishment, gentle although it was, worked when sympathy had not and the girl's frightened voice was now heard between her sobs. "We can't go, Mummy! Grannie will die if we do."

Mary gave a start. Her arms closed protectively round the distressed child. "Who told you this? Grannie?"

The racking sobs began again. "She will die, Mummy. I know she will. We mustn't go. Please, Mummy."

Mary was wondering why she had ever felt sympathy for her mother. At that moment Harry ran back into the bedroom with the baby in his arms. "Let's get her out of here," he muttered. "As quickly as we can."

At his words, Elizabeth began to scream. White-faced, Mary rose to her feet and picked up the hysterical girl. As she turned for the door, she saw Ethel standing there and her voice struck at her mother like a spear. "Is this what you've made her believe, Mother? That you'll die if she goes? If you have, then you deserve to die."

Ethel's face was as white as their own. "I

never said any such thing. As God is my judge, I never did."

At that moment, with the heartbroken child in her arms, there was no mercy in Mary. "You're a liar, Mother! A barefaced liar!"

Ethel's voice was frantic. "But I didn't. I wouldn't frighten my little girl like that. I swear it on the Bible."

Mary started for the door. "We're taking her away from you, Mother. So get out of my way."

Elizabeth was screaming and struggling so violently now that Mary was compelled to hand her over to Harry and to take the baby herself. The disturbance had woken the child and his crying was adding to the tumult. As the distressed couple descended the stairs, Ethel followed them, almost unrecognisable now with her dishevelled hair and tear-stained face. At the front door, she caught Mary's arm. "She's all I've got, Mary! For God's sake don't take her from me!"

Behind her Mary caught a glimpse of the maid, looking upset and frightened. Pushing her mother away, Mary followed Harry down the front path.

Fifty yards down the road, she glanced back. Ignoring the curious glances of passers by, Ethel had run to the front gate and was standing there, a distraught and frantic figure. As Mary watched, she saw Molly take her arm and try to draw her back into the house.

★ ★ ★

Harry found Swanson standing at the bar of the Hare and Hounds with an empty beer glass in his hand. "Sorry I'm a bit late. But it's been one of those days."

"That's all right, old lad. Plenty of time." Swanson nodded at the barman. "Two more of the usual, Jack. And twenty Navy Cut." He turned back to Harry. "So you've done it at last? How does it feel?"

Harry shook his head. "Don't ask me yet. Try me in six months time."

Swanson examined him. "As bad as that, eh? You do look a bit peaky, old lad."

The barman slid two pints of beer and a packet of cigarettes towards Swanson. He paid for them, broke open the packet and offered it to Harry. "It's probably those bloody Capstan you smoke. Have a decent fag and your life'll change."

Harry grinned as he took a cigarette. "Is that how it's done?"

Swanson led him to a table, sat down, and took a long draught of beer. "Your trouble is you don't drink enough of this cat's pee. Didn't you know cat's pee's full of vitamins? Drink enough of it and you'll be on the roof howling your head off with the rest of us."

Harry grinned again. "It sounds like fun."

"It is until the local big Tom takes a dislike to you. Then it's all claws and fur and wish I'd stayed at home, Mum." Swanson's pleasant voice ran on without changing tone. "Tell me all about it. When did you move?"

"Two weeks last Saturday." Harry's mouth

quirked humorously. "Or was it two years?"

"Was it that bad?"

Harry took a sip of beer. "I shouldn't be here. Mary's had a hell of a fortnight. Only she insisted I had a break from it."

Swanson nodded. "You look as if you need it. What's the problem? Elizabeth?"

"Yes. I've never seen a kid so upset as when we took her away. Eventually we had to call the doctor in to give her a sedative. He came again the following Monday and advised us to keep her off school for the week."

"How did the old lady take it?"

"Just as hard. I've never seen her like that before. She was nearly as hysterical as Elizabeth."

"What about Mary?"

"She's been trying to do half a dozen things at the same time: fix up the house, look after the baby, pacify Elizabeth, and show me what needs doing in the office. She couldn't leave Elizabeth alone the first week in case she ran back to Ethel."

"The old lady hasn't closed down the business yet then?"

"Not yet, although she might be trying to sell. That's one of the problems: we don't know what she'll do. We haven't seen her since we left."

"But you're keeping it going in the meantime?"

"We're doing our best. I've been doing Mary's accounts and any urgent jobs in the evenings. The rest of her work we're having to leave until she can take over again."

Swanson made an exclamation of disgust.

"You're both a damn sight more conscientious than I'd be if I thought the business might be sold. So what's the situation now? Is Elizabeth getting used to not seeing the old woman?"

Harry drew on his cigarette. "It's hard to say. We had to make a deal with her that if she promised to come home, she could visit Ethel on Saturday afternoons and Sunday mornings — that's when Ethel takes her to church. So far she's kept her promise."

Swanson's tone changed. "There you are then. She's accepted it. Kids are like that. They make a big hoo-ha at the time but they've got short memories."

Harry shook his head. "No, it's not that way with her. Every time she comes home she's in tears. She says her grannie's not well and it's all because she's missing her so much."

"Isn't that just the old woman up to her tricks again?"

"Yes and no. Ethel will be missing her, there's no doubt about that. The worrying thing is it seems to be affecting Elizabeth's health too. She's lost her appetite and it's an effort to get her to talk. Mary's worried sick about her."

"What does the doctor say?"

"He said he's been expecting something like this to happen. Apparently Ethel had confided in him."

"What did she tell him?"

"Being a doctor, he wouldn't give much away but I could read between the lines. We've used her to look after the girl when it suited us and now, when it suits us, we've taken her away.

How much of it he believes I don't know but he did warn us we could have problems with both her and Elizabeth in the weeks ahead."

Swanson frowned. "Don't you think he's exaggerating? I still think kids get over these things quickly."

"That's what I said but he believes Ethel has the kind of personality that makes a deep impression on a child."

"Do you believe that?"

Harry nodded reluctantly. "Yes. She also plays on a child's imagination and fears. We've known this a long time."

Swanson's solution was quick and uncomplicated. "Then stop Elizabeth going round. Right away. Otherwise how can things improve?"

"If only it were that simple. If we don't give the child a safety valve, she might run round to Ethel one day and not come back. Then what would we do?"

The bachelor in Swanson was never more obvious than at that moment. "Go and drag her back. And tell the old woman if she encourages her once more, you'll burn her house down."

Harry grinned wryly. "I'd enjoy that." Then his tone changed. "Imagine invading an old lady's house to tear away a grandchild who's screaming to stay with her. What a field day that would give her lawyers."

Swanson took his point. "How does Mary feel about all this?"

"The same as I do. Most of the time we're hating the old woman but just now and then we can't help feeling a bit sorry for her."

110

Swanson's scornful laugh brought him curious glances from nearby tables. "Sorry? For an old witch like that? You're both crazy."

Harry shrugged. "Again it's not that simple. After all, she is Mary's mother. And there's no doubt she worships Elizabeth. She must be as lonely as hell in that big house."

Swanson stared at him. "I don't believe this. She's given you both a cat and dog life since God knows when and now you're starting to feel sorry for her." Rising, he picked up both glasses and grinned down as Harry protested. "I know it's your round but you'd come back with more of that cat's pee. I'm buying you a pint of Guinness to put some good, old-fashioned hate into you. So sit there and don't move."

12

MARY lit the gas mantle and led Elizabeth to a table at the far side of the office. "Sit there a moment, darling, while I put some coke on the stove. Then we can get to work."

She raked the stove and opened the damper. As she fetched a shovelful of coke and scattered it on the still smouldering embers, she cast a glance at the girl. She was sitting on the chair swinging her legs back and forth as she waited, making it difficult to judge whether she was being rebellious or merely apathetic.

It was Harry who had suggested she should bring Elizabeth over to help her. The girl was, as Harry said, intelligent beyond her years and to be given a task in the business, however small, might just be the thing she needed to divert her mind from Ethel. Mary had thought about his suggestion for a few days and when she could find nothing against it, had approached the girl.

Elizabeth's first reaction had been sullen and unresponsive. "But, darling, you could be such a help to me. We've got a big order in for some pills and they have to be sorted out into little boxes. With those nimble fingers of yours, you could fill the pill boxes much faster than I. Won't you help me? It's a very important job."

With the girl always a willing helper with household chores in the past, Mary was sure it was her last remark that had tipped the scales. Now, as she closed the door of the stove and crossed over to a cupboard, she wondered if the girl had changed her mind: Pulling out a large cardboard box, she set it down on the table. "These are the little boxes we have to put the pills in. Now let me get the pills for them."

She unlocked a metal cabinet and returned half a minute later with a sealed carton. Opening it, she poured a pile of small white pills into a bowl. "We have to put six of these into each box, darling. No more and no less because they're quite expensive. You can do that, can't you?"

In spite of her unhappiness at being separated from Ethel, the child was looking curious. "What are they for?"

"They're pills to make people sleep, darling."

"Why do they need pills to make them sleep?"

"Oh, for all kinds of reasons."

"Do you need them, Mummy?"

"No, darling. They're mostly for sick or older people."

"People like Grannie?"

"No, darling. Grannie's far too healthy."

Immediately the girl's blue eyes turned resentful. "She's not healthy now. She cries a lot and Molly says she's always in bed."

Mary quickly changed the subject. "Let's see how soon we can finish this job, shall we? The order is for three hundred boxes, so we've quite a lot to do. But be careful to put the right number in each box, won't you?"

As she had hoped, the job occupied the girl's attention and she became more animated as the pile of filled boxes grew. "Is this what you do all the time, Mummy?"

Mary laughed. "No, I've all kinds of other jobs. This is a special order that Daddy got for us. It's for a chain of chemist shops and and they want delivery next week. That why Mr Conway came in yesterday."

"What does Mr Conway have to do with it?"

"Mr Conway? He's a retired druggist who buys certain drugs for us."

"Why can't you buy them yourself?"

Mary was thinking what an inquisitive and lively intelligence the child had when she was relieved of emotional stress. "It's because of something called the Drugs Act. Only a qualified druggist can buy certain drugs from the manufacturers. That's why we've had to use Mr Conway since Grandpa died."

It was an unfortunate reference. The child's expression changed again. "Grannie's never been happy since Grandpa died, has she? She misses him ever so much."

Mary hesitated, then decided it would be too obvious if she tried to divert the child's mind again. "We all miss him, darling. He was a lovely man."

"Yes, but it's worse for Grannie. She's got nobody now." Tears suddenly filled the girl's eyes. "Why did you leave her, Mummy? It's made her so unhappy."

114

The child's genuine distress made Mary's own eyes sting. "Darling, all married people want a home of their own. You'll be the same one day when you get married."

"But Grannie's been so good to us. She looked after you and me when Daddy was away in the war. It's not right to let her be unhappy now."

Mary felt a chill. The brain-washing had been expertly done. "Darling, it was Grannie who told us to go. We're not angry about that but we couldn't leave you behind, could we? What would you have thought of us if we'd done that?"

"But Grannie's so unhappy. How can you let her be unhappy when she's your own mummy?"

Mary had the eerie feeling there was another party in the office orchestrating the conversation. "It's not us who're making her unhappy, darling. We let you go round twice a week and she's free to visit us whenever she wants. It's not our fault if she doesn't choose to come."

"She can't come. She's too sick."

"She can't be that sick if she can take you to church on Sundays. Has she called in the doctor recently?"

"I don't know," the girl muttered. "I suppose so."

Was this Ethel's new ploy? Mary wondered. A campaign of ill health? "You mustn't worry about Grannie, darling. If you like, I'll have a word with Dr Armstrong. I'm sure he'll call round to see her if I ask him."

Elizabeth brightened at that. "Will you, Mummy? Dr Armstrong will make sure she doesn't die, won't he?"

Mary took a deep breath, then walked round the table and took hold of the girl's hands. "Now you listen to me, darling. All this talk about Grannie dying is wicked nonsense. She's as healthy as we are and she's not going to die. Is that clear?"

The child's artless face gazed at her. "That's not what she says."

Mary could not hold back her anger. "Then Grannie should be ashamed of herself. There's no danger of her dying, not for years and years and years. So take no notice of her when she talks that way. It just isn't true."

The girl frowned. "But that's saying Grannie is telling lies. And she always says it's wicked to lie."

Acutely aware of the perils involved in attacking Ethel, Mary took the point no further. "Just believe me, darling. Grannie isn't going to die. Now let's finish our job, shall we? Frank will be wanting his next meal soon and I didn't tell Daddy what to give him."

With her mind occupied again, the child forgot her resentment and fears. Helping her on with her scarf and coat forty minutes later, Mary could not remember feeling more love for her or more sympathy. She was like a piece of human flotsam, being tossed back and forth on a sea of possessive emotions she was too young to understand. If the battle for her mind and her body were not resolved

116

soon, Mary thought, there was no telling what damage might be done.

★ ★ ★

Mary spoke to Dr Armstrong on the telephone the following morning. The bluff doctor's reply surprised her. "Aye, she came round to see me last week. Hasn't she told you?"

"We haven't seen her since we moved house. Can you tell me how she is?"

Armstrong's slight hesitation before replying made her wonder if she were trespassing on medical ethics. "Let's say she's suffering from separation problems, lass. Like that daughter of yours is."

"Does that mean there's nothing seriously wrong with her?"

Again the slight hesitation. "It depends what you mean by serious. She's missing that young girl of yours, I'll tell you that."

She wondered if his words implied criticism. "We had our reasons for leaving, doctor. Pretty strong ones, as a matter of fact."

"Aye, perhaps you had. But you wanted to know what's wrong with her and I've told you."

Mollified somewhat, she went on: "She'll get over it soon, won't she? She's told us she'll probably sell the business and go over to America."

"She's not said anything about that to me. I hope she does. It'll take her mind off things." Before she could say any more, the gruff voice changed its tone. "How are you managing to work and look after that baby of yours? You've a longer journey, haven't you, now you're back at the office?"

She knew she was being side-tracked but felt there was little she could do about it. "I've got a bicycle and Harry's found a local girl to come in and look after Frank during the day. And I'm leaving earlier in the afternoons. It's the best we can manage until we know what Mother's doing about the business."

"I'll drop in next week to see how she's getting on. I take it that your daughter's back at school again?"

"Yes, she's back. You'll know that we're letting her see her grannie twice a week?"

"Aye. The old lady told me. I think that's very wise, at least for the time being. Now that's enough chin wagging. I've got work to do. Bye bye, lass."

There was a click and Mary was left staring at the receiver, uncertain whether or not she was any wiser about her mother.

★ ★ ★

The following Monday morning Mary was busy packing the pill boxes into cartons when she heard footsteps on the outer stairs. As she glanced round, Ethel entered the office.

Mary rose to her feet, feeling both diffident and apprehensive. "Hello, Mother. How are you?"

Ethel, wearing a brown, squirrel-trimmed coat

and matching hat, gave her a cold stare. "What sort of a question is that? How do you think I am?"

"I'm asking you, Mother, because I've heard you've been to the doctor. So naturally I'm wondering what's wrong."

Ethel gave a sniff. "Are you saying you don't know?"

She didn't look well, Mary thought. She appeared to have lost weight and there were dark shadows beneath her eyes. "I'm sorry if you're feeling lonely. Why don't you take Jack up on his offer and have a holiday in America? The change would do you the world of good."

Ethel's laugh was bitter. "You'd both like that, wouldn't you? To get me right away from Elizabeth and be able to do what you like with the business."

Mary sighed. "Mother, you've already told us you'll sell the business if you go to America. So how can we have thoughts like that?"

Ethel's lips compressed. "I ought to sell it after what you've done to me."

Mary was long past caring what she did. "You must do what you want. Only don't you think it's time you told us your plans so we can start making plans of our own? We do have two children to think about, you know."

Ethel opened her mouth to reply, then winced instead and put a hand up to her head. "I haven't come to haggle with you, Mary. I've written to Captain Watson and as soon as I've got his opinion, I'll let you know.

All I've come for now are some headache powders."

Mary showed her surprise. "Headache powders?"

"Yes. I've had a dreadful head for days and the pills I got from the chemist have been no use at all. I remember your father used to make wonderful powders and I thought we might still sell them."

Braced for news that would affect all their lives, Mary felt let down. "Yes, we do. I'll get you some."

She crossed over to the metal cabinet and unlocked it. Behind her Ethel moved to the table where the pillboxes were stacked. "Is this the order Elizabeth was telling me about the other day? The one she helped you with?"

Mary was reaching into the cabinet. "Yes. I think she quite enjoyed helping. I might use her again sometime."

"But isn't it dangerous? Aren't you afraid she might put a pill into her mouth? They're narcotics, aren't they?"

Mary had found the carton for which she was searching and drew it towards her. "I warned her to be careful and of course I kept an eye on her as well. But she's far too sensible to disobey me on anything like that."

Ethel was now standing between her and the table. "Just the same, I'm never happy about drugs where children are concerned. How strong are these pills?"

"Quite strong," Mary admitted. "Although

she'd have had to take more than one to be in danger." She glanced into the carton. "Will four powders be enough? If not I'll have to go to our store."

As she glanced back she saw Ethel was again wincing with pain. "If your headache's as bad as that, oughtn't you to see the doctor again?"

"I have seen him and he wasn't any help." Ethel held out her hand. "Four should be enough for the moment. If I need any more, I'll let you know."

Taking the paper-wrapped powders, Ethel went to the door. Seeing the looseness of her coat, Mary thought again how much weight she had lost. Her sympathetic voice checked the woman. "I hope those powders help, Mother. If they don't, I really think you should see Dr Armstrong again."

Ethel answered her without looking back. "There's only one thing that can help me, Mary, and that's something you and Harry refuse to give." With that she disappeared down the stairs.

Shaking her head, Mary returned to the pillboxes. With the order requiring ten boxes to each carton, she was kept busy for the next twenty minutes filling and sealing the cartons. She had twenty-nine of them stacked in a packing case and was about to fill the last one when she saw there were only nine pillboxes left on the table.

It could mean only one thing, she thought. With her mind on other things, she must have put one pillbox too many in one of the sealed cartons. Impatient with herself, she was about to begin re-opening them when she remembered she had an appointment with a drug salesman in fifteen minutes.

She hesitated, then walked over to the gas ring. There was no urgency, the cartons could wait until later in the morning. In the meantime, unsettled by her mother's visit, she would make a cup of tea to calm her nerves.

* * *

Harry heard the distant cries as he was ascending the stairs to the warehouse office. As he paused to listen, light flooded out on the landing above and he heard Mary's voice. "Is that you, Harry?"

"Yes, love. What's happening out there?"

Mary, showing alarm, appeared on the landing. "I don't know. It's someone crying for help, isn't it?

"Where's it coming from?"

"From the lane, I think. I'd better go and find out."

She ran down the stairs. "I'll come with you."

He caught her arm. "You need a coat. It's bitter out there."

She pulled away. "I'm all right. I want to know what's happening."

He hesitated, then followed her. As they ran out into the dark yard, they heard the cries more clearly. Mary gave a gasp of alarm. "It's Molly!

122

What could have happened?"

Lights were appearing in the back windows of flanking houses as they ran down the lane. Halfway along it they met a coatless and frantic Molly. As she gave a relieved cry, Harry grabbed hold of her. "What is it, Molly? Is it your mistress?"

Too breathless to speak, the frightened girl could only nod and sob hysterically. Harry turned to Mary. "Take care of her while I go and see what's happened."

He found the back door of No. fifty seven wide open. Discovering the kitchen and living room empty, he ran upstairs to Ethel's bedroom. Seeing the door only half open, he paused. "Mother! Are you there?"

When there was no reply, he pushed the door open. Ethel, fully dressed, was lying supine on the bed with her eyes closed. From the colour and laxity of her features, his first thought was that she was dead.

It was only when he approached the bedside that he saw she was breathing, although very shallowly, and froth lay at one corner of her mouth. As he reached out to take her pulse, Mary ran into the room. "Mother! Oh, my God!"

"It's all right," he said quickly. "She's not dead." He pointed at an open pillbox resting on a bedside cabinet. "There's the reason. She's taken an overdose of something or other."

White-faced, she ran over to the cabinet and gave another gasp of shock. "It's from that narcotics order. A pillbox I couldn't find. And it's empty, Harry. She could have taken a lethal dose."

Without another word, he ran down into the hall and snatched the receiver from its hook. "Hello, operator. Get me the hospital, please. Quickly! I've an emergency to report."

13

MARY jumped to her feet as Dr Armstrong entered the hospital waiting room. Anticipating her question, he gave his blunt reassuring laugh. "Stop looking as if we'd lost the war, lass. She's going to be all right."

Her pale face relaxed. "Thank God for that. Is she conscious?"

"She is but she's not in any state to see you. The poor old soul's still vomiting her heart up."

"But they have pumped out her stomach?"

Armstrong's eyes twinkled. "You teaching us our job, lass?"

"No, of course not. But if she took all those pills, it was a very heavy dose."

"We know all about that. Yes, they've emptied her stomach and had her walking round the ward. There's no permanent damage that any of us can see. You can stop worrying about her."

Questions, previously ignored, now began to plague Mary. "I don't understand how she could do a thing like that." She turned to Harry who was standing alongside her. "You spoke to Molly before we left, didn't you? What exactly did she tell you?"

"She said your mother had been complaining about a bad headache and eventually went over to the warehouse for headache powders. When she got back she said she was going to take two and then lie down."

"She didn't have lunch?" Mary interrupted.

"I don't know about that. Molly was still hysterical. But as far as I could gather your mother went to bed in the early afternoon. When she didn't come down, Molly went upstairs to tell her she'd finished work and was going home. That's when she found her unconscious."

"Had she asked Molly to wake her up?"

His expression told her he was following the reason for her question. "I don't know that. But doesn't Molly always tell her when she's going home?"

Before Mary could answer, Armstrong's gruff voice interrupted them. "What are you two getting at? That it was a fake suicide?"

Molly turned to him. "It would be an effective way to influence Elizabeth, wouldn't it? She's already terrified her grannie might die if she's left alone much longer."

Armstrong, heavily-built, with iron-grey hair, gave a grunt of censure. "It's also a damned dangerous one, lass. I know the two of you have had problems with her but this is too far-fetched for words. Come on, let's be fair to her. She loves that little girl of yours and she was shell-shocked when you took her away. She found the loneliness too much and decided to end it all."

"But it's only been five weeks. And Mother's such a strong-willed person." Then, remembering how she had sometimes called her mother unstable, Mary paused.

126

"It's often the strong-willed ones who commit suicide, lass. The others haven't the courage. And remember, it wouldn't be the past five weeks she'd be thinking of but all the years in the future."

"But we haven't stopped her seeing Elizabeth. She sees her every weekend. And she has a man friend in America who keeps asking her to go over. She's not that alone."

Armstrong shook his head. "It was the little girl, lass. She worships her and she was convinced that one day you intended to separate them permanently." When Mary did not answer, Armstrong went on: "Don't forget she did come to me for help. So I do know how badly depressed she was."

Yes but do you know my mother as I know her? Mary thought. Do you know the things she is capable of? Then she had a vision of her mother at the gate of her house when they were taking Elizabeth away. For Ethel, so prim and respectable, to break down that way in front of her neighbours had said more about her state of mind than any private outcry of grief.

"Can we see her later if we stay?" she asked.

Armstrong shook his head. "Not for another hour or two and I'm not sure it's a good idea in any case. I've got a better one. I've no calls tonight so why don't I come home with you both? I think I should be there when you tell your daughter the news."

The prospect of bringing to life all the fears that Ethel had instilled in the child's mind made

127

Mary's heart sink. "Must we tell her tonight?"

"She'll have to hear sometime. And I think it's better she does when I'm there." Before Mary could reply, Armstrong took her arm. "Come on, lass. My car's outside."

★ ★ ★

Armstrong drew the hypodermic needle gently from the hysterical girl's arm. "Shut your eyes, lassie, and go to sleep. Things will seem different in the morning."

The girl screamed, and in spite of her limbs being held by both her parents, her small body arched and stiffened. Then she sank back, her sobs faded, and her frightened eyes grew heavy and closed. As Armstrong nodded and stood back, Mary gave a sob of distress and turned away from the two men.

Armstrong's voice had never been gruffer. "Aye, she's taken it hard all right. It's as well I came back with you."

There was sweat on Harry's face as he tried to comfort Mary. "How in God's name can Ethel affect the child like this? You'd think she'd hypnotised her."

It was clear that Armstrong himself was shaken by the child's reaction. "Did you say the old lady sometimes talked about her death to the child?"

Mary swung round. "Sometimes? She was always doing it. And making Elizabeth promise to visit her grave after she'd gone."

Armstrong rubbed a hand over his chin which

128

was already growing an evening stubble. "You should have told me. I could have warned her what a bad effect it might have."

"Isn't that why she was doing it?" Mary asked bitterly. "To chain Elizabeth to her?"

Before Armstrong could reply, Harry broke in. "We'll have to get the child right away from her. Out of town if necessary."

Armstrong took a look at the unconscious Elizabeth, then turned away. "Let's go downstairs and talk about it."

Realising the doctor needed time to think, Mary tucked the bed clothes round the girl. "Will she be all right on her own?"

Armstrong glanced back from the doorway. "Oh, aye. She'll sleep until mid morning after the shot I gave her. Come on down and let's have a chinwag."

She followed both of them down into the sitting room where Armstrong looked round approvingly. "You've worked wonders here, lass. I meant to tell you when we first came in."

She motioned him to sit down in one of the two second-hand armchairs they had bought. "Thank you. Although it needs a lot more doing to it yet."

Armstrong lowered his bulk into the chair. "Take your time. Rome wasn't built in a day." Fishing in his jacket pocket he pulled out an old pipe and raised his bushy eyebrows at Mary. "Yes or no, lass?"

"Yes. I don't mind. Harry used to smoke a pipe once."

Armstrong threw a glance at Harry who was

showing impatience at the delay. "You should start again, lad. Nothing better to calm a man's nerves. Like a bowlful now?"

"No, thanks. I haven't smoked one since before the war. What are we going to do about Elizabeth?"

Armstrong applied a match to his pipe which began emitting clouds of pungent smoke. "More's the pity, lad. They're a great comfort." He sat puffing away for a few seconds more, then took the pipe from his mouth and glanced at both parents in turn. "As I see it there's only one thing you can do. That's let the girl go back to your mother."

Mary gave a gasp of protest. "You can't mean it."

Armstrong held up a tobacco-stained hand. "Hear me out first. What choice have you got? If you carry on as before, that child upstairs is going to run straight to her grannie and refuse to come back. What will you do then? Bring her back by force? Even if you do, she'll run there again. You can't keep her locked up forever."

Harry interrupted Mary's reply. "Then we'll have to do as I say. Move out of town."

"What good will that do? The girl's going to be more upset than ever if she doesn't know what's happening to her grannie. And Grannie isn't going to stop at one suicide attempt. If she doesn't see the child at all, she's certain to try again."

Mary could feel nothing but hatred for Ethel

at that moment. "Then she'll have to do it, won't she? She's no right to blackmail us like that."

"That's where we differ, lass. I'm sure it was a genuine attempt. That's why I'm certain she'll do it again."

"But it's still blackmail. She's trying to manipulate our lives by threatening to take her own. We can't let her do that."

Armstrong shook his head. "You talk that way now but I've known you since you were a girl and I know what a tender heart you have. If your mother did kill herself out of loneliness, you'd never forgive yourself. Look at the way you acted tonight."

At that moment she hated him almost as much as she hated her mother. "That's not fair. Do you realise you're advising us to give away our own child?"

Armstrong gave an impatient grunt. "Isn't that a bit of an exaggeration? If she stays with the old woman you can see her whenever you want. And you'll keep your jobs. Whereas if you go out of town, you'll not only have the girl and your mother to worry about, but you'll be out of work as well. And that might be quite a problem these days."

She opened her mouth to argue, only for words to fail her. In her distress she turned to Harry. "You're keeping very quiet. Why don't you say what you think?"

With his own nerves strung tight, he showed resentment. "I've kept quiet because she's your mother, not mine."

131

"What's that to do with it? Elizabeth's your child, isn't she?"

"Yes," he said quietly. "And if I'd my way she'd never see your mother again."

"Then that's all right. We both agree."

"Yes, but as the doctor says, there is just one thing. You have to promise not to blame yourself if Ethel attempts suicide again."

"Do you think I would?"

"Yes, I do. You were almost doing it tonight."

The knowledge he was right made her deliberately misinterpret his words. "You're making it sound now as if I want Elizabeth to go back to her."

"Don't be ridiculous. I never said anything of the kind."

Realising they were close to quarrelling, Armstrong broke in quickly. "You say your mother has a man friend over in America. Do you mean someone she's thinking of marrying?"

Relieved by the interruption, Mary turned back to him. "We're not sure. I know she's written him to get advice on what to do with the business. So he must be involved with her plans in some way."

"Couldn't that be your answer? Let her have Elizabeth until that affair's resolved. If she feels as lonely as her actions suggest, isn't it likely she'll agree to marry him sooner or later?"

Harry was frowning. "How would that help us?"

Armstrong put another match to his pipe before replying. "Marriage and sex can change people's allegiances, lad. She might not want the burden of a child when on her honeymoon. Or afterwards for that matter."

Mary gave herself no time to be tempted. "No. That would be the worst thing possible for Elizabeth. She'd think nobody wanted her then."

"Not even if I spoke to your mother myself and told her all the things she mustn't do or say to her?"

Although aware he was only trying to help, Mary could not keep the contempt from her voice. "You couldn't change my mother's behaviour in a hundred years. She's a law unto herself." Then her tone changed. "I'm sorry, doctor. I know you're trying to help us and you're right in thinking I'd probably feel dreadful if my mother did kill herself. But I can't sacrifice my daughter because of that."

Armstrong sighed. He puffed on his pipe a couple of times, pressed down a glowing flake with a thumb, then glanced back at both parents. His voice was sympathetic. "I didn't want to have to say this but there's one thing you're both forgetting. If you do as you say and the worst happens, then you're absolutely certain to lose your daughter. Have you thought of that?"

Mary threw an alarmed glance at Harry. "I don't know what you mean."

"Think, lass. If the old lady kills herself, Elizabeth will know why. That means she'll never forgive you. And there'll be no way of turning back the clock. It'll be too late."

Mary felt her blood run cold. "But she's only

133

a child. How could she feel like that?"

"Children are all feelings, lass. Sometimes illogical ones. In any case, she won't be a child much longer."

Suddenly Mary's legs would not support her and she sank into a chair. Armstrong's words were like a torch, revealing a dark truth in her mind that until this moment she had refused to acknowledge. Seeing Harry's pale face, she knew he had the same thought. Ethel had unsheathed the one weapon they could not defeat.

As Harry, showing concern, moved to her side, she gave a sob and caught his hand. "He's right, Harry. She's won, hasn't she?"

His voice was harsher than she had ever known it. "Yes, love. She's won as she always intended to."

She clung to his hand as if it were a lifeline. "What are we going to do? Whatever happens we mustn't lose Elizabeth's love."

He turned his face away so she could not see his pain. "There's only one thing we can do. We'll wait until your mother's out of hospital. Then we'll make arrangements for Elizabeth to go back to her."

134

Part Two

Part Two

14

THE trawler was heading towards the open sea, its bow wave jaunty against the sunlit water. In the sky, white barges of cloud were beating up river for the safety of harbour and home. As the breeze brought a smell of salt and seaweed, Jack Watson took a deep appreciative breath. "So this is the Humber? It's some river all right, Harry. Do you come here often?"

The younger man alongside him nodded. "If I'm travelling in these parts I sometimes bring my sandwiches on the pier."

Watson turned his gaze to take in the seven miles of cranes and derricks that reached out on either side. "It's some port too. I didn't get a chance to see any of this when I came during the war. Where do the trawlers go?"

"The Arctic. Iceland. It's mostly deep sea trawling from Hull and Grimsby."

Jack Watson, a round-faced, genial, overweight man, had arrived in England two weeks previously. What stories Ethel had told him neither Harry nor Mary could guess, but in the one visit he had paid them, he had shown no signs of second-hand hostility. Instead, he had brought round flowers for Mary, whom he had last seen during the Armistice when Harry's fate was still unknown, cigars for Harry, and a box of American candy for Frank. "The little feller's changed a bit since I last saw him, Mary. How old is he now?"

"He'll be three in October, Jack."

He had reached down and solemnly taken the boy's chubby hand. "Hiya, Frank. I'm the guy who used to read your sister stories about America when you were a little baby."

Mary's laugh had been rueful as the boy's blue eyes had gazed solemnly up at him. "You'd better not do that to him or he'll be wanting to go to America too."

His avoidance of any comment or any mention of Elizabeth's living with Ethel told them he had been given some briefing but of what kind they could only guess. The only thing they could be certain of was that Ethel had made no mention of her attempted suicide. A week prior to Watson's arrival in England, she had paid a visit to Mary's office when Harry was out on his rounds. From her appearance and her tone, Mary had been unable to decide whether she was making a plea or a pronouncement.

"As you know, I hadn't expected Captain Watson to come over this year. In some ways it is a nuisance because I'm not ready for him but I can hardly put him off. So I'm taking it that I can rely on your discretion."

Not absolutely certain what she meant, Mary had progressed cautiously. "Discretion in what, Mother?"

When Ethel was in the embarrassed mode, her instinct was always to attack. "You know perfectly well what I mean. I don't want him to know why I had to go into hospital."

138

"I won't say anything about it, Mother. But what about Elizabeth? Isn't there a chance she might blurt it out?"

"No. I've spoken to her and she's promised me faithfully to say nothing. But that still leaves Harry? Can I trust him to keep his mouth closed?"

"Harry's the last one to be spiteful, Mother. But I'll mention it to him just the same."

When discussing Ethel's request afterwards, the young couple had wondered what Watson's reaction would be if he knew about the attempted suicide. One thing was certain, Harry thought dryly as Watson stood watching a paddle steamer churning the water into foam as it headed across the river towards New Holland, with the hope that the American might marry Ethel and so get her off their backs, they were the the last people in the world to mention it to him.

Harry's presence on the pier was due to Watson's request the previous week. "Who knows, Harry, I might come over here and stay one day. So how about being a good guy and showing me the sights?"

For the last two hours Harry had been doing just that. They had been to the Wilberforce Museum, to Trinity House, and to Hull's magnificent Holy Trinity Church. Then round the market and back to the old town which had fascinated Watson. "Look at these names, Harry! Land Of Green Ginger, Blackfriargate, Lowgate . . . It'd kill my kid brother if he could see this. And take a look at these old Georgian houses.

Aren't they beautiful?"

For over half an hour he had kept Harry walking round the labyrinth of narrow cobbled streets. Although by this time most of the houses had been converted into lawyers' offices, Watson had kept pausing to peer through the grilled, dust-stained windows into the gaslit rooms inside. "Take a look at this one, Harry! Isn't that a sight straight from Dickens?"

The American's enthusiasm had remained unabated when Harry had taken him to a restaurant in Whitefriargate for coffee. "Geez, just look at this place, Harry. All these old beams and oak tables. And look at all that brasswork. Is the coffee as good as the atmosphere?"

By this time Harry had realised Watson's enthusiasm was sincere and found himself liking the ingenuous American. "We think so. But you're the experts on coffee. So we'd better wait and see."

When the coffee arrived, Watson's approval had been unequivocal. "Just like Ma used to make. I'm going to bring Ethel here. And Elizabeth too, of course, if she'd like to come."

It was the first time that day that he had spoken the girl's name and his pause before doing so seemed significant to Harry. He waited while Watson pulled out his cigar case and held it out. When he shook his head, the American pulled a face. "Aw, c'mon, Harry. This is a special occasion. We're getting to know one another."

Feeling he could no longer refuse, Harry took one. Opposite him Watson was making something of a ritual in lighting his cigar, giving Harry the impression he was searching for the right words. He felt his suspicion was justified a few seconds later when Watson expelled a cloud of smoke.

"That little girl of yours, Harry. She's very fond of Ethel, isn't she?"

Alerted, Harry nodded. "Yes, she is."

Watson puffed out smoke again. "Yeah, I've noticed. And it's clear enough Ethel feels the same way. How did all that come about, Harry? Was it because she and Mary used to live with her while you were in France?"

Unsure what the outcome of the conversation might be, Harry choose his words carefully. "Yes, I suppose it must be."

Watson's attempt to keep his question casual was not entirely successful. "Is that why you left the kid there when you moved? So Ethel wouldn't be lonely?"

The temptation to tell him the truth was strong but with dangers everywhere, Harry was forced to prevaricate. "Elizabeth did go with us for a few weeks but Mary felt sorry for Ethel. After all, it is a big house and it must have seemed empty with all of us gone."

"It was some gesture for you both to make. I sure appreciate it. But then it's only for a limited time, isn't it? You'll want the girl back as soon as Ethel's fixed up?"

Harry was hoping that 'fixed up' meant what he hoped it meant. "What do you think? She's our daughter. Of course we want her back."

Watson's changed tone suggested considerable

relief. "You two kids are really something. You really are. Ethel's a lucky woman." He drained his cup of coffee and then grinned expansively at Harry. "Well, what's next on the agenda? You're going to show me the docks, aren't you?"

Harry had felt both shame for Watson's praise and relief at his attitude when he had led the American towards the river. Unless Watson had been pumping him on behalf of Ethel, which he did not believe, there seemed little doubt that Watson was not happy with the present situation and could well be a valuable ally in the future.

Watson's question interrupted his thoughts. "Hear that, Harry? It's a couple of aeroplanes, isn't it?"

Listening, Harry could hear the drone of engines over the city. Turning, he squinted up into the bright August sky. "It could be. No, wait a minute. It might be the R.38. The papers said she might be flying over Hull today."

The heavy drone grew louder and a few seconds later shouts of excitement broke out from dockers and fish hands as a long slender shape emerged from a cloud bank above the city. Alongside Harry, Watson gave a wry grimace. "It's not the Krauts coming back again, is it?"

Harry laughed. "No, it's the R.38 all right. I'd forgotten she was coming this way today. They say she has some Americans on board."

"Americans? Why's that?"

"I believe she's doing trials for them."

The airship could be seen clearly now, a fish-shaped giant whose symmetry was only broken

142

by the gondola slung beneath her silver body and the pods that carried her engines. As the sun broke out of a cloud, iridescent haloes glowed round her spinning propellers. Watson gazed up admiringly. "She's a pretty sight, kid, isn't she?"

Harry was thinking about the Zeppelin that had destroyed their first home in 1916. "She is. But I'm glad she's one of ours."

The huge droning airship passed almost directly over them and began to turn up river. As he watched, Harry thought he saw a wrinkle appear in the fabric on her near side. When the airship continued to sweep majestically forward he believed it was only a trick of the sunlight. Then a second wrinkle appeared and without further warning, the entire structure suddenly buckled in its centre. Watson gave a gasp of shock. "My God, Harry! The damn thing's breaking up!"

Around them men began shouting and Harry heard a woman scream. For a moment the two ends of the airship seemed to rise, leaving the centre section, with its gondola, at the bottom of a silver V. Then the gondola itself split open and small dark objects began toppling out from it towards the river below. At first Harry thought it was ballast being thrown out but then, as he saw arms and legs waving, he realised the falling objects were men.

Beside him, gripped by shock and horror, Watson was swearing softly. The screaming of women, who had run out from the fish gutting sheds, rose as the toppling bodies smashed into

143

the water. Above, there was a dull explosion as the massive framework caught fire. As tongues of flame seared out and enveloped the gondola, more men could be seen leaping out. Here and there parachutes could be seen but most men fell unaided to their deaths.

With its huge ballonets of gas ruptured, the airship was now a blazing inferno. Yet as if it were determined to prolong the scene of horror as long as possible, its descent was slow, almost majestic. For a time it seemed it might drift back over the docks before sinking down but as the naked framework began to show through the hundred-foot flames, it began to fall faster and faster. A flock of sea gulls, feeding out on the river, rose like thrown confetti as it struck the water about half a mile from the shore. A hiss of boiling water sounded, then a huge cloud of steam billowed up through which the flames glowed obscenely.

Although men and women on the quayside were still shouting and screaming, patrol boats were already casting off and making towards the wreck. Watson, his round face pale, turned to Harry. "What the hell happened, Harry? Why did it break up like that?"

Harry shook his head. "God knows. A change of wind, perhaps, that buckled the frame."

Watson turned back to the blazing wreck. "Poor bastards. I wonder how many of them survived."

Boats began bringing in the bodies half an hour later. One berthed at the quay where Harry and Watson were still standing. With its sailors unprepared for the emergency, they carried off the bodies to a waiting ambulance on sailcloth and blankets. As one party went past Harry, he was able to see the charred remains of what had been a man only an hour before. Another body, with a spark of life remaining, was making sounds that were barely human. Watson, who had wanted to learn how many men had survived, gave a shudder and glanced at Harry. "I shouldn't have stayed to see this, kid. Let's get back home."

* * *

That night the sights he had witnessed gave Harry his nightmare again. Star shells were bursting in a crimson sky and men running forward and clambering over the broken walls of a redoubt. To his right flashes were jetting from a pillbox and the running figures were collapsing like broken dolls. Crawling towards the pill box, he waited until its machine gun ceased firing, then poured fire from his Lewis gun into the embrasure. As he sank down into the mud, he heard a thin cheer and saw two familiar khaki-clad figures running towards him. He tried to shout a warning but in his nightmare his voice locked in his throat.

The two men could be seen clearly as another star shell burst in his mind. One had a young face that was full of hero worship. Once again he tried to shout a frantic warning but now it was too late. Like a dragon's tongue, a long jet of flame roared out from the redoubt's shattered

145

walls, enveloping both men in a cloud of oily black smoke. When the reptilian tongue drew back, men that had become living torches were now visible, One, with eyes burned away, staggered forward and collapsed into a shell hole, bringing up a white cloud of steam. The younger man, still able to see and think, began dragging his incinerated body towards Harry.

The smell of burnt flesh made Harry gag as he bent over him. The buckles of the youth's carbonised webbing burned his hands and brought hideous imaginings of the agony locked within the quivering body. As the youth's shredded mouth shaped two words, Harry wanted to scream and run but the nightmare held him in merciless bondage.

The ghastly lips moved again and a charred hand clutched pleadingly at the Lewis gun he was still holding. With the night spinning round him, he gave a cry of despair and fired one long downward burst. Then he turned and ran like a madman towards the redoubt.

The time sequence of the dream slipped a cog and brought him face to face with the two German *flammen werfer* operators. With their hands in the air, they were standing alongside a khaki-clad figure. Ignoring their captor's cry of protest, he fired a long murderous burst at both men that almost cut them in two. Then, as he dropped to his knees in shame, he heard Chadwick's voice above him. "You shouldn't have done that, Miles. They were only doing their duty."

His head bowed lower as the familiar voice

146

continued: "Just the same you've done wonderful work tonight, Miles. In fact, I'm recommending you for the Military Medal."

There was no opportunity to protest. Only a dazzling flash from the tormented sky and then his painful return to the present with Mary's distressed voice sounding in his ears.

15

ELIZABETH was beginning to pout. "But I want to go with you, Grannie. Why can't I?"

"I've told you why, dear. Captain Watson wants to take me to the theatre afterwards and we know you wouldn't like the play. Apart from that, you'd be home far too late for a young girl."

"But you always take me out with you on Saturdays. And it doesn't matter if I get to bed late. I don't have to go to school the next day."

"I'm sorry, dear, but this time I can't take you. You'll be all right with your mummy just this once. It'll give you a chance to play with your brother."

"I don't want to play with Frank. I want to go out with you and Captain Watson." An element of resentment began to enter the girl's voice. "It's not you that doesn't want me to go, is it? It's Captain Watson."

Ethel frowned. "You mustn't say things like that. Captain Watson's been very kind to you since he's been over here. Think of the times he's bought you sweets and toys. And the books he has given you."

The girl's lips were quivering now. "Just the same he doesn't like taking me out when you're with him."

148

"Why do you say that? Has he said so to you?"

Elizabeth gave a tearful sniff. "No, but I know it just the same. He likes to have you to himself."

Ethel, handsome in a high-necked bronze dress, was caught between a smile and another frown. "That's not because he doesn't like you, dear. All men behave that way sometimes."

The girl's voice turned curious. "Is that because he's going to marry you, Grannie?"

Ethel stiffened. "Really, young lady, I don't know where you get your ideas from. Whoever told you that?"

"I heard Mummy saying so to Daddy one day. She thinks he's in love with you."

"It's a pity your mother hasn't more to do than tittle tattle about my affairs. And you shouldn't listen to such gossip. Captain Watson and I are just good friends. So don't go getting such ridiculous ideas."

The girl's face brightened. "Then aren't you going to get married after all, Grannie?"

Ethel stared at her. "Not if I don't want to. But why wouldn't you like me to marry Captain Watson? I thought you liked him."

"I do like him," the girl muttered. "Only . . . "

"Only what, my pet."

Elizabeth gave a sob and turned away. Ethel drew her back. "What is it, dear? Why have you turned against the Captain?"

For a long moment the girl did not reply. Then she burst into tears and flung herself into the woman's arms. "If he marries you, he'll take

149

you away and I won't see you again. And that would be awful. Absolutely awful."

Smiling, Ethel rocked her back and forth. "You silly child, of course he's not going to take me away from you. Wherever did you get such an idea from?"

"You nearly went away before," the child accused. "You nearly died and left me."

"That was different, dear. That was because of what your mummy and daddy did."

"But that's what Captain Watson's going to do if he marries you. Take you all the way to America so I'll never see you again."

"Don't be silly, dear. Grannie would never leave her little girl like that."

"You might if he wanted you to," Elizabeth sobbed.

"Rubbish, girl. Who's filling your mind with these ridiculous ideas? Is it your father?"

The tearful girl nodded. "Daddy doesn't think Captain Watson likes me to live with you."

Ethel's voice immediately hardened. "Did your father say that to you?"

"No. I heard him talking to Mummy in the garden. Is it true, Grannie? Doesn't he like me being here?"

Ethel's arms tightened round the girl. "Of course it isn't. Hasn't he shown you already how fond he is of you? Just the same I'll talk to him when he comes home so he can tell you himself. Now you go off to bed and in a few minutes Grannie will come up so we can read a story together."

Ethel emerged from Elizabeth's bedroom and nodded at Watson. "She's awake, as I thought she would be. Shall we do it now?"

Watson nodded and followed her into the room where Elizabeth was sitting up in bed. Ethel gave the girl a smile. "Here's Captain Watson, dear. I've told him about your fears and he's come to tell you what a silly little girl you are."

Watson, who looked distinctly embarrassed, sank down on the bed. "Hello, honey. What's all this about my not liking to take you out? I love taking you. It's just that we know you wouldn't like the play on Saturday, that's all."

When Elizabeth, too shy to look at him, did not answer, Ethel took up the cudgel for her. "It's not just that, Jack. She's got the impression from her parents that you don't like her living here with me."

Watson hesitated, then cleared his throat. "It's none of my business where you live, honey, as long as you're happy. And you sure seem happy enough with your Grandma. If you heard your mummy and daddy say that, they must have gotten the wrong impression. O.K.?"

The girl's voice was muted. "I suppose so."

"Then that's O.K., isn't it?"

There was a pause and then Elizabeth shook her head. Glancing at Ethel, Watson leaned forward. "Then what else is worrying you, honey?"

The girl gazed at him, then flung herself down

and buried her face in her pillow. Ethel turned towards the American. "She's afraid you might take me on holiday to America and leave her behind. I've told her you wouldn't dream of separating us like that."

This time Watson gave a start and looked distinctly uncomfortable. "I guess I wouldn't like to," he muttered.

"Only we couldn't take her without her parents' consent, could we?"

The child's reaction was instantaneous. "Then you are taking Grannie away to America! You are, aren't you?"

Watson's discomfort grew. "I did ask your Grandma, yes. But we haven't settled anything yet."

Elizabeth turned her tearful face to Ethel. "I knew he'd ask you. And Mummy and Daddy will never let me go. So you are going to leave me. And you said you never would."

As she burst into tears, Ethel gave Watson a look, then sank down on the bed and took the girl in her arms. "Now don't start all that crying again, dear. You don't know what your parents will say until Captain Watson has asked them. And he is going to, aren't you, Captain?"

Watson frowned uneasily. "Yeah, I suppose I could. But they'll never agree, will they?"

Elizabeth's sobs intensified. "They won't, they won't! I know they won't!"

Ethel ran a hand over the girl's hot face and then down her long, braided hair. "Be quiet and listen to me. Let's wait and see what happens after Captain Watson has spoken to your mummy and daddy. He'll tell them that you'll get a proper education over there and be well looked after." She glanced up and smiled at the discomforted Watson. "Captain Watson is a very persuasive man and I know your Mummy likes him very much. So let's wait and see before you cry any more, shall we?"

The possibility of seeing America made the girl's eyes start to brighten. "Do you think they will let me, Grannie? Do you really think they will?"

"We can only wait and see, darling. But as I say, Captain Watson is a very persuasive man and we know he'll do his very best."

"When will he ask them, Grannie?"

Ethel glanced again at Watson. "I'm sure he won't keep us waiting long, dear. He knows how much it means to both of us. Perhaps he might even go to them tonight."

"Tonight?" Watson muttered. "Will they be in?"

"One of them will be. They have a baby to look after."

Watson hesitated for a full thirty seconds before sighing and lifting his considerable weight from the bed. "O.K., if that's what you want. I guess the sooner we find out the better. I'll go and get the car."

Turning so that Elizabeth could not see her face, Ethel showed her appreciation by pursing her lips in a silent kiss. In one so naturally prim, it was a response that would have astounded Harry by its erotic promise. Clearly pleased by it, Watson moved towards the door with more enthusiasm. When he disappeared, Ethel turned to the girl. "There. Let's see what he can do."

In the way of children, Elizabeth's mood changed again. "What if they say no, Grannie? Will you still go to America and leave me? That would be just awful."

Ethel folded the girl in her arms so that her expression could not be seen. "Stop worrying, dear. Just trust your grannie and everything will turn out all right."

* * *

Watson was showing more than a little embarrassment as his eyes travelled from Mary to Harry. "Well, I guess that's it. How do the two of you feel?"

The young couple, who were seated in their living room with the American, glanced at one another. When neither spoke, Watson frowned. "Neither of you seem surprised. How come?"

Mary answered him. "We expected Mother would want to take Elizabeth if she went to America. The thing we didn't know was whether she'd be going."

"I'm not sure myself yet," Watson told her. "I've asked her half a dozen times over the last two months but she keeps on stalling me. I guess Elizabeth is the reason; she doesn't want to leave her behind."

Mary glanced at Harry again. "I'm sure she doesn't. She hates leaving her for long."

"Yeah, I've noticed that. She's real fond of that kid. That's why it's maybe unfair of me

154

to ask her over to the States if Elizabeth can't come with her."

"I don't think it's unfair at all," Mary said. "A trip over there will do her the world of good."

Watson rubbed his chin, a characteristic gesture. "I guess it might if she'd come. But without the kid I doubt it."

Harry broke the silence that followed by picking up a poker and turning over the coal fire. As flames leapt up in the grate, Watson turned to him. "You haven't said much, Harry. How do you feel about it? You've got my promise the kid would be well looked after and receive a good education while she was over there."

Harry replaced the poker into its stand. "Ethel asked you to talk to us, didn't she?"

Watson looked slightly taken aback by the question. "Why, yes, she did. But I guess she felt you'd want to hear from me personally how we'd look after Elizabeth. Ethel's like that. She's a mother herself and knows how mothers feel about their children."

"Was any of this discussed in front of Elizabeth?"

Watson was nothing if not honest. "Yeah, it was. But that was because the kid had gotten the idea I didn't like taking her around with us. I went up to her room to tell her that was all baloney and that's when the holiday business came up."

"Who brought it up?" Mary interrupted. "My mother or Elizabeth?"

Watson's forehead wrinkled. "I think Ethel said the kid had mentioned it and was upset she might be left behind. So we talked it over and decided I'd have a word with you both to see how you felt."

"What was Elizabeth's reaction?" Harry asked.

"Elizabeth? She almost bounced out of bed at the thought of seeing the States. She's just crazy to go. But you two know that already." When neither Harry nor Mary spoke, Watson's voice turned apologetic. "I guess it's my fault. I should never have gotten her so interested."

Seeing Harry's expression, Mary could read his thoughts and for a moment her voice turned bitter. "You're quite right; you shouldn't. She's been nagging Ethel to take her ever since."

Watson winced. "Yeah, it was stupid of me. But I'd no idea during the war that things would work out this way."

There was a moment of silence before Harry spoke again. "So at this point you don't know how long Ethel would stay over in America?"

Watson shook his head. "No, we've never gotten that far. I just want to get her over to meet my brother and the rest of my family. I guess I'd like her over there for three or four months but if you let Elizabeth go with us, you could name your own time. I guess that's only fair."

How little you know about my mother, Mary was thinking. She leaned forward. "Can I ask you a personal question, Jack?"

The American gazed at her, then grinned. "Shoot and I'll tell you."

"Do you intend to marry my mother? If she agrees to marriage, of course."

156

Her question made Harry frown. Watson looked almost bashful. "I'd sure like to, Mary. I was gone on her the first time we met. But it's not just up to me, is it?"

"Have you asked her?"

"Are you kidding? A dozen times at least."

"Does that mean she's refused you?"

"Not exactly. She keeps on stalling me. Says maybe next year or the year after that."

"Are you prepared to wait that long?"

"Yeah, I guess so. I've lasted all these years as a bachelor so another one or two shouldn't make all that difference."

"She's a lucky woman," Mary said.

Watson grinned. "Lucky? A lady like that? I think she's crazy even considering me, only don't tell her that, will you?"

Mary was thinking how much she liked this modest man. "You know it's Elizabeth that's preventing her saying yes, don't you?"

"Yeah, I figured that out some time ago. That's why I was thinking if I could get her over to the States and she liked it there, she might make the break."

"You mean make the break from Elizabeth?"

"Yeah. I know it's none of my business but I can't help feeling the kid ought to be with her own parents. Not that I don't think it's a hell of a thing you two have done to help Ethel, but if a marriage could take Elizabeth's place, it might be the best thing for everybody."

Mary realised Harry was right. They had an ally in this man. "But wouldn't your taking

157

Elizabeth with you to America defeat that purpose?"

Watson gave a rueful grin. "I don't think I'll get her over there to find out unless Elizabeth goes with us. And I can't stay here indefinitely. I might sell out my shares in the business to my brother in a year or two but right now I'm needed over there."

Mary took a deep breath. "I'll be honest with you too, Jack, and admit I hate the idea of Elizabeth going away for so long. On the other hand I can understand your problem." Pausing, she turned to Harry. "What do you think, darling?"

The light was casting a shadow on Harry's face, making it difficult for her to see his expression. At the same time she knew his thoughts. Elizabeth was waiting in No. fifty-seven for the outcome of Watson's visit. If they refused permission again, Ethel would use it ruthlessly to widen the breach between them and the girl.

The bitterness in Harry's voice confirmed her belief. "I think we'll have to let her go. I don't see we've any choice."

Watson made an immediate protest. "Wait a minute. There's no pressure on you. If you'd rather the kid didn't go, say so. I'll understand and I'm certain Ethel will too."

At that moment there was a cry from upstairs. As Mary rose to her feet, Harry checked her and rose himself. "I'll see to him. You stay with Jack." He went to the door, then turned to Watson. "I said you can take her. Only for

God's sake take care of her and don't be long away." With that he turned and ran up the stairs.

Watson, looking troubled, turned to Mary. "I don't get it, Mary. You two don't have to say yes. So why is Harry acting like that?"

The temptation to tell him the full story was almost overwhelming. "He's very fond of her, Jack. He only sees her three times a week as things are now and he's going to miss her badly if she goes to America."

Watson was showing distress now. "I think you two kids have been wonderful. But don't worry any more. I'll tell Ethel it can't be done. She'll be the first to understand."

She wanted to laugh at his innocence and cry at the same moment. "No, Jack. Harry meant what he said and I agree with him. Elizabeth's crazy to see America so this time we can't disappoint her. Only take great care of her, won't you?"

"Are you sure, kid? Really sure?"

She rose to her feet. "Yes, we're sure." As more cries came from upstairs, she went on: "I'll have to see to Frank. He's restless tonight. You go back and tell Elizabeth her good news."

16

1921 SLIPPED into 1922. Ethel returned with Elizabeth in April of that year, leaving behind Watson who was unable to accompany them because of business commitments. Although Harry and Mary would have liked to have met the couple in at Liverpool, their involvements with the business and difficulty in finding a baby sitter for Frank that day, forced them to be content with meeting them at Paragon Station.

They had feared Elizabeth might have been spoiled by her four months in America and be discontented at her return. To their relief this was not apparent, at least not when the girl stepped from the train and saw her parents and Frank waving at her. She ran forward, kissed both parents, and then bent down and gave Frank a big hug and kiss. As the boy showed his pleasure at seeing her, she hugged him again. "My, how you've grown. You're becoming a big boy, aren't you?"

Even Ethel was friendly in her fashion when Mary asked if she had enjoyed herself. "Yes, thank you, dear. It's been a nice change. Although it's good to be back in England again." She smiled at Elizabeth who was chatting animatedly with Frank. "I think my little girl feels the same way, don't you, dear?"

The agreeableness of the reunion made Mary overlook the possessiveness of the remark. "Do you, darling? Are you glad to be home again?"

The girl nodded. "Yes, Mummy. Mind you, I liked America. It's ever such fun over there."

Harry, whose delight in having his daughter back was almost palpable, swung her up into his arms. "You've grown too, do you know that? But where's your American accent? I thought you'd be talking like Jack when you came home."

At that Ethel gave a sniff. "Not on my life. Every time she came out with one of those slang words, I gave her a good talking too. I like Americans but, oh dear, that dreadful language of theirs."

After collecting their luggage, Harry drove them all to No. fifty-seven in the old Ford which he was now using for work again. On the way Ethel chatted quite amicably to Mary. "Jack introduced me to William's brother while we were over there. He took us out sightseeing quite a few times when Jack couldn't take time off from work."

"Does he look like Dad?" Mary asked.

"Yes, quite a lot. Not so tall but with the same strong build. He said I had to tell you that if ever you visit America, you can stay with him as long as you like."

The conversation remained amicable for the rest of the day. Molly, whom Ethel had retained in employment on condition she visited the house every day and kept it clean, was awaiting their arrival and Ethel invited the young couple to have tea and scones with her before they left. During the conversation she offered each one a pound a week rise, saying it was something she

161

ought to have given them before she left the country. In truth the rise was long overdue and both were certain they had Watson to thank for it.

Nevertheless it was welcome, not only because they badly needed the money but because of the new relationship with Ethel it seemed to herald. Ethel even suggested that in the future they should use the Ford to bring Mary to work, an offer that brought a wry and amused comment from Harry when they drove off with Frank two hours later. "It must be the climate over there. Or has she missed us?"

Mary laughed. "I doubt that. More likely Jack has something to do with it."

He gave her a mischievous grin. "Do you mean he's been a good lover?"

She felt herself blush. "Don't be so naughty."

He laughed. "I can't think of anything else that would put her in such a good mood, can you? And it was you who said she was hot blooded."

"She is. But if it was Jack, her mood's soon going to change, isn't it, now that they're three thousand miles apart."

He grimaced. "Don't say that. Maybe she's agreed to marry him and that's why she's purring."

"No, I think she'd have told us if she had. Certainly Elizabeth would. Perhaps Jack's coming over again this year."

"Let's hope so," he said. "What do you think of Elizabeth? She's becoming quite a young lady, isn't she?"

"Yes, she's growing up fast. I thought she looked very well and pretty."

His tone expressed his surprise and relief. "I'd half expected her to be disappointed now she's back home. Do you think she didn't like it over there?"

She shook her head. "I thought the same at first but it's not that. When you were taking mother's cases upstairs, she told me she thought America was a wonderful country."

He laughed, clearly delighted by the news. "Then perhaps she really is glad to see us again."

She desperately wanted to believe it herself. "She did seem to be, didn't she? And I loved the fuss she made over Frank."

He laughed again and threw a glance over his shoulder at the little boy sitting on the back seat of the Ford. "You were glad to see her too, weren't you, Scamp? Perhaps she'll come over to play with you this weekend."

She could not remember when she had seen Harry so happy. With Elizabeth showing such pleasure at their reunion, he had every cause, she thought, and she ought to share the same sense of relief. Yet, try as she would, she could not dispel the feeling that there was another reason the girl was glad to be home.

★ ★ ★

During this period of relative goodwill, after carefully checking with Ethel that she had no objections, Harry used the Ford occasionally to

163

take his family out at weekends. As Saturday was one of the days Elizabeth spent with them, he usually managed to take her along too.

These were days everyone enjoyed. With few cars yet on the roads, it was the practice for motorists to salute one another and the two children drew great fun from this, leaning out of the windows and waving their arms energetically at every vehicle that passed by.

For Mary it was the happiest spring and summer she had known since the war. Harry's health seemed to be improving, Elizabeth to be content with her life style, and even Ethel to be more reasonable than she had been since William's death. Both Mary and Harry felt they owed much to Watson's influence.

Their weekend tours were varied. On one Saturday they would go to the seaside at Bridlington or Withernsea and let the children build sand castles or go into the sea. Elizabeth, now an attractive, willowy girl of nine years, had learned to swim at her private school and was totally unafraid of the water. Frank, now a sturdy three year old, wanted to follow her into the waves and would cry lustily in frustration when his laughing parents restrained him.

On other Saturdays Harry would take them to Flamborough Head where the children would play for hours climbing among the rocks, searching rock pools for crabs, and sometimes, under Harry's supervision, clambering into the cool, dark caves that the restless sea had gouged into the chalk cliffs.

Then they would take trips into the country.

A favourite place was Beverley where, on the Westwood above the ancient town, the children would fly the kites Harry had bought them. At other times they would climb the Wolds at Brantingham Dale and at the top lie panting and listening to the skylarks.

But for Mary the golden day of that year was their trip to Burton Stather to see Harry's grandparents. She and Harry had spent their honeymoon in the couple's cottage and she had often longed to return there.

The couple were very old now but their joy at seeing the young couple and their children was unrestrained. After a meal cooked lovingly for them by Agnes Leason, Mary and Harry left the children with the old folk while they walked down to the river that held so many memories for them.

To Mary's relief it had not changed. Dragonflies still hovered over its gently-moving water and as she walked arm in arm with Harry along its banks, the tall grass still released its pollen on her dress.

The spell of the past was on Mary and the glance she gave Harry was almost shy as they approached a copse of trees. "Do you remember?"

He squeezed her arm. "Of course I do. Every moment."

After the sunlight outside, the shade within the trees was cool on her face and arms. As she gazed around, he laid his jacket on the grass and urged her down. His voice was gentle in her ear. "It was the first time we made love, wasn't it?"

She swallowed and nodded. "Yes. And you said wonderful things to me."

"Things like 'you're beautiful? The most beautiful thing I'd ever known'?"

She eyed him in wonder. "You've remembered every word!"

"Why not? You're still the most beautiful thing in the world."

At that, tears filled her eyes. "So much has happened since then, Harry. So many ugly things. We didn't have any idea, did we?"

He hushed her. "Let's be as we were then. Young and innocent and full of hope. Shall we?"

He was smiling down at her. Above him leaves were moving gently against the sky and sunbursts of light were glowing and fading. Inside her something seemed to burst and flood her mind with an emotion that had no name. "Love me, Harry," she whispered. "Love me as you did that day."

He bent down and kissed her. A moment later the sun paused in the sky as it had paused eleven years ago and huge wings lifted her towards the leafy cathedral above. The organ note of summer grew louder until it burst and echoed back from the far end of the world. Under his shirt, her hands tightened and drew him deeper within her. "I love you, Harry," she sobbed. "Oh, God, I love you. Every gentle, manly thing about you."

His eyes, still dazed from his lovemaking, stared down into her own. He tried to speak but instead sank down beside her. As her

166

arms closed around him, a ray of sunshine burst through the vaulted roof. It seemed to shower them with golden dust and as the hum of summer became hypnotic in its insistence, their eyes turned heavy and closed.

★ ★ ★

It was late afternoon when they returned to the cottage and joined the old people in the warm kitchen they used as a living room. They had only been back a few minutes when Bill Leason began talking about Chadwick. "Things have changed, lad, since the old squire died. The young 'un's a different breed to his father. But then you'll know summat about that, seeing you served under him in the war. Didn't you have some trouble with him?"

Harry gave Mary a smile. "Just a bit now and then. But in fairness to him he was a good soldier."

"Aye, so I heard. He got a medal or two, didn't he?"

"Quite a few. He was in his element during the war."

"Aye, he always liked a scrap. Do you remember the one you had with him when you were both little 'uns?"

None of the adults noticed that Elizabeth had lowered her book and was listening to their talk of Chadwick. "I remember it," Harry said. "But what changes has he made here?"

The old man gave a grunt of disgust. Wearing an old waistcoat and corduroy trousers, he was

167

sitting at one side of the fireplace in which a coal fire burned summer or winter. He had a churchwarden pipe in his hand on which he would suck every now and then. This act was usually followed by his aiming a glob of spittle into the fire. It was a habit that infuriated Agnes, particularly as Bill Leason made no compromise when she had a cooking pot on the grate, although it had to be said in the old man's favour that he was a deadly shot and could put his bullets through the pot handles with unerring accuracy.

To Agnes's cry of protest, he sent one sizzling into the fire now before answering Harry's question. "The bugger's sold me land for one thing."

Harry frowned. "Sold it? When?"

"Two years ago. Some bloody company owns it now."

Agnes gave another cry of protest. "Stop swearing like that! You've got children in the room."

As Leason looked round, Elizabeth lowered her face into her book. The old man looked suitably chastened as he turned to Mary. "Sorry, luv. It's just a bad habit. No offence meant."

Mary, who had been amused during her honeymoon by the interplay between the pair, was hurting herself in trying not to laugh at his antics with the pipe. Harry came to her rescue. "That's all right. Elizabeth's got more sense than to repeat swear words and Frank's a bit too young yet. What about your cottage? Chadwick didn't sell that too, did he?"

168

Bill Leason scowled. "He wanted to sell 'em all but I think the local council persuaded him not to. But all the land 'cept the garden's gone."

Agnes intervened again. "What does it matter? You're too old to have gone on farming it. Don't you realise you're over eighty?

Leason gave her a scowl. "Don't be a silly old fool. Course I could have farmed it. And so could all the others."

"But you are all right?" Harry asked. "You can manage?"

Agnes replied for him. "Now don't you go worrying about us, lad. We get a bit of a pension, we've got a bit tucked away, and there's the garden too." She turned her wrinkled face to Leason. "I've got to say this about the old man. He just about feeds us from that garden of his."

"Aye," Leason grunted. "At least when those red-coated buggers aren't tramping all over it."

"Do you mean the local Hunt?" Harry asked.

"Aye. Chadwick's lot. They go wild now and then. They chased a fox though here last month and took a couple of rows of beans with 'em. And ruined a dozen or so cabbages."

"Didn't you complain to the police?"

"The police? Chadwick's got 'em all in his pocket. He's the Chairman of the Bench and you should see the sentences the bugger dishes out. One old tramp got three months' hard labour for pinching a bottle of wine from one of his bloody garden parties."

Harry's old dislike of Chadwick was back. "I'll

169

talk to him about your garden. He shouldn't let his hunt ride roughshod over it like that."

Mary could not hold back her protest. "No. You mustn't get involved with him again." Unaware of Elizabeth's curiosity, she turned to Agnes. "He gave Harry a dreadful time during the war. I don't want all that bad feeling to begin again."

Although Agnes knew next to nothing of the details, her support was immediate. "You're quite right, dear. It's best nothing's said about it. It only happens now and then, and in any case we don't want to risk losing the cottage. Let sleeping dogs lie, I say." With a glare at Bill Leason, she put a kettle of water on the grate. "Let's have a cup of tea. You two must feel like one after your long walk."

The old man waited until the kettle was in place on the hob. Then he sucked on his pipe, took aim, and sent a bullet straight through the kettle handle.

There was a sudden scamper of feet and Frank ran in front of the fireplace. His young, excited face gazed admiringly at the old man. "Do it again, Grandpa. Please do it again."

Everyone laughed, including Mary. Yet at the same time she knew that the talk about Chadwick had spoiled for her what had otherwise been a perfect day.

17

THE armistice between the young couple and Ethel lasted longer this time than was usual, continuing throughout the winter and into the following year. It was not without a few eruptions — with Ethel a participant that would have been too much to expect — but nevertheless they were minor ones and did not scatter lava as high and wide as in earlier days.

For this improvement in relations, Mary felt Jack Watson must take the credit. While it was obvious Ethel was the dominant personality of the two, she was nevertheless a woman of her time in that she paid some attention to the opinions of her man friend, and from his letters alone there seemed no doubt that Watson had a genuine affection for her daughter and son-in-law.

At the same time, without looking a gift horse too closely in the mouth, Mary could not help wondering why Ethel had chosen Watson to be the new man in her life. While she, Mary, liked Watson very much, he was a far cry from the huge and impressive personality that had been her father. Perhaps, as Harry had suggested, he was a good lover. Good relations, if not permanent relations, have been founded on less and Mary had no doubts about her mother's strong sexuality.

Not that Watson was without other assets. He had an excellent sense of humour, was extremely good-natured, and as far as Mary could establish, he was a reasonably wealthy man with good social contacts in the States, something which would appeal greatly to the snob in Ethel. Indeed Mary often wondered why Ethel had returned home after only four months in America, even though she had promised to stay away no longer.

To some extent this question was answered when Watson announced he would be paying another visit in the late summer. From Ethel's barely concealed pleasure at the news, it was clear that her overseas trip had deepened her feelings for the American and made both Mary and Harry wonder if this time she would accept his offer of marriage.

If they were looking forward to Watson's visit, however, one member of the family was not. As soon as Elizabeth heard the news, she began to show discontent. Although at first Mary said nothing to Harry, her suspicions about the girl's behaviour on returning to England surfaced again. She had not forgotten how morose and sullen the girl had been during Watson's last visit to England when he had taken Ethel out and left Elizabeth behind with her parents.

At first Mary had blamed these moods on simple resentment at not being invited but now she felt certain Elizabeth had become jealous of Watson's claim on Ethel's affections. This, she felt, could well be the reason the girl had been glad to get her grandmother back to England.

It was a suspicion that waxed hot and cold in her thoughts. At one moment it seemed melodramatic to ascribe such possessive feelings for her grandmother to a ten-year-old child. Then Mary would remember the morbid sentiments Ethel had inflicted for years on the girl's developing mind and it became all too probable.

That summer during Watson's visit she took particular notice of Elizabeth's behaviour and felt her suspicions were confirmed. When Harry, who seldom criticised the girl, made a comment on her moods, Mary felt the time had come to explain them.

"She's jealous of Jack. Haven't you noticed she's always like that when he's alone with Ethel?"

He gave a laugh of disbelief. "Jealous of Jack? You can't be serious."

"I wish I wasn't. But she is. She feels he's stealing Ethel's affection from her."

"Has she said so?"

"Of course she hasn't. She probably isn't aware of it herself yet. But that's what it is."

His love for the girl and his relief at her new interest in Frank would not let him take Mary's belief seriously. "I know she has moody spells but don't all kids suffer that kind of jealousy from time to time? Sometimes it's over a teacher at school or a friend. Isn't it just something she'll grow out of?"

Although she felt there was a world of difference between a grandmother and a

173

schoolteacher, she did not argue with him. She wanted reassurance, not only because of her love for the child but because she could not face going back to the old cat and dog days with Ethel again. Yet on the days that summer when she found Elizabeth crying in the small room they kept for her at home, instinct warned her the girl's emotion was not natural and it presaged danger in the days to come.

★ ★ ★

The brief ting of the front door bell made Ethel glance up from her needlework to the gilt clock on the mantelpiece. "That must be the evening paper, dear. Fetch it for me, will you?"

Elizabeth, back from school only ten minutes earlier, laid down her book and ran into the hall. Ethel gave her a smile as she returned and handed her the paper. "Thank you, dear. I'll just scan through it and then see how Molly is getting on with dinner."

There were a few seconds of silence while the girl returned to her book and Ethel opened the paper. It was broken by a murmur of acclaim from the woman. "How true. Well done!"

Elizabeth looked up curiously. "What is it, Grannie?"

Ethel continued reading for a moment, then glanced up at the girl. "What's that, dear?"

"You said well done. What's happened?"

"It's something about this wave of strikes we're having, dear. Sir Michael Chadwick has been speaking about them."

174

"He's the officer Daddy served under, isn't he?"

"That's right, dear. He's the local squire now and a very important man in the city."

"What does he say about the strikes?"

With the girl so precocious, there were times when Ethel forgot she was still a child. "He thinks the same as I do, that they're disgraceful. He says the working man should be doing his best to pull the country round after the war and not trying to sabotage it. He says they're nothing but Bolsheviks, like the Russians. I agree with every word he says."

"That's not what Daddy says. Daddy thinks it's a disgrace men are getting such terrible wages after what they did for the country during the war."

Ethel gave a sniff. "I'm afraid that's just what your father would say. Sadly he doesn't know as much about these things as people like Sir Michael."

"But Daddy was poor once, wasn't he? So why doesn't he know how people feel when they're poor?"

Ethel stared at the girl. "It's not that simple, dear. A person has to be educated to understand the problems. Regrettably, your father didn't go to the kind of schools Sir Michael went to. So we can hardly expect him to understand such things, can we?"

"And yet Daddy seems to know a lot about trade unions and the Government. I often hear him talking to Mummy about them."

Almost without Ethel knowing it, her tone

became scathing. "I'm sure he knows a lot about trade unions. It's the unions that are causing all these strikes at the moment. As Sir Michael says, they ought to be ashamed of themselves."

The girl reflected a moment, then changed the subject. "Mummy and Daddy don't like Sir Michael, do they? I heard them talking about him once when we went to Burton Stather."

Ethel looked curious. "What did they say?"

"Daddy's grandpa was complaining that Sir Michael keeps chasing foxes through his garden and doing damage to it."

"Why haven't you told me this before?"

"I didn't think you liked Daddy's grand-parents."

"I didn't mean you shouldn't tell me things about them. What else did they say about Sir Michael?"

The girl's brow wrinkled. "Something about the punishment he gave to an old tramp for stealing a bottle of wine. How could he do that? He isn't in the police force, is he?"

"No, dear. But he's a Justice of the Peace. That means he tries wrongdoers and sentences them to punishment."

"Daddy's grandpa thought his punishments were too severe," the girl said.

Ethel gave a hard laugh. "I'm sure he did. He's probably not above doing a bit of poaching himself. Never take any notice of what people like that say. They're all as bad as one another."

Once again the girl reflected. "Just the same, neither Mummy and Daddy like Sir Michael. Why is that, Grannie?"

"I've already told you, dear. Your father served under Sir Michael during the war. Officers like Sir Michael hold the King's Commission and swear an oath to do their duty. Men in the ranks, like your father was, often don't understand the orders officers have to give and so take a dislike to them. That's why your father doesn't like Sir Michael."

"But Mummy doesn't like him either. In fact she hates him. And she didn't serve under him."

Ethel realised they were reaching dangerous ground now. "Wives often take their husband's side over these things. She was worried when your father was missing and naturally had to blame somebody. In fact Sir Michael was very kind to her. He spent a great deal of his time trying to find out what had happened to your father."

"But then why does she hate him so much?" the girl persisted.

Ethel had the feeling she was being driven into a corner. "You mustn't on any account repeat this to your parents but I think your mother has taken far too much notice of the things your father has told her. The truth is, Sir Michael was a very gallant soldier. Many people believe he should have been given the Victoria Cross."

Elizabeth took the newspaper from her and gazed at the head and shoulders portrait of Chadwick. "He's very good-looking, isn't he?"

The comment, with its hint of pubescence, clearly startled Ethel. "He's a very fine gentleman. I certainly always found him so."

The girl's curiosity was whetted now. "Did you have much to do with him, Grannie?"

"Yes. I saw him every time he came to talk to your mother. That's why I know what a fine gentleman he is."

"Why did he come to see her, Grannie?"

"I've told you why. To tell her the news about your father."

"But there wasn't any news, was there? So why didn't he just telephone her?" When Ethel, taken aback, hesitated, the girl went on: "I'll bet I know why. He liked her, didn't he? Men do like Mummy because she's beautiful. That was the reason, wasn't it?"

Inwardly proud of her brief association with Chadwick, and his admiration of her daughter, Ethel went further than she intended. "If you must know everything, you little minx, he did find your mother attractive. If your father hadn't returned from the war, I think he might have asked her to marry him."

Elizabeth clapped her hands in excitement. "Does that mean she'd be Lady Chadwick today?"

"Yes, I suppose it does."

The girl gave another excited laugh, then her tone changed. "But if he though her so attractive, why does she hate him so much?"

Ethel was already regretting being carried away. "I suppose she felt he shouldn't have shown such interest in her when it wasn't known whether your father was alive or dead. In normal times she would have been right but the war was

178

still raging and Sir Michael was going back to it. So I think he could be forgiven, don't you?"

The girl looked puzzled. "Why did he need forgiving? He hadn't done anything wrong, had he?"

Conscious that she no longer had an innocent child on her hands, Ethel frowned. "You know better than that, dear. It's most improper for a young man to show interest in a married lady. All I'm saying is that I feel he can be forgiven because of the circumstances."

The girl's voice was full of admiration. "He did it because he's so brave. I think it's ever so romantic."

Ethel seldom regretted her words but she was regretting them now. "I want you to promise me you'll never let your mother and father know about this conversation. Do you promise?"

Elizabeth's face was shining with romantic thoughts as she nodded. "It's all right. I won't say anything to them." Then she gave a shiver of excitement. "But I'm ever so glad you've told me."

18

THE wave of strikes that incensed Ethel so much had begun early in 1921. After the short post-war boom had exhausted itself, it became more and more obvious that the productive capacity of the industries on which British prosperity had been based for a hundred years was greatly in excess of world demand. Devastated Europe could not buy from her and nations outside Europe, in particular India and the countries of South Africa, Canada and Australia, having been cut off from British exports during the war, had either sought other sources of supply or industrialised themselves. This led to a drastic reduction in the demand for cotton goods and for shipping, another traditional British industry whose capacity at that time was sufficient to meet the world's entire annual demand. With the iron, steel, and engineering industries affected in turn by this decline in demand, the domino effect spread right throughout the land, causing unemployment and hardship for millions of families.

With this unemployment came great bitterness. Men who had served their country in the most terrible of wars had been promised a land fit for heroes to live in. By 1923 the most chauvinistic Briton would have been hard put to justify that pledge. With some unemployed families near to starvation, protest strikes became commonplace. Between 1919 and 1922 there had been two police strikes, a national railway strike, a three-month engineering strike, a two-month shipbuilders' strike, two national coal strikes, and many violent demonstrations in the larger cities. Indeed it is difficult to see how revolution could have been avoided had not unemployment insurance been extended to workers and the dole being given to them after their entitlement under this insurance scheme was exhausted.

Yet to put things in perspective, in spite of this wide spread unrest, no lives were lost in Britain through industrial violence during that time. The same curb upon violence was not evident in the wider world outside. In Ireland the Black and Tans and the Irish patriots were killing one another with grim gusto; in India Hindus and Moslems had resumed their age-old pastime of religious murder; in Armenia Turks had begun to slaughter Greeks again.

While all this had been going on, President Harding in America had announced that the United States would take no further part in the League of Nations, a body that had been created by his predecessor, Woodrow Wilson, for the very purpose of preventing such horrors and disasters. In spite of the terrible lessons of the Great War, the world remained as blind, capricious and dangerous as ever.

During this time it could not be said that The Hardcastle Drug Company had greatly prospered either. Immediately after the war

181

commodity prices had risen sharply, and with wages falling at the same time, and Ethel refusing to help with any injection of capital, the most Harry and Mary had been able to do was put the business on a sounder footing. This they had done but it was not until 1924, when there was a slight improvement in general trade and a small drop in the cost of living, that they obtained Ethel's permission to take on two extra men.

Although the young couple felt the extra help would allow the business to expand, they began to regret their request when Ethel stubbornly refused to give the other warehousemen a rise. "Why do they want more money? With two extra men they don't have to work so hard."

"Mother, we've taken on extra help to increase our turnover, not to reduce our work load. The men haven't had an increase for three years. With the cost of living going up all the time, they're getting poorer and poorer."

"It isn't going up," Ethel announced triumphantly. "It's going down. The papers say so."

"It went up two years ago. And I haven't noticed much change since then, have you?"

Ethel had been adamant and Mary's petition had failed for yet another year. During this time, although Ethel kept fending off his offers of marriage, Watson kept on coming to England to see her. He had now sold his business shares and was only needed by his brother in an advisory capacity. As a result the length of his visits grew proportionally longer.

182

It was in May of 1925, just a couple of weeks before the American was due to arrive, that Brown, the ware house foreman, tapped on the door of Mary's office. "Can you spare me a minute, Miss?"

"Yes, of course, Alf. Come in."

The burly foreman looked almost embarrassed. "It's about the men, Miss. If they don't get more money soon there's going to be trouble. Won't you have another word with Mrs Hardcastle?"

Mary motioned him to sit down. "Tell me about it."

Brown wiped his hands on his acid-stained apron before taking the chair. "We're all havin' a bad time, Miss. Webb's little girl's got whooping cough and he can't afford the doctor. Bell says his missus goes hungry so his kids get enough to eat. And things aren't much better for my missus. It can't go on much longer, Miss. Summat has to be done."

Mary went to her petty cash box and took out four pounds. "Give two to Webb and one to Bell and yourself. In the meantime I'll have a talk with Mrs Hardcastle. Tell the men, will you?"

Brown showed some relief. "Thanks, Miss. But do you think she'll agree?"

"I don't know, Alf. But I promise to do all I can."

* * *

Mary went over to see Ethel that lunchtime. Elizabeth was at No. fifty-seven when she arrived, having just returned home for lunch. Making the pretext she had come over to see the girl, Mary chatted with her until she returned to school. Then she turned to Ethel. "I really came over to see you, Mother. I had another complaint from Alf Brown this morning."

Never one to bear complaints from workmen lightly, Ethel made a tut of impatience. "That man's always complaining. What's wrong with him now?"

"I'm sorry, Mother, but he isn't always complaining. He's a very hardworking and patient man. But as foreman, it's his duty to bring me any complaints from his men."

"What are they complaining about? Their wages again?"

"Yes, I'm afraid they are. If we don't give them an increase soon there could be trouble."

Ethel stared at her. "What kind of trouble?"

"They might go on strike. There isn't much else they can do if we go on refusing to listen to them."

Ethel gave a laugh of derision. "Let them strike. We could fill their places the next day."

"That's not true. Brown would have to train new men. But in any case that's not the point. They've been loyal to us so far but now they're suffering hardship." Mary went on to tell her about Webb and Bell. "You surely don't want to get a name for being a bad employer. And these are two good men."

"How do you know that?" Ethel demanded. "In all likelihood they drink their money away as all that class do. If we give them an increase

184

it'll only go into the pockets of the brewers."

"Mother, how can they drink on the wages they get? Could you live on two pounds a week?"

"That's a ridiculous question. Those sort of people don't have the expenses and commitments we have."

"They don't have them because they can't afford them. So that's no answer."

"You don't know what you're talking about, girl. Dad and I were poor once but we never went around looking for charity."

"Mother, these men aren't asking for charity. They simply want a decent wage for a decent day's work. At the moment they're not getting it."

Her persistence was beginning to irritate Ethel. "Where's the money going to come from? You're always telling me we can't afford to take any more out of the business."

"We've no choice here. I think we can afford to give each man an extra ten shillings a week, with the promise we'll give them another increase next year."

Ethel gave a start. "Ten shillings! That's ridiculous. Who's put you up to this? Harry?"

Mary felt her heart sink as she realised how close the armistice was to collapse. "It's got nothing to do with Harry. He doesn't even know yet that Brown has made the complaint."

Ethel's sniff suggested total disbelief. "I'll lay odds he'll stand by the men when he does. His class always stick together."

Mary took a deep breath. "If you're going to

snipe at Harry, Mother, you can handle the men yourself. Are you going to give them an extra ten shillings or not? If you don't, you'd better be prepared to lose a lot more when they go on strike. Don't say I haven't warned you."

Tight-faced, Ethel gazed at her, "I hope you realise one thing. If we give it to them, there'll be no increase for you and your Harry next year."

Mary made a weary gesture. "I'd expected that before I came to see you. Then I can give it to them, can I? From this week?"

When Ethel gave a stiff and resentful nod, Mary walked out of the house without another word. The armistice was already in tatters, she thought. The only question now was when open warfare would break out again.

19

HARRY passed the letter over to Mary to read. "It's from Lena Turnor. Her uncle's died and left the cottage to his daughter in Canada. She's waiting to hear what the daughter intends to do but feels she's certain to sell. So she wonders if we'd start looking for somewhere else to live as she'll probably have to return here."

Mary read the letter, then passed it back. "It's probably just as well. Only I wonder how long we've got."

He was not surprised by her reaction. For some time now they had discussed moving to a larger house. With Elizabeth sometimes wanting to stay the night when Watson was in England, they had occasionally allowed her to use Frank's bedroom and made a bed for the boy on the sofa downstairs.

Boylike, Frank had enjoyed the novelty of sleeping on the sofa but now that he was growing older they did not want him to think that his sister was being given priority over him. It was not likely, for he was a cheerful and happy child not inclined to such jealous speculations, but with Ethel giving Elizabeth almost anything she wanted and giving the boy little more than token presents at Christmas or on his birthdays, it was a risk neither of them liked to take.

The problem had been money. A larger house

would mean less to spend on the children and with Ethel lavishing presents on Elizabeth, the disparity would widen further. For this reason they had hesitated, but now the decision was being taken out of their hands neither was unduly dismayed.

Harry read the letter again. "She hasn't heard from the daughter yet and as she must be given a few weeks' notice, we've time to look around. What sort of place do we want? Will three bedrooms be enough?"

She laughed at his question. "What were you thinking of — a manor house? Of course it'll be enough. But I would like a decent-sized garden if we can afford it. Then Frank won't have to play in the street so much."

"All right," he said. "I'll start looking tomorrow."

Although they needed to be reasonably near the warehouse and Elizabeth's school, empty houses were not a problem. With so many men unemployed and many of those in employment able to afford only slum properties, houses with 'to let' notices stood in every street.

Even so it took Harry nearly a fortnight to find what he wanted: a semi-detached house in Mason Street, on the opposite side of Ellerby Road. It was no further away than their present house from the school and warehouse and had a reasonably-sized back garden. Moreover it had the one thing Mary desired: a living room large enough to take the sideboard her father had left her.

The rent, however, was seven and sixpence a

week, two shillings more than they had been paying in St George's Road, and the one factor that made Mary hesitate. "Can we afford it, Harry?"

He grinned. "With that living room, we'll have to, won't we?"

She reached forward and kissed him. "That's what you've been looking for all this time, isn't it?"

"Why not? You've been waiting for it long enough."

She hesitated. "Is it silly of me?"

"No. Why should it be?"

"Sometimes I think it is. To be so sentimental over a piece of furniture. But for me it stands for everything Dad was. Big and solid, yet warm-hearted and beautiful too." Pausing, she laughed at herself. "Imagine what Dad would say if he heard me say he was beautiful."

Harry did not laugh. "He was beautiful. A beautiful man."

She hugged him. "You understand everything, don't you? Why am I so lucky?"

He grinned again and kissed her. "You won't feel so lucky when you tell your mother you want the sideboard moving here. She's probably forgotten by this time that it belongs to you."

Even the thought of Ethel could not douse her delight at the new house. "Then she'll have to lump it, won't she?"

He lifted a quizzical eyebrow. "Lump it? If your mother hears you using Yorkshire slang like that, you know who she'll blame, don't you?"

189

She laughed with him. "Then I'll tell her she can lump that as well."

★ ★ ★

They moved house a week later. As Harry had prophesied, Ethel showed resentment when Mary asked for the sideboard. "I can't believe your father was in his right mind when he put that in his will. He loved this house and the things he bought for it, and the sideboard is one of the highlights of this room. It'll look empty without it."

When Mary showed no sign of giving way, Ethel tried to discourage her. "It'll look ridiculous in a small house. And it'll leave you no room to move about. Why don't you wait until you have the money to afford a bigger place?"

Exasperated at having to fight for her own possession, Mary went further than she had intended. "If we had to wait for that we might have to wait for the rest of our lives, Mother."

Ethel's lips compressed. "Don't blame me for that, young lady. It's you who insisted on paying the men more than the business can afford. If it wasn't for you and that husband of yours, I'd sell the entire concern tomorrow. I'm tired of all these hints and innuendoes. If you aren't satisfied with what you get, then say so and I'll know what to do."

Mary took a deep steadying breath. "For heaven's sake, Mother, I came to get what Dad left me in his will, not to have a quarrel with you about the business. Are you going to let the removal people fetch it or not?"

Ethel stared at her, then changed her tone. "William bought that sideboard on our third anniversary. It was to celebrate his success in starting up the business and we were both so proud of it. If you want to take it away from me now, then do so. But don't expect me not to feel pain every time I see an empty wall where it used to stand."

★ ★ ★

Two weeks after they moved into their new house, Harry brought a bulldog puppy home. He was holding it in his arms when Mary met him at the front door. "Mrs Jenkins, that widow who has a shop in Haltemprice, offered me this little chap for a couple of shillings. He's from a litter her dog gave her six weeks ago. I thought now we've a garden it would be good for the children to have a dog."

Remembering his love of animals and the way he had with them, she could not help smiling. "Only for the children?"

His grin was almost sheepish. "I have always wanted one and this little chap's a real beauty."

She held out her hands. "Let me look at him."

He handed her the tiny puppy. It was snow white with a pink belly and a jet black nose. As she cupped her hands around it, it tried to lick her finger. She laughed. "He is rather lovely, isn't he?"

His voice was eager. "Then you don't mind? You do realise he'll be a big dog one day?"

"I know that but I expect you or the children will take him for walks, won't you?" When he nodded, she went on: "He might even bring Elizabeth over more often. And Frank'll go crazy over him."

"Where is he now?"

"Playing in the garden."

He took the puppy from her. "Let's go and see his face when we show it to him."

The boy was playing on the back lawn with a friend when Mary called to him. "Frank! Come and see what Daddy's brought."

The child scampered over. With Harry concealing the puppy in his arms, the boy could not see what he was carrying. "What is it, Daddy? What have you got?"

As Harry bent down and released the puppy on the grass, Frank gave a gasp of delight. "It's a doggy, Daddy! A real doggy!"

Both Harry and Mary laughed. The boy's eyes were huge and his face shining with excitement. "Is it for us, Daddy? Can we play with it?"

"It's for you and Elizabeth," Harry told him. "Only you must promise to be gentle with it. It's very small and could be hurt if you're not."

The puppy, still a trifle unsteady on his legs, began to move towards the boy as if by some magical symbiosis. Reaching his feet, it sniffed at them and then began wagging its stumpy tail vigorously. The boy gave a shout of delight. "He likes me, Daddy. He does, doesn't he?"

"He seems to, Frank. Tickle his chest and stroke him."

The puppy's tail wagged faster as the boy obeyed. As it tried to lick his hand, Frank shouted at his friend who was hanging back. "Stephan! Come and see what my daddy's brought."

Mary turned to Harry. "I know it's ridiculous but the puppy does seem to have taken a fancy to him."

Harry grinned back. "You're right. I think they're going to be good friends."

Frank, who had run to fetch the puppy a ball, lifted his rapturous young face to Harry. "What shall we call him, Daddy?"

Harry watched the puppy trying to roll the ball with its paws. "Well, he's going to be a big fellow one day so we have to give him a name he won't be ashamed of. I knew a man once who called his dog Pride. Shall we call him that? I think he might like it."

★ ★ ★

Lena Turnor returned to Hull the following week and Harry met her at Paragon Station.

At first he did not recognise her on the busy platform. Her hair was bobbed in the current fashion and she was wearing a calf length blue coat. "Harry! How good of you to come. But you shouldn't have. I could have taken the tram."

He took her suitcases from her. "It's no trouble. I've got the car these days. It's parked outside."

193

He was surprised by the warmth of her greeting. After such a long time he had expected her to be reserved again but she chatted freely to him on the journey home, although only about his affairs and not her own. "How are the children? Frank must be quite a big boy now."

He nodded. "He starts school this year."

"What is he like?"

He grinned. "He's a normal little boy. Full of chatter and mischief. He has a dog now and you should see them playing together."

"What about Elizabeth?"

"She's living with Ethel but we see her two or three times a week. She's been to America with Ethel while you've been away and come back quite a young lady."

Her voice suddenly went quiet. "You're a lucky man, Harry, aren't you — "

Glancing at her he saw her expression and changed the subject. "Stop talking about me and tell me about your self. Did you make any friends in Hebden Bridge?"

"Yes, I got to know some of the local people."

"What about close friends?"

Although her voice gave no hint of it, he was sure she grasped his meaning. "No. As you've seen, I don't make friends easily."

"That's rubbish," he said. "It's just in your mind. You're the best listener I know and as people prefer to talk rather than listen, you could make friends anywhere you wanted to." Then, feeling he had made his earlier meaning obscure, he went on: "Besides all that, you're an attractive girl."

From the corner of his eye he saw her glance at him. Inwardly damning himself for a remark she might misinterpret, he was forced to halt the Ford quickly as a cyclist swung out in front of him. When the road cleared again and she still had not spoken, he tested the water by changing the subject.

"Why didn't the old man leave you his cottage? That daughter of his in Canada hasn't done a thing for him, has she? So why should she get it?"

To his relief she seemed not to have resented his remark. "Blood's thicker than water, Harry. All the world over. My uncle liked me, I think, and we got on well together but I couldn't expect him to leave me his cottage when he had children."

You were born either a winner or a loser, he thought. There was no doubt what she was. Her voice broke into his thoughts. "I hope this move hasn't made any problems for you and Mary. Only I'd nowhere else to go."

"No. As a matter of fact it's worked out very well. With Frank growing up we needed three bedrooms. So we would have needed to move sooner or later."

She gave a gasp of pleasure as they drew up outside her house. "You've had it painted! How nice it looks."

"Do you really like it? I ought to have asked your permission first,"

"No. I like that colour. And I know it needed to be painted."

She showed equal pleasure when they entered the living room. "You've decorated this too!"

"Yes. All the rooms, I'm afraid."

She ran upstairs, then returned smiling. "It's lovely, Harry. Everything looks so bright and clean."

He was finding her pleasure rewarding. "You'll see we've left a few carpets and fittings. They were the wrong size for our place. But don't hesitate to chuck anything out you don't like. We won't mind."

Her eyes wandering again round the living room. "I feel I ought to pay you something towards all this, Harry."

"Don't be silly. We did it all for ourselves. You don't owe us anything."

She frowned. "We'll talk about that some other time." She glanced at the kitchen. "I'm sorry I can't make you a cup of tea but I'll have to stock up at the grocer's first."

He smiled. "We're not that uncivilised: Mary's left some groceries, a kettle, and a half pound of tea. And I bought a pint of milk this morning. You'll find everything in the pantry."

For a moment he thought her voice sounded a little unsteady. "You're very thoughtful, both of you. I do appreciate it."

During tea they chatted about inconsequential things until he remembered the time. "I'll have to go in a few minutes. I've a customer out at Bilton to see before five o'clock. But can I ask you something first? You won't be angry?"

She gave a faint smile at his caution. "I don't know until you ask me, do I?"

"Are you going to be able to manage here without our rent? You had a difficult time before, if you remember."

There was something of her old apathy in her reply. "I'll be all right. Uncle has left me fifty pounds in his will and I'm still receiving that weekly allowance Sir Michael got for me."

She walked out with him to the car. In her summer dress, with the bright sunlight on her, he thought again how pretty she looked. At the same time he had noticed a change in her since they had taken tea and he thought absurdly of a clockwork toy, wound up tightly for her homecoming but now beginning to run down again. Before entering the car, he turned to her. "Now that you're back, why don't you come and spend an evening with us? Mary would be delighted and we're not far away now."

To his disappointment she shook her head. "With both of you working and with children to look after, you've no time to entertain. But thank you for asking me and thank Mary again for all she's done to the house."

He thought it wise not to press her. He climbed into the car, then glanced at her through the open window. "Then can I pop round some time to see how things are going? We are old friends, aren't we?"

She smiled back. "Of course you can. Now you'd better go or you'll miss your appointment."

She had not changed that much, he thought

as he drove away. In spite of her outward appearance, the real woman was still wearing widow's weeds. It was a thought that brought back with it the spectre of guilt that he had wanted to forget.

20

AS if to punish them for their temerity in moving to a larger house, Harry and Mary found the balance of trade moving against them for the rest of that year. With national exports figures sagging again, industrialists had begun a campaign to force wages down under the pretext that it was the only way to make their exports competitive in world markets. With their customers having less money to spend, shops and pharmacies were in turn forced to reduce the orders they gave to Harry.

The coal miners were among the first to resist this move and for a while it seemed the rest of the trade unions would support them. With a general strike on the cards, Prime Minister Baldwin provided a subsidy to maintain existing wages while a Royal Commission examined the coal industry. Although this appeared like a climb down by the Government, in fact Whitehall used the breathing space to build up transport pools and food depots all over the country in case a general strike did occur. The more prudent of the miners' wives, in spite of the pathetic income they received, made a similar attempt to stockpile food.

This was the situation throughout most of 1925, with both sides girding their loins for a possible showdown. Tension, however, was not a national monopoly. Watson, who made his annual overseas pilgrimage in July that year, had not been in England for three weeks before Mary found Elizabeth in tears in the bedroom they kept for her. "Darling, whatever's the matter? What's happened?"

As always when Watson was in England, Mary and Harry had been seeing more of the girl than usual. This time, however, she had been coming over four and five times a week. At first they had attributed it to the puppy, for in the beginning Elizabeth had been as thrilled by it as Frank was. On her last two visits, however, her interest had been only half-hearted and her mood touchy and irritable. Although Mary guessed the reason, the girl's tearful behaviour tonight seemed excessive.

"What is it, darling?" she asked a second time when Elizabeth did not answer her. "Has it something to do with Jack again?"

For a reply the girl threw herself down in the bed and began sobbing bitterly. Sitting down beside her, Mary cradled her head in her arms and ran a sympathetic hand down her long, braided hair. "You mustn't get so upset when they go out by themselves, darling. It's not that they don't love you. You mustn't think that."

Elizabeth tried to answer but the sobs that were racking her slim body made her words unintelligible. It was a full half-minute before her face lifted. "It's not just that. It's what they're going to do."

"Going to do, darling? What are they going to do?"

Tears were streaming from the girl's swollen eyes. "Grannie's agreed to marry him. She told me so today."

Mary gave a start. "Are you sure?"

"Of course I'm sure. I guessed it was going to happen earlier in the week. And now it has. Oh, Mummy, I'm so unhappy."

Mary's mind was in turmoil at the news. So it was to happen at last. What would the implications be for them all? She wanted to run downstairs and tell Harry but he had gone out that evening to see Swanson. Moreover, there was Elizabeth to comfort. She drew the girl towards her. "You mustn't be upset, darling. Grannie's been lonely all these years since Grandpa died. Now she'll have someone to look after her. You should be happy for her, not sad."

Her words of comfort brought only a fresh paroxysm of tears from the girl. "What's going to happen to me, Mummy? Grannie won't want me any more when she's got him instead."

Flinching with pain, Mary took the girl into her arms again. "It's not going to make any difference to Grannie's feelings for you, you silly little girl. Any more than my loving Daddy makes me love you any less. You'll still be able to see Grannie, just as you always have."

"No, I won't," the girl sobbed. "What if they go to live in America?"

Mary gazed at her. "Have they said they will?"

"Not yet. But I know he'll want to take her once they're married."

"You don't know anything of the sort. You heard Grannie say how glad she was to get back to England."

Elizabeth's face was full of dislike now. "He wasn't with her when she said that. He makes her do all kinds of things she doesn't want to do."

Mary was not letting Ethel get away with that. "Darling, your Grannie is perfectly capable of looking after herself. She won't let Jack take her to America or anywhere else if she doesn't want to go."

Elizabeth's expression showed she was anything but convinced. "She's going away with him to London this weekend. I'm sure she didn't want to go there either but he made her."

"No, darling. Grannie's much too strong-willed to be influenced that way. You mustn't blame Jack for everything that happens."

The girl's face suddenly contorted. "You hate Grannie, don't you? You blame her when she goes off without me but it's not she that wants to. It's not, it's not!"

For a moment the girl's attack was like a blow in the face. Then, as the hostile words echoed back in her mind, Mary realised they were born of pain. "I don't hate Grannie, darling. I'm trying to make you understand things so that you're not hurt in the future."

"You're not! You're trying to turn me against Grannie. Well, I won't let you. I won't, I won't!"

There were tears in Mary's own eyes now. "Darling, I'd never do that to you. I know how much you love your grannie. But for your own sake you must let her live her own life. Otherwise you'll be terribly hurt one day. Can't you see that?"

Elizabeth was not listening. Instead she rose from the bed and went over to a small desk that Harry had bought her. Mary gazed after her. "What are you doing?"

The girl's voice was sullen. "I haven't done my home work yet. I'd like to start it now."

Mary realised she was being dismissed. She made a last effort. "You won't go on fretting about Grannie's marriage, will you? Think how happy it's going to make her. Won't you try, darling?"

A single sob followed her words. Then Elizabeth wiped her face with a handkerchief and turned. "I want to start my homework, Mummy. Why won't you let me?"

Mary stared at her, then stood up and walked from the room.

★ ★ ★

Mary was at the front door that evening the moment she heard the snick of the front garden gate. As she opened it, Harry caught her arm. "You've been crying? What's happened?"

Afraid the girl upstairs would hear, she drew him into the living room and closed the door. "Mother's agreed to marry Jack. Elizabeth told me when she came over tonight."

He gave a laugh of relief. "At last! That's marvellous news!" Then his tone changed. "But what's made you cry?"

She told him about Elizabeth's distress. "The poor child's getting the idea Jack's taking Ethel away from her."

He frowned and removed his jacket before replying. "We can't do much about that, can we? She'll just have to get used to them being together."

"That's what I've been trying to tell her. The trouble is she won't accept that Ethel's as much involved as Jack. I daren't think what she'll be like if they decide to live in America."

He lit a cigarette. "Isn't that the best thing that could happen?"

"In the long run, perhaps. But she's going to be terribly hurt."

He exhaled smoke. "That's always been on the cards, hasn't it?"

"Yes, but have you thought of the effect it might have on her? At the moment she's blaming everything on Jack, which I suspect is her defence against the truth. But think what it might do to her when she finds out Ethel is just as much to blame. She might get the idea that nobody loves her. And you know what that can do to people, particularly children."

"Surely she could never think we don't love her."

Her own fears were frightening her. "She might. After all, we did let her go and live with Ethel, something we haven't done with Frank."

His frown deepened. "But that wasn't our fault. She must know that."

"How can anyone know how a child's mind works? On one level she might know it but on a deeper one she might wonder why we allowed it to happen."

He muttered something and ground out his cigarette. "Is she asleep?"

"I don't know." As he started for the door, she caught his arm. "No! Don't say anything tonight. Leave it until she's less upset. Please, Harry."

For a moment it seemed he would go against her. Then he walked over to an armchair and dropped heavily into it. His question seemed to be addressed as much to himself as to her. "How could she think anything like that? We've always given her everything we've given Frank."

She hated saying it but it had to be said. "Everything but our home, Harry."

He turned to stare at her. "You're not blaming me for that, are you?"

She realised how easy it would be for them both to quarrel. "Of course I'm not. I'm more to blame than anybody because I was worried about Mother. But that's neither here nor there where Elizabeth's concerned, is it?"

He relaxed. "No, I suppose not. Has she suggested we haven't wanted her?"

"No. I don't think that's in her mind yet. I'm only saying it might happen if Mother puts Jack before her."

"Which she's not above doing if Jack gives her a good time," he said bitterly.

"Let's be fair. We don't know yet what Mother intends doing. After all, she's put off marrying Jack all these years. But it's the possibility that I'm afraid of."

He turned and sat staring into the coal fire. His cigarette was half burned away before he glanced back at her. "I suppose all we can do is show her she is wanted here and hope for the best. Do you think your mother will go over to America?"

"I've absolutely no idea. We'll probably be the last ones she'll tell. After all, she hasn't told us about her wedding yet."

At that moment she thought she heard sounds from one of the bedrooms above. Leaving the room, she climbed the stairs quietly and stood outside each bedroom but both children seemed asleep. When she returned to the living room and closed the door, Harry's mood had changed. "Haven't we been looking too much on the black side? After all, Jack doesn't like the situation any more than we do. So he could be a help, couldn't he?"

"I don't see how. All it means is that he's more likely than ever to wean Ethel away from the girl. So how is that going to help?"

"Jack might explain things to her. Tell her Ethel needs a man to make her happy."

"I've told her that already and all it did was make her cry all the more."

He lit another cigarette, an act of frustration and concern. "All right, she's upset at the moment. But children's emotions change like the weather. Couldn't it work the other way? Once she's rid of Ethel's influence, she might listen to us more and become our own child again."

She wondered how much of this he believed and how much he was saying to reassure her. At the same time she desperately wanted to believe him. "It's possible, I suppose. But she's going to suffer a great deal before it happens."

He turned away to hide his expression but the action was enough to remind her of his love for the girl and the pain her fears were causing him. To help him, she changed the subject. "There's one good thing about all this. If she goes to America we'll have a much freer hand with the business."

"Unless she sells it before she goes," he said wryly. "After all, this won't be a four month trip."

She knew anything was possible but felt she had spread enough gloom that night. "I don't think it's likely, not with Connie's husband off work and only on half pay. And Jack likes us, so he won't be in favour of her selling it."

As if appreciating her effort to lift their mood, his shapely mouth twitched. "Poor old Jack. He hasn't a clue what he's getting himself into, has he? Don't you think one of us ought to warn him?"

It was a relief to laugh. "She's got her knife deep enough in you already. So don't you start getting ideas like that."

★ ★ ★

Ethel phoned Mary at the office the following morning. "Hello, dear. I thought you'd like to hear that Jack and I have decided to get married.

Or has Elizabeth told you already?"

"Yes, she told us last night. I'm delighted for you, Mother. Congratulations."

Ethel's attempt to keep her tone matter-of-fact was not wholly successful. "Yes. Jack's asked me to go down to London with him this weekend to get a ring. I don't know why we can't get one here but Americans seem to think London's the only place where you can buy decent things. You don't mind Elizabeth staying with you for the three nights, do you?"

"No, of course we don't. When are you leaving?"

"We're taking the Friday afternoon train and will come back Sunday evening unless Jack wants to stay over an extra day. However, I'll give you a ring when we're back."

"That's all right. I hope the weather keeps fine for you. Have you decided on a date for your wedding yet?"

"Not yet. But as Jack would like his brother and sister to come over, I don't expect it'll be until next year."

With Ethel sounding amicable, Mary felt the question could be asked. "Where will you live, Mother? Here or in America?"

From the change in Ethel's tone, it seemed this might be a bone of contention between her and Watson. "That's something we still have to decide. In the meantime I'd like you not to say too much to Elizabeth. The poor girl seemed quite upset the other night when I gave her the news."

Unable at the moment to think out the

implications if Ethel were told about the girl's distress, Mary decided to procrastinate. "We won't talk about it if she doesn't. If she asks questions, we'll tell the truth and say we don't know."

From her brief silence, it seemed Ethel herself was undecided on the best procedure. The touch of irritation in her voice confirmed it. "I hope she won't be a silly girl and start imagining things. Tell her I'll talk to her next week when we're back home."

Mary mentioned the phone call to Harry when he came in with his orders that evening. "She's obviously worried about Elizabeth's reaction but at the same time I got the impression it's irritating her as well."

"It hasn't stopped her from agreeing to marry Jack, has it?" he said.

She hesitated. "No. But I couldn't help wondering if it might if Elizabeth gets any worse."

"Cancel the wedding? After she's said yes and Jack's making all the arrangements? Surely not."

She found herself unable to unravel her thoughts. "She's so fond of Elizabeth you can't be sure. After all, it's the reason she's put off marrying Jack all these years."

"But has it been?" he asked. "We've assumed it but couldn't it just have been her idea of respectability? You know, allowing a decent time to elapse after your dad's death?"

"After all these years? Isn't that a bit far-fetched?" Then she paused. "I suppose Dad might have had something to do with it. But if it were that, why did she sleep with Jack during the war?"

"That's different. As far as she was concerned, no one knew about it."

It was a point she had to concede although she still believed Elizabeth was the reason for her mother's hesitation. As she walked over to the drug safe to lock it, her bitterness spilled out. "We don't know what we want, do we? Whether we want Mother to go to America and make Elizabeth feel nobody wants her or whether we want her to stay in England and smother her as she's smothered her all these years? How can we make plans, how can we do anything, when we don't know what's best for our own child?"

21

ETHEL and Watson were married in April the following year. The church chosen for the occasion was the famous old Holy Trinity Church in which Ethel had insisted Mary and Harry were married in 1911. Because of its size and splendour, Mary had no doubt the choice had been Ethel's and not Watson's.

Watson's brother, a younger man than Jack, with sandy hair and horn-rimmed glasses, was present, as was his wife Susan, a slim woman with a Bostonian accent and dyed blonde hair, whose treatment of Ethel suggested she was either in awe of her or else in distrust. They spent their two weeks in England at No. fifty-seven, with Watson taking them on sightseeing trips in his car. Accompanied by Ethel and Watson, they also made one obligatory trip to London.

Harry and Mary met them only twice, once at the wedding reception at the Assembly Rooms and once when Watson brought them round to their house to say goodbye. Even so, with typical American hospitality, the two invited them over to the States to stay as long as they liked. Then the couple went and Watson and Ethel were free to go on their honeymoon.

Their choice was Scotland and they stayed up there for two weeks. At this point neither Harry nor Mary knew where the couple were planning to live and neither did Elizabeth who had inevitably been left behind. Confident Watson would sympathise with their need to know, Harry had spoken to him on the phone before the honeymoon. "We have to know, Jack, because of Elizabeth. At the moment the poor kid doesn't know where she stands."

"I sure understand that, Harry, and I'll let you know the moment we've come to a decision."

Harry had not been able to hide his impatience. "Are you saying you don't know yet?"

Watson had sounded embarrassed. "I know it sounds kinda crazy but we're still throwing it about. We'll make up our minds on our honeymoon and let you know right away."

His words had seemed to confirm there was a power struggle between the couple and the outcome was still in doubt. Elizabeth, however, tearful and fretful, had already made up their minds for them. "He's going to take Grannie to America and leave me behind. Just as he has now. I hate him, Mummy! I hate him!"

With Mary feeling pain every time she heard the girl's distress, it was not easy to comfort her. "Darling, he couldn't take you with them on their honeymoon. No one does that. And you can't be certain they're going to America. Why don't you just wait and see?"

But there was no comforting the girl. Not a night passed when Mary did not hear her crying in her room. Moreover Elizabeth's feeling of betrayal infected her relations with her family. Once she had played with Frank and read him

212

stories. Now, when the boy brought her books, she snapped at him, leaving the child hurt and upset. In turn this filled Elizabeth with remorse and added to her misery.

This ambivalence towards her family came to a head a week after Ethel and Watson had gone on honeymoon. The evening paper had just arrived and as Mary turned over the pages she saw a photograph of Chadwick. She read the article below it, then passed the paper to Harry who was struggling to mend a toy Frank had broken. "I see Chadwick's in the news again. He's calling for strong police action if the miners refuse to accept a cut in wages and go out on strike."

Neither of them noticed the curiosity Elizabeth showed on hearing the name. She was sitting in a chair in the far corner of the room reading a book but her eyes were now on Harry as he took the paper.

He read the article, then gave a wry laugh. "I don't suppose you can really expect anything else. After all, how can he and his kind know what it's like to be a miner?"

"That's no excuse," she said. "They can go and find out, can't they?"

"They don't think they need to. That's the basic fault in their education. It gives them the confidence to believe they know everything."

His equanimity was annoying her. "It should make you angry as it does me."

"What's the point of getting angry? It won't change anything and it certainly won't change Chadwick."

She gave a shudder of distaste. "The brute's into everything these days. And now they say he has political ambitions. Imagine Parliament full of people like him."

Harry laughed. "I'd say he's just the type Baldwin's looking for, with all his landed gentry tradition."

There was a sudden cry of protest from Elizabeth. "Why do you keep on about Sir Michael Chadwick? What's he ever done to you?"

Both Harry and Mary showed surprise at the interruption. Mary was the first to speak. "What do you know about Chadwick?"

"I know quite a lot. I know he was a very brave solder who got lots of medals fighting for his country."

"Who's told you all this?"

The defiance in Elizabeth's voice increased. "Grannie told me. She says she met him often during the war. And he was ever so nice to you when Daddy was missing. So why are you always running him down?"

Not knowing what Ethel had said, Mary felt her nerves tighten. "Darling, don't talk like that. We know far more about Chadwick than Grannie does. Your father served under him throughout the war."

"Then he must know what a brave soldier he was. So what's wrong with his becoming a Member of Parliament?"

Although nervous of what the girl might know, Mary could not let this pass. "Brave soldiers aren't always good politicians, darling.

214

Sometimes they make very bad ones."

"But why?" Elizabeth insisted. "Why would Sir Michael make a bad one?"

"Because of what Daddy said a minute ago. Men like him have no idea what it's like trying to live on a couple of pounds a week. You were with us when Daddy's grandpa told us how he treated the little people in Burton Stather. Would you want a person like him in government?"

"But the miners are like the Russians and always trying to have a revolution. They don't deserve any help or sympathy."

For a moment Mary forgot herself as she glanced at Harry. "You know where she's heard that, don't you?"

The girl's face tightened. "Why shouldn't Grannie say what she thinks? Anyway I've seen it said in the newspapers too."

Her words made them realise they were no longer dealing with an innocent child. Harry, who had laid down the toy he was repairing, spoke for the first time. "You mustn't take too much notice of the newspapers Grannie buys, love. They're owned by the same class of people who own the coal mines. So it suits them to call the miners revolutionaries."

"Grannie says they are revolutionaries," the girl insisted. "And I believe her. Otherwise why would they want to drag the country down when men like Sir Michael fought for it."

Harry laughed. "Love, men like the miners fought for the country too. Millions of them. Doesn't that give them the same rights as

215

Chadwick to have a say in its affairs?"

"It doesn't give them a right to cripple it and have a revolution. That's why I think Sir Michael is right."

Although Mary was showing dismay at the things she was hearing, she could see that Harry, with his usual tolerance, was prepared to discuss them, even to welcome them, as evidence of the girl's awakening maturity.

His reply confirmed it. "As you're showing such interest in national affairs, why don't you let me tell you something about the miners."

"I don't want to hear about the miners," Elizabeth muttered. "I think they're horrible people."

Harry shook his head. "No, that won't do. If you want to be an adult and talk about adult matters, then you must listen to both sides of an argument. If you don't do that, people will still treat you like a child."

Conflicting emotions showed on the girl's face. Finally she gave a sullen nod. "All right, if you want to talk about the miners, go on. But I still won't like them."

Harry smiled. "Perhaps you won't. But at least you'll understand them better."

She sat silent while he told her about conditions in the mines, the claustrophobic seams of coal, the wet, the accidents, and the pneumoconiosis suffered by so many miners. "Half of them die before they're old enough to retire, most of them because the coal dust has destroyed their lungs. That leaves their wives and children without a wage earner and so they suffer too." Harry pointed at the coal fire flickering in the grate. "That's the price they pay to keep us warm. The newspapers don't tell you things like that, do they, love? At least not the newspapers Grannie buys."

Watching the girl's face, Mary had noticed her wince at Harry's more harrowing descriptions, a comforting reassurance that Ethel's influence had not destroyed her sensitivity. But a ready surrender to argument is not a human characteristic and Elizabeth was still a child.

"It's isn't just Grannie's newspapers who say it," she said sullenly. "People like Sir Michael say it too."

Harry nodded. "That's because he has never been down a coal mine in his life. In fact I doubt if he's ever been near one."

"Have you?" Elizabeth challenged.

"Yes. I had a friend once who lived in a Welsh mining village and I spent a few days with him there. That's when I found out what a brutal life miners have."

With her case against miners in jeopardy, the girl returned to a safer subject. "I still don't see why you hate Sir Michael so much."

Harry laughed, "I don't hate him, love. Where do you get that idea from? I don't like his ways and ideas, that's all."

Elizabeth glanced at Mary. "Mummy hates him. Don't you, Mummy?"

Feeling Harry's eyes on her, Mary felt her nerves tighten again. "I've reasons not to like him. He did dreadful things to Daddy during the war."

"What things?" the girl asked.

Mary rose to her feet. "I'll tell you one day when you're old enough. Now it's past your bedtime. Come along. Kiss Daddy good night."

The girl turned sullen again. "Grannie lets me stay up longer than this. Tell me first why you hate Sir Michael so much when he was fond of you?"

Seeing Harry's change of expression, Mary felt her cheeks turn hot. "What are you talking about? Sir Michael only helped me because he felt guilty at what he'd done to Daddy. Now come along to bed or you'll make me angry."

"That isn't what Grannie says. She says he found you attractive."

At this, Mary's nerves and temper snapped. "How dare Grannie say such things! If I hear any more of this kind of talk, I won't let you see her again. I mean it."

There was malice in the girl's voice now. "What are you so cross about? It wasn't your fault if he wanted to marry you, was it?"

Mary dared not look at Harry, shaking with anger, she caught the girl's arm and dragged her to her feet. "Get upstairs! This minute! Go on."

Looking half triumphant and half scared, the girl ran across the room and up the stairs. Still not looking at Harry, Mary followed her, expecting at any moment that his voice would check her. When it did not, she followed the girl into her bedroom. "Why did you say those things just now? Did Grannie tell you to?"

The girl pulled off her dress without replying. Mary swung her round. "I asked you a question. Did Grannie put you up to this?"

"No," Elizabeth muttered. "But it's all true, isn't it?"

"Never you mind what's true and what isn't. If ever I catch you talking about me and Michael Chadwick that way again, I'll give you a hiding you'll never forget. Now get into bed and don't let me hear another word from you tonight."

Afraid to face Harry, it was a full five minutes before Mary returned downstairs. She found him gazing into the fire with the broken toy alongside him. The laugh she gave had a cracked ring. "Heavens, she's growing up fast, isn't she? I'm glad you told her about the miners. I could see it made her think."

For a few seconds he did not speak. Then he turned towards her. "What was all that about Chadwick wanting to marry you? Is it true?"

She wished she could keep her voice steady. "No. It was just Mother's imagination. You know what a snob she is. Because he kept coming to see me, she imagined the rest."

"How often did he come to see you?"

"I can't remember. Four or five times, I suppose."

"Even though he had no news of me? That doesn't make sense."

She knew she had to give him some reason for Chadwick's attendance or his suspicions would grow. "I suppose he did like me." When he opened his mouth to question her, she broke in quickly: "I didn't encourage him, Harry. I hated

219

seeing him, in fact. But what could I do? I was afraid if I refused to see him he'd stop trying to find out about you."

A tinge of bitterness entered his voice. "What else did you do for me? Did you go out with him?"

Unsure what Ethel had told Elizabeth and afraid what Harry might suspect if she lied, she decided to tell half the truth. "Just once." Distressed by his expression, she went on: "He blackmailed me, Harry. It was just before his leave ended and he made it clear if I didn't have dinner with him, he'd drop all his enquiries. So what else could I do?"

He turned his gaze back to the fire as if not wanting to see the consequence of his question. "So he took you out to dinner. What happened afterwards? Did he kiss you?"

The temptation to tell him the truth was almost overpowering. It was his very quietness that stopped her. Although he was still gazing at the fire, she had the feeling there was a coiled spring inside him, waiting to be released by her answer. "No," she lied. "He wanted to but I wouldn't let him."

"He wanted to," he repeated. "What else did he want?"

Her attempt to make a joke of it was a failure. "Don't all men try their luck, Harry? Surely what matters is how I felt."

He turned and gazed back at her. The reflections of herself in his brown eyes hid the thoughts behind them. "How did you feel?"

She felt a sudden burn of anger. "That's a stupid question."

"Why? He's a handsome man. And he was a hero."

A memory flashed back to her. Chadwick, handsome and tanned, with his beautifully tailored uniform enhancing his hard, lean body, sitting in a ray of sunlight in her office. The prickle of her skin as for one brief moment the Eve in her had responded to the archetypal Adam. A moment that had lasted only a second but whose memory fuelled her resentment now. "You've no right to make that remark, Harry, I've never been unfaithful to you in my life."

He was silent for a moment, then reached out for her. "I never said you had been. But it does all make it hard to understand why you hate him so much."

She threw herself into his arms and hugged him tightly. "You're not a woman, so you can't understand. Perhaps I hate him just because he tried to take your place."

He ran a hand down her long, golden hair. "You should have told me all this before. Why didn't you?"

Ashamed of the sympathy her lies had earned her, she buried her face into his shoulder. "I suppose I hated the memory."

She could hear the slow steady beat of his heart as she lay against him. "That was stupid," he said. "It would have helped me to understand things better."

Then was she wrong after all? she wondered. Would it not be better to tell him everything

221

while he was in this mood and rid herself of the threat Ethel held over her? She was struggling to assemble the right words when he gave a self-deprecatory laugh. "I say that but the truth is it makes me feel sick to think of any man putting his hands on you. And Chadwick most of all."

★ ★ ★

The moonlight was slanting through the window and lying like a white coverlet over the bed. Lying alongside Harry, listening to his quiet breathing, Mary was wondering yet again why she was so afraid of Harry finding out the truth about Chadwick.

On the surface her fear seemed groundless. She had known him since they were children and never once had she seen him lift a hand to anyone. Her fear that he might get himself into serious trouble with Chadwick if told the facts seemed almost melodramatic.

And yet was it? As she lay there, she remembered the fist fight he had had with Chadwick when the two of them had been children. That had been over a nesting bird Chadwick had needlessly shot. Then there was Harry's hatred of blood sports and his reaction to Gareth's execution. Did they not all say something fundamental about him? He might be slow to respond to personal attack but he had shown little tardiness in springing to the defence of others.

Wasn't it that same hatred of cruelty that

had been behind his need to return to France? Although he denied it now, his dislike of Chadwick and his ways must have been intense to make him face that hell again just to prove himself different.

Thinking about the war made her turn to gaze at his face in the moonlight. The light was bright enough for her to trace his sensitive features and shapely mouth. The face of a gentle and tolerant man, she thought, and yet this same man, as the machine gunner Chadwick had made him, must have killed hundreds of men.

It was a thought she had always tried to avoid, as she guessed a million women did, that the man who made love to her, sometimes excitingly but always lovingly, had blood on his hands. Blood from his country's enemies, perhaps, but blood nevertheless. If a man could kill only once, he must, to her woman's mind, have learned to pull down the barrier between pacifism and violence. And Harry had not only won the Military Medal but had earned Chadwick's accolade of being 'a damn good soldier'.

It did not even stop there, she thought. Harry had admitted to murdering two helpless men in a orgasm of revenge for his friends whom the Germans had killed earlier. How did that fit with the gentle, tolerant man she knew?

It was that thought that frightened her the most. If his protective instincts could drive him to that excess, why should they motivate him differently if he found out what Chadwick had done to the woman he loved?

She knew none of this had the slightest effect on her love for him. Indeed she was honest enough to admit that in a way she dared not analyse, the paradox in his character added an excitement to their relationship.

At that moment he sighed in his sleep and turned so that he was facing her. Watching him, her mood changed again. She was being ridiculous. Millions of men had fought in the war and returned as peace-loving as when they had left. Many indeed were more peaceful now that their masculine aggression had been sated by the horrors they had seen. Why should Harry be any different? She had no cause to believe otherwise.

She knew she was deceiving herself at the same moment she had the thought. That very night a reason had been given her. It was the way his steady heartbeats had suddenly changed their rhythm and begun to beat fast and hard when he had talked about Chadwick laying his hands on her.

22

THE armistice with Ethel, already crumbling on all fronts, finally collapsed a week after her return from honeymoon. Not only did hostilities break out again but this time they took the form that in later years was to be known as Total War.

Perhaps symbolically they coincided with the great industrial strike of 1926 that became known as the General Strike. The Royal Commission that had been set up by Baldwin the previous year to inquire into the state of coal mining recommended that a scheme to reorganise the industry be put into operation as quickly as possible. As this virtually gave permission for the owners to reduce the miners' wages, it confirmed what workers everywhere had suspected: that Baldwin's subsidy had been a ploy to give the Government time to prepare for a general strike.

In a mood of great bitterness, the Miners' Federation called for a strike on the 1st March. In the meantime the Trades Union Congress, ashamed that it had not stood by the miners in their earlier strike, informed the Government it would call out all its members if the miners' rights were not upheld.

It had been felt that this threat of a general strike would force Baldwin to think again and it was true that negotiations were carried out for a while between the Government and the TUC. However, by the spring the hardliners in Baldwin's cabinet had won the day and the negotiations were broken off on the flimsiest of pretexts. This left the TUC with no alternative but to call together its constituent members and remind them of their promise to the miners. The executives voted and a general strike was called for the midnight of the 3rd March.

Thus, on the morning of the 4th, the country found itself without dock workers, trains, buses, electricity, gas supplies, newspapers and a thousand other products and services that make up a modern society. Many people had the fear it was the beginning of revolution, although in fact there was little general disorder and no concerted attempt to effect a political coup.

To some extent the worst effects were minimised by the eager and enthusiastic response of the middle and upper classes who saw it their patriotic duty to side with the Government. Lawyers and clerks, estate agents and journalists, volunteered in their thousands to drive buses and trains and maintain essential services, and within a week a quarter of a million men had enroled as special constables. As a further illustration of the great divide that existed between the classes at that time, undergraduates at Oxford and Cambridge deserted their lectures to 'do their bit' while middle-class girls and women ran canteens.

More professional help came from the Government's secret preparations, made during the time they had bought by their Royal

Commission ploy. Caches of food, and transport pools, were now in position in strategic parts of the country and volunteers were quick to service them. To present their case and to issue their directives, the Government took control of the radio and printed their own journal, The British Gazette. In response, the TUC published The British Worker.

With workers feeling betrayed by the middle class, some of whom had fought alongside them only eight years previously, bitterness was high and it led to tension in many small businesses that had not known industrial strife before. One such business was the Hardcastle Drug Company. On the morning of the 4th, just prior to Harry leaving on his rounds, Brown the foreman came to Mary's office. "Can I have a word with you and Mr Miles, Miss?"

"Of course you can, Alf. What is it?"

Brown cleared his brawny throat. "It's about this general strike, Miss. The lads feel we'll have to join it."

Although Mary and Harry exchanged glances, they showed no surprise. They had been discussing the possibility for weeks. At Mary's request, Harry answered for her. "You're their spokesman, are you, Alf?"

"Aye, sir. Not everyone wants to strike, particularly the older 'uns like me who've worked with you for a long time. But Prescott and Mayfield say they're goin' to set up a picket line on the gate. The rest of us don't feel we can cross a picket line even if we're not union men."

Harry nodded. "I agree. You can't."

His compliance took the foreman by surprise and added to his embarrassment. "I don't like it, Mr Miles. You two have always been fair to us. Maybe if Mrs Hardcastle had given us better wages, I might've been able to keep the younger 'uns in line. But as it is we all think we ought to show some solidarity with the rest of the workers."

"Do you think there's any point in my talking to Prescott and Mayfield?" Harry asked.

Brown shook his head. "No, sir. They're set on it. Talking to 'em would only make matters worse."

Harry shrugged. "Then that's it. Tell everybody we'll do what we can to help them while they're out. But don't expect much. Remember we don't control the purse strings."

Brown looked relieved that the ordeal was over. "The men know that, sir. I hope we won't be out too long."

Harry gave a wry grin. "So do I, Alf. Good luck."

The foreman hesitated, then held out his huge stained hand. "Good luck to you, sir." He then turned to Mary. "I'm sorry about this, Miss. I really am."

"I know that, Alf. We'll look forward to seeing you again when it's all over."

Harry glanced at Mary as the foreman's heavy footsteps were heard descending the stairs. "Poor devil. He hated doing that, didn't he?"

"You're on their side, aren't you?" she said.

"Who can't be? The miners have been cheated

all the way down the line. It's heartening to see the rest of the workers are supporting them this time."

Unsure for the moment of her own feelings, she gave a half smile. "Do you think it's Gareth's Brotherhood of Man coming about at last?"

He grimaced. "No. The Government hold too many cards. It'll all collapse sooner or later and the miners will go back to eating coal dust again."

"Then what's the point of it?"

"The point is it'll give the Government a nasty shock. They won't be so quick next time to throw their weight behind the employers at the expense of starving kids."

Feeling he might be misunderstanding her sentiments, she gave him another smile. "Then I take it you won't be joining the rest of the middle class in manning the trams and trains?"

His frown turned into a grin. "The only thing you might see me doing is pinching the control wheels or sabotaging the trolley wires."

As he spoke she heard voices below. Moving to the window she saw half a dozen workmen pushing their bicycles towards the warehouse gate. As Harry came to her side, they saw two men remain at the gate while the rest cycled away down the lane. "Those are the pickets," Harry said. "At least one of them will stay there until the strike's over."

She moved away from the window. "Mother's going to spit blood when she finds out what's happened."

"It's her own fault," he said. "Just as it is with employers everywhere. If she'd paid the men a decent wage they wouldn't be cycling away now."

"That's not the way she's going to see it. And I can't see her paying us our full wages while it's on either."

"I don't expect she will. She'll probably blame me for everything that's happened."

"Perhaps she'll listen to Jack," she said hopefully. "He must have been in situations like this over in America."

"I doubt if she'll listen to anybody. But in any case wasn't Jack going to London today on some business matter?"

Remembering he was right, she turned towards the gas ring and the kettle. "Well, we can't do anything about it, can we? So why don't we have a cup of tea before we go over and tell her the news? I don't see any point in your going round looking for orders we can't meet."

* * *

They did not need to visit Ethel at No. fifty-seven. Before the kettle had boiled, angry voices could be heard below. Running to the window Mary saw her mother, holding an umbrella in her hand like a weapon, quarrelling with the two pickets on the gate. Although they were attempting to argue with her, they were mere men confronted by a modern Fury. As her voice increased in decibels, it looked for a moment as if she were about to strike the taller of the two men. Instead she gave them a last withering glare, flung open the gate, and strode towards the warehouse.

Mary turned to Harry. "Let me handle her. At least to begin with."

He shrugged. "If you want to. But don't let her upset you."

Ethel, with two red spots burning in her cheeks from her encounter with the pickets, wasted no time on a preamble. "What on earth's happening? Where have the staff gone? And why are you allowing those two wretches to stop everyone coming through the gate?"

"They're pickets, Mother. They're there to stop supplies coming in."

Ethel swung round on Harry. "What in heaven's name are you doing to allow such a thing? Why don't you go down and sack them on the spot?"

Mary intervened quickly. "Harry can't do that, Mother. If he sacked the pickets, we'd lose the entire work force."

Ethel was fuming with anger. "Lose them? We've already lost them. I'm going to give every man jack of them his notice from today."

Mary showed alarm. "You can't do that. It's not the men's fault. They'd be thought blacklegs if they defied the pickets."

Medusa herself was barely a match for Ethel when in this mood. "Whose side are you on, girl? They're a bunch of ungrateful scoundrels and if you think I shall take them back after this, you're as stupid as they are. I want a notice in the paper at once that we want new warehousemen."

"But, Mother, it's happening all over the city and all over the country. If we employ blacklegs, there'll be trouble at the gate. The pickets will call back the rest of the men and there'll be a fight."

"Will there indeed? Then we'll call in the police and have them thrown into the cells. That'll cool them down, I can tell you."

"Mother, don't you understand? This is a general strike. Workers everywhere have laid down their tools."

Stymied for the moment but still breathing fire, Ethel swung round on Harry. "I suppose it was you who put them up to this. You and your Bolshevik friends."

It was inevitable it had to come, Mary thought. The only question had been when. Before Harry could reply, she sprang to his defence. "Harry doesn't have Bolshevik friends, Mother. And he's never said a word to the men about striking. It's been their own decision."

Ethel's lips curled. "Of course you'll defend him. When haven't you? But ask him if he agrees with what they've done and see what he says. Go on — ask him."

Harry's quiet voice gave Mary no time to reply. "If you want the truth, yes, I respect the men for showing solidarity with the rest of the workers. Particularly as they stand to lose a great deal by it."

With a laugh of triumph, Ethel turned back to Mary. "What did I tell you? That's the man you married and who William trusted to help run his business. A traitor who's glad the staff

232

have gone on strike. Poor William! He must be turning over in his grave to hear this."

"There wouldn't be a strike if Dad was still alive," Harry said quietly. "He always paid his men fair wages."

Ethel swung back on him. "And I haven't? Is that what you're saying?"

"Yes, I am. If you'd been fairer to them in the past, I don't think those two men on the gate could have talked them into a strike."

"So all this is my fault?"

Harry was not giving an inch. "Yes, it is. You wouldn't listen to us when we warned you and now you're paying the price for it."

Mary wanted to intervene but knew it was too late. By this time Ethel was shaking with rage. "Paying the price! You common, ungrateful wretch!" She turned to Mary who had stiffened at her words. "Did you hear what this man has just said to me?"

Her attack on Harry drove all caution from Mary. "Harry's right. You've expected us to run the business with our hands tied behind our backs and this is the result. You've got your desserts, Mother."

Ethel gave a gasp of outrage. "You little hussy! How dare you talk that way to me?"

"I'm sorry, Mother, but you forfeit all respect when you attack Harry this way. You ought to be ashamed of yourself after all he's done for you."

"Done for me? What's he ever done for me except pull my daughter down to his level and now try to ruin my business?"

By this time battle was fully joined. Mary's laugh was contemptuous. "Your business! You know as well as we do whose business it ought to be. And don't give me again that sanctimonious claptrap about only keeping it going for our sakes. You've held on to it so Connie can have the quarter share she never does a thing to earn. For that matter you haven't done so badly out of it yourself. So stop being so damned hypocritical."

She knew it was all over before Ethel found enough self-control to reply. All the years of work to build up the business, all the plans and hopes for the future: all for nothing now. The swords with which they had struck one another had bitten too deeply.

She felt numb as Ethel went to the door and turned. "You've got two weeks to wind up the business. Then I shall sell it to the highest bidder. Not to a drug company, so don't think you'll be able to stay on. My solicitor tells me I can get much more by letting a sweet manufacturer have the equipment and the premises and that's what I shall do." Her inflamed eyes turned on Harry. "So you can let your accomplices in the warehouse know there'll be no job for them when they come crawling back. I hope they lay the blame where it belongs."

Mary could not hold back her bitterness as the woman opened the door and walked out. "So you don't care about killing the business Dad was so proud of?"

Ethel's reply was almost brutal as she began

descending the staircase. "I've let sentiment influence me long enough. Your father's dead and I'm not supporting his business any longer so that you two can take advantage of it. I'm selling it and you have two weeks to get out. That's my final word and don't think either of you can change it."

23

SEEING the procession marching along Holderness Road, Harry pulled the car into the kerb and switched off the engine. Lighting a cigarette, he sat watching the column of men approaching him.

A pathetic band of drums, pipes and trumpets was leading it, the discordant notes reverberating from the shops and houses that flanked the road. Behind the band, two men were carrying a home-made banner exhorting the few pedestrians who bothered to watch them to support the workers' cause.

Behind the banner came the workers. They were marching four abreast, a motley crowd, some in cloth caps, others bareheaded, some in overalls, others in patched shirts or threadbare pullovers, and almost all wearing boots or shoes in need of repair.

Yet, in spite of their ragged appearance, they walked in step and with a certain swing that told Harry many of them had been in the Armed Forces. As their vanguard reached him and the long procession began to march past, he could see patches of colour on many of the men's shirts or pullovers. They were wearing their service medals and among those for gallantry he could see Military Medals and even the odd Military Cross and DSO given only to officers.

Sitting there, with unemployment facing him

236

in a few days' time, Harry thought what Gareth would have said had he been sitting in the car. "It's always been the same, boyo. The bastards use you when they need you — they even give you medals and promotion to keep you sweet. But once it's over, it's the bloody grindstone again and don't you dare to grumble about it or you're out on your ear. That's the system, boyo, and mugs like you put up with it."

Poor old Gareth, Harry thought with a smile. He'd probably have been right in the front leading the procession if Chadwick hadn't had him executed.

At that moment the procession was forced to halt and squeeze to one side as a tram rattled down the road. It was manned and filled by well-dressed volunteers who jeered and shouted insults at the procession. In turn there were catcalls, curses, and shouts of 'blacklegs' from the strikers. Nothing Harry had seen so far had made the schism between the classes seem more evident and its ugliness drove the smile from his face.

He knew Chadwick was a power behind the efforts to cripple the strike. One of the local newspapers, which had managed to keep in print, had been using his name in recent days to great effect. His good looks and his title were in themselves enough to convince the middle class they were on the side of the angels. When his war record, with its patriotic overtones, was also taken into account, he emerged as a strikebreaker of considerable influence.

Harry's eyes returned to the seemingly endless

237

procession. What were these men but patriots? he thought. Chadwick had fought bravely — Harry was the last man to deny that — but then Chadwick had possessed things to fight for: wealth, position, a stately home and a glowing future. What had these men to fight for? Many of them had left hovels and gone back to hovels. Yet the array of medals some of them wore told they had fought just as bravely. Who then were the patriots?

In his darker moments Harry had often wondered if the schism between the privileged and the poor would ever be bridged. For the bitterness of the underprivileged to be fully understood, a man had to see his mother slowly killing herself with backbreaking toil, as he had done in his youth. It was like a knife being twisted in the soul and there are no words for that kind of pain.

And now it could happen to Mary, he thought. Unless he could get a job quickly, she might quite easily end up like his mother. Their bank account and their possessions were minimal and the society of the twenties, as the pathetic procession showed, knew little about mercy.

The end of the parade was in sight at last. He waited until it had passed by, and started up the engine. He drove quickly to occupy his mind but fear for his family haunted him all the way to the warehouse.

* * *

238

Harry helped Mary off the tram and led her along the pavement. It was raining and a passing car, squeezing between the tram and the kerb, splashed her coat. As he drew her closer and opened his umbrella, she glanced at him. "It's not far. Just this side of Ings Road."

He did not answer. After a few steps, she glanced at him again. "Stop worrying, darling. God knows you've tried hard enough to get a job."

It was almost an understatement, she thought. Since Ethel had discharged them ten weeks ago, she had lost count of the letters he had written or the vain and endless hours he had spent in the queues that seemed to reach out from every factory in the land.

His hope, which now seemed absurdly ambitious, had been to find work that would enable them to keep their house and pay well enough to keep Frank at the same private school as Elizabeth. Although the boy had never shown the slightest sign of jealousy at the presents and privileges his sister received from Ethel, both Mary and Harry felt it vital that at least he should receive the same education. In addition they desperately wanted to remain within easy reach of Elizabeth.

Yet both knew if they took the shop they were about to visit, they could hardly be further away from No. fifty-seven without moving out of the city, for it stood at the far end of the eastern tram route, while No. fifty-seven stood in almost a similar position in the western suburbs.

During these stressful ten weeks, in which they

239

had seen their meagre bank balance dwindle alarmingly, Ethel had kept her threat and sold the warehouse and its equipment to a sweet manufacturer. How much opposition Watson had put up the young couple could only guess but his apologetic behaviour on the visits he had paid them suggested it had been considerable. "I'm sure sorry about this, kids. I know what the business meant to you both. But Ethel seems to feel it was getting too much for her and she's also worried about Connie. This way she won't need to worry about her if we decide to go and live in the States."

He had been referring to the quarter share of the sale proceeds that Ethel had given to Connie, whose husband had now been forced to retire on a small pension because of his ill health. According to William's bequest, a second quarter should have come to Mary but instead Ethel had put the money in trust for Elizabeth on her coming of age.

It had been a typical move on her mother's part. Although Mary could have legally contested the allocation and had it changed, to have done so might have seemed to Elizabeth, if not now then later, that her parents thought less of her welfare than did her grandmother, who had given her the money. As a consequence, acute although their needs were, Harry and Mary felt they had no choice but to keep silent.

However it had been clear that Watson felt less comfortable about the arrangement even if he had no knowledge of the provisions of the will. "I sure hope you kids are going to be all right. What about these guys who've bought the business from Ethel? Have you approached them for a job?"

"It was one of the first things I did," Harry told him. "But it seems they're bringing in all their own staff."

"That's tough, kid. I'm real sorry. I wish I could do something to lend a hand. Can you think of anything?"

Knowing he had been apologising for Ethel, Mary felt sympathy for him. It was early days to have his first insight into Ethel's ruthlessness and although from loyalty he was doing his best to excuse her actions, it was clear that her sale of the business had shaken him.

"I don't think so, thank you, Jack. I'm sure we'll manage. But you will let us know in good time if the two of you decide to go to America, won't you? We must know because of Elizabeth."

"Sure I'll let you know, honey. The minute we make up our minds. In any case, I'll keep coming round to see you every now and then. That's O.K., isn't it?"

"Of course it is, Jack. You're always welcome. And I know Harry enjoys those little visits to the pub that the two of you sometimes make."

His grin had been both sheepish and conspiratorial. Although Ethel had closed her eyes to his drinking during their courting days, it had become clear that since their marriage her tolerance was becoming less marked.

Nevertheless, Watson's having a drink at home was one thing. Drinking with Harry, Ethel's arch enemy, was something else. The secrecy with which the American occasionally met Harry in a local pub would have been laughable were it not for its significance. The good-natured Watson was no William who, while putting up with some of Ethel's minor prejudices, had never allowed her to change his habits or dominate him. Watson, perhaps without knowing it yet, was already afraid of his own wife.

The way he had made his offer betrayed that fear. "Don't forget what I've said. If you ever need help, let me know. Only let's keep it to ourselves. I wouldn't want Ethel to know you were in bad trouble and worry about you."

To hide her expression, Mary had kissed his cheek. "You're very sweet, Jack. I won't forget. But there is something I would appreciate if we have to move house."

"What's that, honey?"

"I'd be grateful if you'd occasionally bring Elizabeth round to see us. If we have to move far away, that is."

"You've got it, honey. It'll be a pleasure."

It had been Mary who had suggested the shop. She had heard about it from a local shopkeeper with whom she had become friendly in the days when she travelled herself. "It's something we could manage together, darling. And I want to help."

At first Harry had taken badly to the idea. "I don't want you slaving away in a shop. In fact I don't want you working at all. You've quite enough to do at home."

With his role of provider under threat, it had

not been easy to make her case. "Darling, you've lost over a stone in weight trying to get a job. If it goes on you won't be fit to work. If jobs aren't available, then isn't it good sense to make one for ourselves this way?"

"We've spent enough of the money your Dad left you. This would take it all."

"Isn't it better to buy a job with it than to fritter it away failing to get one?"

"But this is a bakery. What do either of us know about confectionery."

"We can learn, can't we? And the shop does sell other things too. Moreover, the bakeress has agreed to stay on, so we won't have to start from scratch."

He remained unconvinced. "Why is the owner selling if it's such a snip."

"The agent says he's going abroad."

"Do you believe that?"

"I've no reason not to. But does it matter? We'll have to go a long way to find a shop with equipment, stock, and goodwill selling for less than two hundred pounds."

"How much is the rent?"

"Ten shillings a week for the house and the shop."

"What about the books? Have you seen them?"

"Yes. I admit the turnover wasn't good during the last year but you have to allow for the effects of the General Strike. Also, if the owner is planning to go abroad, he wouldn't have put his heart into things during the last few months."

His real objection surfaced again. "It's going

to mean hard work for you. Shops have to be manned at all hours, particularly confectioners'."

She knew he had to be reminded of the facts again, painful though they were. "Harry, you must have tried to get a hundred jobs. We've been living out of the bank all that time and if we don't start earning some money soon, we won't have enough left to buy a business. Then we will be in serious trouble. We just can't afford to wait any longer."

When he shook his head but made no reply, she went on: "At least come with me to see the shop. If you don't fancy taking it on, then we won't. That can't do any harm, can it?"

His voice brought her back to the present. "It's a hell of a long way from No. fifty-seven."

She pressed his arm. "Beggars can't be choosers, Harry. And Jack did say he'd bring Elizabeth over to see us whenever we asked him."

"What about Frank? He'll have to go to another school."

"There must be some good private schools around here. And he's an adaptable boy."

"That's assuming we can afford to send him to one. I'm still not convinced about the owner's reason for selling out."

She pushed away her impatience. "Whatever we do there'll be a risk, Harry. At least give it a chance."

He said no more until they reached the shop. It was set back some twelve feet from the pavement, a shop with twin windows and a central door. The right-hand window was filled with dummy replicas of the sweet meats of the day: bars of Frys and Bournville Chocolate, Whipped Cream Walnuts, Peppermint Crisps, and glass jars of fake toffees and boiled sweets. The left-hand window was empty, with only a few grease-stained squares of paper to show it had once contained items of pastry. At one side of the small paved square was a slot machine containing a selection of popular brands of cigarettes.

She turned to him. "You see! Confectionery, sweets and cigarettes. So at least it doesn't just rely on the bakery."

When he made no comment she pressed the bell. Ten seconds later a thickset, balding man with a somewhat plummy voice opened the door. "Ah, good afternoon, Mrs Miles."

"Good afternoon, Mr Harewood. This is my husband."

"I'm happy to meet you, Mr Miles. Please come inside."

The young couple were led into a shop containing two counters. One, glass-topped and glass-fronted and set at right angles to the windows, was clearly designed for bread and pastry although at present it was empty. The other, facing the windows, supported a showcase containing a variety of sweets and cigarettes. The wall behind this counter was lined with shelves carrying further stocks of confectionery. Seeing the shelves were not full, Harry pointed at them. "Is that all the stock there is?"

The agent shook his head and opened doors at the back of the counter. Harry glanced inside, then frowned at Harewood. "I'd expected more stock than this."

Harewood put on the hurt, slightly reproving look endemic to his profession. "The owner is only asking one hundred and eighty pounds, Mr Miles. And that does include the goodwill."

"I was going to ask you about the goodwill. How long is it since the owner closed down?"

"Only two weeks, sir."

"That still means a loss of customers."

Mary broke in quickly. "Did Mrs Fennell manage to come?"

"Yes, Mrs Miles. She is in the house waiting to see you."

The room he led them into behind the shop was surprisingly large for such a modest property. Its only window at the far side looked out over an unkempt garden but Mary's eyes were on the woman who had turned from the window to face them. At first, silhouetted against the light, she appeared as only a tall, gaunt figure wearing a shapeless grey coat but as she moved towards them and Mary saw the strands of iron-grey hair straggling down from her hat, it became clear she was a woman in her late forties or early fifties. Her features were as austere as the rest of her appearance and the tight smile she gave the young couple when the agent introduced her seemed only to accentuate their severity.

As if Harewood were aware of her unprepossessing appearance, his voice became hearty.

"Mrs Fennell says she will be quite willing to continue working for the new owner. As this will ensure the bread and pastry maintain their high quality, I'm sure you'll agree this is a considerable asset in itself."

"What wage have you been getting, Mrs Fennell?" Harry asked.

The woman, whose pale blue eyes had been studying them both, turned back to him. She had a toneless voice with a lugubrious thread running through it. "Two pounds, ten shillings a week, sir. That's from half past six in the morning until three in the afternoon, with Saturday afternoon and Sunday off. And the ovens ready for me in a morning."

"Ready for you?" Harry asked.

"Aye. I can't light' em myself, not if you want fresh bread and pies by half past eight when you open. That's something you have to do yourself."

"When have they to be lit?"

"Half-past five at the latest. Otherwise they won't be hot enough."

Seeing the glance Harry gave Mary, Harewood made a hasty intervention. "Perhaps we'd better go and see the ovens in question, Mrs Fennell."

Nodding, her head very erect, the woman led them through another room, much smaller than the first, along a narrow corridor flanked by a toilet and a second door, and finally into the small bakery itself. Opposite the door were two ovens and along the side wall a waist-high bench for kneading pastry. Shelves and cupboards completed the layout.

Harry pointed at the ovens. "Those are coke fired, are they?"

The woman nodded and pointed at the first door in the corridor behind them. "Aye. The coke's kept back there in the bunker."

"And these ovens have to be lit every morning at 5:30?"

"They have if you want your bread in the shop on time."

Harry turned and grinned at Mary. "I hope you like getting up with the birds."

Mrs Fennell gave Mary no time to answer. "It's no use giving the job to her. You get big clinkers in these ovens and it takes a man to dig them out."

Harry gave a heartfelt groan. "Why didn't someone tell me this sooner."

Not a muscle flickered in the woman's face. "Baking's hard work, sir. You have to put your back into it."

She's either not got a spark of humour or she's nervous, Mary thought. Before she could say anything, Harewood made another hasty intervention. "I'm sure a young couple like yourselves will not find it arduous. Would you like to see the upstairs rooms now?" The flight of stairs that ran from the side of the large room led to four small rooms upstairs. Three were bedrooms and one was a utility room containing a bath and airing cupboard. "When does the present lease expire?" Harry asked.

"At the end of this month. That is why Mr Jones is letting the shop go so cheaply. He doesn't want the bother of collecting the rent when he goes abroad."

They descended the stairs again and entered the large room where Mrs Fennell was waiting for them. Glancing round the room, Harry gave Mary a grin. "I see now why you're interested. You know you can get the sideboard in here, don't you?"

Encouraged by his change of mood, she laughed. "It is a bonus, I have to admit."

Seeing the optimism on the agent's face, Harry turned to him. "We might just be interested if your Mr Jones will take ten pounds less for the business. Tell him we feel he should have kept it a going concern until he sold it. When can you speak to him?"

Harewood's face was showing practised doubt. "I might be able to contact him this afternoon. But I think it most unlikely that he will take any less. As things are he felt he was almost giving it away."

"Try him anyway. And we'll phone you in the morning to find out what he's said." Without waiting for a reply, Harry nodded at Mrs Fennell. "As Mrs Fennell is involved too, no doubt you'll let her know our decision. Thank you both for showing us round."

Harewood followed them to the shop door, then drew Harry aside, his stage whisper loud enough to carry to Mary. "Forgive my saying it but do you think it's wise to risk losing such a bargain for a mere ten pounds? For one thing Mrs Fennell is such an excellent bakeress that she might find work elsewhere if there's any further delay in taking possession."

Harry smiled at Mary. "I think we can take that risk until tomorrow. Thanks again for your help."

★ ★ ★

The rain was still falling when they took the first tram home but the sky was beginning to brighten. As Harry folded up the umbrella and slid into a seat alongside Mary, he gave a laugh. "That woman really believed I was going to let you light the ovens in a morning. Can you believe it?"

Delighted by his improved mood, she laughed back. "Mind you, I think she behaved that way because she was nervous."

"I hope so. Because otherwise I'll bet she could be a real dragon."

The tram clattered over a set of points. She waited until the sound ceased, then turned to him. "What do you think? Are you willing to give it a try?"

His expression changed. "I don't know. We've only got this chap Jones's word that he's selling because he's going abroad. What if the shop's been going downhill recently and he's using the abroad story as an excuse? You don't want to spend the last of your Dad's money on a dud shop."

She knew that if the money were his he would not be so cautious. "We've gone over all that before, darling. If we wait much longer we won't have any money left to buy a business. So what would we do then?"

250

"You're saying we're between the devil and the deep blue sea?"

"Yes, in a way we are. If this fails, at least we've used the money positively."

She could feel his inner conflict as he gazed out through the tram window. A full minute passed before he turned back to her. "Could you really cope with all that work and that dragon of a bakeress?"

Relief flooded through her. "I've coped with a dragon all my life, haven't I? Mrs Fennell will be child's play beside Mother. If she is a dragon, that is."

He took a deep breath. "All right. I'll phone the agent in the morning and we'll take it whether the price has come down or not." He paused, then his mouth quirked humorously. "But there is just one thing."

"What's that?"

"You get up in a morning and light those ovens. Otherwise the deal's off."

She had never been more grateful for his sense of humour as their laughter pushed back her doubts and fears about the gamble they were taking.

24

ETHEL gave a gasp of horror. "A shop? A pastry shop?"

Mary nodded. "Yes. Why not?"

Ethel's voice was hoarse. "Where?"

"At the far end of Holderness Road."

Ethel relaxed but only slightly. "Have you gone out of your mind? You'll be at the beck and call of every Tom, Dick and Harry who wants a ham sandwich."

The conversation was taking place at No. fifty-seven.

Before moving house, Mary needed to make the necessary arrangements about Elizabeth's visits. To avoid any unpleasantness with her mother, she had hoped Watson would be present but had discovered he'd gone into town for the afternoon.

Nevertheless she could not deny feeling a certain satisfaction at Ethel's dismay in finding her daughter was to become a common shopkeeper. "That's a good idea, Mother. I hadn't thought of stocking cold meats. We could, couldn't we?"

Ethel shuddered. "Don't joke about it, girl. How can you think of such a thing?"

Expecting the maximum possible opposition from her, Mary had decided beforehand that she would take no nonsense. "We hadn't much choice, had we, Mother? Not after you put us both out of work."

Ethel stiffened. "You're surely not blaming me for your choosing such a way of making a living."

"Who else is there to blame? You knew full well when you sold the business how difficult it would be for Harry to find a job."

"Rubbish, girl. There are always jobs for men who look for them."

"Look for them! Harry's worn himself out looking for them. Have you seen the queues outside the factories and work places? There are millions of men unemployed."

Ethel gave a disparaging sniff. "I was thinking of men with qualifications, of course. Not tradesmen and their like."

The speed at which Mary's temper came to a head told her much about her present state of mind. "Don't begin that again, Mother. If it hadn't been for Harry, you wouldn't have got fifty pounds for the business. It was he who built it up and you've rewarded him by putting him out of work."

"I put him out of work, my girl, because he sided with those lazy ruffians who went on strike. What did you expect me to do? Keep a man working for me who was a traitor?"

"A traitor? Couldn't you see he was trying to save the business for you? If you'd paid those men decent wages you'd still have a healthy business and be drawing good dividends from it."

Ethel gave a sneer. "Do you think I don't know why you hate me for selling the business?

It's led you to find out your wonderful Harry isn't capable of looking after you on his own, hasn't it? That's why you're acting like this."

Mary found herself shaking with anger. "You poison everything, don't you, Mother? Every single thing!"

"Don't put the blame on me, girl. Put it where it belongs. Harry's not going to be the one behind the counter in this wretched shop, is he? You're going to be the one who'll do all the work. No wonder he talked you into spending Dad's money on a shop. Whatever else he is, he's not a fool, is he?"

The complete falseness of the accusation restored Mary's self-control. "You're wrong again, Mother. Harry never wanted a shop. In fact we almost quarrelled before I got my own way."

Ethel's pause lasted only a split second. "Don't lie to me, girl. No daughter of mine would sink to such a level unless her husband forced her into it."

Mary rose to her feet. "There's only one person forced me into it, Mother, and that's you. But I'm not going to argue about it any more. I came to see you about Elizabeth. I know we'll be at the other side of town so we can't expect her to visit us midweek as she did before. Instead I want her to spend the weekends with us. Jack has promised to bring her, so that shouldn't be any problem."

"What — all that distance away?"

"It's only the other side of town. It's not Australia."

"How can you expect Jack to do that?"

"I'm sure Jack won't mind. But if he does, then she can come by tram. She's quite old enough to make the journey herself." Seeing Ethel was about to protest again, Mary gave her no opportunity. "I insist on these weekends, Mother. Otherwise we shall take her back for good."

Ethel gave her little sniff. "I'm not sure she'll want to stay in a house over a shop. Have you thought about that?"

Mary took a deep breath, walked to the door, and turned. "Now you listen carefully to what I say. The only reason we've agreed to leave her with you is because of her school. We know she's happy there and doing well, so we don't want to upset things for her. But if you fill her mind with these snobbish ideas about a shop, we'll take her from you again and this time she'll never come back. So you watch your tongue when you speak to her."

* * *

Elizabeth came round to see them that same evening.

"Grannie says you're going to have a shop. Somewhere down Holderness Road."

Mary nodded. "That's right, dear. Just opposite the tram terminus."

"Grannie also says you want me to go there every weekend. Is that right, Mummy?"

"Yes, we'd like you to, darling. Otherwise we wouldn't see much of you."

255

"But what about the friends I play with at the weekends?"

Mary glanced at Harry who was reading a book in the armchair opposite. "I know that, darling, and I'm sorry. But you'll have Frank and Pride to play with here, won't you?"

"Couldn't I come one night during the week?"

"How could you? It's dark by half past four in the winter and neither Daddy nor I would want you travelling alone in the dark."

"But I wouldn't need to. Jack would fetch me."

"Darling, we'd see so little of you. We shall have to keep the shop open until eight o'clock and you couldn't stay much longer than that."

The girl's pretty face began to pout. "Why have you to take a shop, Mummy? It's making everything so difficult."

Hypersensitive on the subject, Mary felt her nerves tighten. "Has Grannie been complaining to you about it?"

The girl's slight hesitation sharpened Mary's suspicions. "She doesn't like you going so far away. She thinks it's going to be difficult for me to see you. And it is, Mummy. If you had to take a shop, why couldn't you take one nearer Grannie?"

"Because we couldn't find one we could afford, that's why. I don't know why you're complaining so much. If anyone has cause to complain, it's Frank. He'll not only be leaving his friends, he'll also have to change schools. Yet he's not making half as much fuss as you."

The girl's sullenness grew. "Then why take

a shop at all? Wouldn't some other work have been better?"

Certain now that Ethel had complained of more things than the distance involved, Mary felt in no mood to spare her. "There isn't any other work. That's why it was so wicked of Grannie to sell the business and put us in this position."

Elizabeth's blue eyes filled with resentment. "But she hadn't any choice. The men went on strike for more money and she couldn't afford to give it to them. And Auntie Connie was in trouble and needed some money."

Before Mary could reply, Harry lifted his face from his book. "Stop it, Mary. You're wasting your time."

Mary turned back to the girl. "One day you'll find out the truth about what Grannie has done to us. In the meantime you'll come to see us at weekends. You'll soon make plenty of friends over there."

Elizabeth's sullenness grew. "I want to stay with my friends here. I don't want to go to your shop."

Acutely aware of Harry's feelings as he listened, Mary lost her temper. "Stop arguing! You'll come to us at weekends and that's the end of it."

At that the girl burst into tears. "Why do you always spoil things for me? Why can't you let me do what I want, like Grannie does?"

★ ★ ★

Harry thanked the headmaster, took the boy's arm, and led him down the tiled corridor.

257

Outside the sound of children at play was muffled but as they approached an open door it grew louder. Pausing at the door which led down a flight of steps to a playground, he bent down and gazed into Frank's pale face. "Are you all right, Scamp?"

The boy swallowed and nodded. His eyes, wide and frightened, were staring down at the playground where a hundred or more boys, many raggedly dressed, were yelling, wrestling, or kicking about old tennis balls.

Harry drew him to one side. "I know it's a bit different from your old school but you'll soon get used to it. You do understand why we've had to bring you here, don't you?"

The boy jerked his head again. His voice was very small. "Yes, Daddy. You've told me."

We've told you but do you understand? Harry thought. Can any young mind accept the unfairness of your situation compared to Elizabeth's?

His own heart had sunk at his first sight of the school. Situated in an industrial area of shunting trains and smoking chimneys, with small windows, turreted roofs, and enclosed by high iron railings, the building was a relic of Victorian times and pure Dickens in appearance. Yet from Harry's enquiries he had discovered its academic reputation belied its appearance and with no local private school they could afford, they had been left no option but to enrol the boy.

Harry put his arm round him and felt how he was trembling. "They say it's a very good

258

school but there is just one thing to remember. You talk a little differently to the other boys so at first they might rag you a little. Do you understand what I mean?"

Nervousness made the boy sound impatient. "Yes, Daddy. I understand."

"Then can I leave you as the headmaster said? Remember you're in Mr Canham's class, in room 20. That's it there, at the bottom of the corridor."

The boy did not answer. His eyes were glued to the horde of screaming young barbarians in the playground below. As the two of them stood there, half a dozen of the children spotted them and gathered at the foot of the steps. One of them, burlier than the rest, with sweat-matted hair and socks rolled down to his boots, let out a yell of derision. "'ere's a new kid with 'is Dad. Come an' look at 'im! Ain't he posh?"

In seconds, the foot of the steps was crowded with grinning, jeering children. At that moment time slipped a cog and Harry was back at school himself. A voice at his elbow made him turn. "He'll be all right in a couple of days, Mr Miles. I think it would be wise if you go now while I take him to his classroom to meet Mr Canham."

Harry nodded and stood back as the headmaster took Frank's arm. The white-faced boy took a few paces with the headmaster, then suddenly tore away and ran back to Harry. "Don't leave me, Daddy! Please don't leave me!"

Harry knew that nothing he had done,

or would ever do, would match the effort of handing the pleading boy back to the headmaster. With his mind in turmoil, he pushed through the ranks of jeering children until he was standing outside the main gates of the school. He glanced back and then, as the yelling of the children rose in volume, drove his fist against one of the stone pillars of the gate.

He felt no pain as he stared at his bruised and lacerated knuckles. A man passing by stopped and stared at him. "What's the matter, mate? You all right?"

No, I'm not, his mind raged. I hate this damned world that never fails to punish the poor for their poverty and the good for their innocence. Instead, alarmed by his emotion, he gave an embarrassed smile and finding no suitable words, walked quickly away.

25

SWANSON rose to his feet as Harry entered the pub and waved him over to his table. As Harry approached, he gave a startled whistle. "What's the matter, old lad? You haven't been ill, have you?"

Harry's answer was short. "Of course I haven't. What are you drinking?"

Swanson waved him into a chair. "I'll get 'em. You take the weight off your legs. You look as if you need to."

Harry watched him make for the bar. A young, attractive woman was sitting alone at a table and Swanson eyed her with interest as he passed. In turn she made an almost imperceptible nod at the bar where her boy friend or husband was fetching her a drink. Taking the hint, Swanson gave her a wink and continued his journey to the bar.

The sight of the woman sitting on her own made Harry think of Lena Turnor. Since moving across town, he had not had the chance to visit her again. The lack of a car had been one handicap and although he had often wondered how she was getting on, the time required to pay her a visit had also been at a premium. As he was deciding he must make the effort to see her soon, Swanson returned with two pints of beer.

"Here we are. The old cat's pee." Placing

one glass in front of Harry, he offered him a cigarette, then dropped into his chair. "It's been a long time, old lad. What've you been getting up to?"

Harry took a deep pull on his cigarette before replying. "I haven't been winning the war, if that's what you mean."

Although Swanson grinned, his pleasant voice was sympathetic. "Is it as bad as that?"

Harry shrugged. "We always knew it was going to be tough, particularly when the owner took our lower offer. He'd let the shop run down and neither of us knew anything about the confectionery business. But as Mary said, beggars couldn't be choosers, and as we had the same bakeress we felt we might get the old trade back eventually."

"And you haven't?"

Harry exhaled smoke. "We've got some of it back, I suppose. Just about enough to keep going. But it's still panic stations every time the bills fall due. On the other hand I suppose we ought to be thankful we've survived this long."

"How is Mary taking it?"

"Not a grumble although she's on her feet twelve hours a day, six days a week. And Sundays aren't much better for her because there's stocktaking to do and the shop to clean up and get ready for Monday."

Swanson surveyed his friend's sparse body. "You don't look as if you've been sitting on your bum yourself. What do you do apart from lighting those ovens at five thirty every morning?"

"Not as much as Mary. We both have the impression the customers don't like a man serving cakes and pastry, although I have to help Mary in the shop sometimes. So I spend most of my time out on my bicycle delivering orders or looking for business. I'd like to do more but my role's limited."

This was the man who had won a Military Medal, Swanson thought. Who had taken every threat and every weapon the enemy had thrown at him. And was now reduced to peddling bread cakes round on a bike. Without being sure at whom it was directed, Swanson swore an inner, heartfelt oath. "What's your bakeress like? The one you felt might be a dragon?"

Harry grinned. "She is a dragon. As strait-laced as an Edwardian corset, a stickler for her rights, and with as much humour as my mother-in-law. But to be fair we couldn't possibly manage without her. We didn't even know how to price the goods until she told us. We get on all right as long as we don't interfere with her work. Then she's on her hind legs and breathing fire."

Swanson grinned back. "You're the man for dragons, aren't you? How's the other one getting along?"

Harry took a draught of beer before replying. "We don't see her these days. But I wouldn't think she's changed."

"Doesn't she ever come with Watson when he brings Elizabeth to you?" At Harry's expression, Swanson laughed. "Hasn't she learned to live with your having a shop yet?"

"Live with that? Hell would have to freeze over first. I've a feeling Jack Watson gets a beating just for visiting us and bringing Elizabeth over."

"But at least Elizabeth does come? The last time we met you were worrying she wouldn't."

"Yes, she comes. But that's about all you can say."

Realising it was a touchy subject, Swanson let it drop. "How is little Frank getting along? He'd just started his new school when I saw you last."

Harry exhaled smoke. "He never complains but I know he hates it. It's this damned pronunciation thing. You know how cruel kids can be."

"Cruel?" Swanson spoke with feeling. "I hated the little bastards when I was one myself. They gave me hell when I moved school."

Harry nodded. "Speak differently and you're an outcast. It was one of my old man's set pieces. He used to say the reason the working class was allowed to speak their language so badly was so the upper class could always recognise them and keep them in their place."

Swanson grinned. "Bernard Shaw would agree with that."

So would Gareth, Harry was thinking. Swanson's amused voice interrupted his thoughts.

"Your old Dad must have been quite a character. I'd like to have met him."

Harry smiled back. "He probably had his tongue in his cheek when he said it. On the other hand he had a point. You send two men

264

into a pub wearing the same clothes but one talking with a broad regional accent and see which one's called Sir and which one Jack."

"And your lad's going through this? Only in his case the snobbery's inverted."

"Isn't that often the case? Isn't the working man often his own worst enemy?" With his mind brought back to his son's problems, Harry's voice changed. "It's hard on the kid. He knows his mother's having a bad time so he keeps the bullying to himself. I found him sobbing his heart out the other day. It seemed the little thugs had torn his jacket and because he couldn't tell Mary about the bullying he had to keep quiet when she accused him of not taking care of his clothes. But he was terribly hurt that Mary felt he didn't care."

"What did you do?"

"I had a word with Mary. But it'll probably happen again. It's a hell of a shame because he's such a willing little chap. He never grumbles about making deliveries for us."

Deciding children were not the subject to brighten up the evening, Swanson changed the conversation yet again. "I see Michael Chadwick's back in the news. Did you see that report the other day that he might put up as a parliamentary candidate at the next election?"

Harry nodded. "I suppose he'll be putting up as a Socialist?"

Swanson grinned. "What else? Just like my old man. Up with the workers and down with the capitalists. That'll be the day, the old bastard."

Harry laughed. "He's still hammering you down, is he? What are you doing now? Cleaning out the toilets?"

"No, I've had promotion. My new job is putting the pips in the jam."

Harry stared at him. With Swanson one never knew where humour ceased and reality began. "Putting in the pips?"

"Yes. They're slivers of wood. Didn't you know that?"

"Come off it. They can't be."

"They are, old lad. Cross my heart. Only don't tell anyone or I'll lose my inheritance."

They talked for another hour and then Harry glanced at his watch. "I'll have to be going. I promised Mary I'd be back in time to unpack some cigarettes and fill up the counter and machine. Can I get you another beer before I go."

Swanson shook his head and rose with him. "No, if you're leaving I'll pop round and see my new girl friend. She wasn't going out tonight."

Harry stared at him. "You didn't put off seeing her for me, did you?"

Swanson took his arm and led him to the exit. "Of course I did. That's the way you keep 'em — don't let 'em think you're too keen. Don't you know anything about women?"

It was a cold night and the wind brought a shiver from Harry as they came out into the car park. There was concern in Swanson's eyes as he watched Harry draw his bicycle out from the cycle rack, although his voice carefully masked it. "You're getting as skinny as we were in that

266

bloody German POW camp, old lad. So don't make it another four months before we have another drink. If that cat's pee does nothing else, it puts a bit of weight on you."

Harry tucked his scarf inside his coat collar. "I'll do my best."

"Do that, old lad. Give me a ring soon."

Harry nodded and rode off into the darkness. Swanson watched him for a moment, then shook his head and climbed into his small car.

★ ★ ★

Harry ran into Chadwick only two days later. He was delivering an order to a client when he heard a car hooting behind him. Turning his head, he saw a Rolls Royce was following him. When he waved it on and it did not pass, he jumped off his bicycle and walked back. About to ask what was wrong, he recognised Chadwick at the wheel.

"Hello, Miles. I thought it was you. How are you getting on?"

"I'm all right," Harry said. "What about you?"

"I'd like a talk with you, Miles. Do you think we could have it now?"

Harry was about to refuse when curiosity overcame him. "I suppose I can spare a few minutes. Where do you want to talk? In the car?"

Chadwick glanced through the windshield. "No, there's a cafe along the road." He eased his fashionably-dressed, elegant body out of the car.

267

"Come and have a cup of coffee with me."

The waitress who served them, although middle-aged, responded to Chadwick's good looks and style as unctuously as a young girl. "Coffee for two and scones, sir? Yes, of course. You will have cream with your coffee, sir?"

Chadwick smiled at her. "Yes, of course we will. And bring us some fresh raspberry jam, will you?"

"Just coffee for me," Harry interrupted.

Ignoring him, Chadwick nodded at the woman who smiled back. "Right away, sir. Thank you."

As she hurried away, catching the winking eye of a colleague as she went, Chadwick turned his smile on Harry. "I'm glad I ran into you today, Miles. As a matter of fact I've been wanting to contact you for a couple of weeks now."

Harry accepted the Balkan Sobranie cigarette he was offered. "You have? Why?"

Chadwick held out his gold cigarette lighter. "You've taken a shop now, haven't you?"

Harry wondered who had told him. "Yes. Six months ago."

"It's a pastry shop, isn't it?"

Harry did his best not to sound defensive. "Yes, it is."

Looking amused, Chadwick released a cloud of blue smoke. "What on earth made you take a shop? And a pastry shop of all things?"

"Isn't that my business?"

"My dear chap, of course it is. Only it seems such a waste, a man like you going around on a bicycle delivering eclairs and jam tarts. I was

268

quite shocked when I heard about it."

Harry's voice was thick with sarcasm. "I hope it didn't upset you too much."

Chadwick gave his light, pleasant laugh. "I know how all this must sound, but remember you were one of my men so I have a natural interest in your welfare."

"I'm touched," Harry said. "I really am."

Chadwick smiled. "All right, Miles. I'll come to the point. I took over a business a few weeks ago and I want a good manager. I thought about you right away."

"Why?" Harry asked. "I told you ages ago I wasn't interested in working for you. So what's different now?"

"You were working for your mother-in-law in those days and came out with some sentimental tosh that you couldn't let her down. It seems that as a reward she sold the business over your head. So it occurred to me you might show better sense now."

The arrival of the coffee and scones prevented Harry's reply. The glance the middle-aged waitress gave Chadwick was almost coquettish. "Is there anything else, sir?"

Chadwick pressed a coin into her hand. "No, thank you. This is just what we wanted."

The waitress stared down at the coin. "This is half a crown, sir. Do you know?"

Chadwick put his finger to his lips. The woman blushed. "Thank you, sir. Thanks ever so much."

As she hurried away, looking as if she had been given an engagement ring, Chadwick turned back to Harry. "Let's be honest with one another. Look what this shop life is doing to you. I've never seen you looking so down at heel, and what about your wife? She must be working just as hard or even harder. Is it fair to her when you could have a job that would allow her to give up work and have a little luxury?"

Harry realised he had done his homework well. Before he could speak, Chadwick held out the plate of scones. When Harry shook his head, Chadwick broke one in half and buttered it. "There are your children too, Miles. Don't you want them to have the best education possible? You could give it to them if you worked for me."

Harry sat watching Chadwick pour out two cups of coffee and pass one over to him. "What is this business you've taken over?"

Chadwick poured cream into his coffee before answering. "It's a timber yard down at the docks. I need a good manager and I'll pay him well. A starting salary of £400 a year and I'll throw in a car for good measure." He set down the cream jug and gazed at Harry. "It's not even a new trade for you, I believe."

Harry knew he was playing for time as he made his reply. "Carpentry's hardly buying and selling timber."

"It's near enough for me. Think of it, Miles. You can take your wife and children out in the car at weekends and you can buy them the little presents they deserve. Isn't that better than working yourselves into an early old age in a pastry shop?"

Harry felt a surge of his old dislike. "Don't patronise me, Chadwick."

Chadwick raised an apologetic eyebrow. "I didn't mean to, old chap. I just don't like to see a good man wasting his life."

Harry was fully aware that his sarcasm was an attempt to ward off temptation. "So this offer is for my sake? A generous gesture because we once fought together?"

Chadwick shook his handsome head. "Not a bit of it. I want you because I know what a good man you are and I want only the best men to run my enterprises. So there's no sentiment involved."

Harry gazed at him for a full ten seconds before replying. "I'll have to talk to Mary first."

Chadwick frowned. "Must you do that? Can't you make a decision yourself?"

"I could but I'm not going to. Give me your number and I'll phone you tomorrow."

Chadwick handed him a card. Harry slid it into his pocket and rose. "I'll have to go now. Thanks for the coffee. I'll be in touch tomorrow."

From the cafe window Chadwick watched him walk to the pavement edge, pick up his bicycle, and ride away. A close observer would have noticed frustration in the squire's eyes as he turned back and poured himself a second cup of coffee.

★ ★ ★

271

"No!" Mary's reply was adamant. "You're not to work for Chadwick. Not now or ever. No!"

Harry took hold of her hands and opened them out in front of her. "Look at them. Chapped and sore already. Think what they're going to be like in a few years' time."

She snatched them away and held them behind her back. "Never mind my hands. At least we're our own masters here. Do you think you'd be that if you worked for Chadwick?"

He drew her down to a stool that stood behind the shop counter. "Listen a minute, love. It isn't just ourselves we have to think about. What about Frank's school? What about birthdays and Christmas presents? What about necessary things like good food and clothes? Let's not fool ourselves. We've given it six months and we're still barely able to pay our bills. It's not going to get any better in the future. You know it isn't."

Although her eyes filled with tears, her voice was as determined as ever. "We're not going to put our lives in Chadwick's hands, Harry. Not again."

"Love, it wouldn't be like that. I'd be his manager, not his slave. I could always quit if I had to."

"How could you quit? We'd get nothing for the shop as things are, so we'd have no money to start another business. You'd be at his mercy just as you were during the war."

"But I'd give him value for the wages I got. So why should he behave differently from any other employer?"

Her voice struck at him. "Because he's Chadwick, that's why. Why can't you understand that he's always been jealous of you."

He laughed. "Jealous? That's only in your mind, love. How on earth can he be jealous of me?"

She knew that was something he would never understand. She also knew that with his concern for his family so deep, there might be only one threat that would deter him. "Harry, do you know something?"

"What, love?"

"If you were to work for Chadwick, I should have to leave you. Don't look at me like that. I mean it."

He laughed, then his voice changed as he saw her expression. "You're not serious?"

"I am, Harry. Deadly serious."

"But, love, that's ridiculous. I'm not suggesting going to live with another woman. I'm talking about a job."

Her lovely pale face gazed up at him. "If I'd to choose between Chadwick and another woman, Harry, it would be another woman every time. That's how I feel about Chadwick."

Baffled by her behaviour, he half-opened his mouth to question her. Then he shook his head and moved away. "All right, if you feel so strongly about it, I'll ring and tell him. But I think you're making a bad mistake."

273

26

THE event that was to change their lives in a number of ways occurred two weeks later. Late one Wednesday evening, just as Mary was about to close the shop, Watson drove round and brought Elizabeth with him. "Hello, honey. Can I come in?"

Delighted to see Elizabeth, Mary did not at first notice the girl's expression. "Of course, Jack. It's lovely to see you both. Go through to the living room while I lock up the shop and call Harry. He's out in the garden repairing a fence."

Watson and the girl were sitting in silence in the shadowy living room when she emerged from the shop and switched on the light. It was only then she saw Elizabeth's tear-stained face. She pulled up short. "What's the matter, darling? What's happened?"

The girl jumped to her feet. "Is my room ready?"

"Yes, of course. It's always ready. But why? Are you going to stay the night?"

The girl gave a sullen nod. "If I can."

"If you can? What a silly question. Of course you can."

"Then I'll go upstairs now. Is Frank in bed?"

"Yes. He went up fifteen minutes ago. I think he's asleep."

"Don't worry. I won't wake him. Good-night."

"Aren't you going to say good-night to Daddy before you go?"

"No, I want to go to bed. Say good-night for me, will you?"

Without another word, the girl disappeared up the stairs. Puzzled, Mary turned to Watson. "What's happened, Jack? Has there been some trouble at home?"

Watson was looking embarrassed. "It's all a bit complicated, honey. Maybe it'd be a good idea if you get Harry in before I explain."

Harry entered the room half a minute later, wiping his hands on a towel Mary had given him. "Hello, Jack. It's good to see you. What's the problem?"

Watson lifted his hand to rub his chin, his characteristic gesture of concern. "It's all come about from some news I got from the States three days ago. My brother tells me some of the local folk would like me to put up for mayor in the elections they're having next year."

Mary gave a laugh of pleasure. "That's splendid news, Jack. Aren't you pleased?"

Watson gave her a doubtful grin. "It's not that simple, honey. It means my going over to the States to live, at least for a couple of years and maybe more, and I wouldn't think of going without Ethel."

Mary was beginning to understand. "What does Mother say?"

"She didn't seem sure at first but now she says we ought to go. She feels it's an honour

275

for me and I ought to accept it."

I'll bet she does, Mary thought. Every social climbing instinct in her character would be alerted. "What do you think your chances are, Jack?"

Watson's natural modesty had never been more obvious. "I think they're pretty good, honey. Mostly 'cause there aren't many other contenders."

"Don't give us that, you old fraud. They like you over there, don't they?"

"It's more to do with the number of guys we employ, honey. And all the other folk who depend on them. These things count in the States."

"They count here too," Harry said. "So you've decided to move over there. Is this what's upset Elizabeth?"

Watson's troubled expression returned. "Yeah. She's pretty cut up about it." His eyes turned to Mary. "Mind you, between the three of us I think it's the best thing for her. I never thought she ought to grow up without her parents."

Mary was still trying to assimilate the news and its implications. Before she could speak, Watson dug into his jacket pocket and drew out an envelope which he handed to Harry.

Harry gazed down at it. "What's this?"

"It's yours, kid. Open it."

Harry obeyed and drew out a cheque. He gave a puzzled frown. "Two hundred pounds? What's this for?"

"Just a little gift, kid. For everything you and Mary have done for me."

Harry stared at him. "What have we ever done for you?"

"More than you think. Take it, kid. To please me."

Harry glanced at Mary, then shook his head. "We can't, Jack. I know you mean well but we can't."

"Hang on a minute and listen to me. I never liked your taking a shop and do you know why?" When Harry shook his head, the American revealed the business acumen that had brought him success in the States. "By and large shops are a bad bet because they chain you to one place and that means your customers have to come to you. If they don't, you're through. There's only one answer to that. You gotta have transport so you can take your goods to them and also go outside the catchment area to find new customers. So I want you to use that money to buy yourself a good panel van. Then you can be selling outside the shop while Mary sells inside it. O.K.?"

Mary's comment broke out involuntarily. "It's true, Harry. A van would make all the difference."

The American turned to her. "Thank God for a woman's commonsense. Hell, I don't want to brag but this money's peanuts to me. So it would be crazy for you two kids to go on struggling when a few bucks can sort things out."

Mary turned to the frowning Harry. "Jack's right, darling. It will make all the difference to us and I think it'll make Jack happy too."

Watson grinned at her. "That's my girl."

They both turned again to Harry who was clearly having a mental battle. "C'mon, kid," Watson said. "You have to do this for Mary."

A few seconds passed before Harry gave a reluctant nod. "All right. Put that way I suppose I can't refuse. But only on one condition: that we treat it as a loan and pay it back as soon as we can."

Watson rolled his eyes to the ceiling. "God save us from these stiff-necked British." Then he gave a relieved laugh. "O.K. if that's the way you want it. Now get it into the bank before you change your mind."

With her eyes brimming with tears, Mary ran across the room and kissed him. "Thank you, Jack. It really is a godsend and we'll never forget you for it."

Clearly moved, the American cleared his throat, then rose to his feet. "I'll have to be getting back, kids, but we'll be in touch again before we go."

"When do you expect that'll be?" Mary asked.

"It's hard to say at the moment but I'd reckon in a month to five weeks."

"Will you sell the house?" Mary asked as they walked with him to his car.

"No. Ethel says she'll let it on a longish lease. Then we can always change our minds later on." Watson jumped into the car, wound down the window, then motioned Mary towards him. His voice dropped as she bent down. "There's just one little thing, honey. I think it's better if you don't say anything about this money to Ethel. O.K.?"

"Of course, Jack. If you don't want us to, that is."

"I'd rather you didn't, honey. Tell Harry, will you?"

She gave him a sympathetic kiss, then stood back. They waved as he drove away and he pipped his car hooter in return. As the car disappeared into the distance, Harry turned to her. "What was that about?"

He shook his head as she told him. "Poor devil. It's happening to him already."

He led her back to the shop. As they entered it, the full implications of the gift seemed to strike him for the first time. Throwing an arm around Mary's waist, he gave a laugh of disbelief. "Do you realise what this means, love? I can play a full part in the business now."

She hugged him back. "I know. Jack's a lovely man, isn't he? Mother doesn't deserve him. The only thing is . . . " She paused as he began to lock the shop door, not wanting to spoil the moment for him.

He turned to her. "What, love?"

She kept her voice low in case Elizabeth was still awake. "We'll have to be very gentle with Elizabeth for a while. She must be very upset that Mother's chosen to leave her."

For a moment her reminder sobered him. "Yes. It must be a shock to the poor kid. But never mind. We can make it up to her now."

She wanted to believe him. "Do you think we can?"

"Of course we can." He caught hold of her again and lifted her clear off the ground, his brown eyes shining at her. "Think of it, love. We're a complete family again, Ethel's getting off our backs, and we've the money to make a fresh start. I'm not dreaming all this, am I?"

She had not seen him so happy for a long time and although her maternal instincts were sending her warning signals about Elizabeth, she had no wish herself to spoil the moment. Laughing, she returned his kiss. "No, you're not dreaming, darling. Our luck's changed at last."

Part Three

Part Three

27

MARY lay listening to the silence. It was magnified by disparate sounds: the hoot of an owl, the clip-clop of a carrier's cart bringing in produce for the morning market, and, every quarter of an hour, the chime of bells from the Anglican church down the road. The clatter of the trams that halted and reversed at the terminus had ceased hours ago.

She heard the hum of the approaching car just after the church clock had struck the hour and instinct told her that her vigil was over. Half a minute later the car halted outside the shop and the sound of its engine ceased.

Believing Harry was asleep, she drew aside the blankets carefully and eased herself from the bed. Tiptoeing to the window, she drew back the curtains. A street lamp was still alight on the far side of the road and enabled her to see the expensive sports car parked below. A full minute passed before its nearside door opened and a girl stepped out. She leaned down, whispered something to the driver, and blew him a kiss. Then, stepping as quietly as she could on her high heels, she made for the shop.

Mary heard the faint click of the lock below. At the same moment the car started up and drove off. She was tip-toeing towards the bedroom door when Harry's voice halted her. "What's the time, love?"

283

Reluctant to tell him, she hesitated for a split second, then prevaricated. "Some time past one, I think."

He began climbing out of bed. "I'll go and talk to her."

Her voice quickened. "No. It's better I do. It is, really. Please."

He hesitated a moment, then dropped back. "All right. But you must be firm with her. Promise?"

Firm with her, she thought. That's precisely why I'm going myself. You forgive her too easily. "Yes, I'll be firm," she said. "You go to sleep."

She closed the bedroom door before crossing the dark landing. As she reached the light switch, there was a faint creak from the lower flight of stairs before she clicked the switch down.

The sudden flood of light revealed Elizabeth halfway up the stairs. She was carrying her high-heeled shoes in her hand and her expression as she stared up at her mother was a mixture of surprise, resentment and defiance.

Although angry, Mary kept her voice low. "Do you know the time? It's gone two o'clock."

Shrugging, the girl continued up the stairs. "I couldn't help it. The party went on longer than I thought."

"What has that to do with it? You didn't have to stay to the end, did you?"

Elizabeth reached the top of the stairs. At seventeen years old, she was almost a facsimile of her mother, with the same attractive features, large expressive eyes, and luxuriant golden hair.

If anything, she was an inch taller, with a body a model would have envied for its high breasts, slim waist, and long slender legs. To heighten her attractions, she was wearing a tight, black satin dress that fitted every curve of her body and set off to perfection her mass of blonde hair.

At the moment, however, her beauty was marred by her resentment. "We didn't stay to the end. These parties go on all night."

"I know all about these parties. And I don't think you should be going to them."

The girl's voice turned sarcastic. "Why not, Mother? Aren't I good enough to go?"

"Don't talk like that. You know perfectly well what I mean. Those people have different standards to ours and neither your father nor I like those standards."

Elizabeth's sarcasm grew. "You mean you don't like the way they enjoy themselves. It's wicked to laugh and dance and to have parties. It's only moral when you spend your life serving people behind the counter of a shop."

Knowing to go too far would be counter-productive, Mary held back her temper. "You know well enough we want you to enjoy yourself. But men like Rodney Stone are too old for you. They're also playboys. They take you about because you're a beautiful girl but it'll never go further than the physical level. All they are doing is using you. Can't you see that?"

"In other words, stay in your class. That's what you really mean, isn't it?"

"Don't be ridiculous. I don't mind who you

go out with as long as they're decent boys and respect you."

"But you'd prefer poorer ones, wouldn't you? The kind you get round here who haven't two pennies to rub together."

"Money isn't everything, Elizabeth. You'll find that out one day."

"It's meant plenty to you and Dad," the girl said bitterly. "I haven't lived with you not to find that out."

"That's not fair. We've needed money to survive and bring up a family. Men like Rodney, who have money, do nothing but play around and tempt young girls with it."

For a moment Elizabeth had seemed to regret her words. Now her beautiful face tightened again. "So you think he's tempting me?"

"Yes, I do. He's trying to buy you with expensive presents and promises he'll never keep."

"How do you know that?"

"Because I've met men like him before."

The girl's voice became malicious. "Who, Mother? Sir Michael Chadwick?"

Mary stiffened but managed to control herself. "I'm telling you that men like Rodney are all tarred with the same brush. They've no respect for young girls, particularly if they have no social status. They just use them."

Elizabeth eyed her mockingly. "I don't see why you should hate Sir Michael so much. After all, he fancied you, didn't he?"

Mary took a deep, steadying breath. "Stop talking about Michael Chadwick, Elizabeth. I've

286

warned you about it before."

The girl laughed again. "Why not? After all, I have met him and he isn't a bit the way you say he is."

Mary gave a violent start. "You've met him?"

"Yes. He was a guest of honour at a party Rodney took me to last month. Rodney introduced us." Seeing Mary's expression, the girl went on defiantly: "Why not? Rodney's father's the Chairman of the Chamber of Commerce, so we could meet on equal terms."

"Why didn't you tell us?"

"What was the point? I knew you'd only kick up a fuss."

"Why did you want to meet him?"

Elizabeth shrugged. "I suppose I wanted to see if he's as bad as you paint him. And he wasn't. In fact he was charming."

"Did he know who you are?"

"Yes. I've just told you, Rodney introduced us. Although Sir Michael said afterwards that it wasn't necessary: he would have recognised me anywhere from my likeness to you." There was malice in the girl's voice again. "I think he still fancies you, Mother."

Mary took another deep breath. "I think you'd better go to bed before your father comes out. I'll have another talk with you in the morning. Go on."

The girl opened her mouth to answer, then noticed her mother's expression. With a shrug and a toss of her head, she turned and disappeared into her bedroom.

287

Harry was sitting up in bed when Mary returned. She wondered how much he had heard. "You've been a long time," he said. "I nearly came out to you. Has she been difficult again?"

She got into bed before answering him. "They've been to a party. One of those county affairs Rodney takes her to. They left before it ended and I suppose it was quite a long ride back."

His voice was half quizzical and half serious. "And that was why your voices were raised? Come on, love. Let's have it all."

She sighed. "She didn't like me attacking Rodney and his friends."

"Perhaps that's a mistake. Maybe we ought to let her find out the truth herself."

There were times when his tolerance annoyed her. "That could be too late. Have you thought of that?"

"Hang on, love. We've always taught her to respect herself. You surely don't believe she'd sleep with Rodney, do you?"

"I'm not as sure as you," she said. "She's a hot-blooded girl and she hates working in the shop. You can't be certain what she might do to get out." Ignoring his protest, she went on: "But that isn't all we had words about. She told me she'd been introduced to Michael Chadwick."

"Chadwick? Where?"

She explained how it had happened. "I'm sure she asked for the introduction. She's always been interested in him ever since Mother made him sound such a glamorous figure."

288

He asked the same question she had asked. "Did she tell him who she was?"

"I gather she didn't need to. He recognised her likeness to me."

He stared at her a moment, then sank back on his pillow. "I suppose it doesn't matter except it shows the kind of circles she's moving in."

"That's why it does matter, Harry. I don't want her mixing with people like him. And neither should you."

Humour entered his voice. "What are you trying to make me, love? An inverted snob?"

She bit her lip. "It's not funny, Harry. She's only tolerated because of her looks. She could get hurt one day."

"Wait a minute, love. God knows I've never been an admirer of the privileged classes but even I know there are plenty of decent people among them. Socially blind, I'll give you that, but not ogres. She might just stand as good a chance of meeting a decent lad among them as anywhere else."

"Among Chadwick's friends?" she demanded.

Before he spoke, he drew her towards him. "I know she's a problem, love. But you haven't forgotten why, have you?"

Forgotten, she thought. Forgotten that when Ethel abandoned her and went to America, it must have seemed to the young and sensitive child that no one in the world wanted her or could be trusted? No, Harry, I haven't forgotten.

Nor have I forgotten that when the shock and the heartbreak were over and bitterness had taken their place, there had to be someone to punish. If Ethel were not there, then who better to punish than her parents who themselves had seemed not to want her when she was a child?

Feeling cold, she nestled against him. "I know, Harry. It was a terrible mistake we made. We should have called Mother's bluff and taken no notice of the doctor. But all the same, how many years must it go on? I don't have your patience. Also she seems to taunt me more than you."

"That's because the two of you are so alike, love. At times you look like sisters."

She found little comfort in that. "Sometimes I think she sees us as enemies, not as parents."

"Don't all children do that? Isn't it a part of the business of growing up."

"But not like this. Not going out with a married man as she did last year and then telling us about it. She seems to like giving us pain."

"As you've said, that's because she's had such pain herself. It'll go, love. If we're patient it'll gradually work out of her system."

She clung to him tightly. "God, I hope so, Harry. Because tonight she frightened me."

★ ★ ★

She lay awake long after Harry had fallen asleep. The scene with Elizabeth seemed to have cracked the frail shell into which her mind had sealed its problems and now they were harassing her again. Was their livelihood once more in danger? she wondered. Until 1929 all had seemed well. With a van that could search out customers beyond walking distance of the shop and with enough capital in the bank to insure them against unforeseen bills, they had turned the corner and if they had not actually prospered, at least they had survived and been able to afford little luxuries denied them before.

The steady solving of their problems had not been so apparent within the family. It had been more of a slog up hills and down into depressions. On the positive side, in 1928 Frank had taken the examination necessary to attain secondary school education and had gained a high enough mark to receive a free place in the school nearby. It was a school with an excellent record and the boy had liked it from the onset.

On the negative side Elizabeth had never ceased to cause problems. Although Ethel had left her enough money to move to another private school nearer her parents, she had taken a dislike to this new school from the beginning and made no effort to reach the academic standards of which she was capable. Nevertheless, with Harry believing in equal education for both sexes, she had been kept there until the school leaving age of sixteen. At that point, with her attainments totally inadequate for higher education, there had been no other role for her but to help Mary in the shop. From that moment on she had grown progressively more difficult to manage.

Flinching from her fears about Elizabeth,

Mary found her thoughts returning to the shop. Although the newspapers of October 1929 had been full of the news of the Wall Street Crash, neither she nor Harry, nor, she suspected, the average man in the street, had any idea of the deluge to come. Few Britons at that time had the money to buy stocks and shares and so the crash of the stock market in far off Wall Street had seemed of little consequence. Indeed the stories of men throwing themselves out of skyscraper windows had seemed to Mary either newspaper fiction or the over-reaction of a somewhat hysterical people.

What she had not known was that the catastrophe was causing the American Government to withdraw its foreign loans and also driving its industrialists to recall the massive capital they had invested in Britain and other European countries.

The result was like a wasting disease. As one firm was forced to close down and no longer needed components, it brought down others in its wake. If there had been unemployment before, it was endemic now. If ex servicemen had once been bitter, now they were desperate. The song, 'Brother, can you spare a dime', was soon being sung just as fervently in the slums of Britain as in the slums of America.

In the way of wasting diseases, the full impact had not made itself felt in Britain for well over a year. The latest unemployment figure was given as three million and many people, Harry among them, suspected that figure was rigged. But, true or false, the hardship was massive. Very

292

few wives worked or could find work and with the 'dole' desperately inadequate, some families were literally starving.

In one way Mary knew they were lucky to have a bakery. Hardship or not, people had to eat and so they were one of the last shops to be affected by the scarcity of money. But although the sales of staples like bread had remained constant, luxuries like cakes and pastry had shown a sharp decline as people drew their belts even tighter. As the profit margin on pastry was higher than on bread, Harry had been travelling even further afield and Mary keeping the shop open longer in the evenings in their attempts to halt the decline.

The latter move had not pleased Elizabeth. "We're open late enough now. If we stay open another hour, it'll be too late for me to go out."

"Darling, I don't expect you to help out every night any more than you do now. Two nights or even one will be a help. I must have some time off to do the accounts and to clean up the house."

"I don't know why Dad ever took a shop," the girl had complained. "Nobody else works so hard as you do. You haven't had a single holiday since we came here."

Although Mary suspected afterwards that the girl's complaint had been sympathetic rather than critical, her attack on Harry, mild though it was, carried too many connotations to be taken patiently. "Don't blame your father. You know well enough where the blame lies."

Although she had meant to put the blame on Ethel, Elizabeth's reaction had shocked her with its bitterness. "What could you expect from that old woman? You should have known what would happen?"

Since Ethel's departure to America, Mary had never been able to decide where her emotions lay. At one moment she would feel relief that Ethel's power over the girl seemed broken at last, and in the next moment concern and sympathy that a girl so young should have her faith in people devastated. In one way or the other, she thought, it seemed Ethel's baleful influence would always blight their family.

There seemed little doubt that Ethel had felt remorse for during her first year away she had written to Elizabeth almost weekly. Elizabeth, however, had refused to reply and passed the letters over to her mother. Mary, who received a letter a month from Ethel, replied to both at once, making excuses that the girl was a poor letter writer and busy with her school work. With Ethel so far away, there seemed little point in keeping the bitterness alive.

For the next three years, however, the stream of Ethel's letters had turned into a trickle. The reason was betrayed by their content. Watson had been elected mayor and Ethel was too busy preening herself and socialising in his reflected glory to keep her family ties active.

Then, without any reason given, her letters began arriving frequently again. Although they gave nothing away, Mary's instincts began to ring bells. Perhaps it was only that with Watson a mere citizen again, Ethel had more time to write. And yet she felt certain there was another, less innocuous reason.

The sudden clangour of the alarm made her start. Beside her Harry fumbled for the clock and the din ceased. He lay still for a moment, sighed, then climbed out of bed.

He moved quietly as he dressed. She had grown used to his early rising and often slept through the din of the alarm clock. Not wanting him to know she had not slept, she remained quiet while he tiptoed across the room and made his way down to the bakery.

As always she felt regret that he had to rise so early. Moreover she had always felt low in spirits in the early hours of the day. They reminded her of the mornings when Harry had to return from leave to France and she had lain with him in the darkness, clinging to every minute as if it were a jewel of infinite value. In those days the dream of peace when they could face life together had seem like a dream of heaven itself. No problem her mind had been able to conceive had remotely matched the grim reality of war and separation.

These were the very days of which they had dreamed, she thought. Of being together, of having a family and their own home. Was it always the way with dreams? Was the reality that followed the dream always doomed to disappointment?

Or was the human mind, with its capacity to dream, its own enemy? Instead of comparing its dreams with reality, should it not compare reality with reality and find its comfort there?

Ashamed of her sombre mood, she knew that was the answer. She was an mature woman now, with middle age approaching. A woman old enough to know that life without problems existed only in the the mind of a child. In spite of their problems, they were still lucky in having an intact family and the blessings that went with it. Comforted by the thought, seeing the dawn seeping through the curtains, she willed herself to sleep in the hour left to her.

28

HARRY drove down the familiar street, parked against the kerb, and switched off the engine. Peering through the windshield at the house ahead, he saw a light was shining through the sitting room curtains.

For a moment he wondered if she were alone: he did not want to embarrass her. Then he shrugged and threw open the van door. She had always seemed glad to see him in the past and the chances did not come that often.

Her face lit up as she opened the door. "Harry! How good to see you."

"Hello, Lena. Can I come in?"

"Of course you can. How are you keeping?"

He followed her into the sitting room. "I'm all right. How are you?"

She ignored his question, her eyes running over him. "You're still very thin, Harry. Aren't things any better since I last saw you?"

He sank into an armchair. "I don't expect they'll get any better until this slump's over. You must be feeling the pinch worse than we are."

"Yes, things are bad. Just about all we sell these days are wreaths and wedding bouquets, and buyers have cut down drastically on both. They sacked my younger assistant last month and I'm expecting Deidre to go any time. That'll just leave me to run the shop." She smiled, making a joke of it. "It's a good job

I'm the manageress."

"That must mean a lot of work for you."

"Not really. Trade's too bad." Her tone changed. "But let's talk about something else. How is your family?"

"They're all well, thanks, although Mary's working much harder than I like."

"What about the children?"

"Frank's doing well at school. He must have grown six inches since he moved there. He hated the other one so much I think it must have stunted his growth."

She laughed. "What about Elizabeth?" Noticing his change of expression, she went on: "Aren't things any better there?"

"Not really. She keeps saying she wants to get out of the shop and find work elsewhere. Mary will miss her help but I don't see how we can stop her. It won't be long before she's eighteen and quite a few of her friends are leaving home."

"Perhaps that might be the best thing. Most people don't appreciate their home and parents until they leave them."

He gave a wry grin. "That's what I told Mary. But it's poor comfort to a mother."

"What about your mother-in-law? Do you hear from her very often?"

"More than we used to. Mary has the feeling she wants to return to England."

"Do you think she will?"

"It's possible. Jack's finished his term of office so that attraction's gone."

"How does Elizabeth feel about it?"

"She couldn't care less. If Ethel thinks she'll be running back to No. fifty-seven, she'll have a shock coming."

"How long can you stay?" she asked.

He glanced at his watch. "Oh, an hour or so. If you can stand me that long, that is."

Her eyes twinkled as she rose from her chair. "I think I'll just about stand it."

"Good. Then where are you going?"

"I thought you might like a drop of whisky. I've still got half a bottle left."

He hesitated. "All right. If you'll join me."

His eyes followed her as she walked over to a cabinet. She had changed in so many ways, he thought, from the pitiful young widow he had first visited in 1919. Although she was still a slim woman, time and maturity had given a smoother outline to her face and figure. Moreover, she now paid more attention to her appearance and her clothes, although how much of that was due to her going out to work he had never been quite certain. She had taken a job in a local florist's a few months after her return from Hebden Bridge and had now become its manageress.

Yet in one essential way she had not changed, he felt. She had not escaped from her loneliness. Not that she hadn't had men friends. The first had been an estate agent who had bought flowers from her shop. He had visited her weekly for eighteen months until his wife had learned of the affair. The second relationship, also with a married man, had lasted for two years until his firm had posted him down to London only a few days earlier.

She had not allowed these affairs to interfere with their friendship: indeed she had asked him to continue seeing her whenever he had the wish and the opportunity. Trusting him at last with details of her private life, she had discussed both men with him. "I know what people might say about me, Harry, but the lucky ones forget one thing. Three-quarters of a million men were killed during the war, and at least another half million were crippled. So where does a woman like me find a single man of my own age? I've never asked either of them to leave his wife. I know too well how it feels to be left alone. But am I supposed to go unloved for the rest of my life because of a war neither Arthur nor I wanted?"

He had never felt inclined to criticise her. Two short affairs in twelve years seemed little enough in a young widowed woman with no relatives to succour or comfort her. In fact, when he had witnessed the brief happiness she had found, he had felt almost a warmth towards the men and made certain that his visits had not clashed with theirs.

It had not gone unappreciated. "It's thoughtful of you, Harry, but you don't need to be careful. You're an old and dear friend. No one will ever stop me seeing you." Her tone had changed when she tried to lighten her words. "Not even if the neighbours' curtains do twitch every time a man visits me."

He had felt a surge of irrational anger. "Don't let that worry you. People like that are just emotional cripples."

300

Remembering that she would be missing her recent lover, he made mention of him while they were sipping the whisky she brought over. "I'm sorry to hear about Dennis having to move to London. Was he expecting the posting?"

Her shrug had a fatalistic quality. "I'm not sure but something was bound to happen sooner or later. All things end, don't they, Harry?"

Yes, her loneliness was still there, he thought. Locked in her heart as if it were a shrine. She drained her glass, then smiled at him. "Shall we have another?"

Her question surprised him. In all the time he had known her she had never taken more than a glass of sherry. "If you like."

She took his glass and returned to the cabinet. "There won't be any more after this. So I'm glad you're here to finish it with me."

His first thought was that she was in financial trouble again. Then he remembered. Whisky had been Dennis Morrison's favourite drink.

There was a moment of silence after she returned. She drew her armchair nearer to the fire as if she were cold and as she sipped at her glass he could see the firelight touching her dark hair and sombre eyes. The sight brought back memories of Nicole Levrey and the night in France when he had felt himself the loneliest man on earth and his sympathy for Lena grew.

As if reading his thoughts, she suddenly left her chair and sat down on the floor at his feet. "Shall I tell you something, Harry?"

He had never seen her as demonstrative

301

as this and smiled down at her. "It sounds important."

"It is important. Thank you for coming tonight. I'm very grateful."

He cleared his throat. "You're missing Dennis, aren't you?"

She frowned at the question. "Yes, I suppose I am. But not so much him as . . . " Her frown and gesture said things her mind could not express. Instead she laid her dark head against his knee. "Drink doesn't help, does it, Harry? It only makes things worse."

As he sat gazing down at her, her face lifted and he saw there were tears on her cheeks. It was the first time he had seen her cry but before he could speak, she gave a little sob, rose, and threw her arms around him. "Oh Harry. Isn't life awful sometimes?"

His arms closed around her. At first he believed she only wanted comfort. "I'm sorry, Lena. It's a damned shame he had to leave. But won't he come up and see you occasionally?"

"No. He'll find someone else. That's the world we live in, Harry. It's such a lonely place, isn't it?"

He had expected her to draw away when her tears were spent but instead her arms tightened. A few seconds passed and then he heard her low appeal. "Don't go tonight, Harry. Please don't leave me."

A memory of Nicole Levrey came again. The woman who had understood the crying need of loneliness. The woman who had taught him things about life that had changed his

302

perceptions and his beliefs.

He never remembered what he said to her. He only remembered taking her into her bedroom and lying down beside her.

She was crying now as if her heart would break. "Harry! Oh, Harry! Love me this once. Just this once."

He helped her remove her dress. She drew his hand to her breasts. She was crying and smiling at the same moment now. "You never guessed, did you, Harry?"

He bent down to kiss her. "No. You never gave me any idea."

She drew his face down to her breasts. "I've wanted to, Harry. I've wanted to all these years."

He tried to quieten her. "It's all right. I understand."

"No, you don't. You must have thought I didn't like you. And it wasn't that at all. You were so kind to me. And you seemed so happy with Mary and your family . . . " Suddenly she gave a gasp and her eyes widened.

"What is it?" he asked, startled.

She shrank away from him. "No, Harry. No!" Before he could speak, she jumped from the bed and snatched up a dressing gown. As she threw it round herself, he caught hold of her. "What is it, Lena? What's the matter?"

She pushed him away and ran down into the sitting room where he found her trembling in front of the fire. "Lena, what's happened? You must tell me."

For a moment she would not look at him: He

took her into his arms and turned her distressed face towards him. "Did I do something wrong?"

Tears squeezed out of her closed eyes as she shook her head. "I'm sorry, Harry," she whispered. "Forgive me."

"Forgive you for what?"

She leaned against him for a moment, then drew away. "I realised I couldn't, Harry. You'd have been so full of guilt afterwards."

He shook his head. "No, I wouldn't. Not tonight."

She was not listening. "There's Mary too. You've talked about her so much it's as if she's become my friend. And you've all lived in this house together. Suddenly it was like making love to you before her eyes."

Paradoxically he felt more like making love to her at that moment than he had upstairs. She blew her nose, wiped her eyes, then turned and smiled at him. "You've seen me in my true colours tonight. I'm not a very nice person, am I?"

"I think you're a lovely person," he said quietly. "But then I always have."

She gave a faint shudder, then moved away from the fire. "I think you'd better go, Harry. I'm not fit company to be with tonight." When he hesitated, she affirmed her wish. "Please, Harry. It's better for us both."

At the door she caught his arm, her voice anxious. "You won't stop coming though, will you? Not if I promise to behave myself and never to drink whisky again?"

He laughed. "No, I won't stop coming. Not

304

even if they twitch every lace curtain in the street."

She showed gratitude for his humour. She gazed at him for a moment, then leaned forward and kissed his cheek. "I owe you so much, Harry. God bless you."

He hesitated, unable to find the right words to say. When he believed he had them, he found himself facing a closed door. His thought as he drove away was how little one knew about other people's hopes and fears, even if one lived with them for a lifetime.

29

HARRY stared at the letter. "The 10th of next month! That doesn't leave us long, does it? What will you do? We can't close the shop for the day."

"I'll drop a line to Molly," Mary told him. "I've got her address somewhere. I don't think she has any children yet, so I'm sure she'll prepare them a meal. She might even be willing to go round a day or two beforehand and clean up the house."

"I certainly don't think you should take it on. You've more than enough to do here."

The letter was from Ethel. She and Watson had finally made up their minds and were returning to England. The present tenants would be vacating the house at the end of the month and would Mary please arrange to get the keys from the agent and have a meal awaiting them when they arrived on the 10th?

It was a letter typical of her mother, Mary reflected. No thought for the problems of others, of how her daughter could spend an afternoon cooking a meal when she had a shop to look after at the other side of town. "What about Connie?" Harry asked. "Can't she come down and do something?"

For a moment Mary was tempted to write to her sister and suggest it. Then she shook her head. "She won't come down. She'll use

306

her husband's illness as her excuse. No, I'll drop a line to Molly. I'm sure she'll help out if she can."

In the event Molly did help out and Ethel and Watson arrived back to a clean house and a hot meal. Ethel phoned Mary that same evening. "Hello, dear. How are you?"

"Hello, Mother. Welcome back. What time did you get in?"

"Just after four o'clock."

"Did you have a good crossing?"

"Yes, quite good. But what happened to you this afternoon? Jack and I thought you'd be at the station to meet us in."

Nothing changes, Mary thought. "How could we, Mother? We couldn't close the shop."

"Oh, the shop!" The disparagement in Ethel's voice was barely hidden. "I'd forgotten about that. But the children could have come, couldn't they?"

"Frank had a football match this afternoon. He'd like to have got off but his teacher said they needed him."

"Then what about Elizabeth? You gave her the afternoon off, didn't you?"

Mary wondered why she should answer all these questions. "Yes, Mother, I gave her the afternoon off."

"Then where was she?"

"I don't know, Mother. You'll have to ask her. She's a woman now, you know. Not the little girl you last saw in 1926."

In the short silence that followed Mary was certain she heard Ethel give her little sniff. "I

307

still think she might have met in her old grannie who's been so good to her, don't you?"

Aware she was hurt, Mary tried to soften the blow. "Young people can be thoughtless, Mother. I'm sure she didn't mean anything by it."

"Can I speak to her now?"

"I'm sorry but she's gone out for the evening. I'll tell her to ring you tomorrow, shall I?"

Ethel sounded resentful. "Oh, very well. Now what about the weekend? I take it you can leave that shop on Sunday, can't you?"

Mary hesitated. "I usually catch up on the housework on Sundays. You couldn't both come round here, could you?"

Ethel gave a tut of impatience. "Good heavens, girl, you're not chained to the place, are you? Surely you can spare a few hours in the afternoon or evening to see your mother again?"

Realising Ethel would never visit the shop, Mary had little option but to capitulate. "All right, Mother. We'll come round in the early evening. Between six and six thirty."

★ ★ ★

Sunday evening was not a success. It was handicapped from the onset by their arriving at No. fifty-seven in the van. From Ethel's look of disapproval when she came to the front door, she obviously believed every housewife in the district was peering through her lace curtains to see what tradesmen she was entertaining.

To be fair she did make an effort afterwards to be motherly, even to the extent of pecking Harry's cheek. But the effort was clearly an ordeal for her and none of the adults looked comfortable.

To add to the strained atmosphere, there was a marked difference in the way Ethel treated Jack Watson. As the younger couple had noticed, she had started to impose herself on him even before their departure to the States but both had assumed her deference would return once he received his civic honours. Whether that had happened or not, she certainly showed him no deference now. Her voice turned sharp whenever she addressed him and she would break into his conversation in a way that was almost contemptuous.

Moreover both Harry and Mary were startled by his appearance, His face, once round and genial, was now shrunken, with a yellowish tinge, and he looked twenty pounds lighter than when he had left for America.

They had a glass of sherry and then Ethel distributed presents which, although she made no reference to Watson, were obviously gifts from him also. There was an expensive opal brooch for Mary, a pair of roller skates for Frank which brought a whoop of joy from him, and a necklace made from Canadian gold for Elizabeth. Harry's gift from Ethel was a small leather wallet.

They had supper at eight-thirty. Mary wanted to help Ethel prepare it but her mother waved her away. "You look as if you've done enough work today." She turned and smiled at Elizabeth who had said little since receiving her present. "I'm sure my little girl will help me. Then we can have a chat at the same time, can't we?"

Elizabeth threw a glance at her mother, then sighed and disappeared with Ethel into the kitchen. Left with the opportunity to talk to Watson alone, Mary was about to ask him about his health when Harry turned to him and said casually: "You've lost weight, Jack." Knowing how tactful Harry could be on such occasions, she sat back and waited.

The American grinned ruefully. "Just a pound or two, kid. Didn't I need to?"

"Have you been slimming then?"

"You could say that. No, I've been a bit off colour lately. I'll tell you about it sometime." Before either of them could pursue the subject, Watson turned to Frank. "You'll have to ask your daddy to take you to a skating rink now, won't you?"

Unused to expensive presents, the boy's face was shining. "Can you skate, Uncle Jack?"

"I used to, kid. I used to play ice hockey once. But that was a long, long time ago."

"Can you play hockey on roller skates?"

"Sure you can. I often used to play on 'em in the summertime."

"Could you teach me to play, Uncle?"

Watson grinned at Harry. "I could teach you the rules, kid, but don't ask me to skate with you. Those days are over."

Ethel and Elizabeth returned fifteen minutes later with hot sausages and buttered rolls. Half an hour later Mary nodded at Harry and rose. "We'll have to get back now, Mother. We've some parcels to unpack before tomorrow." Hating her lie, she glanced at Watson to make it less mendacious. "It's good to have you both back and thank you for the nice evening." Then, determined to include Watson in the tribute, she turned to the two children. "Thank Uncle Jack and Grannie again for their lovely presents."

Ethel stood in the porch to wave them goodbye but Watson walked down to the gate with them. As they drove off, Mary gave a relieved laugh. "Thank God that's over."

"You weren't alone in thinking that," Harry said. "Ethel's never stopped sweating the whole time the van's been standing outside the house."

They laughed together. Then Mary's tone changed. "I didn't like the look of Jack. I thought he looked terribly ill."

"So did I. Perhaps he'll tell me more on Friday night. We've arranged to have a beer together."

She glanced over her shoulder and then realised that with the two children in the back of the van she could not be overheard. "I wonder what's happened between them. Did you notice the way she spoke to him?"

He nodded. "Maybe I'll find out on Friday." He drove a minute more, then fumbled into his pocket and pulled out the small leather wallet. "You know what this represents, don't you?"

"No. What?"

He grinned. "It's what she thinks of my

earning power. The smallest wallet she could find."

Her urge to giggle got out of control when she saw his droll expression and a moment later her hysterical laughter could be heard by the children in the rear of the van.

★ ★ ★

It was past eleven-thirty on Friday night when Harry parked the van outside the shop. He found Mary in the sitting room listening to the wireless. She switched the set off as he entered and the strains of a dance band died away. "Sorry I'm a bit late, love. But Jack had taken the tram to the pub, so I ran him home."

"How is he?" she asked.

He dropped into a chair. "Not too good, I'm afraid. He's got heart trouble."

She gave a start. "When did that come on?"

"The doctors think he's had it some time but it only got bad two years ago. He didn't say so but it's my guess the Wall Street Crash brought it on. Apparently he'd invested much of his capital in stocks and shares and it all went down the plug hole when the market collapsed."

"Are you thinking what I'm thinking?" she asked.

"What else? He was Ethel's blue-eyed boy when she thought he was rich and influential. It's a different story now."

"But that's awful. It's not his fault."

"Since when did responsibility affect Ethel's thinking? She had dreams of being a fine lady

312

and he's let her down. So in goes the knife."

"Did he admit this to you?"

"Yes. He's a loyal old boy but there's a limit."

"What about Ethel's money? Was that lost too?"

"No. She'd kept that under her own name."

"So they're not in any real financial trouble?"

"No. In any case, Jack has some money invested in land and property. But he's not the rich man she married any longer and, knowing Ethel, I expect she feels she's been cheated."

"Poor Jack," she said. "No wonder he looks so ill."

He nodded. "He's been hit from all sides and not just from Wall Street. Apparently Ethel had taken a dislike to his brother's wife from the start and it just went on from there until the whole thing blew up. I think that got to Jack more than anything."

"In that case it's a wonder he came back with her, isn't it?"

He shrugged. "She's his wife and I suppose he still hopes she might mellow as the years roll on."

She took a deep breath. "She's incredible, isn't she? No matter where she goes, she causes trouble." When he did not answer, she went on: "There are times when I wonder if she can help it. Whether something got into her after Dad died and makes her do these things."

He grinned. "You're not turning superstitious on me, are you?" Then his voice changed. "Let's hope you're wrong because she's back home now

313

and seeing Elizabeth in town tomorrow."

She frowned. "So that's why Elizabeth asked for the afternoon off. But I thought she'd turned against Mother. So why didn't she tell us she was seeing her?"

"She doesn't tell us much about anything these days, does she? So that's not necessarily significant."

"But why does Mother want to see her on her own? Do you think she's going to try to get her back?"

"I think it's likely, particularly now she's turned against Jack."

"What does he think?"

"He also thinks it's likely, although he promised to do all he could to stop it."

"A fine chance he'll have," she said bitterly "Mother wouldn't part with Elizabeth when she respected him, so she's not going to listen to him now." She glanced at the clock. "I think I'll wait up and talk to Elizabeth when she comes in."

"No, I wouldn't do that. You know what she's like these days. If you interfere, you might antagonise her and drive her back. She's a woman now and has to make her own decisions." When she hesitated, he went on: "In any case, we might be making a mountain out of a molehill. Ethel might only want to have a talk with her or buy her a present."

Although she felt it unlikely, she finally gave in and went upstairs with him. But she took apprehension with her. Earlier she had hoped that Ethel's talent for mischief-making had been

314

blunted or even destroyed by her marriage and her years in America. Now that she knew better, she was wondering if it might reach full flower again now that Ethel was back with her family.

30

ETHEL held out the plate of cream cakes. "While you're thinking about it, have another cake, dear. The cream's real, you know."

Elizabeth, who was looking sullen, shook her head. "No, thanks. I don't want to put on any weight."

Ethel looked amused. "You don't need to worry about your weight. You've got a marvellous figure. In any case no one in our family has been overweight except your grandfather, God rest his soul, and that was only because he liked his beer and drop of whisky. Have just one more."

Lines of irritation showed on the girl's smooth forehead. "Please, Grannie. I've said I don't want one."

They were in Fowler's cafe in Hull, renowned for the excellence of its cakes and pastry. Ethel had clearly taken pains over her appearance. She was wearing an expensive green velvet dress and a hat to match. In contrast the girl was wearing one of her cheaper skirts and a faded jumper, apparel that had earned Ethel's disapproval from the onset, although she had taken care not to mention it.

Ethel put the plate of cakes back on the table. "Then have another cup of tea? That won't fatten you if you are so worried about your weight."

316

Elizabeth held out her cup. "I'm not worried about my weight. I just don't want to put on any more, that's all."

Ethel, who had left the girl when she was a pliant child, was clearly taken aback by this tall young woman with a mind of her own. She filled both tea cups, then forced a smile back on her face. "We've a lot of catching up to do, haven't we? Have you been working in the shop ever since you left school?"

The girl gave a moue of disdain. "Yes."

Encouraged by her expression, Ethel went on: "I never wanted your mother to take a shop. I knew how dreadful it would be for you all."

The girl frowned. "I don't see she'd much choice."

"No, I suppose she hadn't. Not after your father made up his mind. But it was a bad mistake."

"It wasn't Dad's fault either. He tried everywhere to get a job."

Ethel gave a patient smile. "Not everywhere, surely."

"Yes, he did. He lost a stone and a half in weight trying. It wasn't Dad who wanted a shop. He didn't want Mum to have to work so hard."

Ethel realised the conversation was not going the way she expected. "Perhaps I know things you don't know, dear. So let's drop the subject, shall we?"

"What things?" the girl demanded.

"Just things, dear, that's all. Things I'd rather not talk about."

Elizabeth was not letting her off so lightly. "I don't know what you mean but I do know none of this would have happened if you hadn't sold the business and gone to America."

Ethel was beginning to realise there was a great deal of slack in the rope to be taken up before she could draw the girl back to her. "I'd no option but to sell, dear. The men had gone on strike and your father was supporting them. Anyone would have done the same in my position."

"A lot of people didn't sell. Some people thought the strikers had a case." Before Ethel could reply, Elizabeth went on: "Anyway, you didn't need to go off to America."

Aware of the girl's resentment, Ethel proceeded carefully. "Dear, it wasn't I who wanted to go. It was Jack who'd been offered that mayoralty. How could I stand in his way? Yet it nearly broke my heart to be taken away from my little girl."

"You still went though, didn't you?"

"I've explained why I had to. One day when you're married you'll understand."

The girl opened her mouth to argue, then glanced at her watch instead. "I'll have to go soon," she muttered. "I'm going out tonight."

Relieved to change the subject, Ethel put on her most ingratiating smile. "Is it a boy friend?"

Elizabeth nodded.

"Can I ask his name, dear?"

"He's Rodney Stone. The son of Alderman Stone."

Ethel's eyes widened. "Really! Have you known him long, dear?"

"Just over six months."

"Your mother and father must be delighted."

Elizabeth shook her head sullenly. "They're not. They don't like him."

"Why on earth not?"

"I don't know. Perhaps they think he's too rich. They don't believe he can be serious."

"That'll be your father," Ethel declared. "He has these strange ideas about rich and influential people."

Elizabeth stared at her. "Why do you always blame Dad? Mother's worse. She's always nagging at me about coming home late."

Ethel was seeing her way at last. "Then why don't you do as I suggest and come back to live with me? I wouldn't mind your going out with Alderman Stone's son. In fact I'd approve of it."

The girl's expression told she was making a fresh appraisal of the offer. "You wouldn't nag at me if I came home late after going to a party?"

Ethel was willing to make any promises at that moment. "I don't see why I should, dear. Not if I knew you were with someone respectable."

Elizabeth gazed at her, then shook her head. "It wouldn't work. Jack never liked me living with you before. So why should it be any different now?"

Ethel's face set. "He'd have nothing to do with it. I'm in my own house now and I'll do as I like."

"But he's friendly with Mum and Dad. He gave them all that money before you went to America. So why would he let me come when he knows they wouldn't like it?"

Ethel's voice turned sharp. "What did you say about money?"

"He gave them two hundred pounds." The girl faltered as she saw the woman's expression. "Didn't you know?"

Ethel made a huge effort to control herself. "Never mind that. Jack's a sick man and I'm the mistress in my own house. If you come back to live with me, you won't have to work any longer in that wretched shop — in fact you won't have to work at all."

Elizabeth shifted uneasily in her chair. "It would be hard on Mum and Dad. They'd have to get someone to replace me and they really can't afford it."

Ethel felt she had the rope tight now. "You can't afford to lose Rodney either, can you? And aren't you more likely to hold his interest if you live with me than if he sees you as just a shop girl?"

"I don't know," the girl muttered. "Let me think about it." She glanced at her watch again. "Do you mind if I go now? Otherwise I'm going to be late. I'll give you a ring when I've made up my mind. Is that all right?"

Ethel watched the graceful girl hurry out of the cafe. She was hers again — she was certain of it. Then, as she remembered what the girl had told her about Watson, her self-satisfaction died. She was right about him. He had taken sides against her even before they left for America. Her voice was sharp again as she addressed the startled waitress. "Hurry up with that bill, will you, girl? I've other things to do but sit here waiting for you."

* * *

Watson shook his head. "I still think you're wrong. The girl belongs with her family. She always did."

Ethel gazed at him with dislike. "What do you know about it? I was taking care of her years before you and I ever met."

"That was only because of the war. Harry and Mary are her natural parents. You've no right to try to get her back."

Red spots were appearing in Ethel's cheeks. "Don't you tell me what's right or wrong. What about the money you gave to that worthless Harry? Why didn't you tell me about it?"

"I've told you why. Because you'd have bitched about it. You were always down on the poor kid and yet a nicer guy I've never met."

"And you're a good judge of people, are you?"

"I reckon I'm a damn sight better judge than you are, Ethel." At her sneer, Watson found something of his courage. "Anyway, whose goddam money was it?"

Ethel stiffened. "Don't you dare swear at me. I've told you about it before. I won't have those disgusting American expressions used in my house."

"*Your* house," Watson said bitterly.

"Yes, my house. And because it is, I can invite whom I like to stay here."

As always when he was quarrelling with Ethel, Watson could feel his heart hammering. He made one last effort. "Can't you see the girl isn't a child any more? She's a woman, and a precocious one at that. In no time at all she'll be running the show and where will we be then?"

"Don't be so ridiculous. If she's a little difficult at the moment, it's because she's been living in an environment she dislikes. Once she's here and doesn't have to be a shop girl any longer, she'll be her old self again."

With an effort Watson rose to his feet. "I'm going upstairs to lie down for a while." At the door he turned. "You're years out of date, Ethel. That girl doesn't care for you any longer. She lost all that when you left her to go to the States."

Ethel jumped to her feet. "And whose fault was that? Who wanted that mayoralty?"

"You did," Watson said.

"That's a lie. I went for your sake, fool that I was."

Watson could feel the tightness in his chest turning into a pain. "You're kidding yourself, Ethel. They've all got you weighed up and I reckon Elizabeth has too."

The red spots in Ethel's white cheeks were vivid now. "It isn't just your heart that's sick, it's your brain too. Go up to bed and leave me alone."

31

CHADWICK caught sight of them as he was driving along Alfred Gelder Street towards the Conservative Club Headquarters. Driving past them, he stopped the car and slid into the passenger seat. As they reached the car, he opened the door and stepped out. "Hello, Mary. It's been a long time."

She gave a violent start as she recognised him. His name fell involuntarily from her lips. "Michael!"

He was not displeased by her reaction. "I thought it was you. You haven't changed at all." He transferred his gaze to the tall, graceful girl alongside her. "Hello, Miss Miles. How nice to see you again. Are you both doing a spot of shopping?"

Elizabeth's eager smile betrayed her pleasure at the meeting. Before she could speak, however, Mary caught her arm and tried to pass him. "I'm sorry. We're in a hurry."

He smiled and checked her. "Surely you can spare a minute after all these years."

Mary turned to the girl. "Go to the shop and wait for me. Go on."

Elizabeth frowned. "What for?"

"Don't argue with me. Just do as I say."

For a moment it seemed the girl would disobey her. Then, giving Chadwick a shrug and an apologetic smile, she walked a few

323

paces away and halted.

Giving her an angry look, Mary turned back to Chadwick, her voice low and curt. "We've nothing to talk about, Michael. You ought to know that better than anybody."

He gave a sigh of regret. "Mary, that was thirteen odd years ago. There was a war on and none of us were ourselves. Surely you can forgive me after all this time."

She stared at him with scorn. "Forgive you? The great Sir Michael Chadwick! What do you care if I forgive you?"

He glanced at the watching girl, then moved closer to Mary. "But I do care. I'm not proud of what I did. That's why I keep asking Harry to work for me. Why don't you let him? I know your shop isn't doing well and I don't like to think of you having to work so hard."

Contempt marred her lovely face. "So you're thinking about us?"

"Of course I am. I want to make amends."

"For having Harry's best friend executed? For making Harry's life hell for nearly four years? For what you did to his pregnant wife? You think you can make amends for all that?"

He sighed. "At least I'd like the chance to try. Won't you give it to me?"

Her expression was as adamant as he had ever seen it. "No! Never! There's only one way you can make amends to me and that's to keep away from Harry. You nearly destroyed him once and I'm not going to let you do it again."

"But I don't want to destroy him. I want to give him a good job."

She tried to step round him. "Let me pass, please!"

Aware of the watching Elizabeth's curiosity, he disguised his words by smiling. "Don't you want to give Harry a better life? Have you the right to deny it to him?"

"A better life? Getting in your clutches again? I know what you want, Michael, and I'd die rather than give it to you."

He moved closer again. "What do I want?"

"You want to prove to yourself that I was wrong in what I said that night. That's behind it all, isn't it?"

Without his realising it, his handsome face darkened. "I don't know what you're talking about. How can my giving him a good job prove anything except that I respect him?"

"I don't know. Perhaps you don't know yourself yet. But don't tell me that you like Harry, Michael. You've hated him ever since you found out he was a better man than you. That was behind everything, wasn't it?"

Although he managed a smile, the look in his eyes betrayed him. "You're obsessed with the past, Mary. At least let us meet somewhere another day to talk about it."

Her low voice tightened. "I never want to see you or talk to you again, Michael. Let me pass or I'll call out that you're molesting me."

He hesitated, then, with an exclamation, stood back. Remembering the girl, he threw her a smile. "I'm sorry we haven't had an opportunity to talk, Miss Miles, but perhaps we'll get the chance another time."

Elizabeth was quick to take revenge on her mother. "I hope so, Sir Michael. Don't forget that dance you promised me."

Chadwick laughed. "I won't. I'm sure we'll have it soon."

Their conversation had made Mary stiffen. Hurrying to the girl's side, she caught her arm. "Come along. We've wasted too much time already."

With a last glance at Chadwick, who smiled again and raised his hat, the girl pulled away. Her voice struck at Mary. "How can you humiliate me like that? If it wouldn't have caused a scene, I'd never have obeyed you. Don't you realise we've been introduced?"

She knew the girl had a right to be angry. "I'm sorry, darling, but I don't want you to get involved with that man."

"What do you mean — involved? Why don't you tell the truth? You didn't want me to hear what the two of you were talking about, did you?"

"Don't be so stupid. I only wanted to keep you away from him. I've told you before — he's a very unpleasant man."

Elizabeth's lips curled. "Don't lie, Mother. There's a secret between you, isn't there? What happened when Dad was away?"

Frustration made Mary's words more severe than she intended. "I don't intend spending any more of the afternoon talking about Michael Chadwick. Do you want that new costume or don't you?"

The girl backed away, her eyes suddenly

326

brimming with tears. "No, I don't. I don't want any favours from you. I'm packing up my things and moving back to Grannie. At least she wouldn't humiliate me like that."

Mary's frustration gave way to dismay. "Darling, I didn't mean to offend you. I'm sorry, I really am, but I hadn't any choice."

She was talking to herself. Elizabeth had turned and was running away down the pavement.

★ ★ ★

Left alone, Chadwick dropped back into his car and watched the two women exchanging words on the pavement. As Elizabeth turned and ran away, he believed he could guess the reason and for a moment a malicious smile played around his mouth. Then his eyes returned to Mary, who, showing distress, began walking slowly away after the girl.

Sinking back, he watched her. Damn her for her long beautiful legs and white, erotic body! Damn her for being the one woman he had desired for over a decade. Damn her for turning his desire into violence and then into humiliation.

He lived it again as he sat there. The moonlit night, the hill overlooking the shining river, the distant cry of a night bird. Her face, lovely in the moonlight but resentful of his advances. Then the predatory swoop of a white owl on a helpless vole that in some elemental way had triggered off his own violence.

She had fought him tigerishly, only for her resistance to fuel his aggression. Violence was an ingredient Chadwick had always needed to perform the sex act and her fierce struggles had provided him with a rare excitement. He had ripped open her bodice and as her breasts had tumbled out, his lips had seized on them so avidly that she had screamed and screamed again.

She had so nearly been his. His hands had torn away most of her lower garments and exhaustion had weakened her resistance. But then his intense excitement had turned into his enemy. As she had struck at him again and her breasts had swung erotically against his face, his body had gone into spasm and pumped his seed into her clothing instead of into her body.

His humiliation had been complete when he had warned her to tell no one about the incident. Jumping out of his car outside No. fifty-seven, she had swung round and made an accusation he had never been able to forget. "This was because of Harry, wasn't it? Because you found out he's a better man than you. You could never defeat him in France, so you've tried to harm him this way. Through me, his wife. You, the great war hero!"

He had struck her across the face then but it had not stopped her taunt. "Dead or alive, Harry will always be a better man than you. And all your life you'll know it."

He could not count the times he had censured himself for allowing that taunt to prey on his mind. Who was she? A druggist's daughter. A shopkeeper's wife. A nobody. And he a squire, the chairman of a dozen enterprises, and in all probability soon a Member of Parliament. On any count his obsession was absurd.

And yet, absurd or not, it had festered within him all these years. He had lived with it until today when she had stood before him again in all her scornful beauty and he had known to his shame that he still desired her. As Chadwick watched her reach a street corner and disappear, he knew he could live with her taunt no longer. One way or another he must take his revenge on her and exorcise his humiliation forever.

32

ETHEL'S slightly protruding eyes were huge as she pressed the telephone receiver to her ear. "Yes, I can hear you, Sir Michael. No, I'm afraid she's out at the moment. But I'll get her to call you the moment she comes home. Unless you'd like to give me a message, that is."

Chadwick's pleasant voice sounded slightly amused. "Yes, as she's staying with you now and so in a sense you're her guardian, perhaps I ought to ask your permission first. I'm throwing a little party at The Grange next week and I'm wondering if she and her friend, Rodney Stone, would care to come. Would you mind?"

Ethel had never sounded more surprised or more unctuous. "Of course I don't mind, Sir Michael. And I'm sure Elizabeth will be delighted. I'll get her to phone you the moment she gets home."

"Good. She can get me at The Grange any time after five o'clock. I'll look forward to hearing from her."

"Thank you, Sir Michael. I'll tell her."

Ethel replaced the receiver and gazed at it in disbelief. A personal invitation from Sir Michael Chadwick. She had never dreamed her grandaughter was moving in such exalted circles. Perhaps the girl was going to make up for her disappointments over the lowly marriages her daughters had made. She glanced at a clock and waited in growing impatience for Elizabeth to return.

★ ★ ★

Elizabeth looked puzzled. "But why did he phone me instead of Rodney?"

Ethel had wondered the same thing. "I think you must have impressed him, dear. After all, you are the image of your mother and he was very fond of her once." Her tone changed. "Isn't it wonderful? I couldn't believe it when he said who he was."

The girl's eyes were shining with excitement. "Do you know what the party's for?"

"No, he didn't say. But you can ask him when you phone. You must be correctly dressed."

The girl's mood was oscillating between delight and curiosity. "It must have something to do with Mother. It must have."

Ethel was certain of it. "Perhaps it did originally draw his attention to you, dear. That's very possible."

Elizabeth's voice lowered. "But that could mean . . . " She hesitated and gazed at the hall door. "Where's Jack?"

"He's upstairs sleeping. You don't need to worry about him. What were you going to say?"

The girl lowered her eyes. "Mother and I do look alike, don't we?" She hesitated, then her cheeks coloured. "Do you think that is the reason?"

Ethel examined her and made her decision. "What if it were? Would you mind?"

Elizabeth hesitated. "He's rather old, isn't he?"

Ethel laughed. "Good heavens, girl, he's still in his thirties. And have you ever seen a more handsome man? I doubt if there is a woman in the county who doesn't hanker after him."

The girl nodded. "I noticed that when we were at the ball. He was surrounded by women."

"Then there you are. That's the man who has just invited you to a party. Aren't you a lucky girl?"

"Yes, I suppose I am." Then the girl's tone changed again. "But he has invited Rodney too. And his father's the local chairman of the Conservative Party. Couldn't that be behind it?"

Ethel had no intention of letting doubts of any kind spoil the moment. "He could hardly ask you on your own, could he? And why did he phone you and not Rodney? Stop looking gift horses in the mouth, dear. You're the luckiest girl in town to get a personal invitation from someone as influential as Sir Michael." She glanced round as the ornate clock on the mantelpiece began to chime. "It's five o'clock. So off you go to phone him. You don't want him to think you're not keen."

★ ★ ★

The large elegant hall was alive with animated conversation. Fashionably dressed women and

332

men in evening dress were standing in groups beneath its gleaming chandeliers while waiters, carrying trays of cocktails manoeuvred expertly between them. Elizabeth, looking lovely in an emerald chiffon dress bought especially for the occasion by Ethel, was standing with Rodney Stone near the foot of a wide curving staircase. Her eyes were fixed on two men and two women chatting beneath a large oil painting opposite them. As one of the women gave a laugh, Elizabeth turned to the man alongside her. "Who are those two women talking to Sir Michael and your father?"

Rodney, a tall, fresh-faced man of twenty-five with wavy brown hair, followed her gaze. "The older one is Sir Michael's mother, Lucinda. The younger one is Antonia McKenzie." Noticing the girl's curiosity, he went on: "Father says she's the woman Lucinda wants Sir Michael to marry. She's the heiress to a fortune."

Elizabeth's eyes returned to the younger woman. She was in her late twenties, a tall woman with strong but attractive features. Expensively and fashionably dressed, with her dark hair worn in the new 'page boy' bob, she was reflecting the new self-assertion of women by smoking a cigarette in a long holder.

Watching her, Elizabeth leaned towards Rodney. "They're not engaged, are they?"

Rodney, whose propensity to pass on titbits of scandal was not discouraged by his three glasses of champagne, gave his somewhat juvenile grin. "Not yet. But from what I've heard Father say to Mother, they ought to be."

She glanced at him. "You don't mean . . . ?"

Rodney grinned again. "That's what all the rumours say. Sir Michael's got a bit of a name where women are concerned. That's probably why his mother wants to get him married off soon."

With her interest quickened, she glanced back at the group again. Chadwick, elegant and handsome in his evening dress, was saying something that made all three of his companions laugh. Then, as if sensing the girl's eyes on him, he turned. A moment later Elizabeth felt her pulse quicken as he nodded to the others and started across the floor towards her.

"Hello, Rodney. Good evening, Miss Miles. How good of you to come tonight. And might I say how lovely you look?"

She felt her cheeks burn. "Good evening, Sir Michael. Happy birthday."

He laughed. "So they've told you, have they? Are you enjoying yourself?"

"Yes, thank you. Very much."

He took her arm and smiled at Rodney. "I want a little chat with this lovely girl. You can't expect to monopolise her all night, you know." As the younger man attempted a smile, Chadwick motioned at the grey-haired, distinguished-looking man talking to Lucinda Chadwick. "Go and talk to your father for a few minutes. I won't be long."

With Rodney obeying in the manner of a sixth-former being given an order by his teacher, Chadwick turned to Elizabeth. "I'm glad you

334

came tonight, Miss Miles. There is something I want to ask you."

She was feeling slightly breathless. "Won't you call me Elizabeth, please? Miss Miles sounds awfully formal."

He laughed. "All right. Elizabeth it is. Tell me, Elizabeth. Would you like to do some work for me in the near future?" At her look of surprise, he went on: "As you might have heard, I'm hoping to represent the Conservative Party in the forthcoming by-election. If I'm chosen, I shall need canvassers to go round the constituency asking people to vote for me. I'm a firm believer in using attractive canvassers and a lovely girl like you would be ideal for the job."

She felt her cheeks burn again. "But I wouldn't know what to say."

He gave his pleasant laugh. "With your looks, I doubt if you'd need to say anything, at least not where male voters are concerned. But seriously, you'd be fully briefed before you were sent out. What do you say?" She gave herself no time to think. "Yes. I'd like to do it. When would you want me?"

"Quite soon." His smile and nod were aimed at the elderly man talking to his mother. "Alderman Stone seems to think my chances of becoming the candidate are very good. But I'll let you know. In the meantime, however, you will have to be careful if you want the job."

"Why?" she asked. Then, with a sudden recklessness that made her blush again. "Is it because of Mother?"

His smile died. "Yes, I'm afraid she would object to your working for me. It's very sad but it's true."

She lowered her eyes. "I'm terribly sorry she was so rude the other day. I felt awful standing there."

He shrugged. "It wasn't your fault. Don't think any more about it."

She hesitated, then her curiosity overcame her. "Why does she act that way towards you, Sir Michael? My grandmother says it's because you were fond of her once. Is that why?"

In her embarrassment she did not notice how the muscles around his eyes tightened and then relaxed. "Yes, I think so. She feels it was wrong of me to admire her when your father was still alive. What she forgets is that we all thought he was dead."

She looked puzzled. "I don't see why she should feel that way because you liked her. I don't dislike men who like me."

He laughed. "Then you must like many men. But there's another reason you'd better say nothing to your parents about my request. Your father doesn't share my political convictions so I'm sure he wouldn't like you canvassing for the Tory Party."

She had not thought of that. "I know what you mean but Dad's very fair. He always says every man should have the right to vote where he pleases."

"I'm sure he does but all the same I don't think he'd like you working for the Conservatives. However, if you don't say

336

anything, he's not likely to find out. I'll be standing for West Hull and he's in the East Hull constituency. And he doesn't do any deliveries out our way, does he?"

Elizabeth shook her head. "Not as far as I know. Although I did notice his van coming out of St George's Road the other day. I waved to him but he didn't see me."

Chadwick's slight start went unnoticed by the girl. "Did you say St George's Road?"

"Yes. I didn't think we had any customers down there. But perhaps he was calling on a supplier or a friend."

Disguising his interest, Chadwick stopped a waiter, took a glass of champagne from his tray, and with a smile handed it to the girl. "Then it's all settled. I'll contact you at your grandmother's when I begin taking on extra staff. Now you'd better get back to Rodney or he'll feel I'm doing the very thing I complained about and monopolising you."

★ ★ ★

Chadwick made a private phone call from his study the following morning. "Moss? This is Sir Michael. I want you to keep an eye on Harry Miles again. I've reason to believe he's visiting a woman called Eleanor Turnor at 126 St George's Road. I want to know the dates he sees her and the time he spends there. Don't report back here. Send me the details to my office in town."

33

WATSON reached out to his bedside lamp, switched it on, and glanced at his watch. Alongside him Ethel stirred, then opened her eyes. "What are you doing?"

Watson turned to her. "Do you know it's four o'clock and Elizabeth isn't home yet."

Ethel, wearing a frilled, high-necked nightdress, stared at him, then sank back. "Go to sleep."

"Ethel, this is the second time this week. And she's still only a kid. What would Harry and Mary say if they knew?"

At that Ethel lifted her head. "What does that mean? That you're threatening to tell them?"

Watson, suspecting another quarrel was coming, felt his heart thudding again. "There won't be the need if you talk to her. It's not right for her to be out all hours like this. She ought to get a job like other folks so she's more tired at nights."

Ethel, who had said nothing to him about Chadwick's offer of work, gave her sniff of defiance. "She'll get a job when she feels like it and not before. And don't think about telling tales to Harry or Mary." Before he could reply, she went on contemptuously: "Not that it would make any difference. She'd never go back to that life again."

In spite of his amiable nature, there was a certain doggedness in Watson that became evident when his sense of injustice was aroused. "Don't you ever think about the kid herself? Those folks she mixes with are all wrong for her."

At that Ethel sat erect. "What's wrong with her friends? Go on. Tell me."

In spite of his thudding heart, Watson felt a surge of rebellion. "They're not her kind. They just use good-looking girls like her. I've seen the same thing in the States."

Ethel gave a laugh of contempt. "In the States? There aren't people like Rodney Stone and his kind in the States. So talk about things you know or keep quiet."

Watson was wondering how he had ever found this woman well-mannered and well-bred. "I reckon I know what goes on in the States better than you, Ethel. And they're all of a kind. Money makes 'em think they're something special and have the right to use people."

Ethel's face was a mask of dislike. "This is Harry talking, isn't it?"

"Harry's a good guy, Ethel. I've never understood why you don't like him."

She gave an exclamation of disgust. "Harry's a nobody. And a Socialist in the bargain. Did you know that? You Americans are supposed to hate Socialists, aren't you?"

"Are we? I know this, Ethel. I've never known a nicer guy or one I'd trust more."

Her lips curled into a sneer. "You know why that is, don't you? You're two of a kind. I learned that when I was over there. What was your father? A factory hand?"

339

Watson felt his heart fibrillate and then begin racing. "Jesus, you're a snob, Ethel. The worst I've met."

Ethel leapt out of bed and grabbed her dressing gown. "In that case you won't want to share the bed with me, will you? Tomorrow you'll move into the spare room. I'm not sharing a bedroom any longer with a man who insults me."

At the door she paused and flung her final barb. "I'm not going to miss much, am I? You never were half the man William was and now with your bad heart you're not a man at all. My God, I wish I'd never met you."

With that the door slammed and Watson was left with his heart whose pounding seemed to fill the room.

★ ★ ★

Elizabeth shrugged off her wet coat, hung it on the hall-stand, and gave a shudder of distaste. "What a foul day."

Ethel, who had hurried to the front door to let her in, eyed her solicitously. "Has the rain gone through your coat, dear? If so, you must go upstairs and change."

Ignoring her, the girl entered the living room and sank down on the sofa. Misreading her mood, Ethel followed her. "I'm sorry, dear. Jack should have fetched you but he said he had an appointment in town. It's always the same these days. He's never here when I want him."

340

Elizabeth frowned and shook her head. "It's not that. We can't expect him to be at our beck and call all the time."

Ethel dropped on to the sofa alongside her. "Then what is it, dear?"

The girl's frown deepened. "I heard Mrs Fennell and her niece talking yesterday . . . "

"Her niece?" Ethel interrupted.

"Yes, didn't you know? Some time ago she said she'd have to have more help and demanded that her niece, Jenny, worked with her. That's why Mum and Dad can't afford to employ anyone to take my place."

With no wish to hear about Harry and Mary's problems, Ethel cut short the girl's explanation. "You were saying you heard Mrs Fennell talking to her niece."

"Yes. I'd gone round to the back of the bakery to fetch some firewood so they didn't know they could be overheard. Mrs Fennell was complaining she was tired of working for other people and saying how much she'd like a shop of her own. Jenny said it would be nice and couldn't they do it?"

Ethel was showing interest now. "What did Mrs Fennell say to that?"

"She said she didn't have enough money. But if ever she had, she'd leave and open a shop tomorrow." The girl gazed at Ethel. "Don't you think that's disloyal? Mum and Dad have done everything they can for her and they let her have free cakes and pastry at the weekends."

Ethel shrugged. "She probably feels it's because of her the shop has paid its way.

Did you tell your mother and father what she'd said?"

"No, I don't want to worry them. After all, she hasn't got the money and might never get it. But it would be awful if it happened, wouldn't it? Mum and Dad would never be able to keep going without her."

Ethel's voice was ripe with satisfaction. "Your father should never have taken on a shop. I warned them both but they wouldn't listen."

Not for the first time the girl showed resentment. "You keep on saying that but what choice did you give them? You must have known Dad wouldn't be able to get a job."

For a moment Ethel forgot her carefully nurtured image of gentility. "You know nothing about it, girl. So don't put the blame on me."

Elizabeth gave her a sullen look. "I don't see who else you can put it on. If you hadn't acted the way you did, we'd all be far better off today."

Ethel kept her temper only with an effort. "I'm not going to argue with you while you're in this mood. Do you want your supper now or later?"

The girl rose to her feet. "I'll have it later. I want a bath first."

"That's a good idea. You'll feel better after a nice warm bath. You're not going out with Rodney tonight, are you?"

"No. He's doing some work for his father."

"Good. Then perhaps we can listen to the wireless together. There's quite a good programme on."

Without replying, Elizabeth left the room. As the door closed, Ethel's motherly expression faded. She had been wrong in thinking the war had been won when the girl had returned to her. It was now becoming clear there were still some significant battles to be fought.

★ ★ ★

The following week Ethel had a telephone call from Harry. "Mother! I have to talk to you. I'll come round tonight."

The tone of his voice made Ethel bristle immediately. "What do you want?"

"It's about Elizabeth. Tell her I want to see her as well."

"I can't tell her. She's gone out for the day with friends. And she won't be home until late."

"Where has she gone?"

"I don't know. I don't keep a track of all her movements."

"Then it's about time you did. But we'll talk about that tonight. I'll be round after the shop closes. About 8.30."

Incensed by his tone, Ethel bridled again. "I don't know I'll be in. You should have given me earlier notice."

"You'd better be in, Mother. Or I'll stay on the doorstep until you get back and make a scene you won't forget. Somehow I don't think you'd want that."

★ ★ ★

343

Harry's van arrived outside No. fifty-seven a few minutes before eight-thirty. Ethel, who had been watching out for it through the lace-curtained windows, turned to Watson whom she had virtually ordered to be present. "I'm not running after him. You let him in."

Looking concerned, Watson went to the front door. "Hello, Harry. What's the problem?"

Harry, who was still in his working clothes, ignored his question. "Is she in?"

"Ethel? Yes, she's inside. But what is it, kid? What's happened?"

Ignoring him, Harry pushed into the living room where Ethel was sitting stiffly in an armchair. He glanced around. "Isn't Elizabeth back yet?"

Ethel was determined not to give him an inch. "What's happened to your manners? Don't you say good evening when you burst into my house?"

Harry ignored her. "I asked if Elizabeth was back?"

"And I told you this morning she had gone out for the day and wouldn't be home until late."

"By late you mean tomorrow morning, don't you?"

Ethel gave a start, then her voice turned icy. "I don't know what you're talking about."

From his expression it was clear Harry was keeping himself under control only with an effort. "Oh yes, you do. A customer of mine saw her and Rodney Stone driving past at five o'clock this morning. I don't believe she's gone

344

out again. I don't believe she came home this morning."

Ethel's expression gave her away. "Stop talking nonsense."

Harry moved forward and in spite of herself Ethel drew back in her chair. "I understand now how you got her back. You bribed her by telling her she could do as she pleased, didn't you?"

Ethel gave a contemptuous laugh. "Don't talk such nonsense. She's a woman now. None of us can stop her doing what she wants to do."

"What sort of a grandmother are you? Would you let her stay out all night if her friends weren't Stone and his set?"

Ethel's lips curled. "It's precisely because she's with those people that I know she's safe."

"Are you really such a fool and a snob as to believe that?"

Ethel went pale to the lips. She swung round on the embarrassed Watson. "What are you doing, just standing there? How long are you going to let him insult your wife like this?"

Harry turned his attack on Watson before the American could respond. "Why didn't you tell me what was going on? I thought we were friends."

The unfortunate Watson reacted with distress. "I tried to drop a hint or two, Harry, but I knew it would only worry you. And Ethel's right. There's nothing you can do to stop her."

"Isn't there? You both forget she's not twenty-one yet. I could go to the police and have her stopped."

Ethel gave a gasp. "You wouldn't do that?"

"Wouldn't I, by God? If you don't stop her, I will."

Ethel recovered quickly. "You daren't go to the police and I'll tell you why. If you did, you and Mary would never see her again. I'd see to that, make no mistake."

"You know what you are?" Harry said. "You're a bitch! A wicked, scheming old bitch!" He turned again to Watson. "I'm sorry, Jack, but it's true. We ought to have warned you beforehand what you were getting."

Ethel gave a cry of outrage and jumped up from her chair. "How dare you, you guttersnipe? How dare you?" She swung round on the dismayed Watson again. "Don't just stand there, you useless fool. Do something!"

When Watson only shook his head, she swung back on Harry, her voice rising into a scream. "All right, he's a coward. But don't think your marriage is so wonderful. You've never been told what happened when you were a prisoner, have you?"

Harry, making for the door, did not look back. "Don't bother, Ethel. I know all about Chadwick and Mary. She's told me everything."

"Oh no, she hasn't. She's been too scared. She's never told you Sir Michael had her clothes off on Swanland Hill, has she?"

As Harry stopped dead, Ethel gave a laugh of triumph. "I thought not. And that wasn't all. She came back with her face bleeding where he'd struck her and said he'd tried to rape her. She said he'd only tried but then she would, wouldn't she?"

Harry's voice was hoarse. "You're lying. You're lying as you always lie!"

In her triumph Ethel forgot everything in her desire to hurt him more. "You've thought you've known everything about her, haven't you? It's you who's the fool, not me. Ask her if you don't believe me. And don't think that's everything. Now Sir Michael fancies your daughter too and has got her promise to work for him. So it isn't just Rodney Stone and his friends you have to worry about. It's Sir Michael again."

The shocked Watson made his protest. "Ethel! For God's sakes, what's come over you?"

She ignored him as she taunted Harry. "If you don't believe me, ask Mary and Elizabeth. Better still, ask Sir Michael."

Harry turned for the door. Seeing his expression, Watson caught his arm. "Don't play her game, Harry, for Christ's sake. Chadwick's a powerful man. He could ruin you."

Harry shook him off and ran down the path to his van. Clinging to the door jamb, Watson watched the van rage off. Then, with one hand trying to slow down his thudding heart, he returned to the living room where Ethel was waiting to attack him. "You call yourself a man? William would have killed anyone who called me names like that."

Fighting for breath, Watson had the feeling it was going to be his last quarrel. "You asked for every one of them, Ethel. It was a filthy thing to tell him about Chadwick."

She laughed exultantly. "Why? He wanted to know everything so I told him everything."

347

"You told him because you know Chadwick can do him harm. In my book you can't get much dirtier than that."

"In your book! What sort of a book is that?"

The room was beginning to swing around Watson. "He was right, Ethel. You are a bitch. In fact you're a sonofabitch. I wish I'd never laid my goddamed eyes on you."

Her eyes turned as wild as a hare's at his words. "You unspeakable creature! You're dirt, that's what you are. Get out of my house. I never want to see you again."

Watson was in no state to go anywhere. The pain in his chest was crushing the life out of him. He sank to the carpet, tried to speak, but instead only a rattle sounded in his throat. With her hysteria ebbing, Ethel moved cautiously towards him. "Jack! What is it?"

The rattle grew louder, then died away. Frowning, Ethel bent over him. "Jack, what's happened? Can you hear me?"

Watson could hear nothing as his sightless eyes stared up at her.

34

HARRY was to remember little of the hour that followed. It was a jerky sequence of sights and sounds, like a motion picture from which huge extracts had been edited out. He was never sure how he found Chadwick. Either he had read that the local Conservative Party was meeting at its headquarters that evening or he drove there because it was the first venue that came into his mind.

Whatever the reason it was the right choice because as he drove into the club car park he saw Chadwick's dark blue Rolls Royce standing there with two men, one in uniform, talking alongside it.

The film jerked again, losing the link of time and motion. He found himself running across the car park as Chadwick and a party of well-dressed men began filing out of the club. He did not recognise the voice that gave an enraged shout. "Chadwick! I want to talk to you. Come here!"

Another jerk of time and space and Chadwick was standing before him. His familiar face and smile seemed to grow until it filled Harry's entire vision. He heard the stranger's voice shout "You bastard," and then Chadwick's handsome features seemed to crumple and blood to spurt across them.

The film ran amok then. Land and sky reeled as he was struck violently from behind and shouting voices rang in his ears. Pain made him retch as boots sank into his body and a red mist with bursting stars swam across his eyes. His last vision was Chadwick's bleeding face close to his own and then he sank into oblivion.

★ ★ ★

He awoke with no memory. He tried to lift his head and winced at the pain that stabbed through it. Lying still, he tried to identify his surroundings. He was lying on a bed but appeared to be fully dressed. Above him was a high ornate ceiling and beside him a small table on which an electric lamp was burning. As he tried again to lift his head, a voice sounded from across the room. "How do you feel, Mr Miles?"

He tried to focus on the man who was approaching his bedside. "Where am I? What happened?"

"You're in my home, Mr Miles. My name is Jonathan Stone. As for what happened, you made a fool of yourself tonight. Don't you remember anything?"

He could make out the man now. He was in his sixties, distinguished in appearance with a mass of white hair and an iron-grey beard. "No," he said. "Nothing at all."

Jonathan Stone sat on the side of the bed. "That will be the effect of concussion. So I'll

350

tell you. Just over an hour ago you drove a van into the car park of the Conservative Club and without apparent provocation struck Sir Michael Chadwick in the face. It so happened he had two members of his staff with him and I'm afraid they defended him a little too robustly. In other words they beat you up. Do you remember now?"

Disjointed memories made Harry frown. Reaching up, he discovered his head was bandaged. "Who treated me?"

"I called in a doctor when I got you home. He said you didn't have a fracture but might have concussion. He wanted to put you into hospital but I thought it better to wait and ask your permission."

With an effort, Harry sat up. "You did right. What's the time?"

"Nearly eleven o'clock."

Harry tried to stand, flinching at the pain in his ribs. "I must get home."

Stone drew him back. "I'll get a taxi to take you back and see your van's brought back to you in the morning. But first there is something I must know. Why did you behave that way tonight and strike Sir Michael?"

Harry gazed at the man, then rose unsteadily to his feet. "I'd like that taxi now, please. I'll pay for it."

Stone checked him again. "Listen, Miles. I'm the chairman of the local Conservative Party and in a day or two we'll be choosing our representative for the forthcoming by-election. As things stand at the moment the vote will

351

almost certainly go to Sir Michael, partly because I'm sponsoring him. Are you following me?"

Harry was trying to keep the room from spinning around. "Yes, I think so. But I've nothing to say."

Seeing the room door was ajar, Stone walked over and closed it before facing Harry again. "Nothing you tell me will go beyond this room. I swear it. But I can't have my name sponsoring a candidate unless I'm certain he is free of scandal. That is why I'm asking for your confidence."

The pain in his ribs made Harry sink back on the bed. "Are you saying you'd believe me if I told you the truth? Against Michael Chadwick?"

Stone nodded. "I saw your face tonight. Unless a man has lost his mind, and you clearly haven't lost yours, he doesn't show that kind of outrage without good reason. You needn't fear I shall penalise Sir Michael unfairly if that's holding you back. But I must know the truth."

Harry's laugh sent another stab of pain through his body. "You think that's my reason? That I'm covering for Chadwick?"

Stone's eyes probed his pale, bruised face. "I understand. Someone else is involved. A lady perhaps?"

When Harry did not answer, Stone sank on the bed alongside him. "I must know everything, Miles. And once again I give you my word that anything you tell me will be in the strictest confidence."

Ethel stood erect while the half a dozen mourners present at the funeral murmured words of sympathy and then drifted away. Watching her from the opposite side of the grave, Mary touched Harry's arm when Ethel turned and followed them. "I must have a word with her, darling. You don't have to come."

From the way he stirred himself, she knew the funeral had affected him. "I don't feel it's right to bury him here in England. Surely it should have been in America where all his relations and friends are."

She sighed. "Perhaps you're right. I don't know." She glanced again at the retreating figure of her mother. "She's treated him badly since they came back, I know, but he was her husband and she must be feeling something, if only remorse. I won't be long."

He hesitated only a moment before following her. She was not surprised: his capacity to forgive had always seemed boundless to her until his assault on Chadwick. Yet she understood him now as never before. He could only be violent when those he was responsible for, or those he loved, were threatened or violated. Attacks on his own person had no effect on him. The malice and spite that disfigured others seemed absent in him.

They reached Ethel as the driver of the undertaker's car was about to open the door. Noticing Ethel's expression on seeing Harry, Mary found her words of sympathy inhibited.

353

"We've come to offer our condolences, Mother. We both liked Jack and we're going to miss him very much."

Behind her veil, Ethel's face had set as hard as granite. "Are you speaking for yourself or for both of you?"

Before Mary could reply, Harry broke in quietly. "We're both very, very sorry, Mother. We want you to know that."

The venom in Ethel's voice made Mary stiffen. "*You* are sorry? You, who killed him? How dare you parade your hypocrisy at his funeral?"

Mary's cheeks turned pale. "Mother, what are you talking about? Jack had a bad heart. That's what killed him."

Ethel gave a harsh laugh. "It killed him all right, but why? That husband of yours came storming round like a madman, accusing me of neglecting Elizabeth in a hundred ways. So what could Jack do but defend me against his lies. That's what killed him, my girl, no matter what else he has told you. Your dear, sweet husband."

Seeing the expression on Harry's bruised face, Mary forgot where she was. "You try to poison everything, don't you, Mother? I know what happened. Harry's told me the whole story."

"Harry has told you nothing. Jack died defending me against your husband's accusations. Harry killed him just as he killed your father during the war. And you wonder why I hate him."

Mary stared at her. "Killed Dad? What are you talking about?"

Ethel sneered. "What is it, girl? Can't you face the truth? If Harry hadn't made you buy that house after your marriage, William would be alive today. Can you deny it?"

"But that wasn't Harry's fault. I wanted our own home just as much as he did. It was the Zeppelin raid and Dad's health that killed him, just as bad health has killed Jack."

"That's right. Blame everyone but your dear sweet Harry. But not me." The glance Ethel threw at the motionless Harry was like a hurled dagger. "I shall pay you back one day. Make no mistake. I will."

Mary's voice dropped into a shocked whisper. "You must see a doctor, Mother. Please ring Dr Armstrong when you get home."

Before Ethel could reply, Harry caught Mary's arm. "Leave her," he muttered. "It was a mistake to talk to her in the first place."

Ethel's cry followed them as they hurried away, bringing curious stares from visitors laying flowers on graves. "That's right. Run away. But don't think I'll ever forget or forgive what you've done to me."

★ ★ ★

Chadwick's secretary, dark and petite, held out an envelope, her eyes straying for a moment to the man's bruised face. "It's addressed to you, Sir Michael. I think it was delivered from the Conservative Party Headquarters."

355

Chadwick took the envelope and dismissed the woman with a nod. For a moment he sat gazing at it. Then, clearly with an effort, he tore it open and extracted the letter.

It was only short and he read it quickly. Although his features did not change expression, his cheeks paled and his hand clenched and crushed the letter into a ball.

He sat for a full minute before pulling himself together and picking up the telephone. "Moss? Have you any news for me yet?"

His expression changed at the answer he received. "Are you certain of this? You are? Then you know what to do. Get on with it."

He replaced the receiver and lit a cigarette. At least the revelation could not have come at a better time, he thought. It would pay them back to some extent for what Miles had done to him. At the same time it was not enough to pay back Mary for her taunts. That needed a different kind of revenge. He thought about that until the cigarette burned away and he had to crush it into his ashtray. Making his decision, he clicked down a switch on his intercom. "Get me Mrs Hardcastle on the phone, will you, Mavis? As soon as you can."

35

CHADWICK glanced at his waiting secretary. "You can send her in now, Mavis."

The girl nodded and left the office, to return a moment later with Elizabeth. "Miss Miles, Sir Michael."

Chadwick dismissed her with a nod, then rose and walked round his desk. "Hello, Elizabeth. It's kind of you to come today. I wasn't sure that you would."

The girl's effort to hide her embarrassment was not successful. "Do you mean because of what happened between you and Dad?"

Although his Party and friends had managed to keep the fight out of the newspapers, Chadwick had felt certain that either the girl's parents or her grandmother would have told her about it. Not knowing what version she had received, he had decided to give her his own. The fact she had accepted his invitation suggested the chances were good she would believe it.

Her appearance also lent weight to his belief. She was wearing a fashionable green coat that clung to and enhanced the curves of her tall shapely figure. With a black choker collar accentuating her smooth neck and her blonde hair massed on top of her head, she looked a picture of elegance and fashion. Only her breathless voice betrayed her youth and embarrassment.

He gave her a rueful smile. "So you've heard the gory details? Who told you? Your parents or your grandmother?"

"Both," she confessed. "My mother and grandmother."

"Not your father?"

"No. Dad hasn't said a word."

"If you've heard it, I'm surprised you accepted my invitation."

She frowned. "I don't see why. Dad's always told me one should hear both sides of a case."

Hiding his expression, Chadwick walked behind her. "Let me take your coat."

She allowed him to remove it. The dress she was wearing beneath it was short enough to reveal her long, shapely legs and tailored to accentuate the high perfection of her breasts.

He hid a smile as he hung the coat on a hanger. By itself the dress would have told him she had not been turned against him by the scandal. Perhaps the reverse, he thought. He indicated a high-backed chair at the near side of his ornate desk. "Sit down there and make yourself comfortable."

She obeyed, crossing one silken-clad leg over the other as he returned to his own seat. Watching her as he sank back, Chadwick thought it could be Mary sitting there and felt his mouth turn dry. "Would you care for a cigarette?"

She hesitated, then nodded. "Yes, please."

He offered her his gold cigarette case and

lighter, noticing with amusement the unpractised way she handled the cigarette. He lit one himself before continuing. "So you've decided to hear my side of the story before putting me beyond the pale. What exactly have you been told?"

Her smooth cheeks turned pink as she hesitated. "My mother said you asked her to go out to dinner. She didn't want to but couldn't refuse because you were trying to find out if Dad was dead or a prisoner of war. On the way back you stopped your car and . . . " She paused, unable to continue for embarrassment.

"She said I tried to rape her," Chadwick said, finding odd pleasure in the remark. "Isn't that it?"

Unable to meet his eyes, the crimson-faced girl nodded. "Yes."

"What did your grandmother say?"

"She thinks Mother made too much of it. She said you were a soldier going back to France; that you believed Dad was dead; and that you were in love with Mother. So what you did was only what any other young man might have done in the circumstances."

Chadwick gave his most winsome smile. "And which version do you believe? That I was villainous or just virile?"

The blushing girl met his eyes again. "I believe Grandmother. I think Mother exaggerated it because she was pregnant and also didn't believe Dad was dead."

In his feigned contrition, Chadwick had never acted better. "I won't deny that I behaved badly, Elizabeth. I ought to have been the complete gentleman and taken your mother straight home. But I'd been in action for years and was going back to France the following day. And your mother was such a beautiful woman." As he spoke his eyes moved over the listening girl with an admiring expression she could not miss. "She looked just like you in those days, enough to intoxicate any man. So I'm afraid I did go over the top a little. But of course I would never have harmed her. I can't think why she believed that."

The girl was blushing again at his compliment. "She's very devoted to Dad. I'm sure that's why she took it that way."

Chadwick gave a laugh of pleasure. "Is that what you believe? Really?"

His seeming relief made Elizabeth smile. "Yes. I could never believe it of you."

The look on his handsome face made her lower her eyes again. "What a sweet girl you are," he said. "I'm touched, I really am. What a pity I shan't be needing canvassers now."

At that the girl's face clouded. "Yes, I saw in the paper that you've decided not to stand for Parliament. Is that because of what happened?"

Chadwick shrugged ruefully. "Yes, I'm afraid it is. I couldn't embarrass the Party over the silly affair and so I resigned."

The girl bit her lip. "It's awful you should lose your chance because of Dad. You must hate him."

"Hate your father? Never. He was only doing what he thought was right and protecting your mother."

360

"Just the same it must be terribly disappointing for you. Will you bring charges against Dad?"

He shook his head. "No. We served in the war together. I couldn't possibly get him into trouble with the police."

The look he received contained more than gratitude. "It'll be a great relief for Mother. She was terribly frightened when she heard what had happened." She paused, looking puzzled. "It was so unlike Dad. He's normally such a kind and forgiving person."

"Never mind," he said. "It's over now. How is your grandmother taking her husband's death?"

His sympathetic air was winning her confidence. "I don't think she's missing him that much."

"Might I ask why?"

"I don't think she was ever in love with him. They were always quarrelling before he died." She gave an embarrassed laugh. "I think it's his will she's more upset about."

He laughed. "Why is that?"

She hesitated, then in a burst of confidence went on: "She found out yesterday that he's left almost everything he had to his relations in America. She's blaming Dad for that."

She missed the slight start he gave. "Why your father?"

"Dad and Jack were good friends. She thinks Dad persuaded him to leave her out of his will. It's ridiculous, of course, but she blames Dad for everything."

He gave another rueful smile. "She's never liked your father, has she?"

"No. Apparently she never wanted Mother to

361

marry him in the first place. She's a terrible snob. I've always known that." The girl gave a moue of impatience. "I'm fed up with everything. Mother and Dad have learned I've been staying out later at nights than they like, so there's more trouble over that. I want to get a job and my own place so I can do as I like. After all, I am eighteen so I ought to be able to come and go as I please."

It was all going better than Chadwick had dared to hope. He was finding his eyes drawn to her legs. For a moment he imagined resting a hand on one silken knee and sliding it up her thigh. As he glanced up, he caught her expression and wondered if she was reading his thoughts. He laughed. "So you still want a job, do you? How would you like a job in one of my companies?"

Her expressive face lit up. "Do you mean it?"

"Yes, of course I do. And if you're that keen to leave home, I might even be able to find a flat for you."

She gave a gasp of disbelief. "A flat?"

"Yes. I think it can be arranged."

The girl's eyes, huge with excitement, were moving over his handsome features and lean body. Chadwick had seen infatuation in too many women not to recognise it now. His pleasant laugh rang out again. "Mind you, I think the job and the flat will have to be out of town, don't you? Or we might have more trouble with your parents."

She showed immediate concern. "Could they make me return home?"

"Strictly speaking, they could until you're twenty-one. But I doubt if any court would uphold it. Not if you showed you were happy and capable of looking after yourself."

She laughed eagerly. "Then will you do it for me? I'll work hard, I promise."

He smiled. "You want it badly, don't you?"

She leaned forward to stub out her cigarette in an ashtray on his desk. When she sat back he saw her dress had slipped another two inches up her thigh. It was going to be easier than he had believed. And pleasurable too. It would be like making love to her mother. Enjoying her and punishing her at the same time.

His mouth turned dry at the thought. "Can you do shorthand and typing?"

She hesitated. "I did them at school, yes."

He had not missed her partial evasion. "I'm sure you'll soon pick them up again. I'll pay you two pounds five shillings a week to begin with and we'll talk about an increase later on. Is that all right?"

"It's wonderful. But where will I work and what about the flat?"

"I'm thinking of giving you a job in my Beverley office. There seem to be quite a few empty apartments in the town. That should be far enough away from your parents and grandmother, shouldn't it?"

She gave a sudden shudder. "Wouldn't it be awful if they could make me go back?"

"I don't think it's likely, not if you behave sensibly. Then Beverley is all right for you?"

"Yes. I don't mind where I go as long as I get away from here."

"Good. Then I'll tell my agent to begin looking for accommodation. When would you like to start?"

Her lovely face was glowing with excitement again. "As soon as I can. Monday if possible."

He laughed and rose from his chair. "It'll take a little longer than that. Certainly the apartment will. Ring me here in a fortnight's time and I'll let you know how things are going. Now let me get you your coat."

At the door, as he helped her put on her coat, he was certain she leaned against him for a moment. In the doorway, she glanced back. "Thank you, Sir Michael. I'm ever so grateful. I really am."

Smiling, he closed the door and walked over to his cocktail cabinet. It was proceeding even better than he had hoped. Even his talk of rape had excited the girl instead of disturbing her. She would not rest now until she had a place where she could entertain him.

At the same time he would have to be careful, he reminded himself. His mother still controlled a large portion of the estate and although she had been tolerant of his behaviour in the past, with his fortieth birthday not far away she was pressing for his engagement to Antonia McKenzie. If Lucinda Chadwick discovered he was involved with a shopkeeper's daughter, many of his plans would come to an ignominious end.

But he could deny his obsession no longer.

He had carried the scar of Mary Miles' taunt all these years and now Miles himself had lost him his seat in Parliament. For his peace of mind he must have his revenge, and fate seemed to be offering it to him in the most rewarding way possible. Savouring the thought, he poured himself a large glass of whisky and drank it with relish.

36

HARRY glanced into the post box on the shop door and saw three letters lying there. Two envelopes were addressed in typescript and he guessed they were bills. The third envelope was printed in ink and he opened it first. It contained a small card with a message written on it in capitals. Looking puzzled he stared at it, then thrust it into his pocket. The bills from the other envelopes he took back into the kitchen for Mary's attention when she came downstairs.

★ ★ ★

The following Thursday evening Harry visited Lena. Seeing him standing at the front door, she impulsively threw her arms around his shoulders and kissed him. "Harry! What a lovely surprise. Come on in."

He halted in the doorway. "Surprise?"

She drew him inside and closed the door. "Why, yes. It's always a surprise when you come round. A nice surprise, of course." Her smile faded as she noticed his expression. "What is it? Why are you looking like that?"

He pulled the small card from his pocket. "Didn't you send me this?"

She took the card from him. The message printed across it read: PLEASE COME NEXT

THURSDAY EVENING AT SEVEN. IT'S VERY IMPORTANT. LENA.

She gave an exclamation. "I never wrote this."

"But it's one of your florist's cards. The name's embossed on it."

"I know that but I never sent it." She looked alarmed. "What does it mean?"

"I've no idea. Could it be someone you know playing a joke?"

"I don't see how it could be. I never talk about you to people in case they jump to conclusions."

"Someone knows about me," he said dryly. "They've even got my address."

For a moment she looked hurt. "They haven't got it from me, Harry. I swear it."

He frowned, then shook his head. "Then I'm baffled. Who the hell knows about us and would send a message like that? What would be the purpose?"

Woman-like, her imagination was ahead of his. "I'm frightened, Harry. Perhaps you'd better not stay in case someone has set this up."

Before he could reply, she ran to the front door and stared out. The light was still good enough for her to see down the street but there was nothing suspicious in the few couples she could see walking along the pavements. Looking puzzled, she closed the door again and returned to Harry who stared at her. "What were you looking for?"

"I thought someone might be watching the house."

367

"You mean you think someone might be spying on us?"

"Yes. What other explanation could there be?"

"It's a hoax," he said. "Someone's playing a game on you. They'll probably tell you tomorrow."

She was not convinced. "Any customer who came to the shop could have got that card, Harry. I don't think you should stay this evening. Not after this."

"Why? Do you think someone might come round?"

"I don't see any other purpose in sending that card, do you?"

He gazed at her for a moment, then sank into an armchair. "If someone's coming, let them come. We've nothing to hide."

She hesitated. "No. But did you tell Mary you were coming round tonight?"

For a moment his voice turned harsh. "For God's sake, you're not suggesting she's set this up, are you?"

She sank down in the armchair opposite. "No, of course not. I'm sorry, Harry. But it's upset me. I don't know what to think."

His anger died. "I don't either. But I'm not going unless you insist I do. If it's some kind of a trick and we give in to it, we'll never feel safe to meet again."

She winced. "I suppose not. But are you sure? I've nothing to lose, but you have. You mustn't risk anything for me."

He tried to relax her by giving a wry smile.

"From the way things are with the shop at present, I won't have that much to lose either."

"I wasn't thinking about the shop, Harry," she said quietly.

He nodded his appreciation. "I know you weren't. But we're not going to stop seeing one another because of a piece of cardboard. Why don't you go and make us a cup of tea? By then one of us might have a bright idea about who's sent it."

Still looking preoccupied by the mysterious message, she nodded nervously and disappeared into the kitchen

* * *

Mary jumped out of the tram and hurried towards No. fifty-seven. Her voice was fraught with alarm as Ethel opened the front door. "What's all this about Elizabeth, Mother? What have you to tell me?"

Ethel checked her. "Come into the sitting room first, dear. We don't want all the neighbours to know."

As Mary followed Ethel into the living room, her anxiety surfaced again. "She was perfectly all right when we saw her two days ago. So what's happened?" She glanced around the room. "Where is she?"

Ethel tried to calm her. "She's gone out for the evening. She's perfectly all right."

Mary stared at her. "All right? Then why did you phone about her and say you needed to see me urgently? Why did you say I mustn't say a word to Harry until I'd seen you? What on earth's going on? Do you realise I've had to close the shop early to get here and leave Frank to find his own meal?"

Ethel nodded. "I'm sorry I had to use her name to get you here, dear. But I knew if I told you the truth, you wouldn't come."

Mary's first sensation was relief. "Then she's not sick or in any trouble?"

"Not at all. On the contrary I've never seen her look happier."

Mary took a deep breath. "Then why have you done this? What game are you playing now?"

Ethel sighed. "I'm afraid it's no game, dear. I'm just sorry that I have to be the one to tell you."

"To tell me what, Mother? Get it out, for heaven's sake."

Ethel took a quick look at the time, then turned back to the incensed girl. "It has to do with Harry, dear. I'm afraid he's having an affair."

In the sudden silence that followed, the tick of the grandfather clock in the hall sounded loud and shocked. When Mary's voice came it was barely audible. "What did you say?"

"Harry's having an affair, dear. And there's reason to believe it's been going on for a long time."

The spell snapped, releasing Mary's fury. "How dare you tell such a lie? How dare you?"

Ethel had never acted better. Pulling a lace handkerchief from her sleeve, she dabbed at her

370

eyes. "I know what a terrible thing it is to hear. I've agonised for days whether to tell you. But I am your mother and it is my duty."

Mary was almost hysterical with anger. "You wicked old woman! You've tried everything possible to destroy my marriage, haven't you? But even you have never sunk as low as this."

Ethel gave a sob. "I don't blame you abusing me, dear. I knew what a terrible shock it would be to you. But what could I do when I got proof? Leave you in a fool's paradise?"

Mary's voice turned hoarse. "What proof?"

Ethel lowered her handkerchief. "Was he going out tonight?"

"Yes. He was going to see a friend."

"That was what he told you, dear. In fact he is going to see her."

"How do you know?"

"I can't tell you that. But I can prove everything I say."

"How?"

Glancing again at the clock, Ethel rose to her feet. "If you come with me, I'll show you. It's only a short walk away from here."

Mary gave a sudden start. "Are you talking about the woman in St George's Road? Lena Turnor?"

Triumph flickered for a moment in Ethel's eyes. "I'm afraid so, dear. I suspect he's been seeing her ever since she came back from Hebden Bridge. I understand she's quite a young and presentable woman."

Despite remembering Harry's concern for the young widow, Mary was beginning to feel panic-stricken. "If Harry has seen her occasionally, it'll only be to check she's all right."

"For all these years?" Ethel asked.

"If he does see her, it can't be that often. He seldom goes out at night."

"What about the daytime? He has the van. It was an afternoon when Elizabeth noticed it."

"Elizabeth? How is she involved?"

"She's not involved, dear. She just saw his van coming out of the road, that's all."

"Perhaps that was one of the times he called round to see if she was all right."

"Then why hasn't he told you? Why did he lie to you tonight?"

Mary bit her lip. "He didn't lie. He said he was seeing a friend."

By this time Ethel had forgotten her sympathetic role and her laugh was contemptuous. "If he said he's seeing a friend, you can bet your life he's having an affair. You're just afraid to face the truth, that's all."

All Mary's anger and resentment returned. "You see dirt in everything, Mother. I trust Harry and I always will."

"Even if he is seeing this woman tonight?" When Mary hesitated, Ethel went on: "If you're so sure of him, why are you afraid to come with me?"

"I'm not afraid. But I won't spy on him."

Ethel laughed again. "You'd rather be made a fool of, would you? Then you're different to me, my girl. I like to face the truth."

At that moment Mary's only desire was to

hurt as she was being hurt. "Did you face the truth about Dad and that woman he left two hundred pounds to in his will?"

From Ethel's gasp and her sudden pallor it was clear the barb had struck home and Ethel had guessed about the mistress William had been keeping before his death. Ethel's effort to control herself was massive. "Don't bring your father into this. He would have been as shocked about Harry as I am."

Ashamed of her malice and her disloyalty to her father, Mary turned towards the door. "I'm going back home, Mother. And please don't get in touch again. It only means more lies and misery."

Her face set in frustration, Ethel followed her into the hall. "So you're too afraid to face the truth? You're going to let him go on with his dirty little affair? What's Elizabeth going to think if you don't do anything? It's a fine example to set her, isn't it?"

Mary swung round. "Have you said anything to her?"

Seeing she had struck a raw nerve, Ethel exploited it ruthlessly. "I haven't told her what's going on yet but I shall if you won't come with me tonight and see the truth for yourself."

It was probably the only thing that could have persuaded Mary to go. Giving Ethel a look that made the older woman flinch, she flung open the front door. "Let's go and get it over. And God help you, Mother, if you're telling more lies."

★ ★ ★

Ethel reached a narrow alley in the street and pointed down it. "Wait in there. Then we can't be seen when he arrives."

Hating herself for what she was doing, Mary obeyed. The sides of houses rose above her but further along the alley they gave way to high walls that enclosed gardens. From one wall a large tabby cat was eyeing them balefully. A chilly wind blowing down the passage made Mary shiver.

Traffic could be heard from the main road but the street was quiet enough for minute sounds to be heard: voices as a door opened and closed, distant footsteps, and faint music from a radio. Then a car drove past and Mary felt her heart momentarily contract.

Her thoughts punished her as she waited. Whatever other words were used to disguise her behaviour, she was spying on the man she loved, the man who in their entire life together had shown her nothing but deep love, kindness and consideration. Could anything justify this? Even if he was having an affair, even if for some physical or mental reason she could not understand he was finding happiness in another woman's arms, his love for her had never seemed to lessen, nor had his deep concern for the welfare of his family.

By inference her thoughts moved to her father. Until his will had been read she had not had the slightest suspicion that the huge, bluff man she had adored had been conducting an affair. Nor, she believed, had Ethel. He had carried out his duties to his family in a way that had

374

earned him the respect and devotion of them all, something that could not be said of many other men whose sexual fidelity was beyond suspicion. They could drink and deny their families the necessities of life; they could be tyrants and bully their children and beat their wives; but none of these crimes matched sexual infidelity in the eyes of the society around her.

These thoughts were new to Mary and almost at once her female self-protective instincts denied them. How could a man love one woman and still gain happiness in the arms of another? If Harry had been deceiving her all this time, how could he still be in love with her?

Yet, even if he was having an affair, was she acting any better by spying on him? Sudden disgust made her move forward. "Mother, I can't do this. I'm going home."

Ethel pushed her back. "Don't be such a fool, girl. He'll be here at any moment now."

"How can you know that?"

"Never mind how I know. Just wait and you'll see."

She was never to know whether her better feelings or her curiosity would have won because at that moment Ethel gave a cry of relief. "Here he is now. Didn't I tell you?"

A blue van had turned into the street. Drawing back, Ethel watched it drive past the passage entrance. As it halted thirty yards down the street, Ethel pulled Mary forward. A moment later she turned in triumph to her stunned daughter. "Now do you believe me?"

37

ETHEL paused. "Are you listening to what I am saying?"

When the white-faced Mary, sitting on the sofa alongside her, did not answer, her voice rose impatiently. "For heaven's sake, it's not the end of the world, girl. Try to pull yourself together."

Mary was barely hearing her. Since seeing Lena Turnor embrace Harry on the doorstep, her mind had seemed unable to grasp the simplest of tasks. "Please, Mother. Don't talk about it any more. I want to get home."

"But we must talk about it. Don't you realise what this means? You can't go on living with him now. So we have to make plans for you."

Mary's stricken eyes gazed at her. "What plans can I make? I don't know what I want to do myself."

"That's ridiculous. You can't live with him. So you must come back here and bring Frank with you. That's the simplest and the best solution."

"But what about the shop? I can't just leave it."

"Why not? It's nearly finished anyway if what Elizabeth tells me is true."

"But I can't leave Harry with all those problems. He wouldn't do that to me if the situation was reversed."

Ethel laughed. "He's done worse than that, my girl. He's left you for another woman. So don't feel any pity for Harry."

Mary felt her eyes aching unbearably again. "But we have to live, Mother. I have to earn money to clothe Frank and to feed him. I can't do those things if I'm living here with you."

Ethel's voice turned quite motherly. "My dear, do you believe I haven't thought of that? If you leave Harry and come to stay with me, you won't have to worry any more about paying bills. Both you and the children will be able to live the way I always wanted you to live." For a moment Ethel's lips compressed tightly. "Thanks to Harry, Jack hasn't left me as much as he should have done but one way and another I've enough to keep us all quite comfortably. In any case it won't be long before the two children start work."

In her confused state of mind, Mary found herself feeling gratitude. "I appreciate that, Mother, but it's too early to make any plans yet. I must speak to Harry first and find out just what is going on."

Ethel's face tightened again. "You'll be a fool if you do. That man knows how to twist you round his little finger."

"But I still have to give him a chance to tell his story. Surely that's only fair."

"Fair? Has he been fair to you? Come to your senses, girl. The man's an adulterer. You can't possibly go on living with him."

Mary rose unsteadily to her feet. "I must go,

Mother. I want to be back before he comes home."

Ethel gazed up at her. "What are you going to say to him?"

"I've just told you. I want to hear his story."

Ethel made no attempt to conceal her threat. "If you are such a fool, remember this. If you go back to him after what you've seen today, you'll get no help whatever from me when the same thing happens again. I shall have lost every scrap of pity for you. Is that clear?"

Mary nodded wearily. "Yes, Mother. It's clear."

Ethel studied her drawn face for a moment, then rose and went to the telephone. "You can't go back in the tram in that state. I'll order you a taxi."

★ ★ ★

Mary glanced at the time. Ten thirty and still Harry had not returned home. She wondered if Frank was in bed yet. With errands to run for the shop he had begun his homework late and was always conscientious in completing it. Needing something to occupy her mind, she went upstairs to his bedroom.

He was lying in shorts and shirt on the bed with his fair hair awry and a school book propped up in front of him. He glanced at her, then gave a start. "What's the matter, Mum? You look awful."

She tried to smile. "I'm all right. How's your

homework going? It's half past ten."

"I've a bit to do yet. It doesn't matter, does it?"

"Not if you're able to get up in the morning. You're not the best of getters-up, are you?"

"I'll be all right." His fresh-complexioned face was looking concerned. "Are you sure you're all right? You look as if you've been crying."

That was earlier, she thought. I don't think I've any tears left to shed now. "Don't be silly. I'm just tired, that's all." She turned away to the door to hide her face. "Don't be too long, will you, or you'll be very tired in the morning."

As she went downstairs, she wondered how she was going to keep the news from him when Harry came home. If their voices were raised he would be sure to hear them. She found the thought as distressing as any that had come to her that evening and switched on the wireless in an attempt to drown it. But the sentimental dance music that flooded the room did nothing to help her mood and after a few minutes she switched it off again.

It was a few minutes past eleven when she heard the sound of a key in the shop door. Immediately, as if her heart had been awaiting the sound, it gave a heavy thud and then began racing madly. A moment later Harry entered the room.

He noticed her pallor immediately. "What's the matter, love? What's happened?"

Her heart was beating so fast she found it difficult to speak. He dropped on the sofa alongside her and took her hand, his voice full

379

of concern. "You're cold. What is it?"

She took a deep, steadying breath. "Harry, where have you been tonight?"

Something flickered in his brown eyes and she was certain it was alarm. "I told you. I've been to see a friend."

She knew she ought to trap him into telling lies but could not bear to hear them from him. "I know who you've seen, Harry. You've been to Lena Turnor, haven't you?"

He gave a slight start, then a wry shrug. "Yes, I have. How did you know?"

His reaction surprised her. She had expected a denial. "I saw you, Harry. I saw your van arrive and then . . . " For a moment her voice faltered. "I saw her greet you on the doorstep."

He stared at her and then his face flushed with anger. "So it was you? My God, how could you be so deceitful?"

Surprise and resentment burned away her misery for the moment. "Deceitful? You accuse me of deceit? What have you been doing to me all this time?"

He jumped to his feet, his voice lashing her. "Do you imagine I'd do such a thing to you? My God, it was almost Machiavellian. Who put you up to it? Ethel?"

She had expected shame, even contrition, and his reaction was confusing her. At the same time it made it easier for her to make her accusations. "She did, but do you blame her after she'd found out about you? I know what a bitch she can be but any mother would give a warning if she

380

discovered her daughter's husband was having an affair."

His voice filled with disgust. "Warning her daughter's one thing. Getting you to take part in a filthy trick like that is another. I'd have bet my life you weren't capable of such a thing."

His disgust bewildered her. "How could you expect me not to go? I had to make sure."

He stared at her, then gave a harsh laugh. "So you are sure, are you?"

"How can I not be after what I saw tonight?"

His finely-shaped mouth curled contemptuously. "Spies sometimes see what they want to see. Have you considered that?"

Although convinced by this time he was having an affair, she longed for him to deny it. "Are you saying I'm wrong?"

"I'm not saying anything. If you've gone to all this trouble, you'll believe what you want to believe. Like your mother always has."

With her nerves stretched to breaking point, his words brought her to her feet. "Don't you cover up your guilt by accusing me of being like Mother! I'm not the guilty one, Harry. You're the one who's been lying to me all these years."

"Is that what you believe?" he asked. "Really believe?"

Her voice rose hysterically. "I saw you in the arms of another woman tonight. After you'd lied to me and said you were seeing a friend. So how dare you act as if I were the guilty one?"

At that moment Frank, whose young face looked stricken, entered the room. He gazed at

Harry and then ran across to his mother. "Are you all right, Mum?"

The last thing she wanted was the boy to be involved. "Go back to bed, darling. Please."

He was fighting back his tears. "But I heard what you said. Is it true about this woman and what Dad's done to you?"

Mary would gladly have died at that moment. "Please, Frank. You're only making things worse. Please don't interfere."

Knowing how he loved his father, she could see the boy's distress matched her own. Yet his instinct to protect her made him face Harry, although his voice faltered and almost broke. "You shouldn't hurt her like this, Dad. It's not right of you."

From Harry's expression, Mary could see it was a rebuke that hurt him more than a knife thrust. He tried to answer but instead shook his head and walked towards the door.

Frightened, she ran forward. "Harry, the boy doesn't understand. He's only trying to protect me."

He pulled away but not before she saw the glint of tears in his eyes. As the shop door closed behind him, she gave a cry of despair. A moment later she heard the van start up and drive away.

38

MARY'S thoughts were bitter as she lay in bed listening to the sounds of the night. Did love between men and women always end this way? Did the golden days of youth and promise always darken into the chill and decay of winter?

It seemed the pattern of life, she thought. The blossom that thrilled the heart soon fell to the muddied ground. The flower that opened to the sun had only days of beauty before it blackened and died. Was love as transient?

She felt she might have forgiven Harry if he had admitted his infidelity. He was nearing forty now and would not be the first man, nor the last, who sought his lost youth in the arms of a younger woman. Instead he had acted as if she were the wrongdoer by taking steps to discover his deceit.

She found that difficult to understand. In all the time she had known him, he had never been anything but fair. How often had she accused him of being too scrupulous in trying to see another's point of view? Yet when she was involved in an issue that affected her so deeply, he had tried to make her appear the guilty one.

Lying there alone in the bed she had shared with him since their marriage, she found this discovery painful. Until today, she had believed him a man of total integrity: in fact, she knew that in her heart she had idolised him. To find out he was capable of the same meanness of mind as other men was a discovery as crushing as the discovery of his infidelity.

Inevitably, as the night wore on, her misery began to give way to the practical problems that now faced her. With Harry gone, how was she going to manage the shop? There were the ovens to be cleaned and fired; the deliveries to be made; the supplies to be brought in. She might be able to prepare the ovens but she could not drive and in any case he had taken the van. As she wrestled with the problems, her resentment returned. Did he intend leaving her to face every task herself? If he did, then surely he was everything Ethel had accused him of being.

As one emotion faded, another took its place. Where had he gone? Had he gone back to Lena Turnor? Was he in her bed at this moment? Thoughts, some painful, some harrowing, some exquisitely nostalgic, tumbled in and out of her mind as the hours dragged by.

It was almost three o'clock when she heard the faint squeal of brakes on the road outside. Heart hammering again, she leapt out of bed and ran to the window. A cry of relief broke from her when she recognised the dark shape of his van. Whether he had come back to ask her forgiveness or simply to collect his things, she did not know. But at least there would be a fresh chance to learn his intentions and to clarify her own.

Trying not to awaken Frank, she hurried down the stairs. As she reached the inner door that led into the shop, she heard the sound of his key in the lock. Swallowing with nervousness, she stepped into the shop and waited.

The outer door opened. With his back to the single street lamp at the far side of the road, his face was cast into shadow. She tried to speak but her throat seemed to be closed.

He moved round the counter and paused. How long they stood facing one another she never knew, for time stood still for her. Then, as if some magnetic switch had been thrown, they were suddenly in each other's arms and sobbing their relief. "Harry, oh Harry, thank God you've come back! I'd have died if you hadn't."

She could feel the wetness on his cheeks as his arms crushed her against him. "I'd have died too, love. It's been the worst night of my life."

All the love and protectiveness of womankind was flooding out to him at that moment. He had come back to her. He still loved her. Every instinct she possessed affirmed it. She could handle the problem of Lena Turnor now. She returned his kiss, then drew him into the living room. "You're cold. I'll go and make you some tea."

They said nothing about Lena Turnor until they were sipping tea together. Then he reached out and took her hand. "I haven't had an affair with Lena, Mary. I really haven't."

At that point of time she did not believe him but the night had taught her things she would never forget. She lifted his hand to her lips and kissed it. "You're still cold, darling. What have you been doing all this time?"

"Just sitting in the van and thinking." When she said nothing, he went on: "It's because I haven't mentioned her that you don't believe me, isn't it?"

She reached out for the teapot. "Don't talk about it, Harry. Not tonight."

He checked her and turned her towards him. "But we must. We can't leave it to fester."

She knew he was right and took a deep breath. "Then why didn't you tell me you were seeing her? And why wouldn't she come round to see us when I invited her?"

His brow furrowed. "I don't know. I suppose I was afraid you might think I was having an affair. Why she would never meet you, I don't know. I think she's just shy at meeting people."

She knew why. She knew now that Lena Turnor loved him. "How often have you seen her, Harry?"

His frown deepened. "That's the point. Not often. At first I was just worried about her — I could never forgive myself for Turnor's death."

"And then?" she asked quietly.

"We just became friends, I suppose. But I couldn't see her very often. I'd just call when I'd a spare few minutes during the day or a spare evening. You know how seldom that is."

She wanted to ask him if he had ever made love to her but found she could not. "Doesn't she have a man friend?" she asked instead.

386

"Not at the moment. But she's had one or two in the past." When she made no comment, he took her hand. "Let me take you round to see her tomorrow. That'll clear everything up."

She wondered if it would. "I'll go one day. But not yet."

"Why not? When you've talked to her you'll understand everything I say."

There was one thing she could not understand. "Harry, if you only saw her at irregular intervals, how did Mother know you were going round last night?"

For the first time since his return, resentment came back into his voice. "Surely you knew about the card?"

"Card? What card?"

Frowning, he drew the card from his pocket and passed it to her. Her eyes widened as she read it. "Did you believe I had sent this?"

"Of course I did. Otherwise how could you have known about my visit?"

Missing pieces suddenly fell into place. "So that's why you were so angry. That's what I couldn't understand." Overjoyed by the discovery, she threw her arms around him. "My poor darling. You must have hated me."

He drew back to stare at her. "Are you saying you didn't know?"

"Of course I didn't know. I hated myself just for walking down St George's Road. If I'd known about this card, wild horses wouldn't have dragged me there."

He shook his head at the implications of Ethel's perfidy. "My God, she'll stop at nothing

387

to break up our marriage, will she? Only how did she know in the first place that I was seeing Lena Turnor? Do you think she's been spying on me? Or has she paid someone to do it for her?"

"I don't know. I'd put nothing past her now." She went on to tell him about Ethel's offer. "She expects me to phone her in the morning to say I'm going back to live with her."

His smile told her his sense of humour was returning. "With business as it is, I'd accept. Only tell her I'll be coming with you. That'll make her day." Then his tone changed. "You'll explain everything to Frank, won't you? The poor kid was so upset."

Knowing how hurt he had been by the boy's attack, she kissed him again. "Don't worry. I'll explain everything. Now come to bed. We've still got two hours before morning."

★ ★ ★

She rang Ethel the next morning after Harry had gone off on his rounds and Frank off to school. "Mother, listen to me carefully. I've found out what you did in order to get Harry round to Lena Turnor's house and I've never heard of anything more despicable. It's made me ashamed to be your daughter."

There was a pause in which she could see Ethel as clearly as if the woman were standing before her, with her pale blue eyes bitter with disappointment. "What difference does it make, you stupid girl? All it did was make it possible for you to see what's going on."

"It was a dreadful thing to do. It makes me feel dirty just to think about it."

"And what Harry is doing isn't dirty? Didn't you see that slut throw her arms around him? What's the matter with you, girl? Haven't you got any pride?"

"I'm not going to argue with you, Mother. This time you've gone too far. From now on I want you to keep out of my life. Don't phone me and don't write. Live your life and let me live mine."

"Then you are turning down my offer?"

She almost laughed. "I wouldn't live with you, Mother, if you were the last person on earth. You poison and destroy everything around you."

Ethel's voice took on a note she had never heard before. It sounded both threatening and hysterical. "You ungrateful girl. I've done everything I can for you and this is my reward. Very well. If you choose to stay with that adulterer, then you're as bad as he is and I've no further pity for you."

"I don't want your pity, Mother. I just want nothing to do with you in the future."

"Is that so? All right, my girl, but don't come crawling to me if you live to regret it. Because you are going to, mark my words."

Mary was about to reply when the line went dead. She wondered why she felt so chilled as she replaced the receiver.

★ ★ ★

Two weeks later Mary was setting the table for Frank's breakfast when Mrs Fennell, dusting flour from her hands, came out of the bakery. "Can I have a word with you, Mrs Miles?"

Something in the woman's astringent voice gave Mary a stab of presentiment. "Yes, Mrs Fennell. What is it?"

The expression on the woman's gaunt face was a mixture of embarrassment and defiance. "I want to give you two weeks' notice, Mrs Miles."

Mary stiffened. "Notice? But we gave you another increase only three months ago. Isn't it enough?"

"It's nothing to do with my wages. Jenny and I are going to open a shop of our own. It's something we've always wanted."

"But, Mrs Fennell, you've never said a word to us about this. And we rely on you."

"Aye, I know that, and I'm sorry. But you can't expect us to turn down a chance to work for ourselves, can you?"

Mary could not hold back the question. "What chance, Mrs Fennell? What's happened?"

The woman took on a look of caution. "That's our business, Mrs Miles. But we've got a shop and we can start the week after next."

"Have you said anything about this to my husband?" Mrs Fennell shook her head. "No. He'd gone when I arrived this morning."

"It's going to be as big a shock to him as it is to me. If only you'd given us some warning, we could have advertised for another bakeress. Couldn't you stay on for another six weeks? Even four?"

390

Shame turned the woman's voice sullen. "If we did that, the shop might go. You can't expect us to risk that."

Mary was trying to think what the loss would mean and could see only disaster ahead. "Not if we offered you both double wages for the extra time?" When the woman shook her head, Mary's voice rose in spite of herself. "We've been fair to you, Mrs Fennell. Don't you think you ought to be fair to us?"

It was a mistake. Her attack was what the woman wanted to fight off her shame. "It's business, Mrs Miles. It's nowt to do with whether it's fair or not. Anyhow, we are being fair to you. We're giving you two weeks' notice instead of one."

Mary pulled herself together. "Where is your shop going to be?"

Mrs Fennell hesitated, then her voice turned sullen again. "Down Ellis Street."

"Ellis Street! But that's just along the road. That's wicked, Mrs Fennell. You're doing it to steal our trade."

The woman hid her shame by turning towards the bakery. "Sorry but in this world you've got to look after yerself. No one else will. I'll give Mr Miles my notice in writing when he comes home."

★ ★ ★

Harry dropped on to the sofa as if his legs had suddenly turned into jelly. "She's opening a shop? In Ellis Street?"

391

"That's what she said." Mary handed him an envelope. "Here's her notice."

He read it quickly, then let it fall on the sofa. From his expression she knew he had the same fears as herself. "We've got to get another baker or bakeress fast," he muttered. "Otherwise we'll be out of business."

She sank down beside him. "Even if we get one, will we keep our trade? She's almost certain to let everyone know she used to work for us."

He cursed and lit a cigarette. He exhaled smoke, then turned to her. "You know what's puzzling me? Where has she got the money from? I know she hadn't any herself from the things Jenny has told me. So where has it come from all of a sudden?"

"Perhaps someone in the family's died recently and left it to her."

"Who? Her parents are dead and Jenny's parents are as poor as church mice. In any case neither of them has died recently."

She stared at him and then gave a start. "You're not thinking . . . Oh, surely not. Ethel hardly knows Mrs Fennell."

He grimaced. "You're right. I'm getting as suspicious as she is." He drew in smoke and shrugged. "Whoever's left it to them isn't the issue, is it? It's how we can survive. Our first job is to try to replace her and get a new assistant. I'll scout about during my rounds and put an advertisement in the paper." Seeing her expression, he put a hand round her waist and drew her towards him. "Don't look so

392

frightened. We've been in worse wars before."

You have, she thought. You seem to have been in wars all your life. Just as one seems to be over, another one begins. Tears were stinging her eyes but knowing they would distress him, she pressed forward and buried her face in his shoulder.

39

THERE was a worried look on Elizabeth's face as she jumped from the tram and made her way towards No. fifty-seven. As she reached a telephone box, she hesitated, then entered it.

She emerged a couple of minutes later, her expression transformed. At last a flat was ready for her! Although it was true Sir Michael hadn't given her a date to begin work and move into a flat, she had believed it was only a matter of a week or two before he kept his promise. Instead six long weeks had passed with every day adding to her frustration.

The delay had worried her in other ways. His behaviour had convinced her he found her attractive and although her young mind was still unsure of her own responses, she found it intensely exciting that a man of his distinction should have noticed her among all the elegant women he met. The effect of the long tantalising delay had been to make her wonder if his feelings towards her were cooling and convinced her she must work harder to restore them again. She was too young to understand this was precisely the effect Chadwick intended.

But now both a job and a flat were awaiting her. She wondered what her father would do if he found out who the provider was. The thought brought back the concern she had felt after her recent visit to the shop. Perhaps she ought to ask Sir Michael to wait until the crisis was over. It hardly seemed right to be going away at a time like this.

Then, with the optimism and self-justification of the young, her mood changed again. What could she do if she stayed? Unemployed as she was, she could not provide the aid her parents needed. But if she took the job, she might be able to help later.

The thought revived her excitement and lightened her step. A whistle broke into her thoughts. Glancing round, she saw a young man in working clothes eyeing her admiringly. Used to her power over men, she tossed her head disdainfully, although a twitch of her full lips betrayed her pleasure. It was wonderful to be young and beautiful. It was also wonderful to know that soon she would be seeing the same admiration in Sir Michael's eyes.

* * *

Ethel frowned. "Eighty pounds? Did they tell you to ask me?"

"Of course they didn't. I thought of it. After all, you are Mum's mother and you can't want her to go bankrupt."

Ethel's sniff was an effort to hide her deep satisfaction. "I warned her this would happen but she wouldn't listen."

There was reproach in the girl's voice. "I don't see that listening would have been much help to her, Grannie. Not after what you did. Will you

395

lend them the money or not?"

Seeing the lie of the land, Ethel chose her words carefully. "I wish I could, dear, but all my money is tied up to give me a monthly income. It's a pity but there's nothing I can do about it."

"Then what about money you've put in trust for me? Can't you draw on that?"

"Good heavens, no. That can't be touched until you're twenty-one."

"But there must be some way to help them. If they go bankrupt they'll lose their home, won't they?"

Ethel sighed. "Yes, I'm afraid they will."

"But that's awful. It'll break Mother's heart."

Ethel nodded. "If only she'd listened to me after she found out about your father. But she always thinks she knows best."

A furrow appeared on the girl's smooth forehead. "I don't believe Dad was having an affair. He loves Mother too much."

Ethel sighed again. "I'm afraid there's no doubt about it, dear. Your mother saw the woman with her own eyes."

"But Dad says she's only a friend. And Mother believes it now she's met her."

Ethel was unaware her voice was hardening. "Your mother's a fool. Look at the mess it's got her into."

"So you're not going to help them?"

"I can't help them, dear. I've just explained why."

The girl sat gazing at her, then gave a sigh of relief.

"Thank God I'm getting away from it all."

Ethel frowned. "What did you say?"

"I said I'm glad I'm getting out. Sir Michael's just told me he's found a flat I can have. One out of town. I can move into it whenever I like."

Ethel looked as if she had been struck across the face. "You never said anything about going away! You only said he was finding you a job."

Elizabeth feigned surprise. "Didn't I? I must have forgotten. Does it matter?"

"Does it matter? You can't live on your own, a girl of your age. Particularly out of town."

"Why not? I'm over eighteen."

Ethel was looking pale with shock. "For heaven's sake, girl, it's too dangerous. You'd be unprotected."

"Who from? Men?"

"If you must put it so crudely, yes. There's nothing men like better than girls living on their own."

Elizabeth found she was enjoying the woman's distress. "There's only one man involved, Grannie. And that's Sir Michael. I thought you were thrilled that he was interested in me."

Ethel looked horrified as well as shocked. "What are you saying? That he's proposing to live with you?"

"No. He's hasn't suggested it. But he has found me the flat." The girl's voice was mocking. "Won't that mean I owe him something?"

"What's come over you, girl? What on earth are you saying?"

"He can't be doing it out of the goodness of

his heart, can he? Particularly after what Dad did to him."

"Are you telling me . . . ?" Ethel tried to frame the words but could not.

The gleam in Elizabeth's eyes was malicious now. "Am I saying he might want to sleep with me sometimes? Yes, I am. Why should you look so shocked? You've always said what a marvellous catch Sir Michael would be."

Ethel's face was a battleground of emotions. "I meant marriage, girl. Not a squalid affair."

Elizabeth laughed. "I don't think it would be squalid with Sir Michael. It would be caviar and champagne all the way."

Ethel shuddered, "Don't talk like that. You've been brought up to be a good girl. Don't you even think of living any other way."

"Not even with Sir Michael? I thought you admired him."

"Not with anybody. Men don't marry girls who let them behave that way. At heart they despise them."

Realising if she went too far, Ethel might call for help from her parents, Elizabeth stopped her taunting. "If you want the truth, Sir Michael's never mentioned anything like that. He's giving me a flat and a job because he knows I'm tired of all the squabbling between you and Mum and Dad."

Ethel frowned. "I hope you're not blaming me for that."

"Come off it, Grannie. As I see it, you've been behind almost everything."

For a moment Ethel forgot her role as the

loving and caring grandmother. "How can you say such a thing? I've done everything I can for your parents and all I've had back is ingratitude."

The girl's resentment, dammed back so far, began to spill over its restraining wall. "Why don't you tell the truth for a change? You've hated Dad ever since he married Mum and you've done everything in your power to come between them. Look at you now. You won't even give them eighty pounds to save them from bankruptcy, even though you'd never miss the money. So don't tell me what you've done for them."

Ethel's temper, always unstable, cracked at her words. "You insolent young hussy! How dare you talk this way to me? I, who have given you everything ever since you were a baby."

The suddenness at which they had become enemies startled them both. Elizabeth's expressive eyes suddenly blazed with a long-held resentment. "I know what you've given me, Grannie. Years and years of tears."

"I've given you tears?"

Elizabeth jumped to her feet. "Yes! You! You pretended I meant so much to you that you faked suicide to get me back, but what did you do when Jack wanted you to go to America? What happened to all your love then?"

The ferocity of her attack momentarily stunned Ethel. "But I had to go. I'd no choice."

"Don't lie. You'd found somebody else who could give you a good life over there and so you forgot all about me. You never thought what it did to me or how it made me turn against everybody. But now Jack's dead I'm suddenly important again, aren't I?"

"That's a dreadful thing to say. I wanted you back because I loved you. But you're not the girl I used to know. You've grown hard and cruel."

"If I have, it's because of you. You've never loved anyone but yourself. There's only one reason why you want me back now. You can't face being left alone with your thoughts. I'm not surprised. I couldn't either, if I were in your shoes."

Ethel was recovering now and in her fashion was seeking to return blow for blow. "You've got your father in you! I see it now. You're just like him."

"What if I have?" Elizabeth sneered. "I'd rather be like him than you?"

No words could have enraged Ethel more. A shiver ran through her and then her voice rose hysterically. "You ungrateful wretch! Get out! Get out and don't ever come back."

The girl laughed and walked towards the stairs. "Don't worry. I can't get away fast enough."

With that she disappeared upstairs. Trembling and white-faced, Ethel sank down on the sofa. Five minutes later Elizabeth entered the room carrying a suitcase. "I'm going now. I've left my keys on the dressing table." At the hall door she glanced back. "Don't try to get in touch with me. I'll never come back, whatever you do."

The front door slammed and she was gone. With the seething anger within her extinguished by the girl's words, Ethel ran to the front window. Seeing Elizabeth push open the garden gate and start along the pavement, she gave a sudden cry of pain. "No! Don't go! Please don't leave me. Please, Elizabeth."

The cry echoed round the empty house and mocked her. Clapping her ringed hands to her face, she gave a moan of distress: "Oh, God, what have I done? What have I done?"

She dropped back on the sofa, her face disfigured by torment. Delirious, fragmented thoughts blazed and died in her mind. It wasn't true. It couldn't be true. Elizabeth loved her. This was just to frighten her. She would come back in a few minutes.

The silence of the large house mocked her again. Looking suddenly old, with tendrils of hair straggling down her face, she heard her own voice whispering to her. She must not be left alone with her memories. Not with those demons that laughed and taunted and stabbed her with spears. Elizabeth knew this and would come back. Elizabeth would come back because Elizabeth loved her.

40

HEARING a tap on the door, Elizabeth ran forward and threw it open. A moment later she gave a gasp of pleasure. "Sir Michael! So you did manage to get away after all?"

Chadwick, elegant in a grey cashmere suit, gave her a smile. "I couldn't let you spend your third evening in your flat alone, could I? It was a pity I couldn't get away sooner. May I come in?"

She laughed. "Of course you can. After all, it is your flat."

He smiled again as he entered the small sitting room. "No, my dear. It's your flat as long as you live here. How do you like it?"

Her expressive eyes shone at him. "I love it. And how thoughtful of you to have those roses sent. They're beautiful."

He dropped into an armchair. "Did the champagne come too?"

"Yes. Would you like a drink?"

"I think it's a good idea, don't you? To celebrate your new freedom."

He watched her run into the kitchen. As when he had interviewed her in his office, she was wearing the short dress that clung to her shapely body and exposed her long legs. He wondered if it were deliberate for he was certain she had noticed his interest. The only difference lay in her blonde hair. Then it had been massed upon her head. Tonight it was hanging in long tresses that reached down to her waist. Watching her dress slide up as she reached into a cupboard, Chadwick felt his mouth turn dry again.

She returned carrying a bottle of Veuve Clicquot. "Will you open it? I don't think I know how."

He rose and took the bottle from her. "Fetch two glasses."

She hesitated. "I don't think there are any champagne glasses."

"Never mind. Wine glasses will do."

She obeyed and a moment later there was a pop and a spurt of froth. "Quickly," he said.

Laughing happily, she caught the foaming champagne as he filled both glasses. He took one from her and clinked it against her own. "To your new job and your new home. Let's drink to both."

She took a sip from her glass and giggled. "I love champagne."

He dropped on to the sofa. "There's plenty more where that comes from. So enjoy it."

She sank down on the sofa beside him and stretched out luxuriously. "Oh, I'm so happy. I never thought I could be so happy."

He was acutely conscious of her nearness. "Then Mrs Bowers hasn't been working you too hard?"

"She's hardly given me any work at all. And she's been letting me off at four o'clock every day."

He shrugged. "So she should. After all, it is your first week."

"That's due to you, isn't it? You told her to make it easy for me."

His eyes twinkled. "How could you think such a thing? As if I'd ever interfere in the affairs of my managers."

"But you have in this case, haven't you? I can tell from the way she speaks to me."

He reached for the bottle of champagne and filled her glass again. "Perhaps I did have a little chat with her. But not a word about it to any of the other girls or I'll have a revolution on my hands."

Her eyes were on his handsome face. "Why did you do it?"

"I didn't think from what you told me that typing and shorthand were your stronger assets. Aren't I right?"

"But then why did you give me the job?"

Fully aware that she was fishing, he found pleasure in teasing her. "You're the daughter of my one-time sergeant. Isn't that a good enough reason?"

Her red lips pretended to pout. "Is that all?"

A smile played around his mouth as he lifted his glass. "It's all you're going to hear, young lady."

"Just the same, I know it's not true."

"How do you know that?"

"You haven't done Dad any favours by getting me away from Grannie. He and Mother will throw a fit when they find out I've gone."

She could hardly have said anything that

404

pleased him more. "Your grandmother will tell them, won't she?"

"She might. I don't know. But in any case Grandmother hasn't my address."

"And you don't intend to give it to any of them?"

"Not on your life. They'd only try to spoil things."

"Spoil what?" he said, teasing her again.

The champagne was taking its effect on her. Under her long lashes, her eyes moved to him and then lowered. "That's not for me to say, is it?" When he did not answer, she reached for the half-empty bottle. "Shall we finish it off?"

"Yes, why not? I can see you're enjoying it."

As she filled his glass he heard raised voices, followed by the slam of a door. His eyebrows raised. "What was that?"

She pointed at the wall behind them. "There's a young couple in there who seem to quarrel a lot. I think the wall must be thin because they sound quite loud sometimes."

He frowned. "I'm sorry. My agent should have checked that out."

"It doesn't matter. It doesn't worry me." She moved a few inches closer to him. "What do I call you?"

With his mind momentarily diverted, he gazed back at her. "What did you say?"

Alcohol was having its effect now. Her young eyes were growing heavy with desire. "I asked what I could call you. I can't say Sir Michael all the time, can I? It sounds so awfully formal."

"Oh, I see. When I'm here you can call me

Michael. Does that make it easier for you?"

She sighed and almost imperceptibly moved closer to him. "Yes. Much easier. Why are you so good to me, Michael?"

He stared down at her. Her dress had inched up above her knees and her golden hair was brushing his shoulder. He felt his loins stirring. "Am I nice to you?"

"Yes. You know you are."

He reached for her and instantly she melted into his arms. He gripped her for a moment, then drew her to her feet. "Come along. Let's go into the bedroom."

She clung to him to steady herself for a moment. Then she led him into the adjacent room. There she threw herself on the bed and held out her arms to him.

As he stood looking down at her, his voice suddenly turned harsh. "Take your dress off!"

She gazed up at him uncomprehendingly. His voice rose. "Take your dress off or I'll tear it off."

She giggled, stood up, and wriggled out of it. Then, clad only in brief underwear, suspender belt and stockings, she dropped back and held out her arms again.

This time he threw himself on top of her. One hand caught the front of her brassiere and ripped it away while the other sank deeply into her groin. Her cry was a mixture of pain and excitement. She tried to reach his face with her lips but his mouth was searching for her breasts. Gripping her groin harder, he seized one breast with his free hand and squeezed it until she gave a gasp of pain. Then he rolled her on her side and tore away her remaining underwear, leaving her naked but for her stockings and suspender belt.

Her protest and cries were an incitement to them both.

As he unbuttoned himself, she tried to lift up on her elbows but he threw her back. Quickly ready, he slid his hands down her slender body, then gripped her knees and forced them apart.

Exposed to his eyes now, she murmured something and tried again to rise, only to fall back as he threw his weight on top of her. He was lying between her legs now and was no longer in a flat in Beverley. He was on a hilltop above the river many years ago and it was Mary's white body lying beneath him.

But why wasn't she struggling? That had been the provocation that had triggered off his virility. Without a fight there could be no conquest and no revenge. It would be the same as it had been with women of his own class that he dared not hurt. Humiliation for him and contempt from the women, even if his social position did prevent them from making their contempt known.

He had the answer when Elizabeth lifted her head and tried to kiss him. Inexperienced though she might be, her response told him she found excitement in a degree of violence. He had not hurt her enough to make her fight him.

He drew back his face to gaze at her. There were her white shoulders and her swelling breasts and the rest of her body beneath him. Plenty of places to hurt and make her seek to deny him. Then he could enter her and it would be rape and the revenge he needed.

It was a man's shout and a crash of glass that checked him. With these damned walls so thin, the girl would be heard if she were made to cry out and fight him. There would be witnesses if she filed a complaint and even if she did not, people would talk and the story would spread.

Her puzzled, uncertain voice broke into his thoughts. "What is it, Michael? What's the matter?"

For a moment the temptation to punish her was almost overwhelming. Then, conquering it, he rose and turned away to adjust his clothing. "I'm sorry. It's these people. They sound as if they are in the room."

"But they're not. They can't see us." She began to cry with disappointment. "Don't go away, Michael. Please."

He felt irritable now. "I'm sorry but I've always been sensitive about such things. You were crying out and I was afraid they might be listening."

"But how can you stop now? I thought you liked me."

Damn her whimpering! He wanted to slap her across the face to end it. "I do like you. But I can't help being the way I am."

She was sitting up now, with the sheets pulled around her to hide her nakedness. "But that means you're never going to make love to me here. That's awful. I thought that was why you wanted me to come."

Finishing his dressing, he turned to her. "I'll see if I can't find you another place. In the meantime you can come up to The Grange. Mother's leaving for her annual two months in the south of France next Monday, so we could be alone there, particularly if I give the servants a night off. So stop crying, for God's sake."

Her disappointment and his change of mood was making her sullen. "It sounds all right, I suppose," she muttered. "When could I come?"

"Quite soon. Probably Tuesday. I'll phone you to confirm and I'll pick you up in the early evening. That suits you all right, doesn't it?"

She rose from the bed and with her back to him threw on a dressing gown. "You are sure about this? You do still want me?"

Realising how her confidence had been shaken, he fought back his irritation and took her into his arms. "It wasn't you. Can't you understand that? You're a very beautiful girl and I want you more than ever. I'll prove that to you next week."

She began to brighten. "Will I see you over the weekend?"

"No, I've a dozen things to do before Tuesday." When her face dropped again, he pulled out his wallet and laid a couple of notes on the table. "I'll make everything up to you next week. In the meantime enjoy yourself. Have a meal and go to the cinema."

She frowned. "I don't want your money."

Ignoring her, he glanced at his watch and adjusted his jacket.

"Are you going now?" she asked.

"Yes, I must. Mother has a few guests she

409

wants me to meet before she leaves."

Looking disconsolate, she went to the door with him. "You will phone me?"

"Yes, I promise. And I'll definitely see you next week."

She lifted up her face for him to kiss. He touched her lips, smiled, then made for the lift. She watched until the lift doors closed, then went back inside. Her lovely face was troubled as she dropped on the sofa and lit a cigarette.

She inhaled, coughed, and ground out the cigarette in disgust. Rising, she went into the bathroom and threw off her dressing gown. Her naked body, full of shape and beauty, reflected back at her in a wall mirror. She turned left, then right, then shook her head impatiently.

It had nothing to do with her, she decided. He would not have taken the flat and gone to all the trouble over her job if he did not find her attractive.

Then was it him? But how could it be when everyone said how popular he was with women? It must have been the sounds next door, she told herself. She had heard that men were often put off by things women hardly noticed.

She walked back into the sitting room. There was no need to worry. It would all come right next week when he was among familiar surroundings. Reassured now, she crossed the room and switched on the radio.

41

HARRY drew the auctioneer aside. "Must you take the sideboard? It means a great deal to my wife. Her father left it to her."

The auctioneer, a large florid man with a heavy paunch, gave him a pitying look. "Don't be daft, mate. It's the only thing you've got that's worth anything, apart from the van."

"But it means so much to her. As soon as I get a job, I'll pay what it's worth to the Receiver."

"I've heard that before, mate. Anyway, the bailiff's got an inventory, so what can I do about it?"

"You could leave it a few days, couldn't you? Until I see if I can borrow the money."

"If you can borrow any money, mate, you can pay some of your other debts, never mind worrying about a bloody sideboard."

"You enjoy your job, don't you?" Harry said with sudden aversion. "It's written all over your face."

The auctioneer grinned at him and pushed past to enter the sitting room where his three assistants were preparing to move the sideboard. Because of its size, it had been left to the last: the rest of the furniture was already packed into the furniture van outside.

It was a school holiday and Frank, looking pale and distressed, was standing beside Mary in

411

the doorway that led to the kitchen. The oldest of the three assistants, a man in his late forties with thinning dark hair, turned to the auctioneer as he entered the room. "She'll have to go out through the window, Mr Preston, and then out through the passageway. But I think we'll need a couple more men even then."

Preston gave a jeering laugh. "What's up with yer, Joe? You gettin' past the job these days? We'll get the bugger out, don't worry." He grinned again at Harry. "Unless Mr Miles here would like to give a hand?"

Ignoring his taunt, Harry moved across to Mary and the boy. "Why don't the two of you go for a walk?" he muttered. "There's nothing you can do just standing here."

Mary, who had seemed frozen in shock since the auctioneers had arrived a hour earlier, shook her head. "It's still my home, Harry. I'm not leaving it while they're here."

He did not argue. To gain the space they needed, the men were having to take off the top of the sideboard and remove both panes of the window. Seeing his mother's expression, Frank gripped her hand, then turned to Harry. "Why are you letting them do this, Dad? Mum loves that sideboard."

When Harry shook his head, Mary came to his rescue. "It's not Dad's fault, darling. It's what happens when you go bankrupt."

The boy was trembling and in spite of his efforts to hold them back, tears were squeezing from his eyes. "It shouldn't happen! You couldn't help it. It's wicked!"

The window was open now and the four men began easing the sideboard away from the wall. As they dragged it to the window and began lifting it, its weight swung it sideways, bruising its satiny surface against the window ledge. It brought a faint cry of protest from Mary and a hand rose to her side as if the injury were to her own flesh.

The sight of her distress was too much for the boy. Pulling away from Harry, he ran forward and began striking at the auctioneer with both hands. Startled by his attack, the man almost lost his grip on the sideboard and cursed as he lowered it to the floor. "You little devil! What d'you think you're up to?"

Crying out, the boy continued to strike him. Before the auctioneer could retaliate, Harry grabbed the sobbing boy and dragged him back to the doorway. A laugh from one of his men brought a growl from Preston. "You'd better get that kid out of here, mister, or he'll feel the weight of my hand."

Harry was holding the boy tightly. "I'm sorry. But he knows what that sideboard means to his mother."

"You'd be a damn sight more sorry if the bloody thing had fallen on my foot. Why don't you take the two of 'em away until we've finished?"

Harry took Mary's arm and nodded at the sobbing boy. "Come on. We're only making things worse by staying here."

This time she obeyed him and they retreated into the empty bakery where Pride, now a huge

413

dog, was being kept away from the men. Fifteen minutes later they heard a shout. "That's it. We're finished. We've left your three beds upstairs and the gas stove belongs to the house. You'll hear from the Receiver tomorrow."

They returned into the empty sitting room. As Mary's eyes moved to the bare wall where the sideboard had stood, Frank gave a sob and threw his arms around her. "I'm sorry, Mum. It's awful for you, isn't it?"

Mary took a deep breath. "It's awful for us all, darling. It's just as bad for you and Dad."

"But you loved that sideboard so much. Why did they have to take that too?"

"When you go bankrupt, they take just about everything, darling. Except the beds. They have to leave them."

"But what are we going to do?"

Mary glanced at Harry. "The rent's paid until the end of the month, so we can stay on for nearly three weeks. We'll manage somehow. We always have. Haven't we, darling?"

His grimace was for her courage. He sat down on the bottom of the stairs and stared down at the uncarpeted floor. She moved nearer to him. "You'll get a job, love. Our bad luck can't last forever."

He did not move. Anxious, she put an arm around his shoulders. "Cheer up, darling. It wasn't our fault. No one could have worked harder."

To her dismay his shoulders began to shake. She fell on her knees beside him. "Oh, my love, I know how you feel. But it isn't the end of the world. We'll get over it somehow."

At that he lifted his head and she saw that he was not crying but laughing. She stared at him in amazement. "What is it? What's making you laugh?"

He put an arm round her and reached out for the distressed boy. "I don't know. Perhaps because I'm happy. Why else does one laugh?"

"You're happy," she repeated.

"Yes." His eyes were on the boy. "Did you see the way Frank went for that bailiff? He was fighting for you, his mother. We've got a real man growing up. Isn't that something to be happy about?"

Although astonished at his mood, she nodded and hugged the boy. "Yes, of course it is. I thought you were very brave, darling. Thank you."

Harry's tone changed as he turned her face towards him. "I know how you feel. We've lost our possessions, we'll lose our home soon, we're down as low as we can go. Perhaps that's it. There's only one way left and that's up. Does that make any sense to you?"

She snuggled closer to him. "Go on."

He paused a moment and then frowned. "Perhaps it has something to do with the war. It put things into perspective. After all, we haven't lost one another, have we? We're still young and we're healthy and we're all prepared to fight for one another. Doesn't that really mean we're rich, not poor? Am I right or am I crazy?"

She had thought she had known everything about him until that moment. The dam in her mind that had blocked her tears since the auctioneers had arrived suddenly cleared and allowed them to burst out in a torrent. Laughing and crying at the same moment, she flung herself into his arms. "You're right. Yes, of course you are. I'm the luckiest woman in the world. I have a brave son and a husband that nothing can defeat." She kissed him until his face was drenched with her tears. "Oh, God, I love you, Harry. I've never loved you more."

★ ★ ★

It was just before six p.m. the following Tuesday when the door bell rang. Entering the shop, Mary halted as she saw the gaunt figure of Mrs Fennell framed in the glass doorway. Recovering, she moved forward and drew back the latch. "Yes, Mrs Fennell. What do you want?"

A large carrier bag was hanging from the woman's arm. Her expression was a mixture of defiance and misgiving, with another element Mary could not define. "Can I come in for a minute, Mrs Miles?"

Mary hesitated, then drew back. "Yes, I suppose so."

The woman's eyes took in the bare shelves and the absence of furniture as she entered. Mary could not hold back her comment as she closed the door. "You'll see it's all worked out the way you wanted. The auctioneers came yesterday."

The woman avoided her eyes. "Aye, I know. Jenny passed by in the afternoon and told me.

I couldn't come earlier because of the shop."

"What have you come for?" Mary asked. "To see for yourself?"

"No," the woman muttered.

"Then why, Mrs Fennell? You haven't come to gloat, have you?"

To Mary's surprise the woman winced. "No, it's nowt like that. Is your husband around, Mrs Miles?"

"No, he's out looking for a job." Mary felt no reason to spare her. "If he doesn't get one soon, we'll all be out in the street, never mind out of business. Why do you want to see him?"

The woman lowered her eyes. "I wanted you both to know how sorry I am for all that's happened."

"Oh, come off it, Mrs Fennell. You knew this would happen all along. You've even let customers know you were our bakeress so as to win them over. So don't play the hypocrite now."

"It wasn't meant this way, Mrs Miles. I never wanted to bankrupt you."

"I don't believe you. Everything you've done had that in mind. So why start lying now?"

"But it wasn't Jenny and I who wanted it. We just wanted a business of our own. It was your mother who's done the rest."

Mary stared at her. "What did you say?"

"It was your mother who gave us the money. We wanted to open up a shop far enough away not to hurt you but she made us take the one in Ellis Street. And then she made us advertise I'd been your bakeress. We didn't want to but

417

she only gave us so much money at a time, so we hadn't any choice."

It took Mary a moment to pull herself together. "Are you saying she did all this deliberately to bankrupt us?"

"Yes. I don't think it was you she wanted to hurt but she seems to hate Mr Miles. She said there was some trouble between the two of you and she wanted you to walk out on him. When you wouldn't, she said you'd have to go down with him."

"Is this the truth, Mrs Fennell?"

"Cross my heart it is. Neither Jenny nor me liked it but what could we do?"

"Why are you telling me now?"

Mrs Fennell motioned at the bare shelves. "I suppose neither of us thought it'd come to this. Now it has, we feel bad about it." She hesitated, then held out the carrier bag to Mary. "We wondered if you'd accept this from us both."

Mary gazed at the bag. Before she could speak, the woman went on: "It's just a few tins and some bread and pies. We thought they might help until things get better." When Mary hesitated, her voice faltered. "Don't say no, please."

Mary saw the tears of shame in her eyes, hesitated again, then held out her hand for the bag. "Thank you, Mrs Fennell. And thank Jenny too. Tell her they'll be a great help."

At that tears began rolling down the woman's gaunt cheeks. "We shouldn't have done it, I know. Only I wanted my own place so much I didn't give much thought to the game she was playing." When Mary did not speak, she blew her nose and then went on: "Mind you, Mrs Miles, I think she's paying a price for it now."

"Why is that?"

"She makes one of us go to her house every Saturday to show her the figures. Jenny took the books last week and said she was in a dreadful state."

"Don't tell me she's feeling remorse."

"No. It's because your daughter's left her. I don't think she can bear being alone. The house hadn't been cleaned and from the way she was talking, Jenny thinks her mind's going."

Mary had heard only one statement. "Did you say my daughter had left her?"

"Yes. Hasn't she told you?"

"Nobody's told us. Do you know where she's gone?"

"Jenny says the old woman was babbling something about her getting a job with a Sir Somebody and going off to live in a flat with him. But whether it's true or her mind was wandering, Jenny couldn't say. It all sounds a bit far-fetched to me."

The blood had drained from Mary's cheeks. "Does Jenny know when Elizabeth left her?"

"I don't think so. But the old lady hasn't been acting funny that long, so it can't have been more than a week or two."

Trying to stifle her panic, Mary glanced at her watch. With most factories and places of work closed, Harry ought to be home soon. Mrs Fennell's voice broke into her thoughts. "So you

419

didn't know your daughter had left her? I hope I haven't given you more to worry about."

With fears attacking her from all sides, Mary felt it was a stranger who opened the door and smiled at the curious woman. "I'll have to go and attend to my son's dinner now, Mrs Fennell. But thank you for coming round and bringing those things. I know how difficult it must have been for you."

She remembered nothing that Mrs Fennell said in reply but managed to remain smiling in the shop doorway until the woman vanished behind the yew hedge of the adjacent garden. Then she ran inside and sat counting the minutes until Harry's return.

42

HARRY had barely set foot inside the shop before Mary ran towards him. "Elizabeth's left Mother, Harry. And I think she's gone to live with Chadwick. We've got to find her and get her back."

He stared at her. "Chadwick? But that's impossible."

"No, it isn't. It's just what he would do to take his revenge on us. We've got to find out where she is, Harry. Tonight."

"Who told you all this?"

"Mrs Fennell. It was Mother after all, Harry. She lent her the money for the shop."

He drew her into the living room. "Try to calm down and tell me everything."

Although trembling with shock, she did her best. "It's desperately urgent. Elizabeth might have been with him for days, even weeks. God knows what he might have done to her."

He was feeling the same urgency now. "We must get to your mother and find out all we can. Have you any money for a taxi?"

When she shook her head, he sat silent for a moment, then jumped to his feet. "I'll phone Swanson. We'll need a car if we're to find Elizabeth. Wait here."

He returned five minutes later, breathless from running back from the telephone kiosk. "Everything's been happening to Swanson. His father's in hospital after having a stroke and he's been given the business to run. He says there's a good job for me whenever I want one. He didn't know we'd gone bankrupt or he'd have been in touch with me before."

The irony did not escape her. If they had heard the news a few hours ago they would have turned delirious with joy. "Can you have his car?"

"Yes. His father's taken a turn for the worse today, so he can't come himself. But we can borrow his car and he'll use his neighbour's if he has to rush off to hospital. Tell Frank where we're going while I lock up. We might be late back tonight."

Without transport to Swanson's lodgings, it took them an hour to pick up the car and then drive to No. fifty-seven. Leaving the car parked outside, they ran to the front door and rang the bell urgently.

There was no reply. When they rang again without a response, Mary turned to Harry. "We can't waste too much time. Perhaps she's gone out."

He shook his head. "We can't do much until we know exactly what's happened. Didn't Mrs Fennell say she wasn't well?"

At that moment they heard the shuffle of feet at the far side of the door. Hands fumbled with the latch and then the door swung ajar. Mary was into the hall before it was fully open. "Mother, what's all this about Elizabeth? Where has she . . . ?"

Her voice broke off at the sight before her. Her

mother's hair, once so well-groomed and styled, was hanging down in uncombed strands over her shoulders. Her haggard face looked wild and distraught and there were tea stains down the front of her dress. Even worse was the unwashed smell that came from her. Mary's voice was hushed. "Mother! What's happened?"

Ethel peered at her as if her sight was failing. Then she gave a cry of heartfelt relief. "Elizabeth! You've come back! Thank God! But then I always knew my little girl wouldn't leave me for long."

"Mother, it's Mary, not Elizabeth. Don't you recognise me?"

Ethel peered at her again, then gave a moan of disappointment. "Mary? Is it you?"

"Yes, Mother. We've come to find out what's happened to Elizabeth. Do you know where she is?"

The woman clutched Mary's arm. "I've been so lonely, Mary. So terribly lonely. Have you come to stay with me?"

Even her voice had changed. Instead of its haughty confidence, it was now self-pitying and frightened. With Mary's fear for Elizabeth dominating her mind, she ignored the implications. "Mother, we must know about Elizabeth. When did she go away?"

Suddenly Ethel's voice rose wildly. "Elizabeth's a wicked girl. Your dad was angry with her. But now he's gone away too and I'm all alone."

At that Mary went ice cold. "Mother, what are you talking about? What's happened to you?"

Harry pushed past her and took Ethel's

arm. "Let's get her into the living room," he muttered.

As the trembling woman sank down on the sofa, Mary turned her shocked eyes on Harry. "What is it? Has her mind gone?"

His own face was pale. "It looks that way. Go on trying to find out about Elizabeth while I phone for the doctor. Does she still use Armstrong?"

"Yes, I think so."

He ran back into the hall. Ethel, who was crying piteously to herself, had taken a cushion from the sofa and was picking aimlessly at it. Seeing the length of her nails and the dirt beneath them, Mary felt she had entered a nightmare. Shuddering, she dropped on her knees before her. "Mother, try to remember about Elizabeth. Did she go away with Michael Chadwick?"

The name clearly struck a chord in the woman's deranged mind for her crying ceased. "Sir Michael? He's been a big help to me recently. Did you know that?"

Mary started. "What do you mean, he's been a big help to you?"

Ethel was not hearing her. "He's the squire, you know. He liked you once, Mary. He told me so."

"I know that, Mother. What has Chadwick been doing? Is Elizabeth living with him?"

"You were such a silly girl, Mary. He would have married you if you'd encouraged him more."

Mary wanted to scream. "Mother, for God's

424

sake stop talking about me. I want to know if Elizabeth has gone to Michael Chadwick. Won't you please try to remember?"

Ethel stared at her, then gave a cry of torment. "They hate me, Mary. They won't let me sleep. Tell them to go away. Please tell them."

In spite of her suspicions, Mary could only feel pity for her at that moment. "We're getting the doctor to see you, Mother. He'll give you something to help you sleep."

Ethel's terrified eyes showed no understanding. Her cries and whimpering suggested that in her deranged mind she was having concourse with demons. Unable to watch her suffering, Mary was about to join Harry in the hall when she heard him cease speaking and replace the receiver. A moment later he appeared. "Armstrong's coming straight round. He said he was always afraid something like this might happen if she were left alone."

"Does he know anything about Elizabeth?"

"No. Nothing." He glanced at Ethel. "He asked if we would get her upstairs. He wants to examine her."

They helped the sobbing Ethel up to her bedroom, then returned to the living room to await the doctor. Frantic for Elizabeth's safety, Mary kept glancing at the time. "What are we going to do if Armstrong can't get anything out of her? Where can we go?"

"I suppose we can always go to The Grange. If Chadwick isn't there we might find out his address in town."

Although Mary had had the same thought, the

idea frightened her. "It could be dangerous. His staff might set on you again. And he's not likely to be there himself, is he? Not on a Tuesday?"

He dismissed her fears with a shrug. "We'd have no choice. We'd have to start somewhere."

The doctor arrived ten minutes later. Mary found the wait agonising while he was upstairs examining Ethel. When he returned to the living room, she ran up to him.

"Did you find out anything about Elizabeth?"

Armstrong gave her a frown. "No, I didn't but let's put first things first, lass. Just now I think you need to worry more about that old woman upstairs than about the goings-on of a daft young girl."

As Mary stared at him, Harry broke in quickly. "There are things you don't know, doctor. How did you find her?"

"She's away in another world and a lonely one at that. I can't say I'm surprised." Armstrong turned back to Mary. "Your dad's death nearly broke her: she could never accept it. I realised that when she tried to commit suicide."

"But she didn't. That was just a trick to make us leave Elizabeth with her."

Armstrong shook his head. "That's something we still don't agree on, lass. Anyway, she's gone over the edge now. I'm going to phone for an ambulance: She needs to get the kind of help I can't give her."

"Will she get better?"

"I'm no psychiatrist so I can't say. But I think you ought to be prepared for the worst."

As Mary shuddered, Harry took hold of her

426

arm. "We've reason to believe our daughter might be in danger. So need we wait for the ambulance?"

Armstrong frowned again. "Not if you don't want to. I'll have to stay with her, so I can lock up the house. You can pick up the keys from my surgery later."

Aware Armstrong thought them callous, they ran outside. Inside the car, Harry turned to Mary. "It'll have to be The Grange now. It's the only address we have."

In spite of her fears for Elizabeth, the memory of his ordeal at the Conservative Club made her hesitate for the first time that evening. "You don't think Mrs Fennell could be wrong about him?"

He frowned, his hand on the starter button. "Do you?"

She thought of all that had happened between her and Chadwick and then of the way he had looked at Elizabeth when they met in town and knew her instincts had never doubted it. "No, I don't. Particularly after the things Mother said. He's been helping her to ruin us and Elizabeth would complete the revenge for him."

He nodded. "I think the same. It suits his style too." He depressed the button and the engine burst into life. "We'll go to The Grange and see if we can find him."

★ ★ ★

They left the car on the road and walked through the open main gates. The Georgian

427

manor, perfect in its proportions and bathed in cold moonlight, stood before them. The night was still and Mary found herself whispering. "Why is everything so quiet?"

Only two lights were burning. One in the huge Palladian entrance and the other in a window on the fourth floor. As they listened, the eerie hoot of an owl made Mary start. Her pale face turned to Harry. "What's the time?"

He held up his watch in the moonlight. "Nearly midnight."

She relaxed slightly. "Then perhaps they've all retired. What should we do?"

He pointed back at the gates. "You wait in the car for me. I won't be long."

Afraid for him, she made an immediate protest. "No, you're not doing this alone. I'm coming with you."

Knowing it was futile to argue, he pressed her arm and they started up the drive again. The silence accentuated the crunch of the gravel beneath their feet and made her expect a challenge any moment from the outhouses half hidden among the flanking trees.

They reached a courtyard and climbed the wide flight of steps that led up to the porch. In the light that shone from it, Mary felt as exposed as if a spotlight were on them. Her nervousness grew as Harry drew out a polished brass knob and a bell began jangling inside the house.

She felt her heart thudding as she waited. The hoot of the curious owl came again but the house fell back into silence. When Harry tried the bell a second time without success, she found herself whispering again. "Where is everybody?"

He led her back down the steps and pointed at the light behind a balcony on the fourth floor. "Someone's up there. They probably can't hear the bell. Let's see if we can find an unlocked window."

She stared at him. "You're not going to break in?"

He was moving away as he answered her, his voice as determined as she had ever known it. "We're not leaving without finding something out. Try the windows to see if any will open."

They had worked their way to the back of the house before she heard a tinkle of glass. Hurrying towards him, she found him standing on a low wall with his hand reaching inside a broken window pane. Withdrawing his arm, he drove both hands against the frame until the lower sash of the window slid up a couple of inches. Heaving it fully open, he turned and gazed down at her. "I'm going to see who's in that upstairs room. I won't be long."

She tried to climb up alongside him. "I'm coming with you. Help me up."

"No. Go back to the car and wait for me there."

"But it's safer if I'm with you, Harry."

"I don't want you with me. Go back to the car." Before she could protest further or find anything to climb on, he squeezed through the window and lowered himself down.

He appeared to be in a lumber room. The faint moonlight showed him piles of crates and pieces of old furniture. Treading carefully, he reached the door. As it creaked open, he found himself in a long, dark corridor. To the right, moonlight could be seen slanting through windows. He made for the light and found himself in the great hall where Chadwick's party had been held.

The silence was intimidating and making him move like a thief. The thought angered him. He was here to find people, not to hide from them. He took a deep breath. "Hello! Is anyone here?"

His voice, echoing back, made his heart beat faster. He gazed around but nothing moved in the moonlight. Walking to the foot of the curving staircase, he tried again. Once more only the echoes stirred the silence and mocked him.

It was the house, he told himself. The ceilings were high and the doors were thick. If he wanted to be heard and receive attention, he would have to climb up to the floor where the light was shining.

He ran up the great staircase. As he reached the second landing, he thought he heard a muffled cry. Pausing, he listened but could only hear the blood thudding in his ears.

Afraid, although unsure why, he ran on to the fourth floor, now switching on lights as he went. Oil portraits in huge gilt frames swam past him and chandeliers blazed in crystalline light. Reaching the wide landing, he paused. Doors were lined around him and he could not identify the one he was seeking. As he paused again, he heard another cry and then a scream of pain.

It was Elizabeth. He knew it and his blood ran cold. As another scream sounded, he gave a shout. "Elizabeth! Where are you?"

The cries suddenly ceased as if a hand were being clapped over the victim's mouth. Still unable to identify the room, he ran across the landing and began throwing open door after door.

The rooms were empty except for furniture covered in white sheets. Sweating with fear at the time he was wasting, he shouted again: "Elizabeth! Which room are you in? Try to tell me."

There was no reply but he could now see light shining beneath a door. Running towards it, he burst into the room.

It was spacious and masculine in decor. Photographs were everywhere, mostly of men in uniform. Ancient pistols and a sword and scabbard hung from the walls and a stag's head was poised over the fireplace. But Harry's eyes were fixed on the large double bed where Elizabeth was holding a sheet to cover herself. At first she seemed too paralysed to respond to his entry. Then, with an hysterical cry of relief, she dropped the sheet and ran towards him. "Dad! Oh, Dad, thank God you've come!"

He stood holding her naked body in disbelief. Her lips were swollen, her cheeks bruised, and there were abrasions on her shoulders and breasts. "Elizabeth? In God's name what's been happening?"

She tried to speak but instead dropped her face on to his shoulder and sobbed as if her

431

heart would break. As he kissed her tousled hair, his eyes lifted to the far side of the room where Chadwick was finishing adjusting his clothing. His voice was thick, a stranger's voice. "Why, Chadwick? Tell me why?"

Chadwick, showing no concern at his appearance, was smiling. "It was a little unfinished business, Miles. Mary would understand. Have you brought her with you? I hope so."

Elizabeth was clinging to Harry as if her life depended on it. He could feel the heat of her tears through his shirt. "He hurt me, Dad. Why did he have to hurt me so much?"

Harry's eyes rose to Chadwick who smiled again. "It's over, you know, Miles. You arrived too late."

Hate came to Harry then. It welled up from every pore in his sweating body and burst like a bomb in his mind. He was no longer in the present as he stood the sobbing girl aside. He was back in France, staring at the charred bodies of his two comrades that the enemy had incinerated.

Chadwick saw his expression and recognised it. He showed no fear, only the caution of a soldier preparing for combat. "I wouldn't if I were you, Miles. Remember the other times you've tried. Go home and take that stupid little bitch with you."

At that Harry went straight for his throat. Chadwick moved away with the skill of a trained boxer and struck a blow that buckled Harry's knees and dropped him to the floor.

He heard a woman's scream but felt no pain. Death itself would not have stopped him at that moment. He rose and fell again to another blow. Chadwick stood over him laughing. "Give it up, Miles. There's no way you can win."

There was still no pain: Only a brain filled with whitehot fury. Grabbing Chadwick's legs, Harry brought him down to the floor and a moment later the two of them were rolling over and over on the carpet.

All traces of civilised behaviour had vanished from them now. Their one aim was to kill. They crashed into the fireplace and brought down a heavy poker and shovel. Grabbing the poker, Chadwick forced it against Harry's throat and using all his strength drove him back to the floor. As the poker cut off his breath, he heard Chadwick's mocking laugh. "So you're different from me, are you, Miles? Where's the difference now?"

Calling on his hatred for strength, Harry smashed a fist into his face, rolled away, and scrambled to his feet. As Chadwick cursed and swung the poker at his head, he ducked, then dived headlong at him. The collision sent the two men crashing through the French windows to the balcony outside, scattering the two wicker chairs that stood there and hurling the men against the protecting rail that ran round it.

The impact saved them from the sixty foot drop to the courtyard below, although it fractured three of the wooden stays and broke the handrail above them. But in spite of the gap that now yawned between the stays,

433

neither man gave thought to his personal safety. Fighting like animals, they rolled back and forth until Chadwick's superior strength forced Harry against the rail at the side of the balcony.

He had no doubt of Chadwick's intention. The excitement of the kill was written all over his handsome, exultant face. "It's self-defence, Miles. You broke into my house and attacked me . . . "

Neither man had noticed Mary run out on the balcony or heard her cry of fear. Harry was fighting for his life as he was driven further and further over the rail. Chadwick's hands were on his throat but he knew if he released his grip on the rail to ease the stranglehold, he was certain to topple over to his death.

With stars bursting behind his eyes he did not see Mary run up behind Chadwick and try to pull him back. It was only when the pressure on his throat ceased that he saw Chadwick turn and strike her.

The sight of her crumpling to the floor brought back his hatred. As Chadwick turned to him again, he kicked out with all his strength. The blow caught Chadwick on the left hip and spun him round towards the gap in the rail. Staggering, the man tried to regain his balance, only for his foot to slip over the edge. Lunging out desperately, he caught hold of one of the splintered stays, his hand sliding to the bottom of the post as he fell.

Coughing, sobbing for breath, Harry crawled towards him. Chadwick's free hand was scrabbling for a hold on the balcony edge but the tiling was wet with dew and his fingers kept slipping away.

There were shouts coming from below now and torches flashing but Harry could could see nothing but Chadwick's upturned face. He could see no fear there, only shock and disappointment. For a moment only one wish dominated his mind: to see Chadwick fall and be crushed on the flagstones below.

Then the madness in his mind lifted as he realised the man's helplessness. Pushing one foot between two intact stays, he twisted round and seized Chadwick's left wrist with both hands. "Hold on," he panted. "I'll pull you up."

That was the moment when fear sprang into Chadwick's eyes. "No! Leave me! I can get back myself."

Harry could see his scrabbling right hand and its failure to gain a grip on the balcony. "Keep still or you'll fall." Gazing round, he saw with relief that Mary was struggling to her feet. "Come and help me! Quickly."

Chadwick's voice rose in a shout of despair as Mary threw a hand round Harry's waist to aid him. "Damn you, Miles! I don't want your help. Get away from me."

In the long minute that followed Harry was once again back in time, struggling to heave the wounded German up the railway embankment to safety. Although Chadwick struck at him with his spare hand, it was doubtful if anything but a wrench could have broken his grip. With muscles cracking and lungs sobbing, with his stomach retching with the strain, inch by inch he drew Chadwick over the balcony edge until the man was able to drag himself to safety. Then he dropped back and fought for air like a drowning man pulled out of the sea.

When his eyes cleared Mary was bending over him. "Harry! Are you all right"

When he nodded, she bent down and gave him a long, fierce kiss. Rising unsteadily, he saw Chadwick had dropped into a wicker chair and was staring at him with eyes that were bleak and haunted in the moonlight. About to speak to him, Harry changed his mind and walked into the bedroom where the terrified Elizabeth, now wearing a coat, gave a sob of relief and ran towards him. "Dad! Can we go home now?"

He turned and saw Mary was saying something to Chadwick. What it was he never found out, but although the marks of the night were etched on her face when she walked back into the bedroom, her eyes shone bright and proud when she kissed him again. "I was right, wasn't I, my love? I was even more right than I thought."

Before he could ask what she meant, she turned to Elizabeth and held out her arms. As the girl ran forward and clung to her, she smiled and kissed her. Then she held out her arms to Harry. As he moved forward to embrace them both it seemed to him that her voice had a singing sound as she answered the weeping girl. "Yes, we're going home, darling. And this time we're all going home together."

Epilogue

THERE was much happiness in the neat, semi-detached house in the suburb of Sutton that day in October 1935. The house was full of laughing young people and no one was enjoying the occasion more than Harry and Mary.

They were celebrating two events: Elizabeth's engagement to a young solicitor and Frank's 17th birthday. The boy had passed his matriculation that year with two distinctions and recently begun work in the city. Elizabeth, now apparently recovered from her youthful traumas, had never seemed more contented as she and her fiancé moved among the guests.

With loud music on the radio competing against the chatter and laughter in the living room, Harry and Mary moved into the dining room where Harry poured out two glasses of wine. He handed her a glass, then turned and eyed the celebration through the open door. Seeing him take a deep, appreciative breath, Mary gave him a smile.

"Are you thinking what I'm thinking?"

He grinned. "Probably. I usually do."

"We're not dreaming," she said. "It's happened. We've survived." As he nodded, she took his hand and gripped it. "You never lost faith, did you? I still remember you laughing at the foot of those shop stairs. It was the bravest thing I'd ever heard."

He shrugged. "Life's like a roller coaster. What goes down has to go up. It's not a bad thing to remember."

At that moment Frank appeared in the doorway. Fair-haired and powerfully built, he was already taller and broader than his father. "What are you two doing in here? Come and join the party."

"Go away," Harry said. "We've come in here for a bit of peace."

Frank took them both by the shoulders. "You can't have any peace today. We're celebrating. Come on. We want Mum to play the piano."

As they were speaking, the radio music in the living room gave way to the news. A moment later a harsh voice was heard haranguing a wildly cheering mob. Someone gave a shout. "That's Hitler. Turn it off. Mrs Miles is going to play the piano."

The harsh voice sent a shudder through Mary as if a cold draught had entered the room. Then, as Harry pulled her to her feet and they followed Frank back into the living room, she chided herself. The past had made her too distrustful of happiness: she must learn to accept the good times as well as the bad. They had come through the fires and were now united as a family. Whatever the roller coaster might do in the future, this was a golden time and she must enjoy it to the full. She sat at the piano and a moment later the house was filled again with music and laughter